JODI TAYLOR

HEADLINE

First published in Great Britain in 2021 by
HEADLINE PUBLISHING GROUP

1

Cataloguing in Publication Data is available from the British Library

ISBN 978 1 4722 7320 8

Typeset in Times New Roman by CC Book Production

Printed and bound in Great Britain by Clays Ltd, Elcograf S.p.A.

Headline's policy is to use papers that are natural, renewable and recyclable
products and made from wood grown in well-managed forests and other
controlled sources. The logging and manufacturing processes are expected
to conform to the environmental regulations of the country of origin.

HEADLINE PUBLISHING GROUP
An Hachette UK Company
Carmelite House
50 Victoria Embankment
London EC4Y 0DZ

www.headline.co.uk
www.hachette.co.uk

AUTHOR'S THANK YOU

Most of this book was written during the Covid-19 lockdown. I should make it very clear that Max's views on the hard-heartedness of the nursing profession are hers and hers alone. I'd like to take this opportunity to thank everyone in the NHS for their selfless dedication and determination.

And I'm pretty sure that whatever Markham says, nurses don't actually throw people out of windows in the pursuance of their duties.

DRAMATIS THINGUMMY

ST MARY'S PERSONNEL

Dr Bairstow	Director of St Mary's.
Mrs Brown	Aka – Lady Blackbourne. North's mother. High-ranking member of the Civil Service. Busy lady.
Mrs Partridge	PA to the Director.

HISTORY DEPARTMENT

Dr Maxwell	Head of the History Department.
Miss Van Owen	
Mr Clerk	
Miss Prentiss	
Mr Sands	Historians. But possibly not for much longer.
Mr Roberts	
Mr Bashford	
Miss Sykes	
Mr Atherton	
Rosie Lee	PA to the Head of the History Department. Time-travel virgin. But not for much longer.

TECHNICAL SECTION

Chief Technical Officer Farrell	Sensibly not very involved in this one. Too busy whisking the younger generation off to a place of greater safety.
Mr Dieter	Turning a blind eye.
Mr Lindstrom	Never says much.

RESEARCH AND DEVELOPMENT

Professor Rapson	Head of R&D. Exploring the possibility of bypassing gravity. Proud rapid chicken-firing gun owner.
Miss Lingoss	Charioteer and bride.

OTHERS

Dr Dowson	Head Librarian. Who else would take a rapid chicken-firing gun to a church?
Mrs Enderby	Head of Wardrobe.
Mrs Midgley	Housekeeper. Both of them very helpful in relocating St Mary's supplies to an alternative site. All right – stealing.

Matthew, Mikey and Adrian	They and their talents are being moved to a place of greater safety. Out of the way for the time being but storing up big problems for the future.

SECURITY SECTION

Captain Hyssop	Off to a really bad start.
Scarfe	Half-Wit
Lucca	Another Half-Wit
Glass	Yet another Half-Wit
Harper	And another one
Jessop	Yes, him too.
The one whose name no one can ever remember	Un-named Half-Wit
Evans	Real security guard
Keller	Another real security guard
Gallacio	Yet another real security guard
Cox	And another one
Mr Strong	Caretaker and handyman. Dr Bairstow's first recruit to St Mary's.
Markham	The Con part of Pros and Cons.
Hunter Baby Flora	His family.
Commander John Treadwell	Quite likeable, actually. Unless you're Max.
Halcombe and Sullivan	Released from captivity.

The Reverend Kevin Aguta	The Rev Kev. An impressive example of Christian tolerance and forgiveness.
Martin Gaunt	Security superintendent at the Red House. A man in love with his own authority.
Various Red House security staff	
Josiah Winterson	We never meet him but he gets a good kicking nevertheless.
Jack Feeney	We do meet him. He wishes we hadn't.
Assorted distressed maidservants who suddenly discover what their boots are for	
Sir Richard Verney	He shouldn't be here! What is happening?
Amy Robsart	Look where you're going – whoops – too late.
The mysterious inhabitants of a mysterious litter	Your guess is as good as mine.
People and priests of Babylon	
Abilsin	Son of Sin but quite a nice boy.
A silk merchant and slave owner	
A couple of overseers at the brickyard	

Pennyroyal	An alleged butler.
Lady Amelia Smallhope	A member of the aristocracy. Bounty hunter. Sorry – recovery agent.

I'd forgotten how cold it can be just before dawn. And quite dark, too. On the other hand, I've been clandestinely creeping around St Mary's since the moment I arrived all those years ago. I know every twist and turn. Every creaking door. Every squeaky board. As long as Professor Rapson hadn't carelessly left any half-constructed bear traps or acid baths around the place, I didn't even need a torch.

I ghosted around the gallery and down the stairs, carefully keeping to the edges to minimise the creaks, although the whole edifice does tend to groan like a clipper in a strong wind whether anyone is standing on it or not.

The Great Hall was no problem. I could weave my way in and out of whiteboards, trestle tables, chairs, stools, piles of files, whatever, with my eyes closed. And frequently had.

I passed silently through the vestibule. The front doors were already unbolted. Easing my way through, I paused to zip up my body warmer. The morning was cold, dank and silent. It was lighter outside, although, sensibly, even the birds weren't up yet. Moisture beaded every surface. Tendrils of light fog drifted across from the lake. Perfect conditions for a discreet getaway.

The car stood ready and waiting – a small family hatchback

of an indeterminate grey colour. There must be millions of them around. You can't avoid CCTV cameras completely, of course, but I would bet any money Leon had stowed a couple of alternative registration plates in the boot. I love that people think he's so respectable.

I skipped down the steps, my frosty breath billowing and making substantial contributions to the fog and general non-visibility around me. Actually, skipped is the wrong word. Skipped implies light-hearted, joyful, carefree and so on, and I wasn't any of those. People do leave St Mary's. Sometimes under quite happy circumstances. But not today. Today was not a happy day.

Leon loomed up out of the fog. Very visible in his orange techie jumpsuit.

I tilted my head to one side. 'You do know this is a stealth assignment, don't you? Short of attaching an SAR beacon, is there any way you could be more obvious?'

He put his arm around me because I was just putting on a brave face and we both knew it. I asked him if everything was ready.

He nodded. 'It is.'

I paused.

He said, 'It's time, Max.'

'I know,' I said, staring at my feet. 'I know. It's just . . .'

'I know,' he said, rubbing my shoulder. 'But the moment has come to say goodbye.'

I nodded. No putting it off any longer. Leon shut the boot and I walked around the car.

Hunter was sitting in the back seat. Markham had muffled her up well but she still looked a little pale and tired. Baby Flora was sleeping soundly in her car-crib.

I crouched down to talk to Hunter. 'All right? Got everything?'

She smiled. 'I hope so because I don't think we have room for anything else.' And I laughed because, trust me, the amount of supplies and equipment needed to transport a tiny human from A to B is mind-blowingly colossal. They could probably go off and discover another continent with what they had packed in that car.

I myself had contributed a little to their burden. I'd gone into Matthew's bedroom and taken down the little suitcase of baby clothes that was all that remained of his childhood. Most of it unworn because he hadn't had his childhood for very long. I don't know why I'd kept them. It wasn't as if I'd ever need them again.

'Here,' I'd said to Markham. 'Everything from six months onwards. Babies grow fast and you'll need them more quickly than you think.'

He took the case very carefully. 'Are you sure?'

I nodded. I'd kept back one or two small items, together with the blanket Helen Foster had knitted, but there was no point in hanging on to the rest. The sensible thing to do was to give the stuff to someone who would need it.

Back to the misty morning . . . Hunter gripped my hand. 'Max . . .'

'I know,' I said, near to tears myself. 'But it's not forever. You'll be back before you know it.' I glanced over to Markham who was giving last-minute instructions to Evans. Or talking about the football – it could be either. 'He's done everything he can to keep the three of you safe. I have complete confidence you'll all be fine.'

'Absolutely fine,' she said with a small laugh.

3

'Take care, Di.' I straightened up and shut the door.

As I did so, the front door opened and Peterson and Evans made their way down the steps towards us, both of them looking even less happy than me.

Markham was shaking hands with Leon who was wishing him luck.

Markham nodded and turned to Peterson. They looked at their feet for a moment and then Markham mumbled, 'For God's sake, look after Max – you know what she's like.'

Peterson nodded and shoved his hands in his pockets. The world was utterly silent. Not a sound anywhere. The fog seemed to be thickening.

Markham looked over Peterson's shoulder. 'I ... um ...' He stopped.

'We can only hope your daughter grows up to be more articulate than you,' said Peterson gravely. 'Although that wouldn't be difficult.'

Their laughter had a forced sound to it.

'Should be going,' mumbled Markham.

Peterson clapped him on the shoulder. 'Yeah.'

'OK. Well. I'll be off, then.'

'Take care.'

'Yeah, mate – you too.'

Markham saw me waiting and came over, presumably before either he or Peterson forgot they were British and embarrassed themselves and each other in public. 'Max.'

I couldn't speak and I think he was having some problems as well.

'Max ... I'll never forget what you did and ...'

I nodded because I couldn't do anything else.

4

He swallowed. 'I'll find a way of staying in touch.'

Honour compelled me to say, 'Don't do anything stupid,' which, as futile efforts go, was probably slightly less effective than Cnut trying to halt the oncoming tide.

He nodded.

I said, 'Keep them safe,' and he nodded again, squeezed my hand one last time, climbed into the car and started the engine. There was no cheery toot of the horn, just the crunch of tyres on gravel as he pulled slowly away. The gates were already open. He slowed carefully, indicated right and disappeared into the fog.

Peterson and I stood for a long time, looking at the place where Markham used to be.

Evans clapped Peterson on the shoulder. 'Early breakfast, I think. Before all the scrambled egg disappears.' They headed back into St Mary's leaving me and Leon alone on the steps.

'All right?' said Leon and I nodded, although I wasn't. I don't know why. It wasn't as if this moment had leaped on us out of the blue. We'd been a week preparing for this. As far as the rest of the world was concerned, Markham was simply taking Hunter and Flora away for a spot of family time. No one could blame him for that – St Mary's is not particularly conducive to the successful rearing of small humans, trust me on that. I mean, yes, it's fine if you want your offspring to grow up with an intimate knowledge of all the murkier aspects of History, or how to convert six inches of lace and a teaspoon into a weapon of mass destruction, or how to defy and subvert authority – although all kids seem to have an instinct for that anyway – but St Mary's can do all that and more on an industrial scale.

Anyway, with Markham there were other factors in play. I'm not going into who he is because it's not my secret to tell, but he's someone the authorities would very much like to have under their control and his tiny daughter, Flora, had, by her appearance, upped the stakes considerably. So Markham was taking his little family away to a place of greater safety. No one knew where. No one had asked, actually – as Dr Bairstow had said, it wasn't something you'd want tortured out of you, was it? – and I hadn't been entirely certain he was joking.

And for those of you still puzzling over my comment about the murkier aspects of History – that's what we do. We're the St Mary's Institute of Historical Research. We're just outside of Rushford – out of harm's way, as the authorities so wrongly think – and we investigate major historical events in contemporary time. Especially the murky bits. Please feel free to call it time travel if you like. Dr Bairstow's had a stressful time recently and opportunities for him to vent his spleen don't come often so you'd be doing us all a favour.

And now he was gone. Markham, I mean. The winds of change were blowing again. Guthrie, Grey, North, and now Markham. I sighed and looked around. We had choices. A very early breakfast or . . .

I said to Leon, 'What could we do for an hour?'

'Eh?'

I draped myself enticingly around him and said patiently, 'We have an hour's unexpected free time. What shall we do?'

'I don't understand.'

I remembered I was talking to a techie. I should keep things simple for him.

'Option A – full-on, head-banging sex. Option B – a bacon butty. Choose now.'

'Hmm,' he said, staring into space. 'Tricky . . .'

I was Dr Bairstow's ten o'clock that morning. Something about which he didn't seem tremendously enthusiastic.

I sank gratefully into a chair. I'd partaken fully of Options A *and* B and thanks to that and my very early start, my internal clock now thought it was time to wind down and go back to bed.

'Dr Maxwell, I thought we'd have a quiet word before you resume your duties after recent events.'

Great. The Boss wants a quiet word – just what every employee loves to hear. I smiled brightly to mask my misgivings.

'How is everything?'

'Absolutely fine, thank you, sir. I have a weekly session with Dr Stone, when he forces me to drink cocoa and talk to him.'

All that was true. At my last session he'd asked me how I was feeling.

'Oh,' I'd said, 'completely overwhelmed by the pointlessness of my life. Trying to pluck up enough courage to hurl myself from an upstairs window before I'm enveloped in a miasma of despair and hopelessness.'

'Big improvement on last week, then?'

'I think so, yes.'

I didn't mention any of that to Dr Bairstow.

'No,' he said quietly. 'I mean – how are you really, Max? With everything that has happened – Markham – his past – his future – everything at Mechelen – now that you have had a while to assimilate all this – how are you feeling about that?'

I opened my mouth to say, 'Absolutely fine,' again, but

7

paused. Absolutely fine wasn't quite true in this case so why should I lie about it? Tell the truth, Maxwell. Just for once – tell the truth.

I said carefully, 'I know why, once you realised who Markham was, you had to keep the truth from me. And I can't argue with your reasons. I don't like that you had to do it but that's not really important, is it?'

'Isn't it?' He paused. 'I don't regret my actions, Max, but I do regret the necessity of them.'

'Sir, it's not your job to be nice. I've got that side of things pretty much covered. It's your job to make the right decision.'

I paused. Well, he'd started the conversation. Never ask a question if you're not prepared for the answer. 'You are the Director of St Mary's. To be effective you need to possess certain qualities. Your job is to do the right thing. Not the nice thing or the acceptable thing or the legal thing or whatever, but the right thing. Which, in this case, was to safeguard Markham as best you could. And to protect me, as well. Secrets can be dangerous – this one certainly is and I wish I didn't know anything about any of it – ignorance really is bliss – but now, sadly, I do.'

I looked down at my hands. 'I myself once had to manipulate Mary Stuart into . . . a situation. My job was to ensure she and Bothwell got together and I'm not proud of the way I did it. But, she and Bothwell had to happen because they'd already happened. I had to do the right thing. I didn't have the luxury of sparing my own feelings. My own weakness, my failure to make a difficult decision and live with the consequences, would have brought disaster down upon all of us. It was the same for you with Markham. Unpleasant choices must be made by the few so the many don't have to. It's like Pharaoh.'

He blinked. 'I'm not aware of the similarity to which you allude but I am certain you are about to enlighten me.'

'Pharaoh, sir.'

'Which one?'

'Any of them. Or all of them. Their job was to ensure the sun rose every morning. They knew that if they couldn't make the hard choices then the sun wouldn't come up and everyone would die.'

Dr Bairstow sat for a moment. 'I think I can honestly say I have never regarded myself in that light.'

'Now might be the time to start, sir.'

He nodded. 'I shall certainly bear your comments in mind. Thank you, Dr Maxwell.'

Passing through Mrs Partridge's office, I was struck by a sudden thought. Well – why not? Pausing at her desk, I said, 'Dr Bairstow asked me to tell you he's ready for his Nubian concubines now,' and pushed off while the pushing was good.

Back in the Hall, historians were settling down to start work on our Minoan Crete material. I stood back for a moment and watched them sorting themselves out. We'd had a week or so to recover from the assignment and now it was time to get stuck in.

Bashford opened another box, peered inside, sighed and said to Sands, 'There's a lot here, you know. We're going to be at this for weeks.'

The problem with David Sands is that although he's tall, dark and handsome, he also comes with the world's worst collection of knock-knock jokes. I can't tell you how we've suffered over the years. He'd had a lot of it knocked out of him but, as subsequent events would show, he'd recently regrouped and modified his plan of attack.

He looked up, grinning. 'Tell me about it. We work for Cunard, you know.' He paused, expectantly.

'Do we?' enquired Bashford, never the brightest historian in contemporary time. 'When did that happen?'

'No, no. It's a joke. When I said we worked for Cunard, I'm actually saying . . .'

Bashford appeared confused. 'So we *don't* work for Cunard?'

'Well, no, but . . .'

'So why did you say we did?'

'I was trying to . . .'

'It's very misleading.'

'It's a . . .'

'We work for Dr Bairstow.'

'Yes, but . . .'

'Everyone knows that.'

'I was trying to . . . no, wait, come back . . .'

I found my own stack of archive boxes, whipped the lid off the first one and got stuck in.

The next day, Peterson and I had our usual Wednesday morning update with Dr Bairstow. We seated ourselves around the briefing table and Dr Bairstow opened the batting, saying thoughtfully, 'I find myself uneasy about the future.'

I blinked. 'Ronan's dead, sir.'

Yes, he was. He'd been an evil presence in my life almost since the day I walked through the gates of St Mary's and now he was – finally – dead. I'd watched him die. It hadn't been a good death. Or a quick one, either. But he was gone. The circle had been closed. I was looking forward to a much more peaceful future. A little gentle jumping here and there. More time with Leon and Matthew. Spending long hours in the Library reading papers and actually doing historian things. To say nothing of enjoying a little breathing space.

Dr Bairstow sighed. 'Yes, but he wasn't the only threat out there.'

Well, this was worrying. I exchanged a look with Peterson and asked, 'Do you have a specific threat in mind, sir?'

'Ronan did not operate alone. Whether he employed others or they employed him – or thought they did – I have no idea. Whoever they were and what their plans for us might be – again, I have no idea. However, after our enforced evacuation of St Mary's last year, I have no intention of being caught unawares again. I think we must consider our original remote site now compromised and commence the search for a new one. And as soon as possible.'

He paused for a moment and then said, 'I suspect that our days of operating with autonomy might be coming to an end. Thinking back over the years, I remember those shadowy figures behind Laurence Hoyle. And, of course, the very unlamented and sadly unleprous Mr Halcombe and his friend Major Sullivan and their attempts to control St Mary's. If there is a government connection, however nebulous, we could find ourselves in some difficulties. I am particularly concerned about safeguarding our Archive. Maintaining a true record is what we're all about, and in these days of fake facts and government-sponsored misinformation, it's more important than ever. If anything should happen to the Archive, then all our endeavours over the years will have been in vain because we can't go back and do it again. We should never forget – there will always be those for whom the truth is an inconvenience to be removed as quickly and quietly as possible.'

Peterson stretched out his legs. 'There are a lot of people out there with vested interests in upsetting the status quo.'

I nodded. 'If, right now, the authorities turned up to confiscate our Archive then there wouldn't be a lot we could do about it. Apart from resist and be arrested, of course.'

Peterson looked at Dr Bairstow. 'And having acquired it, what would they do with it?'

He shrugged. 'My fear is that it could be altered, amended, adjusted . . . and re-presented as the official record.'

'Censorship,' I said.

'Indeed. As the Time Police are so quick to say – the Time Wars were all about people thinking they could go back and rearrange History to represent their particular interests – religion, politics and so on – in a more favourable and much less controversial light. Imagine if you could produce evidence the Crusader Sack of Constantinople never actually occurred.'

'The Time Wars happen in the future, sir. As do the Time Police. And I can assure you the Sack of Constantinople did occur, sir. I was actually there.'

'But without the evidence, Dr Maxwell, it is just your word against less well-informed others.'

'Never mind our Archive,' said Peterson slowly. 'Anyone possessing our pods could write their own History.'

Dr Bairstow sat back. 'That is my second great fear. Let us be dramatic for one moment. Those who come to control St Mary's might think they control History as well. From often bitter experience we know better, but how many would have to

12

die before the more fanatical elements would accept that History cannot be changed. We've already endured Mr Halcombe's attempts to prove the crucifixion took place. I am convinced he was attached in some way to the government. Or a part of it. A department so obscure that perhaps even the mainstream government itself is unaware of its existence.' He frowned. 'Mrs Brown is pursuing that particular avenue of enquiry.'

Mrs Brown was a member of the government department that has specific responsibility for St Mary's. Ostensibly, we were part of the University of Thirsk, from whom our funding came. Over the years this government department had more or less kept its distance – I suspected that, deep down, they just wished we'd blow ourselves up and solve their problem for them. They didn't want us, but they didn't want anyone else to have us either. I can't think why not – we're quite delightful.

Dr Bairstow continued. 'I accept I may be overreacting but I think I would rather set up emergency procedures which may never be needed than trust to luck and possibly lose everything. I shall therefore be instructing Chief Farrell to find us a new remote site. I always feel happier when I know we have a safe refuge, while any unpleasantness is dealt with somewhere else. I shall also request Dr Dowson to transfer the Archive to our big pod, TB2, where it will be ready to go at a moment's notice.'

I was sitting down but the sands were shifting beneath my feet. The foundations of my life – never terribly secure in the first place – were slowly crumbling beneath me. St Mary's was my home. It was the place I always came back to. And now there was the possibility it might not be here for much longer. It wasn't a good feeling. Something was coming.

Dr Bairstow still hadn't finished. It was just one damned thing after another this morning. 'You should also be aware I may not always be the Director of St Mary's. The people with whom I set up St Mary's – allies at Whitehall – have mostly moved on. New individuals have taken their place. People with different priorities. Different ways of thinking. It is entirely possible you may wake up one morning to find another in my place. We will need to devise strategies for such a contingency.'

Peterson stirred. 'We successfully challenged Halcombe on the grounds his attempt to take over St Mary's was illegal, but I suspect you are talking about a government-authorised transfer of power and therefore perfectly legal.'

Dr Bairstow nodded. 'I think we should assume so, yes.'

'And that would not be something we could challenge?'

'Not if legally carried out, no.'

Peterson hadn't finished. 'I am assuming also that one of the main reasons for new ownership might be our consistent failure to make any sort of profit.'

'I think we should assume that also.'

'Then, sir, may I suggest we adopt a more aggressive policy of search and rescue? Rescuing historical items from the past. *Valuable* historical items. Raise our profile a little.'

'An excellent idea, Dr Peterson, but we should beware of opening whole new cans of worms. It is very possible the government would consider those items to belong to them, rather than the country in which the artefacts are discovered. There could be controversy. There might even be unpleasantness.'

'With respect, sir, that would not be St Mary's problem. We simply locate the items. What happens to them afterwards would not be our concern. In the same way a doctor gives her patient a new heart but does not necessarily impose any moral or social obligations on that patient to render themselves worthy of a new heart.'

'The logic of your argument is not lost on me, Dr Peterson. And, in the short term, such a course of action would, I think, keep those in charge of the country happy. For a while. People rarely object to additional fame and fortune. Their demands would increase, I'm sure, and to the detriment of our normal duties, but we should be able to buy ourselves a little time. Perhaps you and Dr Maxwell could put your heads together over the next few weeks.'

We nodded. He picked up another file. 'In the meantime, I have appointed Mr Evans as our temporary Head of Security. I shall make the announcement tomorrow. Should anyone ask, Mr Markham and his family are on parental leave and we expect they'll send us a postcard in due course. I don't see that we can do much more to protect ourselves. Not until a tangible threat materialises.'

And materialise it did. The very next day.

2

The following morning, I was down in the Great Hall with
the rest of my department, all of us still wading through the
Crete stuff. Notes, recordings, sketches, holos, everything. Our
bull-leaping holo was particularly spectacular. We'd watched
it several times – once for the actual bull-leaping – once to
focus on the spectators, their dress, social status, ethnicity and
so on – and once to concentrate on the king, the priestess, and
their court in the royal box. The Minoans had been a matri-
archal society, with women taking precedence over men, and
this had led to some discussion. Why there? Was it because
Crete was an island? Was it because they were a trading nation
and in permanent contact with other cultures? In which case,
why hadn't these cultures adopted Minoan beliefs? The discussion became brisk. That's St Mary's speak for no one had
actually come to blows yet. When the discussion became classified as vigorous, I would probably have to step in.

It was a perfectly normal day – Peterson was out of the
way in his office, doing whatever it is Deputy Directors do all
day long. I've never been able to work it out and I suspect he
doesn't know, either. Our liaison officer, Kalinda Black, was in
her office, hopefully massively exaggerating our achievements

to our overlords at Thirsk and securing our funding for the next twelve months. Dr Dowson was assisting the History Department in sorting through our written material. I'd no idea where Professor Rapson was but he was probably with Miss Lingoss so I wasn't too concerned. Nothing was on fire. No sinister green gas was seeping through the building melting everything in its path. Bashford was actually present and conscious. Everything was lovely – St Mary's was functioning exactly as it should do and there was toad-in-the-hole for lunch. You see – we can do it when we try.

I knew a visitor had arrived but I was concentrating on my last recording – the giant tsunami heading towards Crete to bring death and destruction on a massive scale – and, as usual when major events occurred at St Mary's, I was looking in completely the wrong direction.

I was recalled from scenes of the island's utter devastation by Dr Bairstow's voice in my ear requesting the pleasure of my company. My conscience was clear – both on my own account and that of my department because we hadn't been back from Crete long enough to get into any real trouble – so I bounded confidently up the stairs to his office. Mrs Partridge waved me through.

Dr Bairstow had a guest. A square, stocky woman with crinkly brown hair and a professionally blank expression. I thought she looked like an athlete. There wasn't an ounce of fat on her – it was all muscle. I suddenly became very conscious there wasn't an ounce of muscle on me – it was all fat.

'Dr Maxwell, may I introduce Captain Hyssop, seconded from the army to be our temporary Head of Security and . . .'

Her head snapped up. 'With respect, sir, not temporary. I am your new Head of Security. As my papers show.'

I'm an historian and I know an argument when I've just walked into the middle of one. This was one for Dr Bairstow to deal with.

'I'm sure they do, Captain, but St Mary's already has a Head of Security.'

'Who is absent, sir.'

'Who is on perfectly legitimate parental leave. From which he will return. To resume his position. As Head of Security.'

If it hadn't been so serious it would have been funny. I suspected I was in a room with two people accustomed to getting their way in all things. I watched with interest to see who would prevail. Mrs Partridge had also found an excuse to be present and was shuffling files on Dr Bairstow's briefing table.

I had no idea how the powers that be knew St Mary's was temporarily without its official Head of Security. I suspected that, for all our appearance of autonomy, Dr Bairstow was required to send regular reports to someone or other. Probably via Thirsk. I should imagine there's not much goes on here that someone isn't aware of – and it's not as if we're the most discreet organisation in the world. Just talk to Mrs Huntley-Palmer about the incident at the village fête. And it's not as if they were even our goats.

The implications were beginning to sink in. This was serious. Head of Security is a key post. Presumably this Hyssop person hadn't been just passing and decided to wander in on the off-chance of a job. She was an official but unknown quantity. I could well understand Dr Bairstow's . . . disquiet. He selects his own people. Always has done. His face, as usual, gave nothing away, but the signs were there if you knew what to look for and I was an expert. He was seriously not happy.

I decided to weigh in.

'I'm sorry, sir. I'm confused. Isn't Mr Evans our acting Head of Security? Do we actually need another Head of Security? Because then we will have three. Heads of Security, I mean. Where will we put them all? Will there be a rota?'

Hyssop frowned at me. 'Why would you need a rota?'

Great – a Head of Security without a sense of humour. This should be interesting.

'Actually,' I said, 'now I come to think of it – it's four.'

'What is?'

'Four Heads of Security. I forgot Major Guthrie down in the village.' I looked at Dr Bairstow. 'Is this one of those situations where we're about to find ourselves with more Heads of Security than actual people to be Head of Security over, sir?'

Fortunately, no one was taking any notice of me.

Dr Bairstow said evenly, 'Captain, your papers say you are here as a replacement for Mr Markham. Therefore, when Mr Markham returns you will no longer be his replacement. You are, therefore, temporary.'

'If Mr Markham does not return then I will no longer be temporary.'

'Obviously, Captain, you are privy to information I do not possess. Are you so certain Markham will not return?' He peered over his spectacles at her. 'Do you, perhaps, know something we do not?'

She hesitated for a moment and then said, 'It is felt there is a possibility Mr Markham will become engrossed in his new responsibilities and not wish to return to St Mary's.'

Dr Bairstow smiled his spider smile. The one inviting the unwary fly into his parlour. 'I rather suspect wishful thinking on someone's part. However, time ticks on and we have an issue to resolve. Let us decide to regard the word "temporary" as temporary and agree that you are here temporarily as Mr Markham's temporary replacement. We can resume this discussion on his return.'

She hesitated again, trying to work out what he'd just said, but it was a face-saving solution for everyone. Otherwise we could be here all day.

She turned to me. 'I still don't know who you are.'

Well, that was fine by me. Maxwell Top Tip for the Day – never voluntarily reveal your identity to authority.

Dr Bairstow remained silent so in the end I said brightly, 'Maxwell.'

There was a pause. I looked at Dr Bairstow who nodded slightly.

'Head of the History Department.'

She didn't offer to shake hands. 'Miss Maxwell.'

'Miss Hyssop.'

'It's "captain",' she said, frostily.

'It's "doctor",' I said, and we were off to a flying start.

I don't normally insist on my academic title too much but she would have read files on all of us. She'd know who I was. There will always be people who have trouble acknowledging professional women's qualifications – it's just surprising that this one was also a professional woman. Still, I suppose I should be grateful she wasn't calling me Mrs Farrell. Although, to be clear, there's nothing wrong with being Mrs Farrell.

I know Heads of Security aren't usually famed for their people skills but this surely had to be some sort of record. This Hyssop person had been here twenty minutes and was already

20

ruffling feathers. And Mrs Partridge hadn't brought in any tea so presumably she'd managed to annoy her as well. And – without tooting our trumpets too loudly – Dr Bairstow, Mrs Partridge and I were about the most normal and certainly the nicest people at St Mary's, so God knows what Hyssop was going to make of the rest of us.

We were all regarding each other frostily – and who knew how it would have ended – when Evans knocked at the open door. 'You wanted me, sir?'

'Come in, please, Mr Evans.'

I didn't want to be around while Dr Bairstow told him he'd lost his temporary promotion, although as far as I was concerned, Evans would be my go-to guy for Security issues and I was pretty sure everyone else would feel the same way.

I was about to murmur something polite and leave them to it when Dr Bairstow asked me if I'd introduce Hyssop to the History Department, announcing that since the two of us would be working closely together in future . . .

I shot him a look which he promptly ignored and said, 'Certainly, sir. This way, please, Captain Hyssop.'

I led her around the gallery. Now, I walk quickly. I have to because I'm a bit like a bicycle – if I don't maintain forward momentum then I fall over. And if you're going from A to B then there's no point in dawdling, is there? Some people ask me to slow down a bit and I do because I don't always realise I'm doing it. Hyssop simply lengthened her stride and kept pace.

We strode in silence until, halfway down the stairs, she suddenly said, 'Dr Bairstow neglected to inform you that I also have responsibility for Health and Safety within this building.'

I don't see why I shouldn't have a little fun occasionally.

21

'Congratulations,' I said. 'Although I'm sure you won't find that to be a particularly onerous part of your duties. I think you'll find we're more than compliant in most areas.'

No thunderbolt materialised. The god of historians must have been at lunch. By this time, we were downstairs and astonishingly, the History Department was still where I'd left them.

'This is the History Department,' I said, indicating all the blue-jumpsuited people working away with quiet enthusiasm. I very nearly didn't recognise them. 'We're working on the material gathered from our last assignment in Minoan Crete. Each historian had a particular area of responsibility – Agriculture, Commerce, Religion and so forth. We had to leave in rather a hurry because of the volcanic eruption, so the first job now is to make sure no one has mistakenly picked up anyone else's stuff. Once that's sorted we . . .'

At that moment, Sands picked up a box, looked at the label and said to Roberts, 'I think this is one of yours.'

'Oh God,' said Roberts, sighing. 'Not another one.'

''Fraid so.'

Roberts took the box. 'Why is my pile so much bigger than yours?'

'Well,' said Sands, obviously hardly able to believe his luck. 'That's because I work for Cunard.'

'You lucky dog,' said Roberts, stacking the box with all the others. 'Do you get a staff discount on your holiday cruises?'

'No, I mean—'

'Because that would be great.'

'No, when I say—'

'Can you get me mate's rates?'

'What? No.'

'Miserable bugger.'

'No—'

'I'd do it for you.'

'I'm trying to tell you—'

'Can't believe you'd treat a mate like that. Sort your own boxes.'

'No, wait, come back . . .'

Hyssop turned to me. 'What was that all about?'

'Mm?' I said, apparently engrossed in Roberts' report on crocus-growing and refusing to be involved.

'What exactly are they all doing?' said Hyssop, staring around at people rummaging away, making piles, arguing . . .

'I told you – sorting out their material prior to writing up their findings.'

'Who gathers this material?'

'We do.'

She frowned. 'Who's we?'

'The History Department.'

'Under the supervision of the Security Section?'

'No.'

There was a bit of a pause while she waited for me to qualify that statement while I tried not to imagine the History Department flapping its collective ears around us.

Eventually, she said, 'So the Security Section . . . ?'

'Accompanies the History Department at all times, advising on Security and risk issues.'

She was persistent. 'So they have control of . . .'

'No, they don't, but if Mr Evans shouts, "For God's sake, run," then trust me – we run.'

'Would it not be simpler and more cost-effective if it was

23

the Security Section who gathered the material for the History Department to analyse back at the safety of St Mary's?'

There were so many things wrong with that statement I hardly knew where to start. Firstly, that St Mary's could ever be designated as safe. Secondly, the impossibility of the History Department remaining quietly at home under any circumstances. And thirdly, fragile, ancient civilisations had enough on their plates dodging whatever disaster we'd turned up to document and record without having to cope with the Security Section and their bloody great boots crushing everything in their path.

What I said, however, was, 'When the Security Section can successfully demonstrate their knowledge of the differences between Linear A and Linear B, identify the language spoken at Troy, pick out William Marshall in the thick of the Battle of Lincoln, position themselves to avoid being trampled as the English are routed at Bannockburn . . . Oh, wait – they don't need to do any of that, do they, because we have something called a History Department.'

We stared at each other for a moment – as you do – and then she asked to see R&D. I wasn't sure either of them was yet ready to encounter the other but I could see she was the stubborn type who, if you told her not to do something would immediately go off and do it – twice, possibly – so I smiled and said, 'This way,' and took her back up the stairs to R&D.

Which didn't look too bad, fortunately. The last time I'd been in here they'd had Bashford dangling from the ceiling, sewn up in a cow's stomach for reasons which, I now realised, had never been satisfactorily explained. Or even explained at all.

I introduced her to everyone, and she was polite enough. I began to relax a little. And then we got to the Poisons

Cabinet – which was securely locked as regulations demanded. Slightly less regulationary – the key was in the lock. Because, explained dear old Mr Swanson, he was a trifle short-sighted these days and it made locating the key somewhat easier. He beamed at what he thought was Hyssop but was actually the iron maiden I had insisted be returned to Thirsk before we had a serious incident and which seemed to have found its way back to R&D like a massive, spiked homing pigeon.

Hyssop stared at him for a moment and then waved her hand in front of his face. His amiable smile never faltered.

I sighed.

'Can he see at all?' she demanded as we made our way back along the gallery.

'Of course he can,' I said indignantly. 'You couldn't put a blind man in charge of the Poisons Cabinet, could you? That would be ridiculous.'

'Kitchen next, I think,' she said, striding out and making me trot to keep up with her.

'Lovely,' I said, passing a fire axe on the wall and not using it in any way.

I had no fears for Mrs Mack, who listened intently to Hyssop's suggested new healthy-eating regime while firmly gripping the Oven Glove of Calamity and nodding solemnly every few sentences in a way that would have filled any normal person with the gravest misgivings, but which appeared to sail completely over Hyssop's head. She was obviously accustomed to being obeyed without question. I, on the other hand, am accustomed to imaginative historians explaining they hadn't *quite* understood my instructions, so sorry, and was pretty sure Mrs Mack wasn't listening to a word Hyssop was saying. With luck it would be months before Hyssop realised we were still on our normal diet of fat, sugar, cholesterol, starch and empty calories, and that none of us had seen anything green and leafy go by for some considerable time.

Fortunately – because I really didn't think I could handle much more – she requested the whereabouts of Deputy Director Peterson's office, so I dropped her there and trotted off to see Leon, who was preparing Tea Bag 2 for remote-site reconnaissance. Given that you rarely see a techie outside Hawking – they don't do well outside their natural environment – I was surprised to find he was already aware of the recent Hyssop-inspired blight.

'I haven't met her yet,' he said.

'If you push off now then you won't have to,' I said darkly, still seething.

Vast quantities of Archive boxes were piled outside TB2 waiting to be loaded and techies were scurrying up and down the ramp with tools and serious expressions. I gestured at the activity around us. 'You're not hanging around, are you?'

'No point. The sooner I'm gone, the sooner I'm back.'

'I thought you were taking Number Five.'

A word of explanation. Number Five is a pod. As is TB2. Pods are our means of travelling up and down the timeline. From the outside, they resemble small, stone-built shacks with flat roofs and no windows. The sort of timeless design that fits into any landscape at any time. They could be dwelling houses in Mesopotamia, huts in medieval France, or sheds on a modern allotment.

Inside, they're small and cramped and smell horribly of cabbage. No one knows why. It's a mystery. They can also smell of terrified historian, hot electrics and exploded toilet. Although that's not a mystery.

Leon drew me aside. 'How would you feel if I took Adrian and Mikey with me? I'm really not at all sure we want Hyssop – and by extension, her employers – knowing we have a couple of unregistered geniuses living with us. Are you?'

'Good thought,' I said. One of my nightmares is being held responsible for those two. Although I love them dearly. Most of the time.

'And,' he said, more slowly, 'I'd like to take Matthew, as well.'

I opened my mouth to demand why and then closed it again. Mikey and Adrian are, both of them, a bit of a disastrous good ideas factory. By which I mean their ideas are mostly brilliant, but the world isn't quite ready for some of them just yet. Most of them. All right, all of them. We definitely didn't want either Adrian or Mikey or their ideas falling into the wrong hands.

The same arguments could apply to Matthew and his uncanny affinity with the Time Map. All Time Maps. Ours and the Time Police's. The same arguments *should* apply to Matthew as Adrian and Mikey, it's just . . . I'd rather looked forward to a little Max/Matthew time.

I hesitated.

'I know,' said Leon. 'But it won't be for long. And it's not as if they won't enjoy themselves. Mikey will have two or three brilliant ideas a day and Matthew and Adrian can build them. I'll intervene occasionally as the voice of reason, sanity and survival.'

I still hesitated.

'And we'll take Professor Penrose with us as Matthew's tutor, and on rainy days, the three of them can work on Markham's PA.'

Matthew and Professor Penrose were building Markham his own personal assistant. Don't ask. Just don't ask. There had been one incident already. In the tea-sodden aftermath someone had jokingly referred to it as R2-Tea2 and the name had stuck. Despite this tiny setback, the professor's and Matthew's enthusiasm continued unabated. Only the other day I'd come across them trying to teach it simple tasks.

The lesson had gone thusly:

'R2-Tea2. What is the weather today?'

'On the third stroke, it will be 12:43 precisely.'

The clock said a quarter to four.

So that was going well, then.

'Hmm,' I said, dragging my mind back to the enticing thought of Adrian- and Mikey-free days. 'Theoretically, the thought of shunting ninety per cent of our troublemakers out of the building and into your area of responsibility is very tempting. It's just . . .'

'I know,' he said again. 'But I think you might have your hands full here and, from a parental point of view, it's not good for a son to see his mother thumping the new Head of Security.'

Indignantly, I drew myself up, considered his words and then let myself sag again, and that can't have been a pretty sight.

'I understand why.' I sighed. 'I just don't like it.'

Leon took my hands. 'It won't be for very long. I don't think things will go horribly wrong here, but if they do, you might be glad Matthew's out of the firing line.'

I nodded. He was right. He often is. No need to tell him that.

'And when we're all jumping from place to place, Adrian

and Mikey can pretend they're still on the run from the Time Police. For them, it will be like the good old days again.'

Further down Hawking someone shouted Leon's name. He looked over my shoulder. 'Yes, I'm coming.'

'I'll let you get on.'

'Try not to worry, Max.'

I nodded and left him and was just crossing the Hall when Peterson called down to me. It struck me he was looking nervous.

'What's up?' I said, climbing the stairs. 'Murdered Hyssop and buried her body in the Sunken Garden?'

'That's Option B,' he said. 'Are you busy?'

'Oh God, yes,' I said, suspecting he wanted me to do something ghastly. 'Tremendously busy, I'm afraid.'

'Do you want to come to church with me?'

And I was right.

I tried not to sound too horrified. 'Church?'

'Yes, the big building at the top of the village with the pointy roof and the dead people in the garden.'

I stepped back. 'Oh my God – you have killed her, haven't you? You've killed Hyssop. That didn't take long. Although I never thought it would be you. Well – the important thing is not to panic. You must distract people . . . somehow . . . and I'll get the body out. I wish Markham were here – this is just the sort of thing he's good at. Although if he were here then she wouldn't be and we wouldn't be having this conversation. The key thing is not to go off half-cocked but to keep our heads. Go and wipe your fingerprints off everything you've touched today and then go and talk to Mrs Partridge. About something or other. She can be your alibi. Where have you left her? Hyssop, I mean. It's vital that we . . .'

29

I trailed off as Hyssop emerged from the Library and turned off towards the Security Section.

I clutched his arm. 'Oh my God, Tim – you've killed the wrong woman.'

He was leaning against the wall with his arms folded. 'When you've quite finished . . . For your information I haven't killed anyone.'

'Oh,' I said. 'That's disappointing. What do you want me for, then?'

'I want you to come with me while I talk to the vicar.'

I said cautiously, 'About . . . ?'

'Getting married. To Lingoss,' he added, bringing me completely up to speed.

I was quite indignant. 'You're getting married in a *church*?'

'People do, you know. It used to be quite traditional.'

'What's the matter with our chapel?'

'Well, the thing is, Max – our chapel here isn't big enough. Felix has a family. And I know how hard this is for you to understand, but some of us do have friends outside St Mary's. So it's the church for us. And Markham's not here so I thought you might like to come and provide moral support.'

Well, anything's better than working, I suppose.

I shot off to change and we ambled out of the front door and down the drive. It was a lovely sunny day. In the distance I could hear the chug-chug of giant machinery, and the rich smell of hay hung heavy in the air. And back I went again. Six hundred and fifty years into the past.

I hadn't said anything to anyone – not even to Dr Stone in our weekly half-hour session on Friday afternoons – but occasionally I still saw St Mary's as it was six hundred and

30

fifty years ago. Just as it had been when I was stranded there in 1399. Occasionally, when I wasn't concentrating – which, let's face it, was pretty much all the time – I still tried to walk through doors that weren't there any longer. Or, more painfully, walked into walls that hadn't been there in 1399. The fact that they were here now – solid, recognisable and painful – in no way mitigated the regularity of these occurrences. Sometimes I'd look up and a faint door would just be closing and I'd swear Fat Piers was on his way to the pantry. Or Margery off to do the laundry. Or a dim chicken – I mean dim as in faint, not dim as in stupid. Trust me, chickens in 1399 could have brought down society if they'd put their minds to it. I don't know why Henry V bothered with archers when he could have just taken a contingent of chickens to Agincourt. Resistance would have crumbled and he'd have been king of France by the end of the week. Where was I? Yes, talking about my occasional problems with seeing things at St Mary's as they were in 1399 and not things as they were now.

Either I was going mad – not as impossible as you might think – or, and the thought wouldn't leave me – it was the result of too much timeline activity. Our normal assignments can last for anything from a single afternoon to about six months, but I'd been at the medieval St Mary's nearly a year. I'd lived as one of them. I'd helped with the harvests, collected firewood, fed the chickens, dug ditches and spread the washing over bushes. I'd become part of their lives. They'd imprinted on me. I wondered if I'd imprinted on them. As a ghost, perhaps. And, as I saw their faint outlines, did they see me? Did they walk around saying, 'Do you remember that funny foreign woman? The one who set fire to everything? I could have sworn I saw her over by the stables just now.' Did they believe I was some sort of hero whose ghost would return in times of crisis to save them? Like Theseus? Or Arthur? Or was I just the weirdo who kept starting fires? Well, I think we all know the answer to that one.

The thing is – and it's a big thing – I'd made more jumps than anyone I knew, and I couldn't help wondering if these flashbacks were some sort of side effect of too much time travel. Do we actually leave a little bit of ourselves behind in each time we jump to? Was I slowly diminishing? Fading away? I looked down at myself. No, I still looked fairly substantial. Perhaps it was pieces of my mind I was leaving behind. Or would it be more accurate to say pieces of my heart? In which case, there was a very large lump of it still in 1399. Should I say anything to Dr Stone? Suppose there was a limit to the number of times a person could safely jump up and down the timeline and I'd exceeded it and they made me stop?

'Nice day,' said Peterson, and my mind cleared and I was just me again, strolling down the road with him on our way to convince the Church of England he was a responsible member of the parish – which was perfectly true as long as nobody enquired exactly what he was responsible for.

We wandered down the hill, Peterson chuntering on about something or other, and me inhaling deeply and forcing my sinuses to earn their keep just for once. We crossed the little stone bridge over the stream which marked the village boundary. Peterson stopped to peer down into the dark water beneath. I did as I always did and looked upstream. Because every now and then, my treacherous dreams take me back to a still and sunny glade beside a pool running with clear, cold water, where a man watched me weave a daisy chain.

In what I told myself was an effort to exorcise these too real imaginings, I did once try to follow this stream, to find the place where I'd sat with William Hendred, but I'd underestimated the alterations to the landscape over six centuries. Not only could I not find the little pool again, but the course of the stream had changed as well. I tramped up and down for ages but it had all gone – the little glade, the pool, the flowers, the dragonflies. I don't know why I searched. Was I once more hoping to see a man smiling at me from the other bank? Or was it truly a tiny moment in time and space that was gone forever?

'You all right?' said Peterson.

I came back. 'Yes, of course. Why wouldn't I be?'

He looked at me for a while and then said, 'No idea. Come on. We don't want to upset the church, do we?'

Personally I couldn't see any reason at all for not upsetting the church – which never seems to care if it upsets me – but given that on this occasion I was Peterson's wingman – poor deluded fool – it was probably best not to incur religious wrath until after he and Lingoss had safely tied the knot.

The village was its usual hive of inactivity. Everyone was at work in Rushford. These days, of course, no one works in the fields all day. Or if they do then it's in a super-luxurious, GPS-guided, fully automated tea-and-biscuit-dispensing harvester sophisticated enough to fly to the moon should it choose to do so.

It was uphill to the church. The road slopes down from St Mary's to the bridge then up again to the church as it watches over the rest of the village.

They'd made some changes since 1399. There was a lych-gate – the traditional resting place for the coffin to pause, out of the rain. The yews had gone, of course – even yews don't last that long and at some point the churchyard had been enclosed by a dry-stone wall. On the other side was grazing land, just as it had been nearly six and a half centuries ago, scattered with horse chestnuts. Sheep clustered under the spreading branches, enjoying the shade on this hot afternoon, just as their ancestors had so often done.

Three or four of them grazed in the churchyard – sheep, I mean, not ancestors – keeping the grass down. When I was little, I used to think sheep were eating the dead bodies. Makes you wonder how I grew up to be so normal, doesn't it?

We pushed open the gate and walked up the path to be greeted by a short wiry individual in running gear who leaped out from behind a weeping angel.

'Hello there. You must be . . .' he consulted something written on the back of his hand, 'Timothy Peterson.'

Peterson nodded.

'Kevin Aguta.'

'Oh,' I said. 'You're the . . .' and stopped just in time.

He grinned. 'The Rev Kev at your service. I think it's got quite a ring to it, don't you? And you are . . . ?'

'Max,' I said, shaking the vicar's outstretched hand.

'Lovely to meet you,' he said, looking as if it actually was, which given that he served on the Parish Council and frequently encountered St Mary's in our embarrassing post-catastrophe moments, was very good of him. 'Do come in.'

'If you don't mind,' I said, 'I'd like to take a moment to look around the gravestones. Professional interest,' and then panicked in case he thought I was Rushford's answer to Burke and Hare and hastily added, 'Historical interest.'

'Of course,' he said. 'It's lovely to welcome our friends from St Mary's.'

I couldn't help but be impressed at this truly Christian display of tolerance and forgiveness. Very few people publicly claim us as friends.

'Besides,' said Peterson, 'we're all pretty sure she'll burst into flames the moment she crosses the threshold.'

The Rev Kev's face lit up. He turned to me. 'Are you sure you won't come in? I've never actually seen that happen, you know. Life in a rural parish is very quiet. Even when that parish does contain St Mary's.'

I grinned and they disappeared off to wherever vicars usher their prospective victims and I looked around the lumpy churchyard. For reader reassurance, I think we can assume the lumps were only old unmarked graves whose occupants slumbered serenely in the sunshine, rather than hastily disposed-of corpses, improperly buried. It occurred to me that if St Mary's ever did have to dispose of Hyssop then this would be an ideal place. They'd never notice an additional hump.

Dr Dowson had said burials from the medieval era were probably congregated in the south-east corner of the churchyard, although no one could be absolutely sure. I stood in the porch and looked around. If the church was oriented in the usual way – east to west – then the south-east corner was over there.

I walked slowly between the graves, hoping the dates would give me some sort of clue. You'd think the earliest dates would be nearest the church, wouldn't you, and then spread outwards in a neat radius, but no. There were graves all over the place. No rhyme or reason to their placement. The same names seemed to occur regularly – local families obviously. There were no

Hendreds anywhere. I knew the line hadn't died out – their descendants, the Hendys, still lived over at Castle Hendred on the other side of Whittington – but it looked as if William Hendred's particular line had died with him.

I knew he wasn't buried at St Mary's and I was almost certain he hadn't been returned to the Hendred clan, which just left this churchyard as his probable final resting place. But if he was here then his grave was unmarked. There had probably been a simple wooden cross but that would have disappeared a long time ago. Was his shade watching me now as I wandered among the haphazard rows of the dead on this hot June day? Did he remember?

A terrible wave of homesickness welled up out of nowhere. It wasn't that I was unhappy with Leon and Matthew – far from it. Oh, I don't know . . . I think if William had gone on to live a long and happy life then I'd feel . . . not happier . . . more reconciled, perhaps. And I'd been happy then and now it was all gone. Had been gone for a very long time. Time is inexorable. The centuries piled up behind me like a cliff-face. I floated in time, rootless and unanchored. Not knowing my place. Here and now? Or there and then?

And time is cruel. It had rolled across the landscape, bringing enough change to make me a stranger in my own time while leaving just enough faint and familiar outlines to pull at my heart. The church was virtually unchanged. The line of the original village street was still there. Even some of the houses were in exactly the same position. Yes, the ford had gone, but the same stream still flowed. And through the trees, I could catch a glimpse of St Mary's. Larger and more modern but still occupying the same place in the landscape. Somewhere over there were stones and maybe a few timbers that had known William Hendred and Joan of Rouen.

'Joan of York,' said Walter in my head. Walter of Shrewsbury had been the steward at St Mary's. It had not been a happy relationship for either of us. Joan of Rouen, I'd called myself then.

But I never got to be Joan of St Mary's.

I found a shady spot by the wall and made myself comfortable. William Hendred was here somewhere. That would have to be enough for me. I sat under a horse chestnut tree with my quiet memories.

I was roused by Tim's voice. He looked cheerful enough, so obviously all his paperwork had passed muster and he'd been considered fit to join the ranks of the soon to be matrimonialised.

We waved goodbye to the Rev Kev who seemed disappointed I had remained unignited.

'That's it,' said Peterson, striding off down the hill at a great pace while I trotted alongside. 'Date fixed. Service fixed. Everything fine.'

'Shouldn't Lingoss have been here?' I puffed. 'Are you actually qualified to make these decisions by yourself?'

'Of course I am,' he said, indignantly. 'As Deputy Director I make life-and-death decisions on an hourly basis.'

'So, no.'

'No. Felix handed me a list of written instructions, together with the appropriate paperwork and declarations, and I simply passed them to the vicar, who said yes that all seemed satisfactory, expressed a wish to meet her before the actual deed, and the next minute I was on the other side of the door. Do you think he could be related to Dr Bairstow, perhaps?'

'Or just keen to get you off the premises.'

'Doubt it,' he said. 'I'm delightful. And thanks for your support.'

'I didn't do anything.'

'You didn't burn down the church. I suspect that would have snookered my chances forever.'

We were passing the Falconburg Arms. 'You may signify your gratitude by buying me a drink.'

'Good idea.'

'And lunch.'

'What?'

'Thanks to me and my absence, the day went smoothly. You owe me.'

'Oh, by the way,' he said, ushering me towards the invitingly open door. 'I forgot to tell you. Dr Bairstow wants you to take Hyssop on a jump.'

'What? Where? When?'

'Somewhere non-lethal were his only instructions. I look forward to seeing you struggle with that one. Afternoon, Ian. Are we too late for lunch?'

The non-lethal part of the assignment turned out to be a bugger since this meant no battlefields, famous assassinations, plagues, epidemics, major geological or meteorological events and nothing religious. Which didn't leave a lot. I scoured History books, data stacks, consulted our list of past jumps and just couldn't seem to find anything quite right. And yes, anyone who thinks that my inability to find something suitable was directly related to my not wanting to take Hyssop on a jump is probably slightly correct.

In and around all this, Leon and Matthew readied for depart-ure.

For a boy who had barely owned the rags he'd once stood up in, Matthew had managed to accumulate a fair amount of kit and most of it was stacked outside TB2.

Clothes, some books – not as many as I would like because he still preferred electronic reading, but any reading was good, I supposed – together with his proudly possessed toolkit – just like his dad's but smaller – his version of the Time Map – on which he wanted to work, he said – and a couple of boxes of unnamed but absolutely vital possessions he couldn't live without.

Leon's slightly smaller pile of baggage lay alongside – all ready to be loaded. Now they'd packed their gear there was an awful lot of empty space in our rooms. People were vanishing before my eyes. Guthrie, Grey, North, Markham, and now Adrian, Mikey, and Matthew as well. And Professor Penrose. And Leon. It occurred to me that whenever I looked forward to a little family-together time something always intervened.

Leon looked at me.

I managed a smile.

'We talked about this,' he said. 'It won't be for long.'

I nodded. 'I know. It's just . . . there have been a lot of goodbyes recently.'

'Yes, but there will be plenty of hellos again. Before you know it.'

'Where are Mikey and Adrian?'

'Already loaded and raring to go.'

Matthew shot into Hawking – tousled, triumphant and unbelievably dirty for someone who'd only shot back to his room to look for his second scratchpad.

'I've changed my mind,' I said. 'Both of you get out of here now and never come back.'

They grinned at me and my heart turned over.

Professor Penrose arrived. By contrast he was carrying just a small backpack.

'Is your stuff already loaded, professor?'

'No, no, this is it. Are you ready, Matthew?'

Matthew nodded importantly and pulled out a familiar remote control. Without exception, everyone in Hawking stepped back. One or two people leaped into the nearest pod and slapped the door shut behind them.

'Excellent,' said the professor, eyes gleaming behind his spectacles. 'Load it up, Matthew.'

Matthew stabbed a button and Markham's PA appeared from a dark corner of the hangar. This was a very carefully designated gender-neutral mechanical device on caterpillar tracks with a dodgy guidance system and a streak of malicious cruelty. Ask Markham about his scalded willy. Just don't let him show you.

As a quick aside, it was Bashford who had filled out the Accident Book after R2-Tea2's spectacular debut. Spelling has always constituted a bit of a hurdle for him and Markham's appendage had figured throughout as 'Mr Markham's scolded willy'. According to Hunter, not as inaccurate a phrase as you might think.

Professor Penrose, Matthew and the robot rumbled up the ramp together and into the pod. There was a small crash as Matthew drove it into the toilet door. Leon tried not to wince.

'Ready when you are,' said Dieter, emerging from TB2.

Leon turned to me. 'It's time.'

I nodded. 'Take care.'

'You too.'

He took my hand in his warm one, kissed it and then my cheek, and turned away. Matthew presented himself for a hug. How did he become so sticky?

The ramp closed behind them. I stepped back behind the safety line.

'Don't worry,' said Dieter, beside me. 'They'll look after him.'

'Look after who? Matthew?'

'Leon.'

TB2 blinked out of existence.

I went back to work.

I pondered the Hyssop assignment some more, pacing around my office and muttering to myself, until Rosie Lee complained I was giving her a headache. I wanted to explain it was the duty of every supervisor to get up their underlings' noses as far and as frequently as possible, but in the interests of world peace and inspiration, took myself off downstairs to the History Department instead. Where, obviously, some sort of trauma had just occurred because Mr Bashford was stretched out on the floor, unconscious. (I've had that put on a hot key.)

Bashford is the Planet Jupiter of St Mary's. In the same way that Jupiter's gravity attracts comets and asteroids and keeps the Earth safe, Bashford somehow manages to hoover up every mishap, accident or injury so the rest of us can continue to live very nearly incident-free lives. For which we're all very grateful.

I took a quick look around. No sign of our new Health and Safety officer anywhere – which I gather is about par for the course when it comes to accidents and H&S officers. Mrs Partridge had charge of the Accident Book – sorry, books plural, because we get through about four a year. I was pretty sure Hyssop would soon be demanding to be Custodian of the Sacred Accident Books and I made a mental note to be present when she tried to wrest them from Mrs Partridge.

Returning to the History Department . . . curiosity overrode my better judgement – the very definition of an historian. Stepping over Bashford, I enquired what had happened here. Since he was sprawled at the foot of the stairs, I think I thought he'd just taken a bit of a tumble.

Mr Sands looked up from the prone body at his feet. 'A rather unfortunate accident, Max.'

'I can see that. What happened?'

'Well, in my latest murder it's vital to show the murderer is left-handed.'

Before anyone runs away with the idea that David Sands is a serial assassin, he writes books. Good ones. Check them out at the library. They need the custom and he needs the Public Lending Rights.

Sands was continuing. 'Anyway, we were discussing with which hand the victim would defend himself if threatened with a weapon. Sykes said survival instincts would kick in and people would use whichever hand was nearest and Bashford said no, people would automatically use their dominant hand. There was animated discussion.'

This was St Mary's speak for a near bloodbath.

'In the end, to keep the peace, we decided on a practical experiment. People put forward their considered hypotheses –' St Mary's speak for placing their bets – 'and I picked up the hardback edition of Leick's *Mesopotamia* and chucked it at Bashford. To see which hand he would instinctively use without having had the time to think about it.'

I sighed. 'Well, obviously that's where you went wrong. Bashford has no survival instincts. He once waved at Boudicca.'

We both stared down at Bashford, still unconscious at our feet.

Sands nodded. 'Well, yes, with hindsight, he wasn't perhaps the ideal choice but he was so keen to prove his theory, Max.'

I sighed again. Yes, he would have been. We stared at Bashford some more.

'Well?' I said, actually quite interested to hear the results of this one. 'Bashford's left-handed so which hand did he use? Left or right?'

Sands shuffled his feet. 'Neither, actually. He stood there like the proverbial pillar of salt and Gwendolyn Leick smacked him cleanly between the eyes and knocked him out cold.'

We all peered again at Bashford who had been arranged neatly in the recovery position by his caring colleagues. At the bottom of the stairs . . . Hmm . . . I'd had an idea.

I roused myself. 'Anyone called Sick Bay?'

'On their way, Max. I think Dr Stone wants to talk to you about having a medical presence permanently on hand in the History Department.'

'Hmm . . .' I said, not listening. 'Well, carry on, everyone.' I wandered off.

Because I'd just had a Brilliant Idea.

I spent a couple of hours in the Library researching, selected my team, checked that Wardrobe could accommodate us at such short notice and danced off to see Dr Bairstow.

Who wasn't in his office – an event so unusual as to be worthy of comment. He takes very great care not to see anything he shouldn't and we make very sure he doesn't see anything he shouldn't. Mostly this is achieved by him remaining quietly on one side of his office door and us remaining on the other. It's a system that works well. Not today, however.

Mrs Partridge was at her desk, banging things around with less than her usual controlled grace.

I said, '. . . Um . . .'

'He's with Mr Strong,' she said, closing a drawer with slightly more force than necessary.

'. . . Um . . .'

'It would appear that Mr Strong has not responded well to being instructed to level the Sunken Garden.'

'Oh.' No, he wouldn't. Along with the South Lawn, the Sunken Garden was his pride and joy.

'He responded even less well when requested to fell the old

mulberry avenue because the trees obscure the sightlines should St Mary's ever find itself under attack.'

Crash went another drawer.

I don't think any of us need three guesses as to where those particular suggestions emanated. Bloody Hyssop. God, that woman was hard work.

'Dr Bairstow is with Mr Strong now.' She paused.

I waited breathlessly for the conclusion to her tale which, ideally, would be along the lines of *and they're burying her under the compost heap even as we speak.*

The door opened behind me and Dr Bairstow appeared. I snuck a look at his hands. Disappointingly clean. No smell of compost, either.

'Well, Dr Maxwell?'

'The assignment for Hyssop, sir.'

'Come in.'

He seated himself and I passed over the file.

'Amy Robsart, sir.'

He sat back. 'Go on.'

'Well, I wanted a jump that St Mary's could get something from – not just a quick sightseeing trip for Hyssop – and when I saw . . .'

I stopped. Bashford had been scooped up and removed to Sick Bay where he now lay, palely recovering and with the reverse classification ƧƐ9 imprinted between his eyes.

'. . . and I saw the stairs, sir, and suddenly thought of Amy Robsart. A low-risk assignment but with the chance of solving a centuries-old mystery.'

He twirled my data stack.

'Quite a small jump.'

'Yes, sir. Me, Hyssop, Sands and Evans.'

'Evans?'

'Well, Hyssop's a bit of an unknown quantity.' Which was me being polite. You see, I can do it. 'What we do is not for everyone and I don't want to be in the position of her not finding that out until it's too late. Hence the inclusion of two big blokes in case we have any quelling to do. Either of contemporaries or, of course, Hyssop herself.'

He nodded. 'Will you brief her separately?'

There's always an historical briefing before each jump, to which Security politely listen, but I know they hold their own later. I also know that, in the interests of inter-departmental harmony, historians are usually excluded from that because, basically, the Security Section sits down and goes through the entire jump, moment by moment, step by step, anticipating what can go wrong, who will screw up what, who's not likely to make it back in one piece and who's not likely to make it back at all. Presumably Evans would brief Hyssop. I wondered how much she would listen. Would she turn out to be one of those bosses who implements new methods immediately for no better reason than stamping themselves on their new department? Quite a lot of babies get thrown out with the bathwater that way.

'I had thought about a separate briefing for her, sir, but on second thoughts, if she's to become one of us, I don't want to emphasise her differentness.'

'Rather worryingly, I take your meaning, despite your eccentric use of the English language. Very well, see to it, Dr Maxwell.'

*   *   *

47

We held the briefing in my office. Rosie Lee bustled about looking important while Evans actually made the tea, which was good of him, and it was only after the meeting had finished that I realised he'd helped himself to all the best biscuits.

'OK, everyone,' I said, when we were all settled. 'Everyone's met Captain Hyssop, I believe, and Captain, you know everyone here.'

Everyone nodded. I always try and begin with all parties agreeing on something. It's usually straight downhill from there. And this occasion was no exception.

'Now then,' Hyssop said, pulling up her chair. 'I've read through your preliminary notes and the mission will proceed along these lines: Evans and I will lead the . . .'

I'm not famed for my social skills and when I don't like someone, the struggle is real. If it had been Sands or Sykes I'd have grinned and told them to wind their necks in. They would have grinned back and wound their necks in and that would have been that. This was slightly more difficult. Some degree of tact was called for.

'Let me stop you there,' I said. 'This is St Mary's. We are the Institute of Historical Research. We are historians. We do the research. We lead the assignments. We call the shots. Our Security Section keeps us safe – for which we are all very grateful. In an emergency you will be expected to take the appropriate action to save everyone's lives, but under normal circumstances, assignments are under the control of the most senior historian present. In this instance that would be me. I think it's always important to be clear about these things, don't you?'

She flushed scarlet but I didn't see what else I could have done. I couldn't wait until the end of the meeting and then take her aside for a quiet word. It would have been too late by then. And, frankly, she'd called me out in front of everyone – she could hardly complain if I'd done the same.

Hyssop obviously thought the Security Section should rule the roost. For what reasons remained unclear. I suspected a great deal of insecurity on her part. Markham had none of those problems – always content to remain in the background and only emerging when needed. And Major Guthrie before him. Hyssop obviously felt she had something to prove – which was understandable – but this thrusting herself into the forefront of every situation was not the way to do it.

To cover the awkward silence, I pressed on.

'To begin, then. England, 1560. Elizabeth Tudor has reigned for two years. She has favourites – all men – and her favourite is Robert Dudley, Master of the Queen's Horse, who is married to Amy Robsart. We don't know a lot about Amy – born 7th June 1532 and died 8th September 1560 at the age of twenty-eight. The daughter of Sir John Robsart of Syderstone Hall, she was married to Robert Dudley three days before her eighteenth birthday. Their marriage lasted ten years but it was a sad sort of life. Amy didn't follow Dudley to court. She never had any children. She never even had her own household. She rarely saw her husband. A kind of non-life, really.

'Anyway, back to the queen and Dudley, neither of whom is behaving particularly discreetly and as far as Elizabeth is capable of it, she probably loves him. Word on the street is that if he wasn't already married then everyone would be looking at England's next king.'

I paused in case Hyssop wanted to ask why Dudley didn't just divorce his wife, but she didn't. She'd brought several files with her and I suspected she'd been reading around the subject, so good for her.

I continued. 'Elizabeth was notoriously unkind to other women so Dudley and Amy live apart. By this time, Amy is unwell. It's thought she had breast cancer.'

'So everyone was waiting for Amy to die?' said Hyssop.

I hesitated. 'On the face of it, yes, but can I come back to that?'

She nodded, scribbling on her pad. I noticed she took notes by hand.

'There are rumours that Elizabeth is pregnant by Dudley. The Spanish ambassador actually reported that Dudley was trying to kill his wife so he could marry the queen. In 1559, Amy moves to Cumnor Place, which in those days was in Berkshire. She's comfortable there – she has at least ten servants, including a maid, Mrs Picto, who is a relative of hers, a Mrs Owens, and a Mrs Oddingsells, whose exact relationship is unknown.'

I brought up several images of Cumnor Place. 'It's unclear how accurate these are. The house was modernised soon afterwards and very little remains of the original.

'On Sunday, 8th September 1560, for some reason that has never been established, Amy orders her entire household to visit the fair at Abingdon, leaving her completely alone in the house.'

I brought up a large-scale map of the area showing Cumnor Place in relation to Oxford and Abingdon.

'She gives everyone the day off. Except there's a problem. Mrs Oddingsells is quite offended because Sunday is the day set aside for the common people to visit the fair and no person of quality would be seen there on that day. There's a bit of an argument and, presumably to mollify her, Amy invites Mrs Oddingsells to dine with her that evening. Apparently this works because Mrs Oddingsells departs – although not to the fair. She and Mrs Owens spend a quiet afternoon playing cards in their private rooms.

'The day passes peacefully and then, at some point, the servants return and discover Amy Robsart lying dead at the foot of a flight of stairs. Cause of death is a broken neck, although she has also suffered two fairly minor injuries to her head.'

I turned to Captain Hyssop. 'Your thoughts?'

She put down her pen and closed her eyes. 'The two women – Owens and Oddingsells – heard nothing?'

'There are reports that at some point they thought they heard a crash but it wasn't loud enough or close enough to warrant investigation.'

'Were there any signs she'd been attacked? Signs of a struggle? Disarranged clothing? Defensive wounds?'

'Apart from the head wounds – no. Although – and I think you might find this interesting – even though she'd supposedly fallen down a flight of stairs with enough force to break her neck, her headdress was still more or less in place.'

'Could she have been killed elsewhere and placed at the foot of the stairs?'

'Very possibly.'

'How far did she fall?'

'Another interesting question. The staircase – made of stone – is described as a pair of stairs. The building of the time is gone now but we do know the stairs were curved around a central newel post – so some sort of spiral staircase. It's thought there might have been a half-landing – a flight of steps, some sort of landing, and then second flight of steps – which would account for the description of a pair of stairs.'

She nodded. 'I see, but surely that means neither flight could be very long.'

'That's right. Probably around only eight steps in each.'

'That's not very many.'

'No, but I've fallen down a flight of stone steps and they're not forgiving. I thought I'd broken every bone in my body and I was covered in bruises.'

'But Amy wasn't. Covered in bruises, I mean.'

'No.'

'I believe bruises can develop after someone has died.'

'They can, but not apparently in this instance.'

'Well,' she said. 'This is interesting, isn't it?' She looked at me. 'Your theory?'

'That she was murdered, but not by her husband.'

'Then whom?'

I hesitated. 'The queen.'

'To ensure she could marry Dudley?'

'To ensure she could *not* marry Dudley.'

She sat for a moment. 'Oh. Yes. I see. That's the point you wanted to come back to just now, isn't it?'

I nodded. 'It's popular and romantic to see Elizabeth and Dudley as a pair of tragic lovers who could never marry, but I think Elizabeth was much too hard-headed to give power away. She'd come too far and endured too much to make herself subject to a husband. Marriage, remember, placed a wife in legal submission to her husband. Elizabeth had no intention of marrying Dudley. She had no intention of ever marrying anyone. She'd seen how her sister's marriage to Philip of Spain cost her a great deal of support. She saw how Mary laboured to please both country and husband. And later, of course, there was her cousin, Mary Stuart, who notoriously wanted it all – throne, husband and child. The acquisition of the last two cost her the first. I think Elizabeth had already worked out that perpetually single and perpetually available was the way to go.

'I also suspect a large part of Dudley's charm was his un-availability. She was all set to play the marriage game with every prince in Europe. The last thing she needed would be Dudley hanging around her neck like a dead albatross. Consider this. Amy was dying – but then what? Dudley would be free to marry her. Factions would develop. He would begin to accrue power. Elizabeth was still in the early stages of her reign and not that secure. So, Amy had to die in a manner that precluded Dudley from ever being in a position to marry her, Elizabeth. With his wife mysteriously dead, suspicion would fall on Dudley, which meant Elizabeth could safely distance herself from him. In fact, her ministers would urge her to do so. I go with those who say Elizabeth never had any intention of marrying anyone. She was popular and she was loved but as soon as she gave birth to a male heir, she'd be out. Kings were the proper way to go. A queen was an affront to all right-thinking people, i.e. men. And she knew it. And no matter how much she loved Dudley – she was her father's daughter. Queens do kill inconvenient men. Her cousin, Mary Stuart, killed her own husband.'

Hyssop nodded. 'Interesting.' She turned to Sands. 'And your theory?'

'Meeting a lover,' he said, promptly. 'She cleared all her household out of the way so he could visit in secret.'

'Even more interesting. Mr Evans?'

I was surprised but pleased to see she thought Security should have an opinion. And she was right – they'd been on as many jumps as us – some History was bound to have rubbed off on them.

Evans grinned. 'Dudley panicked. Elizabeth was being besieged by suitors. He was convinced she would choose one of them. Everyone was – because marriage was the only proper state for a woman. As soon as she acquired a husband, he, Dudley, would be out. He wasn't bright and he wasn't subtle. He arranged for Amy to be killed. Remember, his man, Sir Richard Verney, was unexpectedly discovered not far away. I think Dudley sent Amy a message – arranging some sort of reconciliation perhaps. He urged her to get rid of her household so they could be alone together. Amy waited quietly. Someone knocks at the door, she runs down the stairs to greet him, Sir Richard steps out of the shadows, a gentle shove – no more Amy.'

'Risky, though,' I said. 'Shoving someone down the stairs doesn't always mean a broken neck. She might have just banged her elbow.'

'Not if he broke her neck first.'

'And then threw her down the stairs.'

'Or just placed her at the bottom. Remember the headdress.'

'And you, Captain,' I said. 'Your theory?'

'Having read the material,' she tapped the files, 'I'm inclined towards the accident theory. There was no need for murder. She was dying of cancer and she had brittle bones because of it. Possibly she caught her foot in the hem of her dress – as you say, the staircase was almost certainly made of stone and one of those breakneck spiral affairs – and if it was bright sunshine outside then it was probably quite dark inside – and she snapped her own neck. After all,' she said, 'it's not the fall that kills you – it's the landing.'

I closed my file. 'Let's go and find out, shall we?'

We assembled in Hawking Hangar, outside Number Eight and checked each other over. No jewellery, wristwatches and so forth. None of us are allowed tattoos. We all have long hair – even the blokes have what we call the historian shag. There was a vague rumour that Hyssop had attempted to impose a more structured hairstyle upon her team and her team had resisted the imposition. I don't know how Dr Bairstow had heard of it – except he hears everything – but in an apparently casual meeting on the gallery he'd informed her that it was her section and she must do as she thought fit, of course, and if she truly felt the advantages of smart-looking Security guards outweighed the risks of them undertaking an assignment with an obviously anomalous hairstyle, then she should have at it.

She hadn't – had at it, I mean – which was encouraging. There was no doubt however that some of our working methods were coming as a bit of a shock to her. Now she was staring up at St Mary's staff lining the gantry, waving and making rude gestures.

'What are they doing up there?'

'Seeing us off. If we return safely, they'll be back to witness that too.'

I didn't mention that bets had been placed on how she'd do and that the considerably larger crowd on our return would be there either to collect their winnings or pay up.

She frowned. 'Not a particularly good use of their time.'

'I find it fosters inter-departmental team spirit,' I said swiftly, and she hadn't been with us long enough to realise what a load of old cobblers that was.

'And you tolerate this?'

It had been my idea. Enthusiastically adopted by the History Department and most of St Mary's, for whom anything is better than working. 'Of course,' I said. 'Why not?'

'Well, don't they have projects and deadlines to achieve?'

'They do.'

She paused. I could see her trying to frame the next question tactfully and then giving up. 'Shouldn't they be getting on with them?'

I shrugged. 'I tell them what I want. I tell them when I want it. Anything more might be overloading their tiny brains.'

'And that happens? Don't you monitor or check their progress? What happens if someone has a problem?'

'They come and talk to me about it.'

'Are you sure?'

'Absolutely. Trust me – none of my department has any difficulty kicking their way through my door to bring me a problem.'

She frowned again. 'Do you think you might sometimes be too accessible?'

Oh, for God's sake.

'Let's get you checked over, shall we?' I said, smiling politely and not murdering her even a little bit.

As I said, all female historians have long hair because, for much of History, women with short hair were heretics/witches/ unclean/dangerously ahead of their time and, typically, Hyssop had short hair.

'Hi,' I'd said when we met for our fitting in Wardrobe. 'I'm glad we've bumped into each other. I wanted to ask if you had any plans to grow your hair?'

I deliberately kept my voice light and friendly and most importantly – non-critical. I wasn't going to let her push me into being the bad person in all this.

I suspect the same thing had occurred to her.

'Well,' she said, automatically putting up a hand to touch it. 'I have considered it. The thing is that it's almost uncontrollable when it's long. It's just a giant ball of frizz. I can't help thinking that any contemporaries catching sight of it would scream and run for the hills.'

'I appreciate the problem,' I said, trying hard because so was she. 'How would you feel about shoulder-length?'

'Shall we see? I warn you – it's very possible you'll be telling me to get it cut because I'm frightening the horses.'

I'd laughed longer than her feeble joke deserved and said, 'I look forward to seeing this legendary hair of yours.'

We'd both gone on our way and people came out from behind the furniture.

Women could show a little hair in Tudor times and I made a microscopic adjustment to Hyssop's headdress – a cap worn on the back of her head. The green velvet veil hanging down her back hid her frizzy curls. We'd discussed a hairpiece, which she'd rejected with loathing, and I didn't blame her because with St Mary's luck it would almost certainly drop off at the wrong moment, causing massive alarm and consternation among the contemporaries.

The Elizabethan Sumptuary Laws of 1574 hadn't kicked in yet, but there were still stringent rules over who could wear what. Fortunately, it was summer, so the eternal worry over who was entitled to wear which fur – ermine, mink, fox, vair and so forth – didn't apply.

Both Hyssop and I wore the traditional linen petticoat with stiff bodices to the waist, wide kirtles and matching sleeves. Mine was dark green with a little embroidery around the neckline and Hyssop's was a similar design in russet. I wore an old-fashioned gable headdress appropriate for my only very slightly advanced years.

Sands and Evans were dressed in simple brown doublets and hose. We all looked sombre but respectable, which is about the best we can ever get. I thought we were all good to go. Hyssop, however, was unhappy with her shoes.

If we can't wear our boots – always first choice for the discerning historian – then we tend to go for plain brown leather lace-ups which, like our pods, fit into almost every century.

She was scowling at her feet. 'I would prefer something more modern.'

'I daresay you would,' I said, effortlessly skipping over all the occasions when I'd worn my own boots, 'but these are an effective compromise and over time they'll become scuffed and dirty and grow to the shape of your feet and look authentic. Nothing screams fake louder than brand new. To say nothing of having your throat cut and your body thrown into a ditch because someone wants to steal your smart new shoes. Now, are we all set?'

I knew Dieter had talked her through pod procedures so she knew what to expect. Number Eight is a great pod. My favourite, in fact; we've had some exciting times together. In my new-found role as a tactful, nurturing person, I didn't mention any of them.

The console was to the right of the door. Someone had already laid in the coordinates. Now Leon had gone, it was Dieter who checked them over with me while the others made themselves comfortable.

'We were up most of the night,' he said, in full techie martyr mode, 'but, finally, the toilet is working again. Keep it that way. Other than that, everything's switched on, loaded, charged up, ready and working. Good luck.'

'Thank you,' I said, and he exited the pod. I closed the door behind him and suddenly the inside of the pod was much smaller. I watched Hyssop tense. 'Nervous?'

She nodded. 'Apprehensive.'

A good answer. If she'd said no I wouldn't have believed her. I still remembered my first jump. I'd nearly burst into flames with excitement and terror.

'There really shouldn't be any difficulties with this one. Hardly anyone will be around. We enter the house – if challenged, we're looking for Mrs Picto, whom we know has gone to the fair. Pausing only for a quick *Oh, what a shame we've missed her, never mind, we'll try again tomorrow*, we vacate the premises before anyone becomes suspicious, regroup outside and think up another approach.'

'Why not just ask for Amy Robsart? We know she's there.'

'We could do that – and if everything else fails, then we might have to – but direct interaction can be tricky. Suppose hurrying down to meet us causes her to fall an hour too early. Suppose she was supposed to do something important in that hour and now doesn't? And if she does manage to get down the stairs successfully, she might not go back upstairs again. Suppose she spends the whole afternoon on the ground floor and therefore

59

never has the accident.' I smiled. 'The secret to a successful assignment is to be as unobtrusive as possible.'

Evans coughed and turned away, possibly remembering the one or two times when St Mary's hadn't been quite as unobtrusive as we could have, and Sands, stowing our gear in the lockers, grinned at me.

I sat her down between Sands and Evans. I didn't think she'd have a panic attack – she wasn't the type – but you never know how this sort of thing will take some people.

'OK – everyone set?'

No one said no, which was good enough for me.

I checked everything over. Greens across the board. 'Computer, initiate jump.'

'Jump initiated.'

The world went white.

Our touchdown was smooth, which, since we were trying to impress our temporary new Head of Security, was good. Because I couldn't help wondering: to whom was Hyssop reporting? Other than Dr Bairstow, I mean. Well, whoever it was, they'd be hearing about our textbook landing.

Sands activated the screen and we crowded round to have a look.

It wasn't raining, which is always one of the first things I look for when wearing a long, woollen dress. In fact, it was a lovely day. Warm blue skies, golden sunshine so typical of late summer.

Secondly, no one was screaming. Another important point. No one was running. And nothing seemed to be on fire. It was all good.

We'd landed in a churchyard. I could see Sands gearing himself up for a joke about St Mary's cutting out the middleman and just jumping into an open grave now, or even – *quelle horreur* – informing Hyssop he worked for Cunard. I made haste to intervene. 'Mr Sands, report, please.'

'We're exactly where and when we should be, Max. Around 1500 hours on the afternoon of 8th September 1560. We're in the corner of the churchyard to the east of Cumnor Place and one of the entrances to the house itself should be . . .' he panned the camera, 'over there.'

A gateway led out of the churchyard and we could see the mellow walls and roofs of Cumnor Place, drowsing in the sunshine. No one was around. A tabby cat dozed on a nearby grave, paws neatly tucked underneath him, enjoying the sun. Everything was very rural and peaceful.

Unlike inside the pod, where Hyssop had gone from a standing start to red-hot military efficiency. 'Right, Evans and I will check things out. Everyone else is to wait here until we tell you it's safe to proceed with this mission.'

She didn't seem to notice the pointed silence. Evans looked at me. I wasn't going to embarrass him by making him challenge instructions from his new boss but she was trying it on again and we had to nip this sort of thing in the bud. I said carefully, 'No, as we discussed at the briefing, it doesn't work quite like that. I'm in charge of this assignment – and it's an assignment, not a mission. There's no military element involved here.'

Hyssop knew all this. She'd have studied previous assignments and Evans would almost certainly have mentioned it at their own briefing. The new broom was being wielded. I sighed. This had to be sorted now.

'Standard procedure – as you know – is that a male historian leads the way, possibly with someone from Security if we have more than one. Everyone else in the middle, and me and Markham at the back.'

'You don't lead?'

'When dealing with the past, there are very few times and places where it's acceptable for a woman to lead. Trust me, striding around the place barking orders to all and sundry is asking to take pride of place on the next bonfire. It's why we have briefings. So everyone knows what to expect and what to do when we get there.'

'Seriously?'

'Alas, yes. We aim to get through every assignment as quickly and quietly as possible – not give Tudor England a lecture on the rights of women.' I paused. 'I have to ask – when you were given this job, did they not brief you on this?' and waited to see whether she would give any clues as to who appointed her and what her remit had been.

She didn't. 'Well, yes, but I didn't realise *we* operated according to the rules of the Middle Ages.'

I sighed. 'We do when we're in the Middle Ages. At the moment we're in Tudor England so we behave according to Tudor England rules. And it's the same for Ancient Rome, 19th-century Vienna, 20th-century Sarajevo – everywhere. It's up to you, of course, Security is your section, but I can't allow you to risk my people by exposing contemporaries to inappropriate modern behaviour patterns. You go and do things your way and we'll wait here for your unlikely return.'

Non-return would be more accurate but I didn't want to seem too negative about her chances of survival. Not on her first jump.

'Have you ever thought, Dr Maxwell, that this . . . old-fashioned way of proceeding might be the reason your casualty rate is so high?'

I saw Evans sit back down and make himself comfortable.

Refusing to be thrown on the defensive, I said, 'The reason we occasionally incur one or two minor injuries is that we aren't supposed to be here. We are the piece of grit in the Oyster of

History. We are a virus and History will do what it can to get rid of us. If a thing can go wrong, it will. Hence, we ghost quietly around the landscape, recording, documenting, getting out alive, and not, *not* in any way imposing our own values and behaviour on people who wouldn't understand – and definitely wouldn't be grateful for – a lesson in 21st-century cultural mores. And, frankly, I find it disquieting in the extreme that I need to tell you this.'

I didn't give her a chance to regroup. 'Now, we'll exit the pod. You and Mr Sands will lead the way. Mr Evans and I will follow on behind.' I turned away from her. 'As discussed, Mr Sands – through the churchyard and into Cumnor Place. We should find ourselves in the quadrangle and both entrances to the Great Hall will be ahead and diagonally to our right.'

I turned back to Hyssop. 'There shouldn't be anyone around, but even if there is, we're well dressed and respectable and unlikely to be challenged. If we are, Mr Sands will do the talking.'

'And I suppose I just stand back and do nothing.'

'Now you're getting the idea. Well done.'

I moved to the door. The golden rule of conflict resolution – always have the last word. Well, no, the golden rule is to shoot the bastards before they even start to argue, but the second golden rule is always to have the last word.

You can't keep a good woman down. As we exited the pod, I could hear her asking Sands if he thought his artificial foot ever had any impact on his performance. Unfortunately, Evans tightened his grip on my arm before I could get to her.

The day was very hot. Two of us stood just outside the pod, our faces lifted to the sunshine. Historians don't get out much.

'Aren't you checking for hostiles?' Hyssop said to Evans, who was also rotating slowly in the sunshine. Like a giant chicken on a spit.

'What?' I said.

'Potentially hostile people, meteorological hazards, political or geological situations . . .'

'You'd be better off checking for geese, watchdogs and angry chickens,' I said, and Sands, who lives with Rosie Lee and is therefore accustomed to difficult women, offered Hyssop his arm. She hesitated fractionally and then took it. I noticed she made sure she stood on his left. I assumed she was left-handed and keeping her gun arm free.

I tucked myself on Evans' left – he was right-handed and a better shot than me although I'm not bad – and off we set, picking our way carefully among the scattered graves. The cat couldn't even be bothered to open his eyes.

We left the churchyard via a simple wooden gate, crossed a track with wagon ruts baked hard in the summer sun, passed under an archway with the gates pushed back in silent welcome and entered an enclosed quadrangle surrounded by tall golden walls. The roofs were gabled and tiled with moss- and lichen-covered local stone. The tiles had been laid out in the traditional manner with smaller tiles at the top, graduating down to the largest at the bottom, giving a very pleasing perspective.

It was even hotter in this enclosed space and we paused to get our bearings. Working from left to right, the chapel lay diagonally behind us, with its access to the churchyard. Next to that – for some strange ecclesiastical reason – was the malthouse. Then another archway leading into what looked like the garden. The gates there had been left wide open as well, and I caught a glimpse of a neat terrace and a flash of sunlight on water. On the wall facing us was an unknown room, its door firmly closed, and then, occupying the rest of that wall, directly in front of us, the Great Hall with its two sets of double doors, both standing invitingly open. To let in light and sunshine, presumably. To our right was the former buttery, we thought – because it made sense to adjoin the Great Hall. The buttery was the room we were after because it was the room with the fatal staircase. Up on the first floor, and running virtually the length of the house, were the Long Gallery and Lady Dudley's private chambers.

A lark hung over the churchyard, trilling its little heart out, but other than that there wasn't a soul or a sound anywhere. Cumnor Place slept in the afternoon sunshine. A little oasis of Tudor rural peace. A million miles away from the dark paranoia of the Tudor court. Except that a tiny tentacle of that darkness might be finding its way to Cumnor Place even as we stood here admiring it.

'Straight to the Great Hall, I think,' I said, and we headed towards the nearest set of open doors. They were the usual wooden, grey with age, massively hinged affairs, held open by doorstops of stone into which iron handles had been set.

We knocked very gently because we didn't actually want to attract anyone's attention but, if we met anyone, we could honestly say we had knocked. Passing from bright sunshine into deep shade, we paused for a moment to let our eyes adjust.

Hyssop was worryingly quiet. I hoped this was awe and excitement rather than criticism and disapproval.

'All right?' I said very quietly.

She nodded, her eyes darting from doors to windows and

back again. She was watching our backs. Shame I felt I had to watch hers.

I had forgotten how sparsely furnished Tudor houses are. A wooden chest decorated with a linenfold pattern stood under each of the two windows opposite. A well-polished candlestick stood on each. Their contents were unknown and we weren't going to start rummaging. The windows were old-fashioned – 14th century, I thought – with painted glass that threw pools of colour on to the plain flags.

A substantial, highly polished wooden table ran down the centre of the room. I reckoned it could easily seat a dozen people. An armed chair stood at the head, back to the fireplace, and three lesser, armless chairs ran down each side. The rest stood against the walls. Pewter plates gleamed on the mantel and two large tapestries hung on the north wall where they wouldn't be faded by the sunshine. The floor was of swept stone. Looking up into the dim heights, the roof was richly timbered and decorated. Apart from the pleasant smell of lavender, polish, wood and warm stone, that was pretty much it.

There was a closed door in the left-hand wall. A corresponding door on the right was propped wide open, giving a good view of a large room with another flagged floor – and – and this was the important bit – the last few steps of that infamous staircase. And we'd been right. They were of stone, curving upwards out of sight. They were old. Each step was shiny and worn. Even from all the way over here they looked pretty lethal. Add in dazzling sunshine, wide skirts, a moment's carelessness . . . The coroner had recorded Amy's death as misfortune. Perhaps these stairs already had a reputation . . .

Looking around the Great Hall again, the only thing moving

was the dust, caught in the summer sunlight as it streamed through the arched windows. Everything was swept, polished and sweet-smelling. The furniture gleamed. This was a well-run household.

And an absent household. No pots and pans clashed. No servants bustled about. No doors opened and closed. There wasn't even a dog to bark at us. We'd just walked in and we could have been anyone. Which was interesting.

Evans crossed to the open door and peered through into the buttery. I glanced out of the door to the empty courtyard and opened my mouth to say 'well, this could be easy', when Hyssop tilted her head. A fraction of a second later I heard it, too. Hoofbeats. Someone was coming. Not at a flat-out gallop – just a gentle trot. We barely had time to take that in when a rider emerged from under the northern arch, his horse's hooves clopping loudly in the summer silence, and halted in the middle of the courtyard.

'Quick,' said Evans, shoving us all towards the opposite door because we needed to stay as far away from the infamous staircase as possible.

Hyssop eased it open to reveal an empty room. I mean, there was furniture and such, but no people – which was exactly what we were looking for. We all squeezed through, leaving the door open a crack, just as the rider led his horse to the water trough against one wall and then strode into the Great Hall through the second pair of open doors, slapping the dust from his doublet as he came.

He was well dressed in black, his soft leather boots coated in dirt. Pulling off his gloves, he tossed them on to the table and shouted a greeting.

Shit. I looked over my shoulder into the empty room behind me. There was another door behind us opening into the court-yard. If someone came through that way . . . but no footsteps disturbed the heavy silence. No voice was raised in response to his call. The sun still shone, the dust still swirled, we still waited . . .

The newcomer strode across the hall, through the open door at the other end, and into the buttery. He stood at the foot of the stairs, looking upwards. He shouted again. Short and sharp. Somewhere above us, a woman called out.

Sands turned to me, his eyes gleaming, and whispered, 'Bet you a fiver that's Richard Verney.'

It seemed too good to be true if it was, but we'd argue about it later. I was quivering with excitement because Verney was Dudley's man. It was known that he'd been in the vicinity that fatal day but we hadn't realised he'd actually been here in the house. No one did. I had to say, at this moment, things were not looking good for Dudley. His man, on the spot, on the very afternoon – possibly even at the very moment – his wife died. Dudley hadn't been high on my list of suspects, but he was now.

Upstairs a door opened and closed.

I felt Sands stiffen. He had his recorder ready. I dragged mine out too and glanced over my shoulder again. Evans was watching the other door and Hyssop was checking the windows. Our backs were safe.

Now there were footsteps overhead. We could hear heels tapping on a wooden floor. Quick and light. We heard them crossing the room above us. A woman, almost certainly. They grew fainter, moving towards the head of the staircase. And then they stopped.

For several long moments nothing happened. I stared up at the ceiling, straining my ears, desperate for some clue as to what could be going on up there. No one appeared on the stairs. Nothing disturbed the silence of the house.

If asked, I would have guessed the footsteps belonged to Amy Robsart and that she'd paused at the head of the stairs to gather up her skirts in one hand and carefully make her way down the staircase, the other hand on the newel post for support. That's how I would have done it, anyway.

We waited. There was complete silence. No sound of swishing skirts. No sounds of someone carefully making their way down the shadowed staircase.

We waited and waited. What was happening up there? Why was everything so silent? We knew at least one person was upstairs. Was she still there? If not, where had she gone?

Evidently satisfied that someone had at least heard his hail, the rider – if it was Sir Richard and let's say it was – moved away from the stairs and back into the Great Hall, waiting by the table, his back to us.

He was a tall man, and lean. His dark hair was mostly hidden by his hat, a soft, floppy affair – a bit like a beret with a brim – which he hadn't yet removed. His hair and beard were shot through with grey hairs. This time next year he'd be completely grey. His face was flushed from the heat. I imagined he must be desperate for a drink.

And then, from above – a cry. Of surprise. Of shock. Of fear.

And then – the unmistakeable sounds of someone falling down the stairs. No, not falling – *crashing* down the stairs. At some speed. Closer and louder until, suddenly and violently, a welter of arms, legs, hair and petticoats erupted from around the curve to land with a crash on the flagged floor.

For long, horrified seconds, Sir Richard stood frozen. As did we. I was no longer surprised the fall had killed her. I would have been astounded if she had survived.

I had Sir Richard's face in close-up and he seemed completely taken aback at this turn of events. Then the spell broke. Shouting, 'Lady Dudley,' he ran back into the buttery to investigate.

He was wasting his time. We were at the other end of the house and even we could see the body had that broken look about it. If asked, and given the tangle of loose limbs as she fell, I would say she was dead before she arrived at the bottom of the stairs. It had been the fall that killed her – not the landing.

Amy had ended sprawled, head downwards, half on and half off the stairs, her eyes wide open in alarm, staring sightlessly up at Sir Richard as he bent over her.

There was utter silence. A moment when something important has happened and the world needs a moment to readjust. In my head I could still hear the echoes of her fall. We stood paralysed at the suddenness of events. Less than thirty seconds ago Amy Robsart had been alive and now she wasn't. We'd been expecting this but even so it was a shock to us. But how was Sir Richard reacting?

Actually, he recovered more quickly than we did because, upstairs, loud in the dusty silence – a door opened. And then – silence. The house seemed to hold its breath.

Sir Richard sprang into action. He pulled out a knife from his belt, leaped over poor Amy Robsart – as unregarded in death as she had been in life – and disappeared up the stairs.

'Quick,' I said, because the very last thing we needed was to be discovered here. We'd be magnets for the tsunami of blame and accusations that were about to envelop everyone. I suspected the world would be looking for scapegoats and who better than four strangers?

We were out through the door in a flash.

Hyssop paused. 'Don't you want to see who's upstairs?'

'More than anything,' I said, 'but not so much as to risk being hanged for murder. The sun's going down. Her servants will be back soon. To say nothing of Richard Verney. We mustn't be caught here – or even in the vicinity. Quickly now. Before someone looks out of an upstairs window and sees us leaving.'

'Not back through the churchyard,' said Evans. 'Too overlooked. Through the far door, turn right and out through the north entrance. We'll give everything a wide berth and make our way back to the pod.'

Keeping close to the walls, we whisked ourselves out through the north gate, along the dusty path and across the fields to the road. You could tell it was a road because it was even more rutted than the ploughed fields alongside and with the bonus of added dust. Thick, ragged hedgerows lined the way and would prove useful cover and shade.

'Which direction?' I said to Hyssop.

She nodded to our left. 'That way.'

Behind her back I looked quickly at Evans who nodded a confirmation.

'I saw that,' she said, without turning around.

'Just checking your bump of direction is more reliable than mine,' I said.

'It couldn't be less,' said Sands.

I gave him a hard stare which was wasted because he and Hyssop had already set out and I was glaring at their backs.

'So,' I said, 'comments on what we've just seen.'

'All right,' said Sands over his shoulder. 'Speculation. Sir Richard Verney – who wasn't supposed to be there anyway – is the one person in the world who couldn't have killed her.'

'Unless he was the decoy and someone was waiting at the top of the stairs to push her down,' I said.

'In which case why pull a dagger and go to investigate?'

'To report to his man that she was dead. Job done and go.'

'But the dagger . . .' he said, unconvinced.

'Or it was a genuine accident. Which would be my best guess.'

Sands frowned. 'So who was upstairs? Mrs Oddingsells and whatshername? Why didn't they come down to investigate?'

'They may not have heard anything.'

He shook his head. 'We all heard the impact.'

'I bet you another fiver they were both asleep,' said Evans. 'Two middle-aged women on a hot, sunny afternoon – of course they were asleep.'

'We can speculate back in the pod,' said Hyssop. 'You should be concentrating on our withdrawal.'

I felt the familiar stab of resentment at Hyssop telling us what to do – even though Markham, had he been here, would have been the first to say, 'Oi! Less talking – more walking,' and I'd have been fine with that. I really had to get a grip. It wasn't her fault she wasn't Markham.

Without Hyssop's intervention it is very possible we would have stood there in the hot sun, arguing together for the rest of the afternoon and who knows how that would have ended, but at that moment we heard the sound of horses approaching. Horses, plural. And a grinding, wooden, creaking noise as well. The approaching cloud of dust was certainly large enough to denote horses pulling a coach.

We couldn't afford to take any chances. Back through the hedge it was. Mrs Enderby has a phrase – 'Good God, Max, you look as if you've been dragged through a hedge backwards' – well, today I really had. Twice, so far.

There was a ditch on the other side of the hedge. Fortunately, it had already been cleared in preparation for the autumn rains. All this land had once belonged to the abbey and good land-management habits still prevailed. The ditch made an excellent hiding place and vantage point.

I straightened my headdress, pulled a long bramble off my sleeve and found a gap in the hedge to peer through. *Another* set of hoofbeats was approaching. From the opposite direction this time. We'd obviously hit rush hour.

A familiar big brown horse appeared.

'Shit,' breathed Sands. 'It's Richard Verney. Did he see us? Has he come after us?'

But Verney clearly wasn't pursuing anyone. He'd approached at a trot and then pulled over to our side of the road. He was only about four feet away from us. If I peered through the hedge, I could see the dried mud caked on his horse's legs and four dusty hooves. It was very fortunate we'd tumbled into a ditch and were well below Sir Richard's eyeline.

His horse snorted once and then stood quietly. The coach halted almost directly opposite. I say coach but Guilliam Boonen had not yet brought over his design for spring suspension, which would suddenly make coaches more popular. The combination of primitive carriages and rocky roads meant most people either walked or travelled on horseback. This was some kind of closed litter on wheels. The journey must have been beyond bruising.

Sir Richard doffed his hat. He hadn't removed his hat for Amy Robsart.

Shit. No – it couldn't be. Surely not.

The leather curtains were pulled tightly across the window. It must have been stifling inside the coach. Who would suffer such discomfort on a hot day like this?

Someone for whom secrecy was paramount – that was who.

A part of the curtain was pulled aside. For a moment I couldn't see a thing – the interior of the coach was very dark. I stood on tiptoe – as if that would make any difference – and then a woman leaned out and my theory collapsed into nothing. She was in her late fifties, with a plump face and an old-fashioned gable headdress very similar to my own.

Sir Richard bowed and sidled his horse close to the litter.

They exchanged words. I strained to hear but nothing was distinguishable.

And then the other curtain stirred. A woman's small hand appeared, resting on the edge of the coach window. The dark sleeve disappeared into the darkness of the coach but there, on the fourth finger – a ring.

Beside me, I heard Sands draw a sharp breath.

Other than her coronation ring, there is one ring particularly associated with Elizabeth I. It's known as the Chequers Ring. It's a beautiful thing. A gold ring, encrusted with diamonds, rubies and mother-of-pearl, incorporating a locket supposedly

75

containing a picture of her mother, Anne Boleyn. Elizabeth never took it off. Legend says it had to be cut from her dead body in 1603 and carried to James VI in Scotland as proof that Elizabeth of England was actually dead.

Supposedly the ring dated from around 1575 but I was certain I recognised it here and now. It was a well-known Elizabethan treasure and occasionally it was put on public display, including, by massive irony as it now dawned on me, at Compton Verney in 2008. I was looking at Elizabeth's ring and, by extension, presumably Elizabeth herself. Which meant the other passenger was probably Kat Ashley. My head was whirling. Queen Elizabeth was here. In fact, everyone was here. Amy Robsart, Sir Richard Verney, Elizabeth – it only needed Robert Dudley to come cantering up the road and we'd have the full set.

Why was she here? On this of all afternoons. Why were any of them here? What the hell was going on?

I wrenched my attention back to the coach. Sands was still recording like a hero.

I expected that at the very least Verney would dismount and bow but he did nothing of the kind. Leaning low over his horse's neck he spoke long and urgently.

The hand withdrew sharply. A second later the leather curtain was pulled across with a snap. Sir Richard spoke a curt word to the coachman who lashed his horses. They plunged from a standing start to a canter. The litter lurched badly which must have thrown the occupants from one end to the other. With a thunder of hooves and rattle of wheels, both litter and horses disappeared in a cloud of dust.

Sir Richard wheeled his horse around, and sent it galloping

after them. In seconds the road was empty. Just the dust slowly settling in the late-afternoon sunshine to show that anyone had ever been here.

'Bloody hell,' said Sands, lowering his recorder.

'Agreed,' I said, 'but we really can't hang around here. I strongly suspect this is one of the most dangerous places in England at this moment.' I turned to Hyssop. Time for her to earn her pay. 'Get us back to the pod, please. Quick as you can.'

We followed the road, staying behind the hedge for as long as we could before finally leaving its cover to head back towards the squat church tower in the distance. In all that time the only person we saw was a countrywoman in a wide-brimmed hat and apron, trudging along the hot road with her basket. I wondered if she was on her way back from the fair. And she might not be the only one.

Where Richard Verney had taken himself off to was a mystery. As far away as he could go was my theory. A veritable shitstorm was heading everyone's way.

We approached the church and Cumnor Place with massive caution but there was only silence. Obviously the body hadn't been discovered yet. I pictured poor Amy, lying at the bottom of the stairs as the dust swirled silently around her. Her sightless eyes staring at nothing. Just dust and silence. Which, I suppose, is what being dead is all about.

Hyssop led the way along the rough track that ran between the house and the churchyard. There were trees lining the path and we glided silently from one patch of shade to another. Still the sun blazed down. Sands was at Hyssop's shoulder and Evans and I were right behind. We stuck closely together and we didn't run. Nothing attracts more attention than running. Especially on a day like this and in clothes like these. I could feel a strange tingling between my shoulder blades. Just waiting for the challenge that would end in our arrest. And almost certain death.

We skirted the churchyard wall. A small brown snake basked on a flat rock. The sun was sinking in the sky. Amy's household would surely be returning home at any moment. Half of me wanted to hang around in the churchyard, to try to record their reactions. More than half of me, actually. The smaller, more sensible part was shrieking at me to get back to the pod before we did any damage to this critical point in History. Before the body was discovered and we were blamed. No one was ever brought to justice over Amy's death. We couldn't afford to be caught here.

But . . .

I stopped. Everyone else stopped dead and looked at me.

'What?' said Sands.

'We can't leave it like this. I'm going back to have a bit of a poke around.'

'I'll come with you,' said two voices.

Hyssop compressed her lips. 'I can't allow that. Returning to the house for whatever reason is contra-indicated at this moment.'

I wondered afterwards, if it had been Markham talking, would I have heeded *him*?

I wouldn't have had to. He'd have rolled his eyes, instructed Evans to keep an eye on our rear and probably have beaten me back to Cumnor Place. So I ignored her, telling myself I didn't have time to argue.

'Wait,' she said, pulling at my arm. 'I'm overruling you. I have the authority.'

I was conscious of time passing and taking our options with it. It was now or never. There are no second chances in this job.

'I'm overruling your overruling,' I said. 'Wait in the pod if you're not coming.'

Sands lined up with me. Evans stood on neutral ground between me and Hyssop.

'We can't all go,' I said, wanting to give him an out.

'If someone has to go then it will be Evans and me,' said Hyssop, which wasn't what I'd meant at all.

'You're not leaving me behind,' said Sands, massively indignant.

'I'm leaving both of you behind,' Hyssop said.

I'd had enough. Time was ticking. Unless I wanted to give her a quick zap with my stun gun – and don't think I wasn't tempted – the easiest way to deal with Hyssop was to ignore her, so I left them arguing and quietly set off through the gate towards Cumnor Place again.

The quadrangle was still silent. Still hot. Still dusty. A few small puddles, drying in the sun, showed where Sir Richard's horse had drunk from the stone water trough. The doors were all still open.

I slipped into the hall and made straight for the stairs. Amy was still there, staring sightlessly into the next world. Somewhere, a fly buzzed.

I whispered, 'Sorry,' and stepped over her as carefully as I could and started up the stairs. It wasn't easy. I had great handfuls of dress in one hand and trailed the other along the outside wall for balance. I took it slowly, placing my feet with great care. The light wasn't good and I definitely didn't want the same thing happening to me.

I'd been right about the intermediate landing – not so much a landing as a wide stair, where I suspected the Dudley household would stand a candle at night, but yes, there was room for a person to conceal himself there – pressed back against the wall and hidden in the shadows – and then there was the second flight of steps. Every step was narrow and sloped downwards. Absolutely lethal. Now that I'd had a chance to see the stairs themselves I was no longer surprised she came such a cropper. I was only surprised there wasn't a whole heap of bodies at the bottom.

I made my very cautious way to the top and eased my head slowly above the level of the landing. A long corridor lay before me. Whether this was the famous Long Gallery I had no idea. Nor should I hang around to find out. There were three or four doors, on both sides, all firmly closed.

Someone nudged me from behind, nearly giving me a heart attack. I very nearly did an Amy Robsart and tumbled all the way back down the stairs. Bloody Hyssop had followed me. I scowled at her and made WTF gestures. She scowled back and nodded to the far end of the gallery where a patch of sunlight streamed through an open doorway on to the wooden floor. Whether she was warning me or instructing me to leave immediately wasn't clear. I decided to interpret it as encouragement to explore further.

I was here. Hyssop was with me. Sands and Evans were presumably covering the stairs, because why would they have done the sensible thing and returned to the pod? Everything was still quiet. I could do this. There was time. I set off down the landing, my soft shoes soundless on the wooden floor, and peered cautiously through the open door.

Now this was interesting.

Tudor rooms tend to be small but this one was larger than most. The overwhelming impression was of wood. Softly glowing panelling covered the walls. Wide wooden floorboards reflected the sunshine. The ceiling was supported by thick wooden beams.

It was the layout that intrigued me. A large chair had been carefully set to one side of the empty fireplace. An exquisitely carved footstool had been placed in front of it. Facing the chair on the other side of the hearth was a smaller, lower, altogether plainer chair.

Furniture tells a story. This told me that someone important was expected. This chair had been brought in especially. This wasn't its normal position. The simpler chair lived here – I could see the indentations it had made on the floor. And, most convincingly, a piece of embroidery was lying on the seat of the lesser chair, the needle still pushed through it. Amy's embroidery. The piece she had been working on when Sir Richard called up the stairs. I could see it so clearly. She'd heard his call – she'd cast aside her work, hurried to the top of the stairs and . . .

And what? Fallen headlong was the answer. But how?

A flagon of wine had been set aside but not poured. The goblet was intricate and looked to be made of silver. Definitely not pewter, anyway, confirming my suspicion an important person had been expected. I think we've all worked out who.

As if in confirmation, a covered dish stood nearby. I lifted the lid to see some sort of tiny, sticky, honey biscuit things. Elizabeth had a very sweet tooth. Famed for it, in fact.

I looked around. This was a very pleasant lady's room that

must be part of Amy's apartments. *This* was why she'd sent everyone to the fair. She'd prepared for a visitor and no witnesses were desired. There was something to be said. Something to be discussed. Something very, very secret.

But what? Why would Elizabeth trouble herself with Amy Robsart? It's a bit of a myth that the queen had no women friends at all. There were Kat Ashley and Blanche Parry, to whom Elizabeth showed affectionate loyalty, and who served her all their lives. Then there was Anne Russell, and Catherine Carey, whose death left Elizabeth distraught. But Elizabeth's was a glittering court and all the other women would have been copies of Elizabeth herself – bright, hard, brilliant women, intelligent, educated, able to hold their own in conversations at all levels. None of them would have been small, mousy little women whose entire world was encompassed within their home. What could the queen and Amy Robsart possibly have to say to each other? They didn't even occupy the same world.

This certainly kicked my theory into touch, because if Elizabeth had planned to have Amy killed, she wouldn't risk being seen within a hundred miles of this place. And if Richard Verney was here as go-between, it also seemed unlikely Dudley had schemed to have his wife killed. Was it possible that, after centuries of fruitless speculation, we were in a position to say Amy Robsart's death had been accidental after all?

How panicked must Richard Verney have been? The wife of the queen's favourite lying dead at the foot of the stairs and Elizabeth herself within half a mile of the building. No wonder the driver had whipped up his horses.

The first thing she'd do would be to ditch that stupid litter. As soon as she was safely out of the area, speed would become more important than secrecy. Her people would find her a couple of swift horses. I wouldn't mind betting she was halfway back to Windsor by now, to reappear sometime comfortably far away, cool as a cucumber, all ready to show proper shock and horror at this dreadful news.

Hyssop twitched my sleeve and nodded out through the door. We hadn't made a sound. We hadn't heard a sound either, but we couldn't stay here much longer. I whipped out my recorder and panned around the room, making sure to include the chair, the wine, the goblet, everything. Hyssop moved to the door and listened.

When I'd finished, I stuffed the recorder away and we set off back along the landing towards the stairs. Hyssop motioned me to go first and it's a jolly good thing she did. I seized a great handful of skirt and in the same movement, started down the stairs, grabbing at the central newel for support.

My hand slipped. Suddenly, I was completely off-balance. Already moving forwards at a fair rate, I had no chance to save myself. I just had time to think 'shit, this is going to hurt', when Hyssop grabbed my wide skirts and pulled me back again. I collapsed against the wall, heart going like a hammer, and got my breath back.

I looked down at my hand. Sticky and shiny. I looked at the central newel post. The light was dim but part of it looked darker.

Hyssop produced a tiny glowstick. How about that? I wondered what else she had concealed about her person. Reaching over my shoulder she shone the light on to the newel post. I reached out and sniffed. Beeswax. And turpentine. The newel was greased with furniture polish. Was it accidental? Had someone simply not rubbed hard enough to remove the polish? Or was this something more sinister passing itself off as carelessness? Dammit – just as I'd talked myself into thinking Amy's death was accidental . . . No wonder I'd smelled polish in the house.

I stood like an idiot, trying to take in all the implications at once. Hyssop was attempting to move me on but first things first. This was why we were here, after all. I had no handkerchief and my headdress was virtually welded to my head. I nudged Hyssop and silently indicated I wanted her headdress. She raised her eyebrows and I scowled threateningly back. Sighing, she pulled it off. I handed her back the cap and used her green velvet veil to remove every trace of polish from the newel. No one knew how Amy had died. History is silent on the subject. No evidence of foul play was ever found. But if I left this scene untouched then it would be. Dudley would get the blame. There would be an almighty scandal that would probably bring down the throne. That couldn't ever be allowed to happen. So, I cleaned up after a possible murder. And then I handed Hyssop back her greasy veil. She gave me a look but said nothing.

At the bottom of the staircase, Sands helped us step very carefully over Amy, still undiscovered, although surely not for much longer. I was heading for the door when Hyssop stopped and turned back. She crouched down beside the body. I'd missed something. She was carefully wiping Amy's hand. Shit, I had forgotten she'd have a greasy hand as well, so good for Hyssop. But all this was taking time and even I was becoming nervous. I made sure we exited the hall considerably more quickly than we had gone in.

This time we really didn't hang around. There was a body

back there. Both Hyssop and I smelled strongly of furniture polish. We were strangers . . . no, we didn't hang around.

Long purple shadows lay across the quadrangle. It was getting late. The wet marks around the horse trough had dried. There was no evidence that Richard Verney or his horse had ever been here. All we had to do was get out and there would be no evidence we'd ever been here, either.

The quadrangle appeared very much larger than before and it seemed to take an age to reach the safety of the silent churchyard. All the windows of Cumnor Place were boring holes into my back. At any moment I expected to hear either Mrs Owens or Mrs Oddingsells cry for help.

I could hear my dress rustling through the grass. The cat had gone but the pod was exactly where we had left it, which is always my criteria for a successful assignment. Once, in the Cretaceous period, Dieter and I had watched our pod career off a cliff. And we'd been in it at the time.

And then, in the distance, I heard a man's voice, calling. He was ahead of us on the track somewhere. Another man answered and then a woman laughed. Someone sang a snatch of song. The Dudley household was back from the fair.

'Quick,' I said, and Hyssop and I lifted our skirts and awkwardly ran the last few paces, which turned out to be a bit of a mistake because the cat, flat-eared, came flying out from under a bush and Hyssop tripped right over it. She staggered sideways and fell heavily to the ground. Evans grabbed her and pulled her to her feet. I called for the door. Sands stood to one side, covering us. With one last look around I stepped into the pod. The door closed behind us.

'Well,' said Sands, dragging his sleeve across his forehead. 'I'm not sure that one went quite as well as it could have.'

Evans deposited Hyssop on a chair and we all crowded around to have a look at the damage.

'I went over on my foot,' she said, wincing. 'Painful but not serious.'

'We'll leave your shoe on,' I said. 'Dr Stone will sort you out.'

She was cross with herself. 'I'm not usually so clumsy.'

I beamed at her. Just to rub it in. 'Congratulations – you are now officially a piece of grit in the Oyster of History.'

She didn't seem that thrilled.

I knew we should leave. And we would if things became dodgy, but I really wanted to see how events transpired after Amy's body was found by the returning household. We weren't ideally situated here but even I wasn't going back out there. Sands angled the microphones and we cracked the door slightly for some fresh air, then sat back and waited to see what would happen.

The minutes ticked by.

Right out of the blue, Sands said, 'Do you think they slept together?'

'Who?' I said. 'Dudley and Elizabeth?'

'Yeah.'

'I doubt she'd risk it. Every month her women would be obliged to show proof of her monthly period to court officials. To show she was capable of breeding.'

He shrugged. 'Easily managed.'

I shook my head. 'But the risk of pregnancy. Why would someone as hard-headed as Elizabeth risk everything for a few

87

minutes' pleasure? And if she was pregnant, then why come here of all places?'

'Ah,' said Sands, 'but you're thinking logically. She's come to the throne. She's triumphed over enemies and circumstances. She's queen. She's only twenty-five and she's been spied on and imprisoned for most of her life. She's been the virtuous Protestant princess whose enemies would swoop if she so much as put one foot wrong. Now though, she's in charge and she can do anything she wants. Robert Dudley is handsome. Suppose she does sleep with him and the inevitable happens. Pregnant and unmarried? She'd be a laughing stock. She'd certainly lose her throne. The Scottish queen – at this moment also the French queen – would pounce. Or her French relatives would pounce on her behalf. Suppose attempts to abort the child failed. Or were too dangerous to attempt. What would she do?'

'Oh no,' I said. 'If any of this is true, then this is the last place Elizabeth would come.'

'Not necessarily. I think it's very likely mousey, lonely little Amy would love a baby to care for. Her husband's child. *And* she's sent her people away . . .'

'Speaking of which, what's taking them so long?' said Hyssop, immediately dismissing these fascinating speculations as irrelevant. Barely had she spoken than a woman screamed in the distance. And then another one. A man shouted out. I could imagine the scene. I could see them bending over her, realising she was dead. That she'd died while they were all out at the fair. I could imagine them looking at each other in horror. What would this mean for them?

And then, a minute later, a clatter of hooves grew loud. A man on a big strong horse galloped down the track throwing up huge clouds of dust and stones. Someone was taking the news to London.

'Should we be going?' enquired Hyssop.

'In a moment,' said Sands. 'The last thing these people need at the moment is to glance out of a window and see a vanishing pod. Why risk it? I doubt we'll be disturbed here.'

'I shall put the kettle on,' offered Evans, famous for his excellent grasp of priorities.

Hyssop was examining the sad remains of her headdress and saying nothing. I couldn't decide whether she was in pain from her foot, listening carefully to cogent and well-reasoned historian arguments, or just sulking. Whatever it was, I left her to it while I told Sands and Evans of our discoveries.

'Interesting,' said Sands, taking Hyssop's cap off her to see if he could bend it back into shape. 'So, Amy was murdered after all.'

'It would seem so,' I said. 'Unless a maid was just careless and forgot to wipe the polish off the newel post.'

'It was definitely murder,' said Hyssop, sitting up and taking the cap back again. 'But have you considered Amy Robsart might not have been the intended victim?'

We stared at her.

'Oh my God,' said Sands. 'You could be right.'

'Well, don't sound so astonished,' she said, tartly.

'No, you could,' I said, taking great care not to sound astonished at all. 'Suppose, just suppose, someone knew Elizabeth would be here this afternoon. It's perfect because Amy would set the scene herself. She would be the one to send her people away and . . .'

Evans shook his head. 'Wouldn't work. Amy would still have fallen down the stairs when she went to meet the queen.'

89

'Almost as bad,' I said. 'The queen is discovered with her lover's wife dead at her feet. The scandal would still prove fatal for her.'

'I think it was more carefully planned than that,' said Hyssop. 'Would I be right in assuming the queen takes precedence wherever she goes?'

We nodded.

'Did Richard Verney seem annoyed to find the hall empty?'

We nodded.

'Amy should have been there. In person. To greet the queen. Protocol would demand it.'

'But Amy was upstairs,' I said, remembering that sunny room. 'She's not well. It was warm and quiet. She fell asleep over her embroidery. I bet you anything she fell asleep.'

'She'd greet the queen and take her upstairs,' said Sands. 'The queen would go first. Elizabeth would still fall.'

'No, she wouldn't,' I said. 'When you go up, you use the other hand. The outer hand. As both Hyssop and I did. It's instinct. You trail your hand up the wall – not the newel. No, Elizabeth would have arrived safely upstairs, joined her hostess in a glass of wine on a hot day, talked about . . . whatever it was they wanted to talk about . . . and then they'd go downstairs . . .'

'And the queen would go first . . .'

'She'd reach out for the newel post, just as I did . . .'

'And bang crash wallop down the stairs.'

We sat in silence, thinking about it.

'Or,' said Evans, 'and I just chuck this in because I like upsetting historians – Amy herself greased the pole.'

There was even more silence while we thought about that.

'But . . . she'd have been arrested immediately.'

He shrugged. 'She's dying of cancer. What would she care? The ultimate revenge.'

'Little mousey Amy Robsart plotted to kill the queen?'

Hyssop leaned forwards. 'May I just point out that your supposed murderer was the one who died.'

Evans shrugged again. 'She forgot. She woke suddenly. She's disoriented. She's not well. Someone downstairs is shouting her name. She's late. The queen is in the house and Amy's not there to greet her. She runs out of the room, pauses at the top of the stairs to pull herself together, adjust her headdress, straighten her gown, whatever, takes a deep breath to calm herself, instinctively grabs at the newel post, remembers too late and . . . bang.'

I was watching the screen. People were running about in all directions. There was no reason why they should, but no one appeared to be taking any notice of us here in the churchyard.

'A very good theory,' I said. 'But we've all forgotten the fourth person in their love triangle.'

They looked at me.

'The most powerful man in the land,' I said.

Sands sat back. 'Cecil. Of course.'

'The queen's first minister,' I said to Hyssop.

'I know who Cecil is,' she said, annoyed, so I moved swiftly on.

'He hated and feared Dudley. In fact, they hated and feared each other and Elizabeth went to considerable trouble to keep them that way. But now, she's about to embark on the matrimonial merry-go-round – all those foreign kings and princes Cecil's got lined up for milking while the queen pretends to try to make up her mind. He has a lot riding on that. Worse – Amy's dying. He must have been wetting himself over whether

91

Elizabeth would marry Dudley, because he'd certainly be out on his ear if she did. Even if Dudley didn't have him quietly put away first.'

'I bet,' said Sands, slowly, 'Cecil doesn't know Elizabeth was here this afternoon.'

'Good God, no. When he does – if he ever does – he'll have a heart attack.'

'Do you think she'll tell him?'

I shook my head.

Silence fell.

'Well – there we have it,' I said.

'Except . . .' said Hyssop, and looked at me.

'Exactly,' I said.

'Who was upstairs with her? Who closed the door?'

Bugger. If only we'd been able to put someone upstairs.

'Can't we go back and try again?' asked Hyssop.

Typical – just as I was beginning to feel moderately well disposed towards her – her contributions to our discussion had been sensible and useful – she says something daft like that. She should know we couldn't do that. Daft bat.

Or – I could take a deep breath and remember she was inexperienced. Be a nice person, Maxwell.

'*We* can't, no, because you can't be in the same time twice. Trust me on that. But I could send someone else. We could put someone upstairs, hidden away. It's a possibility.'

In the interests of rounding off the story, as a matter of fact, we did. It was some considerable time afterwards, because many of us were overtaken by other events, but we did. We sent Roberts and Gallacio who secreted themselves upstairs behind a convenient screen. The door opening was Mrs Oddingsells at the other end of the house, presumably looking out to see what the crash had been. Seeing and hearing nothing, she closed the door and returned to her cards.

My theory about Amy dozing in the warm room was probably correct. Roberts and Gallacio saw Amy Robsart whirl past. She was running, they reported. For some reason, she looked frightened. No, they didn't see anyone else upstairs. She ran past them at a tremendous rate, screeched to a halt at the top of the stairs and tried to straighten her headdress, which was all crooked. It took her a while to sort herself out and then she grabbed at her skirts with one hand and started down the stairs, travelling fast. The top of her head disappeared from view and then they heard the sound of her fall. No, there was no one at the top of the stairs with them and no one on the landing, either.

They'd all heard Sir Richard's hail – was she just eager to see him? And why was he there? Announcing the queen's imminent arrival? Was that why Amy was so agitated, that she wasn't there to welcome her? Or had there been another reason? Were other people working behind the scenes? Cecil, the queen's right-hand man and Dudley's sworn enemy might have had a hand in this. I have to say that on this occasion, I don't think we'd done anything to clear up the mystery. In fact, we might have made it worse.

You could say that even without the greasy pole, Amy was moving too quickly for safety and would have fallen. Yes, she might have escaped with just bruising – except that her bones were brittle with the cancer. Did her neck snap by itself?

So there you are. There's almost as much evidence for accidental death as for murder. Apart from us, there was no one in Cumnor Place who shouldn't have been.

Except . . . the last I saw of Amy Robsart, her headdress was lying three or four steps above her on the stairs and her skirts were up around her hips. When her servants eventually found her, someone had replaced her headdress and pulled her skirts down. Who? And why? To cover up a crime? As a sign of respect? It's a mystery. It's a mystery that has come down to us through the ages and still no one knows.

They were all there that afternoon. The queen. Sir Richard Verney. Were Mrs Oddingsells and Mrs Owen in the pay of someone else? Did the little mouse plan revenge on the woman who had stolen her husband? Why was Elizabeth there? Who killed Amy Robsart? You tell me . . .

7

I was dissatisfied with the Amy Robsart jump. In fact, I classed it as a failure. It happens occasionally, but it's not often that St Mary's are on the spot, that we actually witness some controversial event, and come away not only no wiser as to what happened, but even more confused than when we set out. I was in a grumpy mood for a couple of days afterwards. Even Hyssop's better-than-expected performance and positive contributions to the discussions afterwards didn't cheer me up.

Her foot healed in a day or so and as soon as she could hobble around the place in her army-issue sandals, sports, brown, suede, warm-weather, feet-for-the-encasing-of than she brought up her report for my initials. I could see by the expression on her face that she wasn't impressed at having to do this. I rather suspected the day would come when I would have to take my report to her.

I took a deep breath and remembered Peterson's words.

'Try and be a little nicer, Max,' he'd said. Or something like that, anyway. 'You have to establish some sort of working relationship with each other, so put some effort into it. A chance to bond.'

As if I was a tube of bloody Araldite. But he was right, so I sat her down and prepared to be sympathetic.

'Good to see you up and about again. How's your foot?'

'Fine – the swelling's beginning to go down. It was pretty painful for a day or two, but now it looks much worse than it is.'

Remembering to show concern, I leaned over the desk to check out the damage. 'Oh my God – are you sure? That looks awful. You've got toes like giant sausages.'

She said coldly, 'It's the other foot,' and Rosie Lee had to slide off her chair and pretend to be looking for something on the floor and I decided I'd had enough of being nice to people. It never works.

I was wandering around the gallery one day, still thinking about Amy Robsart and trying to devise a strategy for another visit – one that could put us actually right on the spot to discover exactly who greased the newel post – and at the same time compiling a list of so-called profitable jumps as requested by Dr Bairstow, and wondering how Leon was faring in his quest for a new remote site. I really wasn't looking where I was going, and I walked straight into Mrs Partridge.

I apologised and stepped to one side to let her pass, glancing casually out of the window as I did so, and there were Mrs Brown and Dr Bairstow having afternoon tea on the terrace. The Full Monty. There were finger sandwiches, scones, mini quiches and tiny cakes, and Mrs Brown was wearing a very pretty summer frock and pouring out the tea and Dr Bairstow was actually smiling.

Bloody bollocking hell. That was . . . I groped for a word that wasn't 'unsettling', failed, and galloped along to Peterson's office because he had an appropriately facing window where I could see without being seen.

He looked up as I burst in. 'Don't you ever do any work?'

I brushed past him to get to the window.

'What are you doing?'

'Spying on Dr Bairstow and Mrs Brown having tea together. Your office is on the right side of the building. I can see the terrace from here.'

We crowded around the window. Bugger. There was a stupid tree in the way and no time to get it chopped down. I regarded him in exasperation. 'What sort of an idiot has *trees* outside his office?'

'No one asked you to burst in here. Go and find another window.'

We scowled at each other and then, with the air of a man struck by the poleaxe of inspiration, he said, 'R&D.'

There was a bit of a struggle as we both tried to get through the door at the same time, Peterson claiming rank and me claiming ladies first. Peterson has very sharp elbows. Fortunately, there was no one around to see this unseemly tussle between two of the most important people at St Mary's.

Out on the gallery we straightened our clothing, smoothed our hair, put our hands behind our backs and trod the meaningful tread of two senior officers discussing weighty issues beyond the ken of normal mortals. Until we got to R&D, obviously.

Professor Rapson was wearing a welding mask with a sou'wester on the top and holding six feet of copper tubing in one hand and a bottle of vinegar in the other. Normally I would have stopped to enquire but it didn't even register on today's list of weird happenings.

Peterson and I pushed past him and into his cluttered office. A headless skeleton sat in the visitor's chair. I pulled up. I really should enquire as to the possibility of it being Dr Dowson, but first things first.

We craned to see the terrace. Dr Bairstow and Mrs Brown sat in splendid isolation. I don't know whether Mrs Mack was keeping people at bay or whether everyone else was just too terrified to approach.

'Afternoon tea,' said Peterson, wistfully. 'I only ever get a biscuit.'

'Lucky you,' I said. 'Evans ate all mine.'

I looked left and right. Every window along the front appeared to have its own cluster of interested faces. As Peterson said afterwards, we must have looked like the orphans in *Oliver Twist* watching their elders and betters eat while they went hungry.

We watched for a while but apart from eating and drinking, nothing else was happening and then my stomach rumbled and I wandered off to think about Amy Robsart again.

Interesting though, don't you think?

It turned out there was a reason for Mrs Brown's visit – not just afternoon tea. Dr Bairstow had been called up to London and she would be travelling with him.

A word about Mrs Brown. She's one of our Boss's bosses. I'd first met her a few months ago when she turned up to enquire about her daughter, Miss North. Since Miss North was actually Lady Celia North, that made Mrs Brown the Dowager Countess of Blackbourne. Professionally, she's known as Mrs Brown, part of the government department supposedly responsible for us, comprising Black, Brown and Green. It does strike me the

98

Civil Service has very little imagination. If it had been up to me, I'd have named them Peshgaldaramesh, Marduk-kabit-ah-heshu and Ninurta-kudurri-usur. Just for the fun of watching people struggle. However, the Boss always referred to her as Mrs Brown, so Mrs Brown it was.

Anyway, meandering back to the laughable plot, Mrs Brown had visited St Mary's a little while ago to talk to me about North's last jump. To Jerusalem, 33AD. I don't think I need say any more. Officially, the jump never took place but during its unhappeningness, things had got a bit hairy and we'd had to be rescued by the Time Police, which is enough to ruin anyone's day. And North had jumped ship too and was now Officer North of the Time Police. I try not to hold it against her.

Most importantly, however, Mrs Brown and Dr Bairstow – well, I'm not going to say 'hit it off' because I can't imagine either of them doing anything that frivolous but they were definitely getting along. She'd returned to St Mary's several times for the purposes of what would be deemed 'social interaction' if we were discussing lesser mortals, but doesn't seem appropriate for such august personages as Dr Bairstow and Mrs Brown. If anyone can come up with an appropriate term, we'd be grateful.

They'd even gone on a jump together – the infamous Princes in the Tower assignment – all of which has been classified, so anyone with any knowledge of what went down on that occasion can certainly expect a visit from the black helicopters in the very near future.

Anyway, she'd arrived at St Mary's last night, apparently. They'd dined together in Rushford – obviously for the purposes of discussing the agenda and other meetingy stuff – and they were to set off for London first thing tomorrow. Speculation as to how and where they'd spent last night was massive. I daresay Mrs Partridge would have been able to advise but no one dared to ask. And anyway, as Roberts said – it's like the royal family and your parents – not only can you not imagine it, you don't *want* to imagine it.

The two of them drove away soon after breakfast the next morning and the rest of us got on with our working day. I went back to obsessing about Amy Robsart because I don't like failure. I asked Peterson what he thought about stationing someone at the top of the stairs. He sighed and pointed out there was every possibility that St Mary's would be causing the very incident they'd come to investigate. I countered with in that case it was our duty to fulfil our destiny and keep the timeline straight, and he'd threatened me with Dr Stone, and I'd been unable to threaten him back with anything at all because he leads a boring and blameless life and so departed in a massive huff.

And then . . . the very next day . . . the bomb dropped.

I saw a strange car coming up the drive but thought nothing of it. At the time, I was supervising the packing up of all our Crete material. Complaining historians were heaving around archive boxes, injuring themselves and each other. I was staying well out of the blast range as befitted my exalted status when I received a message from Mrs Partridge. All department heads were to report to Dr Bairstow's office immediately.

My first reaction was bewilderment because Dr Bairstow wasn't actually here and then, I don't know why, I suddenly thought – something's happened. I was both right and wrong. Something had happened but what had happened was not what I was expecting. Not what anyone was expecting.

I trotted up the stairs into Dr Bairstow's office. Peterson, as Deputy Director and having the shortest distance to travel, was there already, as were Hyssop and Mrs Partridge. Dieter represented the Technical Section in Leon's absence and Dr Stone was behind me.

There was a stranger in the room. A man of about my own age, possibly a little older, with a nondescript face, close-cropped blond-grey hair and crinkly blue eyes. He was neatly presented in a good suit, a grey striped tie and shiny shoes.

'Good morning. Thank you all for coming. Shall we sit down?' His voice reminded me of Dr Bairstow's. Quiet, but with the edge that conveys, very clearly, that instant compliance is required. Democratically selecting a seat near the middle of the table, he waited patiently for us to settle down.

'I'd like to take a moment for us to introduce ourselves. My name is John Treadwell.' He laid an official-looking ID card on the table in front of us. I picked it up. The royal coat of arms was in the top left-hand corner, but otherwise it was very similar to my own.

'You, I know, are Dr Peterson.' He inclined his head towards Peterson. 'And you are Mrs Partridge.' He looked across the table to me. 'I suspect you are either Dr Maxwell or Captain Hyssop.'

I wondered what would happen if I said, 'Correct. I am,' but humourless Hyssop couldn't let that go.

'I'm Captain Hyssop,' she said, in tones that implied he'd better learn to tell the difference between a shambolic historian and a proper person pretty damn quick.

He looked over at me. 'Dr Maxwell?'

I nodded, wondering what was going on.

'Ah yes, you are Head of the History Department, are you not? Comprising,' he pretended to consult his scratchpad, 'Wardrobe, the Library, and Research and Development?'

He phrased it as a question but he obviously knew the answer.

I nodded. 'Correct.'

'And you are Mr Dieter?'

'Head of the Technical Section,' said Dieter.

'In the absence of Chief Technical Officer Farrell, who is out on field tests, I understand?'

'*Joint* Head of the Technical Section.'

'Dr Stone,' said Dr Stone, and just for once, said no more.

'You are responsible for the provision of medical services here?'

Dr Stone nodded.

I think, just for one moment, this John Treadwell toyed with the idea of making a remark about so many doctors but managed to resist the temptation.

'And your purpose here today?' said Peterson.

He sighed. 'I have been asked to speak to you.' He stopped. The only sound was Dr Bairstow's creaky clock with its irregular tick and virtually non-existent tock.

Treadwell looked around the table. 'I am sorry to have to tell you this, but at around half past two yesterday afternoon, Dr Bairstow's car was involved in a road traffic accident just outside of London. His passenger, Lady Blackbourne, who is a colleague of mine, was airlifted to a nearby hospital. Very sadly, Dr Bairstow was pronounced dead at the scene. I'll give you all a moment, shall I?'

He got up and went to look out of the window.

I stared at the table. No one spoke. We're St Mary's. We're

accustomed to death. I think we all expect to die on the job, so to speak. In a battle, or burned at the stake, or hanged as a horse thief. One or two of us may harbour thoughts of dying quietly in our beds, but I don't think any of us ever expect to die in something so . . . ordinary . . . so contemporary . . . as a car crash. The outside world doesn't impact on us very often but when it does . . .

Dazed, I looked around, searching for something with which to ground myself. I was sitting in Dr Bairstow's office, looking at Dr Bairstow's bookshelves with Dr Bairstow's prints on the wall and sitting at Dr Bairstow's briefing table. None of it was very grand. In fact, I think he once told me his first desk had been salvaged from the municipal tip – however likely that was. All of it was so familiar to me I barely noticed it most of the time, but today I saw it through different eyes.

I closed my eyes and listened to the echoes.

'So tell me, Dr Maxwell, if the whole of History lay before you like a shining ribbon, where would you go . . . ?'

'Dr Maxwell, why are you wearing a red snake in my office . . . ?'

'See to it, Dr Maxwell . . .'

On and on, crashing and reverberating inside my head. Echo on echo. A whole symphony of echoes.

I looked over to the window. John Treadwell – whoever he was – was staring out, hands clasped behind his back.

Still no one had spoken. I think we were all too stunned to take it in. I don't know for how long we would have sat there. I have no recollection of time passing at all, but when I next looked up, Treadwell was seating himself opposite me again.

'I don't believe Dr Bairstow has any living relatives, but

Lady Blackbourne's next of kin have been informed and are with her in hospital.'

He paused and sat silently, giving us time to take it in.

My first coherent thought was for Leon. He and Dr Bairstow had been friends for years. Dr Bairstow had recruited Leon to St Mary's. Leon was out there somewhere and knew nothing of this. What dreadful news to come home to. He would be devastated.

My second thoughts were for myself. There was no grief. Not yet. That would come later. Now it was just shock and confusion and a sudden feeling of disconnection. That something had ended. The heart-chilling fear that something had gone forever. Something fragile had been shattered beyond repair and a cold wind was blowing.

Treadwell was now speaking again. 'I shall call a meeting – an all-staff briefing, I think you call it – this afternoon to inform everyone of this tragic event. I can see this news has come as an enormous shock. I know you've all worked with Dr Bairstow for a long time, which is why I wanted to tell you quietly and in private first.'

He paused as if inviting comment but no one spoke.

'Today is Friday. I think it's quite safe to say people are going to be upset. I propose to give them today and the weekend and pick things up again on Monday.'

Peterson said slowly, 'I'm not sure that will be possible.'

Treadwell shook his head. 'I think once the initial shock is over, people will benefit from the discipline of work. That is my considered opinion.'

'And, forgive me, your opinion is important because . . . ?'

'Because I am the new Director of St Mary's. Effective immediately.'

I think I had to replay his words three or four times before they actually made sense.

'There must be an error,' I said, making an heroic effort to speak calmly. 'Dr Peterson is Dr Bairstow's designated replacement.'

Treadwell's face, his voice – nothing changed. He was still going with quiet and sympathetic. 'I'm sorry – no. It has been decided that St Mary's will benefit from an outside approach bringing fresh enthusiasm and new ideas.'

When I'm upset I get angry. 'Why?'

'I'm sorry?'

'What was wrong with the old ideas?'

'Nothing at all. It's just that every organisation profits from a change at the top. Fresh thinking and so on.'

'How fortunate for you that Dr Bairstow has died, then. Is this standard procedure where you come from? Regular culls to ensure new blood?'

'I am making allowances for emotional distress, Dr Maxwell, but please don't try to push me.'

I opened my mouth to tell him I was born to push but Peterson got to his feet, his face grim.

'Unless you have any strong objections – and actually, even if you do – I prefer to make this announcement myself. I appreciate your enthusiasm for embracing the whole *the king is dead – long live the king* thing, but unless you want people to associate you – irrevocably – with the trauma of Dr Bairstow's death, I suggest you separate the two announcements. I'll break the news this afternoon – Mrs Partridge, if you could organise

105

that, please – and you, Mr Treadwell, can announce yourself on Monday. Dr Bairstow was held in extraordinarily high regard by everyone who knew him, and unless they're given time to process this properly, you may find yourself on the receiving end of even more unfortunate pushing.'

Treadwell paused for a moment. 'It's Commander Treadwell, but very well.'

'Who put you in charge?' I demanded. 'What makes you the right person for the job?'

'My appointment was confirmed by the same department that has oversight of your activities here.' He paused. 'It's natural, I suppose, that you will be doubtful as to my suitability. I can assure you that I am not just some bureaucrat in the same way that you are not just historians. I served seven years in the military. I have seen action. I was wounded twice. Not seriously on either occasion. On leaving the military I was offered a post with . . . intelligence . . . during which I travelled extensively. And now, here I am.'

'And your brief?'

He hesitated.

'Well, go on,' I said. 'You're the new blood. We're waiting to see how it will manifest itself.'

Treadwell was silent for a few seconds, looking down at his clasped hands. 'If they have any sense, new brooms do not immediately sweep clean. I shall study your working practices, make some recommendations and then proceed accordingly. I understand that historians are, by their very nature, conservative, but please try to remember change is not always bad.'

'I'm sure you're right,' I said, 'but we at St Mary's tend to prefer improvement.'

106

'It is natural,' he said, irritatingly calm, 'that well-established members of staff, entrenched in their way of doing things, should feel some disquiet at the disappearance of old and familiar routines, but I think, on mature consideration, they will see the many benefits of proceeding in the direction I shall be indicating.'

'I wouldn't hold my breath,' I said, but by then Peterson had me out of the door. As I left the room, I heard Treadwell ask Hyssop if she could remain behind for a moment. For some reason I found that quite ominous.

We filed out through Mrs Partridge's office. She had seated herself at her desk and was pulling her keyboard towards her. I paused. Her face was a mask.

I asked if I could do anything for her.

'That is exceedingly kind of you, Dr Maxwell. If no one has any objections, I shall organise Dr Peterson's all-staff briefing and then spend some time in quiet reflection.'

Peterson made the announcement that afternoon and even Tread-well had to concede that he, Peterson, had called it correctly.

Shock, I think, was the prevailing emotion. People sat so still you could have taken one of those old-fashioned photographs of the entire room. The ones where people had to sit still for long minutes. Dr Bairstow had been our anchor. Whatever catastrophe was occurring at the time, he'd been there. Solid as a rock and slightly less conciliatory. Whether overcoming the Time Police, Clive Ronan, Malcolm Halcombe – he'd always been several moves ahead of everyone else and now . . .

After the briefing, Peterson went off to break the news to Ian Guthrie. He and Mr Strong had been the first people recruited to St Mary's. Mr Strong was nowhere to be found. We didn't see him for a couple of days.

The weekend between Peterson's and Treadwell's announcements is lost to me. All I remember is moving from person to person, listening and comforting as best I could. I like to think I helped in some small way. I certainly think it helped me. It gave me something on which to focus. I could swallow down my own grief, my own loss, and concentrate on others until finally I was able to get back to my own room.

To sit in the cold and the dark and stare, dry-eyed, at the wall.

He began the Monday briefing well. Treadwell, I mean. For a start, he didn't make the mistake of standing in Dr Bairstow's place on the half-landing. He stood at the foot of the stairs, which oddly brought him closer but made him seem further away at the same time. He still wore his dark pin-striped suit and grey tie. In fact, I don't think I ever saw him out of it.

'Good morning. For those of you who haven't met me, my name is John Treadwell. I don't know many of you yet but I hope to become better acquainted over the coming weeks. As you will know by now, I'm here as your new Director and I'd like to begin this briefing with a minute's silence in memory of Dr Bairstow.'

We stood, heads bowed.

'Thank you,' he said eventually, and we sat again.

'I think firstly I need to clear up a small misunderstanding. I believe some of you were under the impression that Dr Peterson was Dr Bairstow's designated successor.'

'Yes,' I said. 'I was with Dr Bairstow on Crete when he thought he wouldn't survive and he specifically designated Dr Peterson.'

'I'm not arguing, Dr Maxwell. I'm sure that did happen;

109

however, it is felt the appointment of his successor was not Dr Bairstow's prerogative and so I am here today to introduce myself.

'I can understand the anxiety you all feel and I want to assure you – as I have repeatedly assured Dr Maxwell – that I have no intention of introducing sweeping changes to this organisation. But please understand – I am not Dr Bairstow. My way of doing things will be different to his. Obviously, I shall try to be as uncontroversial as possible – it's in no one's interests for us to be at each other's throats – but please be aware – *I* am the Director of St Mary's now. In the same way that Dr Bairstow's word was law – so will mine be.'

I don't know if he was expecting a reaction to that but everyone continued to sit, still and silent.

He continued. 'As I have explained to Dr Maxwell, changes will be wrought gradually. You will be consulted and informed at every stage. Without going into massive detail, my brief is as follows:

'To modernise St Mary's. As part of this, I shall be looking at the staff structure and functions. Please do not be alarmed. Any jobs lost will be through natural wastage.'

Atherton, who leads the Pathfinders and once worked in the real world – at a bank, actually – raised his hand. 'Is that where you make life so unpleasant that people want to leave and then you can call it natural wastage?'

Not a muscle moved. 'No,' Treadwell said, pleasantly. 'In fact, initially I think I might be recruiting. Your ... our ... Security Section, is, in my opinion, very understaffed.

'Secondly, I want to make St Mary's more productive and we will do this together. Together, we will look at new ways to do what we do. Or whether we need to do it at all. Or whether we should move into new areas. Any ideas you might have on this subject will be warmly received.

'Thirdly, to generate additional income streams. I'm sure it will come as no surprise to you to learn that St Mary's is the world's biggest money pit. Please be reassured I'm not about to traffic you –' he paused for a laugh he didn't get – 'but there must be ways of earning money. Even a small contribution from St Mary's to offset its massive expenditure would be greatly welcomed by our employers.

'Which brings me to my next point. We are all employed by the government. You know this. I know this. I know the nature of your jobs here has compelled you to surrender your political rights. That you have, in fact, disenfranchised yourselves. That you stand apart. This is no small sacrifice on your part and one which is recognised by the government. However, the government does feel it is time St Mary's was brought more firmly under their umbrella and it will be one of my tasks to make it so. This will not affect us in the day-to-day workings of St Mary's but I do anticipate the government will expect to have an input in future policy and direction.

'That, broadly, is what I will be looking at over the coming weeks. There will be other areas, too, but these will be my priorities.'

He paused and looked around. 'I am not a fool. I can quite understand your resistance, but I'm not here to wreck St Mary's. Far from it – I'm here to make it work better. I know what you must be thinking, but there really is no need for alarm or despondency. For most of you, life will continue very much as it did before. As Dr Maxwell so firmly pointed out to me on

Friday, change is worthless unless it includes improvements, which is how I am hoping you will regard what could be a bright new future for all of us.'

He took a moment for effect and then said, 'Thank you.'

I thought he would return upstairs to his office but to my surprise, he made his way through the still stunned ranks to stand in front of me.

'If you're not busy, Dr Maxwell, I would very much appreciate a tour of your department.'

I nodded. We might as well get it over with and no one knew better than me how to present my shambolic department in a favourable light.

I nodded. 'Ten minutes?'

'Of course,' he said, while we both pretended he didn't know this was so I could send Mr Roberts on ahead to give people a chance to hide the bodies. Every organisation has bodies. They may not be actual cadavers but everyone has something they don't want the boss to see.

I met Treadwell outside his office and we headed downstairs together.

'Before we begin, Dr Maxwell, have I, on several occasions, glimpsed a chicken in the corridors?'

'Yes.'

Well, what else could I have said?

There was a bit of a silence, possibly while he waited for me to flesh my answer out a little, and then when it became apparent that wasn't going to happen, he said, 'Surely, Dr Maxwell, simple hygiene demands it should be removed as soon as possible.'

'Angus was extremely fond of Dr Bairstow and her invariable

reaction to any trauma is to spot-weld herself to Bashford. So yes, you have glimpsed a chicken in the corridors but only attached to Bashford, so no hygiene issues there.'

'I find the knowledge that a chicken actually lives inside the building to be extremely concerning.'

An efficient and effective leader is always on the alert for possible areas of contention and, anticipating this conversation, I'd already had a word with Bashford yesterday, enquiring where Angus was living these days.

'Mr Strong has her in the stable during the day and she's with me at night,' he'd said.

'On your wardrobe?'

'She likes it up there,' Bashford said defensively.

It never seemed to occur to him that this was a potential face-saving moment for him. He could legitimately have consigned Angus to the only slightly less luxurious stables – which doesn't say much for St Mary's accommodation but what can you do? – and considerably increased his chances of saving his relationship with Sykes.

'Oh no,' he said when I mentioned this. 'She was quite adamant about the wardrobe. Sykes, I mean. About Angus. On the wardrobe.'

And then obviously considering he'd explained the matter sufficiently, he'd wandered off – paused – appeared to reconsider his destination and then wandered off in the opposite direction. He really wasn't getting any better.

But back to the present. Before Treadwell could further explore the subject of Angus's living arrangements, I said brightly, 'And here we are.'

We'd arrived at Wardrobe, which was always a hive of

113

activity. Racks of costumes were neatly arranged, firstly in chronological order and then alphabetically, depending on for whom they had been made. Tailor's dummies stood around with various bits and pieces draped all over them.

Through a door was the fitting room – where Rosie Lee had once memorably slapped a Time Police officer and I'd thought we were all going to die. One wall was given over to rows and rows of shelves where rested various accessories – hats, shoes, swords, fans and so on. Another wall was plastered with photos of us historians, together with our measurements. I should say, having your vital statistics on display for everyone to see is a great incentive for everyone to stay slim. Except me. I live with public shame and chocolate. Rumour had it that one or two of the blokes wandered in occasionally and adjusted someone's inside-leg measurement but I wouldn't know anything about that.

I introduced Treadwell to Mrs Enderby, who, in turn, introduced him individually to her people.

He greeted everyone by name and then gazed around. 'This is very impressive.'

'In addition to kitting us out for all our jumps,' I said, not hesitating to gild the lily, 'Mrs Enderby wins awards for her work in the film, TV and holo industry.' I gestured to the various certificates and awards displayed behind her desk.

'Yes, indeed,' he said, peering at them. 'Some of these are very prestigious. Well done.'

I watched him suspiciously, looking for condescension, but apparently, he was serious.

'I see you did the one about Leonardo,' he said, squinting at a small trophy. 'I actually thought the costumes were the best bit. The history was quite inaccurate.'

Her bosom swelled. Mrs Enderby is one of the sweetest persons on the planet but everyone has their *bête noire*.

'One of Calvin Cutter's,' she said tightly and I had to intervene before she rendered us liable to an action for slander.

I gestured to a group of gorgeous dresses currently displayed on mannequins. 'This is what Wardrobe is working on now. We've been asked to provide designs for Mr Cutter's *Catherine the Great*.'

We all paused for him to make the remark about the horse but he didn't, earning himself not inconsiderable brownie points. Instead, he turned his attention to the rows and rows of costumes accumulated over the years. I wondered whether to tell him there were more upstairs and decided against it. It's never a good idea to burden senior managers with too much information. Always leave them plenty of room to think about what to have for lunch.

He smiled at Mrs Enderby. 'Please do not remove my head from my shoulders, but why don't you sell some of these off?'

'Because,' said Mrs Enderby, 'we reuse them all many times. Like this one, for instance.' She pulled out a plain brown woollen dress that had, to my certain knowledge, been a maid's outfit in the Middle Ages, Female Citizen Number Two in Tudor times and Female Citizen Number One at the storming of the Bastille; the addition of a fichu had rendered it suitable for the late Georgian era. It was nicely worn in with shiny patches at the knees and elbows.

'And when they're completely worn out,' she continued, 'we cut them down to make other costumes. We have already incurred the expense of making them but by reusing them many times, lending them – even hiring them out to third parties – we recoup a lot of that expenditure.'

Treadwell said nothing but I could hear his brain working.

From there we crossed the Hall to the Library where Dr Dowson waited, arms folded in a particularly hostile manner.

Our new leader leaned across to me, whispering, 'Why is there a hard hat on his desk?'

I whispered back, 'Because his locker is too far away.'

'From what?'

'From here. There's no point in keeping your safety gear on the other side of the building, is there?'

'I think the point I am trying to make is that this is a library. He is a librarian. Why does he need a hard hat at all?'

'For protection.'

'From . . . ?'

Easy to see he hadn't been here during rapid-chicken-firing-gun trauma.

'From whatever is occurring at the time.'

'Again, this is a library. What sort of things could possibly occur here?'

Even I didn't dare say *from things you need a hard hat to protect your head from* so I said, 'We're directly underneath R&D here. It's a bit of a hazardous location sometimes.'

He glanced upwards and nodded but said no more.

'Commander Treadwell, this is Dr Dowson, our Head Librarian.'

I took very good care to stand between the two of them, all ready to tell Treadwell how the Library earned its keep by providing research to anyone who wanted it, but it seemed he'd found something else to complain about. Wandering slowly in and out of the bays, he said suddenly, 'Some of these books are almost falling apart. Why are they still on the shelves?'

116

'They're scruffy because they're used. Heavily. The better-looking books are more specialist and not consulted so frequently.'

'Why isn't it all digitised?'

'Most of it is,' I said, beginning to get the hang of this. 'When these eventually fall apart, then they will be too. It's a waste of money to duplicate copies needlessly, don't you think?'

'You could sell them off.'

'We do. We send books to prisons, to other countries, to specialist libraries, to charities and so forth.'

Dr Dowson stood quietly by his desk, making no move to join us. I was terrified Commander Treadwell would ask why such a small library would need such a highly qualified librarian. The answer, of course, was to manage our Archive – previously housed behind the door in the corner – which I really didn't want to get into at the moment because it wasn't there – so I shunted him gently out of the door, back into the Great Hall and the History Department, which I was hoping would be the Big Finish and R&D could be quietly overlooked in the excitement.

Clean, conscious and reasonably presentable historians lined up to be introduced. Everyone was very polite. Never a good sign. A polite historian is an historian looking for a fight.

'Before you submerge yourself in our money-making potential,' I said, 'Dr Bairstow traffics . . . *trafficked* out the History Department on a regular basis. We lecture at schools and colleges, private events and so forth, and occasionally assist in arranging tableaux for museums and exhibitions.'

He blinked. 'They let *you* near children?'

'Actually, I'm quite popular.'

'What do you lecture on?'

117

'Riots, revolutions, battlefields, bloody murders, executions, torture, plague, pus . . .'

'Ah. Mystery solved. What are you working on at the moment?' he asked, surveying the productive chaos around him.

'We're just finishing a major assignment to Crete,' I said. 'The eruption of Thera. Destruction of the Minoan civilisation. The rise of mainland Greece. Climate change around the world.'

He nodded. 'Did you bring anything back?'

'We don't bring things back,' I said quickly. 'We can't.'

'Why not? My understanding was that . . .'

'Pod safety protocols will not allow us to remove historical items from their own time. We couldn't, for example, jump to 1503 and bring back the *Mona Lisa*.'

He frowned. I don't know why some people worry about bringing their boss bad news. I quite enjoy it. 'Why not?'

'Because it has a near six-hundred-year History. If we jumped back and stole it when the paint was barely dry, it would have none of that. Events, lives, many things would be changed.'

I could see this argument wasn't having the desired impact and tried another tack.

'Without that History, its value would be considerably less. More importantly, because neither the paint nor the canvas would be six hundred years old, it would be judged a fake. Even though it wasn't. And once that happened, our reputation – and that of Thirsk – would be shot and everything subsequently recovered – and possibly already recovered – would be similarly tainted. So – as I'm sure you are well aware – we rescue items about to be destroyed because they have no further part to play in History. Having done that, we then hide them somewhere temporally and geographically appropriate so they can be recovered by perfectly legitimate archaeologists in a perfectly legitimate manner. Such as, for example, a small part of the contents of the Library at Alexandria.'

'It seems unnecessarily long-winded.'

'We have to do it that way,' I said patiently, although I thought we'd covered this. 'We have to make sure the retrieved object – say, a wooden carving – has aged correctly Otherwise we'd be in a position of handing over a perfectly genuine artefact but all the experts would say, "Yes, it looks genuine, but it can't be because it's obviously brand-new." So we bury it somewhere safe, leave it to age naturally and then Thirsk discovers it to international acclaim.'

'You bury it here?'

'No, we bury it somewhere appropriate. To bolster its authenticity.'

'At Thirsk then?'

'No,' I said, patience oozing from every orifice because everyone was listening and I had an example to set. 'It's a rule we have. Everything is buried and rediscovered in the country in which it was lost. Because it belongs to that country.'

'So there's no financial return on the discovery.'

'Well, yes, of course there is. Massive acclaim for Thirsk for yet another brilliant archaeological find, which almost certainly leads to increased funding for them and, in the fullness of time, us. Plus massive excitement in the country in which it's discovered. Publicity, cultural pride, renewed interest in History – it's all good.'

'But ours was the initial outlay.'

'Seriously?' I said. 'Let us say for one moment that a possible Chinese equivalent of St Mary's discovers Lady Shrewsbury's garter – the one that inspires Edward III to found the Order of the Garter. They find it here in England but they cart it off to China and bury it there. At the appropriate time it's uncovered just outside Beijing and put in a museum there. A major piece of English History. How happy would you be about that? How happy would anyone feel about that? Was there not enough grief over the Elgin Marbles?'

'But if you buried . . . say, the Sword of Charlemagne in this country, to be discovered here, then that wouldn't arise.'

'Possibly – although I think it would probably lead to yet another European war – but discovery in an improbable location would considerably increase the chances of it being denounced as a forgery or fake. That would only have to happen once and everything we subsequently discovered would be suspect.'

'Hmm,' he said, which is what I say when I'm not convinced by someone's argument but too polite to say so. He might have taken it further, but I'd subtly chivvied him up the stairs, intending to return him safely to his own office where Mrs Partridge could keep him safely corralled for the rest of the day. But somehow he veered off and suddenly we were outside R&D. Where things did not get any better.

I made very sure to knock loudly. I don't normally do that. No one does. We barge in and take our chances and if, for some reason, no one is wearing their trousers that day we simply close our eyes and move on. And yes, that has happened. Last Tuesday, actually – the same day Bashford had been banned from the kitchen for getting a stick blender entangled in his hair. That had been quite an exciting day.

And today was living down to normal R&D standards as well.

Bashford lay on the floor with his arms crossed neatly on his chest. I'm ashamed to say my first thought was one of utter panic.

Oh God, not a dead body. Not on Treadwell's first day. We hadn't even had lunch yet.

And then, thank heavens, Bashford opened his eyes. 'Oh, hello, Max.'

'Good morning,' I said formally, maintaining Markham's standards. From that moment, the conversation proceeded along a well-worn path.

Me – knowing I'll regret it but impelled by my lemming genes towards the Cliff of Catastrophe: What exactly is going on here, professor?

Prof R – standing over Bashford: This is so exciting.

Me – not panicking yet but not far off: Oh yes? What's that, then?

Prof R – vibrating with excitement: Levitation.

Me – hoping against hope I've misheard somehow: Leviticus?

Prof R – making appropriate gestures: No. Lev-it-ation.

Me – still not completely without hope: Are you sure? Only I thought you said Leviticus. You know – the Bible.

Prof R – beaming: No, I said levitation. You know – the action of causing an object to rise into the air by means of willpower.

Me – battling the familiar, cold premonition of disaster and failing: I'm sorry – levitation?

Prof R – concerned: Yes, didn't you do it at school?

Me – still not quite believing this conversation is taking place: No, we did geography.

Prof R – shaking his head at such ignorance: No, Max. That thing where you lift someone up with two fingers. Because they're weightless.

Me – to self: Oh God . . .

Normally, at this point, I could expect things to go one of two ways: either Bashford would improbably waft past at head height, or St Mary's would engage the Second Law of Thermodynamics and begin the inevitable transition from order to chaos. Place your bets now, ladies and gentlemen – this could go either way.

Sadly – or probably not – it wasn't going any way at all today. Not with present company standing at my side.

'A fascinating experiment, professor,' I said with the smoothness of long practice, 'and one with so many practical applications. Please don't let us detain you,' and nudged Treadwell towards the door before the professor took it into his head to use our new Director as an experimental subject and floated him out of an upstairs window. Although now I came to think of it . . .

And then a minor miracle occurred. I don't mean Bashford spontaneously overcame the force of gravity, but Commander Treadwell leaned forwards with an expression of great interest and said, 'I assume this is related to the Casimir Effect – nanoscale levitation, zero friction and so forth.'

The professor beamed. 'Yes, to some extent. I'm looking at practical applications. If we could just overcome the problem of unwanted attraction in . . . oh, I wonder . . .' He petered out and wandered off, apparently overcome by the excitement of it all.

'Interesting,' was all Treadwell said, itself an interesting reaction.

I nudged him out of the door before more specific enquiries dispelled the good impression.

'So,' he said as we strolled around the gallery. 'Tell me about your favourite . . . jumps.'

'Mine?'

'Yes.'

Of course, that's like when someone asks you which is your favourite book. Your mind goes blank and you can't remember a single thing you've read in the last twenty years. It would have been nice to have reeled off a wide-ranging list of jumps demonstrating the depth and variety of St Mary's talents – the Cretaceous, Troy, Agincourt, the Gates of Grief, to name but a few – but for some reason the only one I could remember was Joan of Arc.

'Um . . . well . . . one that stays in my mind is the jump to Rouen in 1431. To watch Joan of Arc's execution.'

'Why?'

'As part of a training exercise.'

'Why?'

Somehow we were back down the stairs again.

'This is oversimplifying things slightly, but a large part of our job is watching people die. At some point, as trainees, we're all faced with the unpleasant-death assignment. To see how we handle it. Because some don't.'

'And Joan of Arc died . . . ?'

'Slowly and painfully.'

'That must have been unpleasant for you.'

'Unpleasant for everyone. But mostly Joan, of course.'

'And yet it was the English who burned her.'

'A common misconception. She was burned by the French church for heresy. The English merely sold her to them with instructions to get on with it.'

By now, we'd passed through the front doors and were strolling around the side of the building. It was a nice morning. Sunny . . . peaceful . . . although God knew for how much longer.

'Why was it necessary for you to be there?'

'As I said, a training assignment. I was Chief Training Officer at the time.' Actually, that sounds grander than it was. I was the only training officer at the time.

'No – I mean, as a woman. Must have been upsetting. Does that happen often?'

'Does what happen often?'

'Women on assignments.'

I blinked. 'All the time.'

'Why?'

'For most of History, the sexes had rigidly defined roles and positions. There are places men can go and women can't and places women can go and men can't.'

'Yes, I accept that as an argument for studying domestic and social issues, but surely you're very much at risk during battles and violent disturbances.'

'Remind me to introduce you to Miss Sykes. She's very sound on the world and its position in the lives of women.'

This wasn't actually the first time someone had tried the 'women should stay safely at home' thing. The idiot Halcombe had made a similar mistake a little while ago. Bashford, entering into the spirit of the thing, had described all women as mere vessels, and Sykes had agreed immediately, declaring herself to be a seventeen-thousand-ton battleship, dreadnought class, with enough firepower to level a city. No one had argued on that occasion and I was willing to bet no one would if she did it again.

'No,' he said. 'I'm serious.'

'So am I and trying, politely, to stop you making an arse of yourself. You must be aware of the identities of Mrs Mack, Mrs Enderby and Mrs Shaw.'

'Obviously I've read the files, but it just illustrates my arguments, doesn't it? One's head of cooking, one's head of needlework and one's a secretary.'

The more discerning among you will have noticed that I'm not as young as I used to be. Marriage and motherhood have taken the spring out of my step. Once upon a time a red mist would have descended and there would have been actions that everyone but me would have regretted, but now I'm older and more mature and it's less a red mist and more a kind of lavender haze. Like poison gas but prettier.

'Ah,' I said, 'you're one of those. *Kinder, Küche, Kirche.*'

'No,' he said patiently, apparently getting the reference. 'I'm speaking as an employer, one of whose duties is to keep his employees safe. Can you give me a reason why you, personally, should be at Waterloo, or Hastings?'

'I'm an historian,' I said patiently in return. 'It's my job. And I *was* at both.'

'Hmm,' he said again.

'I doubt,' I said, 'that your advocacy of children, kitchen and church will find much support at St Mary's. For example, there are any number of educated women here, all with enquiring minds, so the church's only interest in us would be as kindling.'

This was true. I'd asked questions at school. As you're

125

supposed to, I believe. But – and I don't know if anyone's ever noticed – only certain questions are acceptable.

My teacher had batted aside questions about Virgin Births with practised ease. She'd been slightly stumped when I'd enquired about Jezebel, wife of Ahab, and why the dogs hadn't eaten her skull, her feet and the palms of her hands, but it was my criticism of a belief system that encouraged Abraham to offer up his son for sacrifice, solely to curry favour with a god, that had propelled me straight into detention for a week, where I'd very ostentatiously read *The God Delusion* and not understood a word of it.

And I don't cook because there are quicker and easier ways of setting fire to a building than by trying to stir something in a saucepan. And I'm abysmally bad with children. Although, to be fair, it's not all my fault because they're equally bad with me.

However, since I was supposed to be older and wiser, I let the Treadwell idiot live, enquiring whether he himself had ever considered a career in the church.

To my surprise, he laughed. 'I'm fully aware of the point you're making, doctor, but can you honestly assure me a battle-field is a safe place for a woman?'

'I think you might be a trifle hazy on the definition of battle-field. I don't think they're meant to be safe. For anyone.'

'But particularly unsafe for women.'

'Look,' I said, old memories of the time I'd worked with the Time Police bubbling to the surface like marsh gas. 'I'm an historian who happens to be female. Peterson's an historian who happens to be male. There's no difference between a male historian and a female historian. Well, only a very little one. In fact, if I can resurrect an old Time Police joke I once heard . . .'

'What are the Time Police?'

I stared at him, my mouth open. 'You haven't been briefed on the Time Police?'

'Apparently not, but please feel free to make any jokes that may occur to you.'

I looked around for some privacy. The Sunken Garden was just over there. 'Come with me.'

'Are you going to drown me?'

'Only in facts.'

'I don't think that's necessary.'

'Then I'll leave you in ignorance. Do you think your employers have done it deliberately?'

'Done what?'

'Sent you here incompletely briefed. Are you their fall guy, all ready and waiting for the day everything goes tits up?'

'Dr Maxwell, everyone wants to make a success of this – a bright, shiny new St Mary's – a flagship government initiative bringing in prestige and profit.'

Oh God, we were doomed. I said, 'All right – I won't tell you.'

'Tell me what? What sort of stories are you going to attempt to frighten me with?'

I stepped back and smiled. 'None at all. I can see you're much too clever to place an overreliance on actual facts. And as they say, ignorance is bliss. But remember, everyone here knows about the Time Police. Your employers know about the Time Police. The only person who doesn't know about the Time Police is you.'

Well – that could have gone better. It occurred to me I should go and talk reassuringly to my department, but there were too many of us for my office so I shunted us all into Wardrobe. Mrs Enderby shut the door and we all looked at each other.

'Sit down, guys,' I said and they did.

I have a large and vociferous department. I've never known them so quiet.

Eventually, Dr Dowson said, 'Max . . .'

I shook my head. 'I'm sorry, I can't add anything to Commander Treadwell's briefing. You now know everything I know.'

'What's going to happen now?' asked Rosie Lee.

'Again, I don't know. I've exchanged a few words with him and he's assured me he's not going to rush into any major changes immediately but I think we'd be deceiving ourselves if we thought everything's going to remain the same. I do beg of you to approach this with open minds. Change is not necessarily bad. Ask yourselves – if it was Dr Bairstow proposing this new method of working, would we oppose it? Try to see improvement where it actually does exist.'

Atherton nodded gloomily. 'They did this at the bank I worked at. We all had to go on a course where bright, sparkly people with frightening smiles exhorted us to embrace change because those who can't die out. I think they cited the dinosaurs.'

'So they weren't killed by an asteroid at all, then?' said Bashford, astonished.

'Not according to the expensive people hired to tell us that our expertise, the working relationships we'd built up over the years, all our hard work was now utterly valueless – as would we be if we didn't get with the new programme. According to them, it was their inability to adapt to this month's new ideas and working practices that did for the dinosaurs and the asteroid had nothing to do with it. They were quite horrified at our lack of enthusiasm for massive redundancies while senior managers – reluctantly, of course – accepted promotions and pay rises with increased bonuses.'

Van Owen twisted in her seat. 'I'm guessing you weren't with this bank for very long.'

'No one was,' he said, gloomily.

I glanced towards the doors. They were solid and they were closed.

'I don't want to alarm anyone, but we've been through this before with the idiot Halcombe. So just as before – simple precautions, people. Grab bags ready. Shred anything you don't want held against you in the future. The Archive's already safe with Leon in TB2. Be ready to go at a moment's notice.'

'Aren't we overreacting?' enquired Mrs Enderby.

'Very possibly,' I said. 'In fact, I hope so. Then when everything turns out all right, we can sheepishly unpack our stuff and carry on as if nothing has happened.'

I took a breath. There are a lot of civilians in my department.

'Those who wish to leave St Mary's in a more conventional manner may do so. No one will hold anything against you. And you should be aware – if we do have to evacuate, we might not be back any time soon. And – again I'm sorry – but if we do return, it might not be here to St Mary's. We might be in another location. Another country, even. If anyone wants to come and talk with me about this, then Rosie will find you a slot. But – let's not panic yet. Let's wait to see what Commander Treadwell has in store for us first.'

129

9

The next disaster wasn't, in fact, Treadwell-related. Well, only very slightly.

They say bad things happen in threes. Personally, I've always found they happen in multiples of threes. Something goes wrong, which causes something else to go wrong, things begin to spiral out of control, disasters accumulate and then everything drops off a cliff. Which is OK because, as Hyssop had said, falling off the cliff is fine – it's the landing that kills you. The trick is never to stop falling.

Anyway – we'd acquired Hyssop. We'd acquired Treadwell. And then, just when you'd think things couldn't get any worse, they did.

I was in R&D. I can't remember why, because suddenly finding myself confronted with an entire room full of prototype Baghdad Batteries had inexplicably caused more mundane matters to fly right out of my head.

Apparently, Professor Rapson had touched down on Planet Earth long enough to absorb some of Treadwell's cost-cutting idiocy and had hatched some crazy idea about powering St Mary's with a complicated network of copper rods and lemon juice. Most of his section had enthusiastically embraced this

God-given opportunity to undermine the English Electricity Board, its sprawling empire, and possibly all of civilisation, as well.

'Lemon juice,' the professor was saying, from his position beneath a fingerprint-covered sign saying *DO NOT TOUCH*. 'Or perhaps vinegar, but lemon juice has more possibilities, I think. And we could grow our own. Lemons, that is. We'd need extensive hothouses, of course, but they probably wouldn't be as expensive as people say and we'd recoup the cost in a hundred years or so – and think of it, Max – a safe and renewable energy source and if we could patent it . . . well. I'm sure I'll be able to get our new Director interested.'

I opened my mouth and Mrs Partridge spoke in my ear.

'Dr Maxwell, Commander Treadwell would like to speak with you.'

'Sorry, professor, Treadwell wants me.'

The professor's face lit up. 'Do you think he's heard what we're doing already?'

'I wouldn't be at all surprised.'

'Can I rely on you to . . .'

'Put a good word in? Of course,' I said, confident that Treadwell would be even less enthusiastic than I was.

As I left, they were discussing the benefits of urine over lemon juice.

'An endless supply,' said someone.

'And it's the same colour,' said someone else.

'We could have Diuretic Days . . .'

'Or if not to generate power, then how about acupuncture,' said someone. There was silence while powerful minds addressed this new opportunity.

'Except won't the needles get a bit hot?'

'A torture device,' said someone, enthusiastically. 'Massive market for that sort of thing.'

And then, thank God, I was out of the door.

I trotted round the gallery to Dr Bairstow's office. Mrs Partridge was wearing black. She didn't look up as I entered so I went straight through and found myself face to face not only with Treadwell, Peterson and Hyssop, but Malcolm Halcombe and Major Sullivan as well. Evans was standing nearby, cradling one of the big blasters and keeping a very close eye on the pair of them.

I braked to a halt on the threshold and thought, 'shit'.

I suspect another quick word of explanation might be in order.

Malcolm Halcombe was Treadwell 1.0 and most of the reasons why he, Treadwell, was being regarded with such suspicion and hostility. Halcombe, backed by the unpleasant Major Sullivan and his team of thugs, had attempted to force themselves upon St Mary's and St Mary's had promptly buggered off to our remote site. Sadly, a few people had been left behind here and they hadn't fared at all well. Ask Evans, who'd been unable to stand by the time he was rescued. And he's a big bloke so imagine what they must have done to him.

Anyway, in an effort to curry favour with his bosses and earn a spot of cash from St Mary's – hands up, anyone who thinks this seems relevant to our current circumstances – the idiot Halcombe had attempted to force Miss North and me back to the crucifixion for a once in a lifetime bit of recording and documenting. Sadly, everything connected with that event is designated Triple-S – Site of Special Significance – and strictly illegal. I wouldn't even open the door, the pod was threatening to self-destruct and we were all slowly suffocating. Sullivan was about to shoot North as an incentive when, fortunately, and for the first time in their lives, the Time Police turned up and made themselves useful by arresting us all. I went on to catch up with St Mary's and North stayed with the Time Police. They thought she was wonderful and vice versa.

Anyway, Halcombe and his mates were all sentenced to a long prison stretch. I still couldn't believe Treadwell hadn't been briefed on the Time Police. I needed to have a bit of a think about that because I reckoned there was something going on somewhere, and now it would appear Halcombe and Sullivan had been released from Time Police custody. Considerably older and almost certainly none the wiser. I've no idea what had happened to their colleagues. Either they'd been released separately or, more probably, they hadn't survived.

And why us? Why had the Time Police dropped them off here? Because they'd been arrested for a St Mary's-related offence, I suspected. From a Time Police point of view, they were now our problem. They would simply have dropped them on the South Lawn and buggered off.

I was quite shocked at their appearance. They hadn't aged well. Halcombe must now be around seventy – Sullivan a little more. Not great ages – not even at retirement age – but the years had not been kind to them.

We all looked at each other in silence. Their crimes were still fresh in my mind because for me, it hadn't been that long ago. They were lucky North wasn't still here. Sometimes she's not as completely in control as she would like to be and doesn't hesitate to go off on one occasionally – to the appreciation of those around her.

Treadwell was talking to me. 'Dr Maxwell, I understand you were present at the arrest of these people. Perhaps you would care to explain what happened.'

I bit back what I'd been going to say and tried to confine myself to the facts.

'They're your people, Commander. They and you originate from the same source. They also weren't familiar with the Time Police and they paid the price. The one on the right is Malcolm Halcombe, leprosy status unclear, who thought he'd force a couple of historians on an illegal jump and incurred a gaol sentence of – what was it? – thirty years. The snivelling one is Major Sullivan – tasked with enforcing the illegal jump. Unfortunately for them, the Time Police turned up and rescued us. Halcombe and Sullivan were tried, found guilty and imprisoned. Now it seems they've been released into our custody.'

Evans stepped forwards. 'Permission to give them both a good kicking, Max.'

Hyssop spoke. 'Back in line, Evans.'

I ignored her, considering this, my head on one side. 'They're old men – it hardly seems right, somehow.'

Treadwell gazed at them, his face quite expressionless. Sullivan seemed to be out of it completely. I'm not sure he realised where he was. A far cry from the days when he strutted around St Mary's pretending he was in charge.

The Time Police actually don't torture people – at least I don't think they do – but their prison system is brutal. I only know bits and pieces – gossip from the mercifully short time I worked with them – but apparently, they take you off and imprison you in another time. Anyone else taking someone out of their own time would suffer the consequences, which, funnily enough, would involve being taken out of their own time as a punishment. Am I the only one who sees the irony? No one knows where or when their prisons are located, obviously, but there are no comfy cells, regular meals, government inspections, leisure facilities, education opportunities or any of that girlie crap.

There are a variety of different Time Police gaols, depending on the severity of the crime and I've even heard there's one place where they simply dump everyone on a small island somewhere and just leave them to fend for themselves. Supervision is minimal. The prisoners form their own society, hierarchy, laws and methods of punishment. They have to catch or grow their own food and, more importantly, they have to hang on to it. It's a pitiless environment. The strong survive – most of them. Everyone else doesn't. The Time Police turn up occasionally, replenish a few supplies and medical equipment, remove any bodies and notify the next of kin.

And even on release, the punishment continues. Because the Time Police bastards return the prisoners to their own time. Only a few months or a year will have passed for those left behind, but the prisoner has served a sentence of thirty or forty years. They're old and they're sick but their world is just as they left it. Their family – staring at them in disbelief and, often, revulsion – are just as they left them. Think about it – even if, after thirty or so years on that island, you haven't turned feral and should be separated from society for everyone's sake, how do you find your place in the world again? How do friends and family accept you back?

Halcombe and Sullivan had been in their late thirties or early forties when I last saw them. Now I was looking at two old men, old way before their time. They were both thin but

135

not skeletal. The Time Police would always ensure there was food – just not quite enough of it. That prisoners' thoughts were always concentrated on where the next meal was coming from rather than plotting mischief or escape. Although, where would they go? They didn't know when or where they'd been imprisoned. At the back of their minds must always have been the thought that they might be escaping to somewhere even worse.

Sullivan, I think, had given up on the world some time ago. Whatever stood before us was just a shell of a man. Halcombe had lost most of his hair and gained a nasty burn scar on one cheek but his eyes glittered with the old malice. Interesting. You'd have thought Sullivan with his military training would have fared better but Halcombe appeared to be the one least damaged by his captivity.

The silence dragged on. They were looking around the room. I wondered if Halcombe was remembering the time when this had been his office. They both seemed quite bewildered. I suppose anyone would be after thirty years' imprisonment. The Time Police wouldn't waste time preparing them for release. They'd just be scooped up one day and dumped back in their own time and if they couldn't cope then that was someone else's problem.

Now they were both staring at me. North and I had been the last people they saw from this time and here I was, hardly changed, while they themselves were thirty years older. If they hadn't hated St Mary's before, they certainly did now and while I felt the same way towards them, they looked so lost and disoriented . . . Now began the second part of their punishment: their attempts to pick up the threads of their lives.

Treadwell moved out from behind his desk, saying quietly, 'Is there anyone I should inform of your release? Your families? Friends?'

They each shook their head.

Silence fell again. I don't think anyone quite knew what to do. Eventually Hyssop turned to Treadwell and said, 'Your instructions, please, Commander. What would you like me to do with them?' at exactly the moment Dr Stone arrived, his team behind him. He took one look at the two ex-prisoners and said, 'No one is doing anything until they've had a complete medical examination.'

Treadwell nodded, although Dr Stone would probably have gone ahead and done it anyway, and Sullivan and Halcombe were helped away, Evans with his blaster following closely on their heels. I watched them go. I remembered the state of Evans when he was eventually rescued. I remembered North with that thick, black gun rammed into her eye.

Treadwell turned to Peterson. 'Dr Peterson, I understand you commanded St Mary's during the time referred to by Dr Maxwell. Perhaps you could take a minute to brief me.'

Peterson was typically brilliant.

'Yes, of course, but if you want to know the real story behind what happened, you should ask Mr Evans, who was beaten up every day in their unsuccessful attempts to get me to talk. In fact,' he said, 'I'm certain Mr Evans will be delighted to renew the acquaintanceship – as would any member of St Mary's. After what they did to us, I wouldn't have any problem with both of them suffering an unfortunate accident during their stay here. But I do advise you to notify your employers of their return and enquire what arrangements have been made for them. None, I suspect. It will be interesting to see if they're regarded as heroes or inconveniences, don't you think?'

I nodded. After Halcombe's embarrassing failure, I wouldn't mind betting the waters would have closed over his and Sullivan's heads and it would be as if they had never existed. Now they were back. And here at St Mary's. A circumstance I found deeply troubling. However, Leon always says there's no point in running towards trouble – although in my experience running away from trouble is only marginally more successful – so I told myself I'd wait and see what happened next.

Treadwell seemed thoughtful. He went to sit behind Dr Bairstow's desk. I must stop thinking of it as Dr Bairstow's desk.

Peterson and I seated ourselves without being asked. Dr Bairstow always politely asked everyone to sit. Unless you were in really deep shit, of course, in which case you planted your feet, gritted your teeth and endured.

Treadwell frowned. 'I've never heard of either of these two men.'

'There were others,' said Peterson and rattled off the names of Sullivan's team. 'They were arrested when Dr Bairstow led the successful attempt to regain control of St Mary's.'

It was clear from the complete lack of expression on his face that Treadwell had never heard of them, either.

I exchanged a glance with Peterson. Was it possible that Treadwell was not from the same stable as Halcombe? My theory has always been that somewhere out there, there's a tiny organisation. A link between Clive Ronan and the government. Or, since Mrs Brown hadn't known anything about them either, a part of the government no one admitted to. Or even knew about. Rogue, perhaps. Or even – and here's a thought – not in this time. You certainly couldn't get more untraceable than that.

Looking over the desk at the expressionless Treadwell, I wondered if his thoughts were running along those lines as well. Was he, perhaps, querying the real purpose of his presence here? Was he, as he certainly thought he was, the new Head of St Mary's? Or was he someone's scapegoat? An excuse for more punitive action if – when – he failed. And when he failed – as he was meant to do – would the real new Director of St Mary's turn up? I still couldn't believe Treadwell had been sent to us without a proper briefing.

Apparently, neither could he. Getting up, he opened the door and politely asked Mrs Partridge for some tea, please. I was pleased to see he didn't just demand it through his intercom.

We sat in silence until it arrived. And he got the good china. Not the best stuff, obviously, because he wasn't Dr Bairstow, but not the cheap stuff she uses for meetings with the Parish Council, either.

He poured the tea himself. I noticed he knew exactly how I like mine. First out of the pot while it's still weak, a slice of lemon and two sugars. I was beginning to realise just how thorough this man was. He was no Halcombe, that was for sure.

'So,' he said, passing Peterson his own cup. 'Tell me all about the Time Police.'

Peterson shrugged and gestured for me to do it.

'Well, a long time ago in the future, the secret of time travel gets out and everyone has a go. It's chaos, of course, because at that stage, no one, from governments upwards, has any clear idea of the implications. Time begins to break down in places. It's called Bluebell Time. When too many people decide to visit the same time and place, the fabric of time begins to disintegrate and then you have to put in a patch.'

'How on earth do they do that?'

I shrugged again. 'I've only ever been involved once so I can't really say, but I think it's a bit like laying down decking.'

I didn't want to go into any great detail about Queen Jane the Bloody. I certainly didn't want Treadwell knowing that under certain conditions, History can be changed. I could just imagine the results:

Place your bids, ladies and gentlemen. Today's special offer – the Battle of Hastings. Saxon or Norman victory? Just place your bids here and win the opportunity to change History for all time.

And think of Bosworth Field. We'd have the Richard III society on one hand beating up the Henry VII society on the other, as both sides vied to rewrite the battle according to the way they thought it should go. There had been that incident in Rushford, a couple of years ago, when the two sides, both marching to celebrate Bosworth Field Day, had, by some extraordinary lapse on the part of the organisers, met face to face just outside of Boots. It had been apocalyptic, apparently, and St Mary's hadn't even been there.

'The Time Police?' Treadwell said gently, nudging me back to the here and now.

'Yes, the Time Police. They do sort it all out in the end. Most of them aren't bright – and they're certainly not gentle – but they do get the timeline under control again. And their losses were massive, so they deserve some credit. I believe now, having achieved their objective, there's some thinking they've outlived their usefulness – and they do seem to spend a lot of time harassing innocent historians . . .'

'And yet they rescued you and your colleague,' he said gently.

'They did,' I said, 'and don't think we weren't glad to see them. It was a toss-up as to whether Sullivan would exterminate us with his rather unpleasant bolt gun or the pod would self-destruct because we were in a Triple-S zone.'

'Triple-S?'

'Site of Special Significance. Areas we don't – can't – jump to. Religious stuff, mostly. The idiot Halcombe thought he'd send us back to the crucifixion. He had some sort of plan to prove it did actually occur.'

'And did it?'

I looked him straight in the eye. 'Don't know,' I said. 'I deleted and overwrote the record of the jump.'

'Why would you do that?'

'I expect my tiny female brain was overcome by the implications and with no big strong man to tell me what to do I was unable to handle the responsibility of making a decision all by my little self.'

There was a bit of a silence.

'Dr Maxwell, I wish you would not deliberately misinterpret my words.'

'Commander Treadwell, I wish you would not deliberately underestimate my abilities.'

There was a bit more silence.

'We'll leave it there, shall we?' he said, standing up.

Peterson and I got up to go.

'If you could spare me a minute, please, Dr Maxwell.'

I sat back down again.

Peterson grinned at me and disappeared out of the door.

I sighed. Now what?

141

'Dr Maxwell, I have a query about your assignment.'

'Ah yes,' I said, feeling I was on firmer ground. 'Babylon. Nebuchadnezzar. The Ishtar Gate. It should be quite spectacular.'

'Yes. I'm very keen. Lots of potential there, I feel.'

'Oh, sorry, I forgot. It's not the historical aspect that's important these days – it's how much money we can make. Well, to forestall your next question – we're planning a big holo. They always go down well. The one we made of the dinosaurs in the Cretaceous is still one of our biggest earners. I think the grandeur of Babylon in its heyday will play very profitably to many people and organisations.'

'I'm sure it will,' he said, 'but actually, it was your previous assignment I wanted to talk to you about.'

'Amy Robsart?'

'Yes. I've read through your report several times and I still can't see who killed her.'

'We don't know who killed her.'

'But you were *there*.'

'Yes, we saw her fall.'

'So why don't you know who killed her?'

'Because we weren't there at the crucial moment. Which wasn't when she fell but some minutes before.'

He frowned. 'Hasn't the whole thing been rather a waste of time, then? An expensive waste of time.'

'Not necessarily,' I said, more calmly than I felt because he might have a point. 'We sometimes don't get it right the first time. That's why we have Pathfinders. Atherton's team. They jump about establishing precise time and dates for us. But in

142

this instance, another jump with a couple of strategically placed historians to ascertain who greased the newel post and who was in the litter should easily sort that out.'

'You're demanding yet another jump?'

I wasn't going to fall into that trap. 'No, that's up to you. I would *recommend* another jump because otherwise the first jump will always be inconclusive.'

'More expense,' he interrupted. 'Because you didn't do the job properly the first time.'

'We operated on the available data. Prior to the jump, no one was ever aware of the presence of Verney actually on the scene, or the queen, or the greased newel post. The situation is obviously far more complex than anyone realised. Now, having surveyed the site, we know where to place our people for best effect.' Talk about making it all up as you go.

Treadwell shut down the data stack with a final gesture. 'I don't think so,' he said. 'Permission denied.'

There was a note of finality in his voice and I left his office with quite a lot to worry about.

Things continued to hurtle from bad to worse. We woke up one morning to find six new Security guards among us. Hyssop's people. Or Hyssop's Half-Wits, as they were soon known.

One or two, perhaps, we could have integrated. Six was too many. And they upset the balance of the building. They were everywhere, shouting to each other across the Hall, and I had to tell them to tone it down because this was a working area. For some reason the dining room suddenly became the mess hall. Rooms became quarters. Military slang was batted around the building. Not to be outdone, historians started to speak to each other in Latin, Luwian or Ancient Greek. People began to talk in terms of us and them.

'Well,' said Evans, reasonably, when I pinned a small part of him to the wall in an effort to find out what was going on, 'Major Guthrie brought his own people in – why shouldn't she?'

'But why so many of them?'

'I don't know.'

'Where have they come from?'

'Military police – same as her. Same as most of us.'

'Why are they here?'

He shrugged and requested I let him go so he could get some breakfast before it was all gone.

Noisy and visible, Security was now a much stronger presence than before. Actually, they reminded me a little of the Time Police. There was Harper, big and blond. Glass, tall, thin and weedy; Scarfe, whom I disliked as soon as I clapped eyes on him. I made a mental note to ensure I never went anywhere with him if I could help it. Lucca and Jessop, whom I could never tell apart. And the one whose name I can never remember. In fact, I'm not sure I ever heard it.

From the start, they made no attempt to integrate. Following their leader's example, they stuck to their army gear, not the usual Security green jumpsuits. As if they were deliberately marking themselves out as different. I watched their behaviour in the dining room one day, had a bit of a think and then assembled all the historians in my office and instructed them not to engage.

'Difficult, I know, but do not provoke them. Hyssop will use it as an excuse to draft in even more of her own people and the situation will get worse. I suspect a lot of this is deliberate. Don't allow yourselves to be manipulated.'

It was Atherton, their usual spokesman, who expressed the general misgiving. 'Max, I don't want to jump with these people. I don't fancy any of them watching my back.'

'Relax,' I said. 'We'll probably have to take at least one of them along, but I promise you for every one of them we'll have one of ours. And we know we can trust *them*. Remember, it's me who selects the people for every assignment.'

They appeared somewhat mollified and got to their feet. For a moment I thought my well-reasoned arguments had won them over but it just turned out to be nearly time for lunch and they wanted to be first in the queue.

I wandered along to Peterson's office where Mrs Shaw would make us both a cup of tea.

'What ho,' he said amiably. 'Just the person.'

I regarded him suspiciously. I'm not accustomed to being *just the person*. 'What?'

He opened his desk drawer. 'What do you think?'

With great ceremony, he donned a pair of spectacles and I hated him and them immediately because they really did make him look both intelligent and sexy.

I shook my head. 'I don't know what to say. Honesty is struggling with not wanting to hurt your feelings.'

He peered closely at me. 'Dear God – is that what you actually look like? I had no idea. Is it too late to pretend I don't know you?'

I grinned. 'Wait till you see Markham.'

'Yes, I suspect that will be a nasty blow. Why are you here?'

Putting my feet up, I said to him, 'Why do you think they've brought in so many new people? Do you realise we now have thirteen Security guards and only eight historians? That's nearly one and a half guards each. Why?'

145

Peterson took off his new specs, looked at them as if they'd done something wrong and put them back on again. 'Because . . .' he said slowly and stopped.

'What? Because what?'

He checked the door was closed but lowered his voice anyway. 'I suspect they're going to replace historians with Security guards.'

I took my feet off his desk in a hurry. 'What? He can't do that. Why would he do that?'

'Because they cost a lot less than a bunch of overeducated disaster magnets. Because it's easier to train Security guards to record and document than it is to teach historians to become Security staff. You know – like astronauts and geologists.'

I was bewildered. 'I worry about you sometimes. What's like astronauts and geologists?'

'When they went to the moon, they needed geologists to analyse the rocks and bring back samples, but it was easier to train astronauts to be geologists than the other way round. I think they're getting ready to replace historians with Hyssop's people.'

'Treadwell specifically said there would be no redundancies.'

'He won't get rid of us. We'll be utilised in some sort of academic way – analysing the data, perhaps – but the jumps will be manned by trained-up Security guards. How many of us would stick around for that, do you think? Atherton was right. That's how they'll get rid of us. We'll leave of our own accord.'

I couldn't think of anything to say. I tried to think how I'd feel about being handed the results of someone else's jump to analyse and so forth but never actually being there. Never stepping out of a pod again. Never again to experience that heady whiff of woodsmoke and horseshit. Never to hear the chatter of different languages around me. Never again to experience that special mix of exhilaration and pants-wetting terror. And not only never to know any of that again but to have to watch other people depart to do it on a daily basis. People who weren't me. I might as well go and get that office job I'm always banging on about.

I wanted to deny it but there was a horrible logic to Tread-well's scheme. It was clever – replacing the expensive people with cheaper people would garner enthusiastic support. His employers would love it. And he wouldn't be sacking anyone. He'd just be creating conditions where the expensive people – yes, that would be us historians – wouldn't want to stay.

'And,' said Peterson, 'I don't think it's only the historians under threat. I think they're about to replace all our own Security people with army personnel. With one stroke they'll have rid themselves of the two biggest departments – and I'm sure you won't disagree – the two sections likely to give Treadwell the most trouble.'

He was right. Not about the trouble bit, obviously, but right about everything else. R&D could be outsourced to Thirsk. Only the Technical Section would remain – until their secrets had been plundered and then they'd be as redundant as the rest of us. And it was easily done. Leon had come to St Mary's from the army. I sat with all sorts of thoughts whirling through my head.

'Of course,' continued Cassandra Peterson, obviously feeling he hadn't depressed me enough, 'he could go the whole hog and just replace all of us with a couple of drones.'

This was not something I wanted to think about on the eve of the Babylon assignment. And I wasn't going to say anything to him, but what of Peterson himself? Treadwell wouldn't want him hanging around. Dr Bairstow's choice of Peterson as his successor would surely make him the most expendable person in the building.

I was properly indignant. 'How could a non-historian possibly have the depth of knowledge to react appropriately when things don't go to plan? Or to direct the drone to the right place? Suppose they frighten a horse at a crucial point in a battle? And drones will terrify the wits out of people. A swarm of drones hovering overhead is not what religion-obsessed people need to see. Not when they're looking for the next witch to burn.'

'That's just it, Max,' Peterson said heavily. 'I don't think there'll be any more battlefields, or coronations or anything. Remember the lists Dr Bairstow wanted us to draw up? I think, very soon, it's going to be all search-and-rescue-based. St Mary's is going commercial.'

I thought back to the comments Treadwell had made when I'd taken him around the building. 'That makes sense.'

He looked at me. 'You'd better make the most of the Babylon assignment. It might be your last.'

All this was pretty grim – I seemed to spend my days doing nothing but fighting departmental fires and mediating – but night-time was even worse. Night-time was when I shut the door on the clamour of St Mary's and was enveloped in the silence of our empty rooms. This was when I missed Leon the most. Night-time was when I would wonder if I was doing the right thing. There was no doubt my life would be a lot easier if I capitulated to Treadwell. Except that all my instincts told me to fight him every inch of the way.

And I missed Matthew. I even missed our usual twenty-minute argument every night over the futility of washing his face and cleaning his teeth – actions which took only a fraction of the time spent arguing about them. As I frequently pointed out.

And I really missed Dr Bairstow, clever enough to remain in his office and let us get on with it but there when needed. And always several moves ahead of everyone else. All unexpected deaths seem cruel but this one particularly so. He'd been on his own for years – decades even. Trust me, running St Mary's is not a job for the faint-hearted, and just when it seemed he had met someone who was perfect for him – bang! Game over. Life over.

And then I'd have to wipe my eyes on the pillow and try to think of something else.

10

I've forgotten to explain about the Babylon jump, haven't I? Sorry about that, although I think everyone will agree there's been a lot going on. Believe it or not – Babylon was Treadwell's suggestion. I suspected he'd been watching one of Calvin Cutter's more sensational cinematic offerings. Actually, all Calvin Cutter's stuff was sensational but for completely the wrong reasons.

Anyway, back to Babylon. Right from the off, things did not go well. I'd selected my team. Me – obviously – Clerk, Prentiss and Sands – all experienced historians – Evans, and because I had to – Hyssop. Two teams of three. Clerk, Prentiss and Hyssop. Me, Sands and Evans. If Hyssop had the sense to step back and let Clerk and Prentiss get on with things, then it would be a useful training exercise for her, which she could then pass on to the rest of the new Security Section. Their training would be better coming from her, and then gradually – and painlessly – we'd get her people integrated.

Well – that didn't happen. The daft bat produced her own list of personnel, which basically was herself and her six goons.

There was no way I was going out on an assignment this big with six inexperienced Security people and said so. At length and at some volume. And, I said, Hyssop could huff and puff and run to Treadwell as fast as she pleased, but no one else would go out with an inexperienced team either.

It was her section, she said. Her responsibility. She'd choose the right people for the job, not me. I'd never interfered in Markham's choices and she wasn't going to allow me to start now.

I never had to interfere before, I said, because I could completely rely on Markham's judgement, and every single one of his team was experienced and capable. And, I said, not allowing her to get a word in edgeways, the whole point of a Security escort was to provide protection and assistance to the historians whose assignment this was – not undermine that assignment by insisting on inappropriate and inexperienced staff just to make a point.

I had to stop then and draw breath and Hyssop nipped in with the quite valid point that if her people never jumped then they'd never gain any experience would they and I said I was glad she'd grasped my point so easily and we both stepped back from the edge before we killed each other and neither of us went on the assignment.

Four historians and six Security people, she said.

Four historians, I said, and four Security people. Of whom at least two must be real Security guards.

Stalemate again.

All this took place in Markham's office. When I eventually emerged, nearly everyone in the building had found a reason to be in the corridor outside. They scattered as I opened the door.

It didn't end there, of course. The next person to be involved was Treadwell himself.

'Dr Maxwell, our new staff will always remain untrained if no one undertakes to train them.'

I shook my head. 'I am unhappy at having more untrained than trained people on such a crucial jump. We don't know how they will react.'

'They are professionals. You can have every confidence in them.'

'To do what?'

'Their job, Dr Maxwell.'

'Which will be?'

'To learn, Dr Maxwell.'

'Yes, that's what bothers me. Until our change of ownership, their purpose would have been to protect historians as we did our job.'

'And it still is. Close protection requires the same procedures in 565BC as it does today. But if you are having misgivings . . .'

'I am. Mainly over the number of so many inappropriate people I'm being compelled to include. I would so much rather take one or two at a time and do the job properly. Can I encourage you to think long-term on this? Let's take our time and . . .'

'Time is of the essence in this instance, Dr Maxwell.'

'In that case,' I said firmly, before he could boot me off the jump completely, 'your people can form their own team and get on with whatever it is they're supposed to be doing, and I'll take Mr Evans and Mr Keller, who can perform their normal function during this assignment which, since no battles or violence will be involved, I hope you will agree is women-appropriate. I promise if anything looks like it's going tits-up, we'll all sit down and knit something.'

'Ah, the typical Maxwell tactic – masking hostility with humour.'

'Well, let's hope I don't have to move on to the next stage – masking hostility with violent actions. Although I always enjoy that one, so I do hope you won't deny me the pleasure.'

'Four historians, Dr Maxwell, whom you yourself may select. Six Security staff, to be selected by Captain Hyssop.'

I wasn't going down without a fight. 'At least half of whom must be experienced personnel.'

'Name those acceptable.'

'Evans, Keller, Cox, Hyssop and any other two.'

'Evans, Keller, Hyssop, Harper, Scarfe and Glass. My best offer, Dr Maxwell. Evans, Keller and Hyssop will provide the experience.'

I wasn't going to get a better offer. It was like arguing with a polite wall. An amused, polite wall that never gave an inch, and after a while you realised you were just hurting yourself. Sometimes I felt like a butterfly hurling myself at a battleship for all the impact I was having. Everything just glanced off him. He never raised his voice but he got his own way every time. And he wasn't a stupid man, either. I had to make sure I wasn't giving him grounds for dismissing me.

'You leave me with no choice but to accept your allegedly best offer. Please regard this meeting as my formal protest as to the inadequacy of the Security provision and a warning as to the consequences of your unwise actions.'

Treadwell sighed loudly. 'Was there anything else, Dr Maxwell?'

I shifted my files. 'Yes. Since this is your first assignment, perhaps you could tell me how much you want to be involved.

Dr Bairstow was very hands-off – I planned and set everything up, ran it past him for clearance and then got on with it. Would I be right in assuming you want to be involved at every stage?'

He smiled, being Mr Reasonable again. 'You would, but before your worst fears are realised, only because this *is* my first assignment and I want to see how it's all put together. Quite reasonable, I think you'll agree. Nothing sinister.'

I ignored this. 'Well, my first task will be to talk to Dieter about pod availability, then Mrs Enderby about costumes because she'll need plenty of notice. There'll be ten of us – practically an invasion force – so we'll take two pods. We'll land in two separate areas of the city so if there's any trouble there will always be a second pod available. Any questions or criticisms?'

'Not at this moment, although you shouldn't have any expectations that happy state of affairs will continue. I'd like to be with you at every stage of the planning.'

'Shadowing me?'

'Exactly.'

'For what purpose?'

'As I said, to learn the job, Dr Maxwell.'

I took him down to Hawking. I'd selected pods Eight and Five, two of our larger pods. I'd talked about the advantages of having two pods because I didn't want him asking about the whereabouts of our big one. Which was out there somewhere safeguarding our Archive. About which Treadwell had not yet enquired.

He paused just inside the door and looked around. Two rows of pods ran down the hangar, all nestling safely on their plinths.

Thick black umbilicals snaked across the floor to the massive power outlets on the walls. Trays and trolleys of equipment stood everywhere. It looked chaotic but it wasn't. Everything was in its place. Leon runs a tidy ship.

'Where is the pod designated TB2?'

Bugger. 'Out on an extensive field test. Inside, it's much the same as the two we'll be using, just bigger and with the addition of a mezzanine which can be used as living accommodation when we're on a Big Job. The downstairs is our working area. For instance, when we rescued bits and pieces from the Library of Alexandria, we packed some of the scrolls and sealed the urns in there. It's useful to have a large working area out of the sun and rain, and the ramp is useful access, as we discovered when we took normal pods to Florence during the Bonfire of the Vanities and had some difficulties getting the big Botticellis through the door.'

'And where are they now?' he asked eagerly.

'Retrieved, to world acclaim.'

'You didn't think to keep even one?'

Somewhat frostily I told him we weren't art thieves.

There was no denying Treadwell was very keen on the search and rescue aspect of our activities though, and it occurred to me that, if we camouflaged our own historical activities within his own differently prioritised initiatives then this might not be so bad. As long as we gave him what he wanted we could probably continue more or less as before.

He was watching me. 'Yes, I wondered when that might occur to you,' and once again I had the impression I was amusing him. It's not a nice feeling.

I sought to change the subject but he did it for me.

'Chief Farrell is still absent?'

I looked up from frowning over my pod schedule. 'Yes, as I said. Field-testing TB2.'

'For how much longer?'

'I'm not sure. There are a variety of trials and scenarios to work through before a pod passes its field test. Of course, given your recently expressed desire to get everything done as quickly and cheaply as possible, we could easily cut a few corners. I think you'll experience enormous difficulty getting any real St Mary's people into an untried pod, but by all means do invite Hyssop and her team to have at it.'

He ignored all that, which was probably just as well. I made a real effort to rein myself in and scowled back at my schedule.

'Is he alone?'

I shook my head. 'No. We never jump alone.'

'Why?'

'You need at least one more person to bring back the body.' I indicated we should move off down the hangar.

'So who is accompanying Chief Officer Farrell?'

'Matthew Farrell, and Amelia and Adrian Meiklejohn.'

'Your son, Matthew Farrell.'

'That's the one, yes.'

'The one being educated here?'

'Again, yes. But before you suffer shooting pains in your spreadsheets, the cost of his education is being borne by his father and by me. As is his board and lodging. In fact, the costs of everyone's board and lodging is deducted from their wages.'

Again, he ignored that. He'd know it, anyway.

'And these two Meiklejohn people? What do they do?'

'One works in R&D and the other in the Technical Section.'

'But who are they? Their files are almost empty.'

'They're part of a deal with the Time Police. Those are the people you don't want to know anything about.'

'They're Time Police personnel?'

'Good heavens, no.'

'And they are here why, I wonder?'

'As I said – part of the treaty between us and them. And before they also fall victim to your value-for-money drive, they're both geniuses who contribute a great deal to this organisation. You can, of course, save a few pounds and cut them loose, but trust me, you don't want those two being snapped up by a foreign power. Although it's up to you, of course.'

'Hmm.' He looked around the hangar. 'Which pods will you be requesting my permission to use?'

We were seriously winding each other up.

'The two most suited to our purposes,' I said.

We'd been walking down Hawking, dodging techies as we went, and he stopped suddenly and turned to face me. 'Dr Maxwell, I am aware these tactics of yours were tolerated by Dr Bairstow. They will not be tolerated by me. If I ask a question it is because I genuinely want an answer. Not the answer you consider appropriate. Or the answer that doesn't actually tell me anything at all. I want a straightforward response to a straightforward question. If you will please talk me through the mechanics of this assignment, give me an insight into your thinking and how you put things together, I shall be perfectly happy to let you get on with things. But acquire this insight I will. If not from you then someone else. Are we both clear about this?'

I shifted my weight. 'If you expect me to make it easy for you to dismiss St Mary's personnel and replace them with your own, then you will be disappointed.'

'I have no intention of doing any such thing at this moment and I am endeavouring to remain neutral at all times. However, in view of your intransigence I may have no option but to return to my employers and report that St Mary's is unmanageable and needs a clean sweep from top to bottom. I don't want to do so – that course of action will set us back some months and seriously impede our plans for this organisation – but if I have to then I will. Now I understand your anxiety, but if you don't begin to cooperate then your misgivings will actually come to pass. A self-fulfilling prophecy, in fact.'

His voice echoed around Hawking. I suddenly realised everything had gone very quiet. I looked around. All the techies were staring at us. All of IT were watching through their office window. A moment frozen in time.

He lowered his voice. 'Please do not think I don't appreciate the value and uniqueness of St Mary's. I was honoured beyond words to be given this position. I want to do my best for you – all of you – and St Mary's, but I can't do it without your cooperation and if you're not going to give it, Dr Maxwell, then get out of my way.'

The gloves were off. 'This unit is politically neutral. It is built into our charter. No one attempts to influence our findings. And yet, here you are, no historical qualifications, a military man who is an employee of the state, filling the place up with more unqualified military personnel. Tell me again how neutral you are.'

I swear I could actually feel the air vibrate between us.

'Enough,' said a new voice, and Peterson was at my shoulder. I had no idea where he'd sprung from. 'Max, your strong opinions are beginning to compromise the politeness with which we deal with each other here, and Commander Treadwell might possibly be underestimating the apprehension people feel about the future of this organisation.'

He was right but I was buggered if I was going to let Treadwell claim the moral high ground so I said, 'Of course, Dr Peterson. With your permission, I shall confer with Mr Dieter on pod availability for the Babylon jump.'

'A very good idea,' said Treadwell, more difficult to shift than red wine on a white carpet.

Peterson shot me a look and walked off. He doesn't throw his weight about very often. I should listen – before both Treadwell and I said something I would regret – so I gestured Treadwell ahead of me and took him into Number Eight where Dieter and I walked him through everything. The questions he asked were intelligent ones and it did occur to me that if he hadn't replaced Dr Bairstow then I might have quite liked him. Which reminded me . . . as we walked back down the Long Corridor towards Wardrobe, I asked about Dr Bairstow's funeral.

'I had word this morning,' he said. 'There will be a post-mortem and then the body will be released. I'll let everyone know when that happens and we can arrange something. It will be a big affair. There will be people from London, from Thirsk . . .'

'The Parish Council,' I said gloomily, 'even if only to make sure he actually stays in his coffin.'

He said quite seriously, 'I am sorry for your loss, Dr Maxwell. And I wish I'd known him better.'

I honestly couldn't work out if he was a genuinely nice bloke in the wrong job or a smiling knife saying what he thought I wanted to hear. I nodded, not wanting to talk about it, and changed the subject, asking him if he'd yet met the Parish Council personally.

'Yes,' he said, smiling. 'Delightful people, aren't they? I flatter myself that Mrs Huntley-Palmer and I really hit it off.'

I stared at him suspiciously. Not for the first time, I had the impression he was enjoying a private joke, somehow. With very nearly completely concealed misgivings, I politely enquired if he intended to accompany us on this jump.

Equally politely, he said, 'Not on this jump. I feel it's rather early to leave St Mary's to its own devices, but one day soon, yes.'

And then we arrived at Wardrobe for our meeting with Mrs Enderby.

'We are going for the average-citizen look,' she said. 'In the words of St Mary's: too poor to rob – too posh to kick.' She gestured to a work table piled high with sumptuous fabrics. A whole spectrum of colour on this dull morning.

'Costumes for both men and women are basically similar,' she said. 'We'll start with the usual undertunic – for modesty and to provide pockets – covered with shawls of various colours and designs. You and your people will need to put in some practice, Max – the way a shawl is wound around the body denotes status and can sometimes send a subtle message. You will need to make sure any messages you do send are the right ones. Did you say something, Commander?'

'No, no,' he said quickly. 'Just slightly amused at your use of the words "Max" and "subtle" together in one sentence. Do please continue.'

'Well, there will be headdresses for the women and caps for the men. Everything will be ornate and overdecorated. We'll pare things back for ease of movement, Max, but you'll all need to remember to move smoothly and gracefully.'

We both peered suspiciously at Treadwell who appeared to be examining one of the rolls of material. 'This looks . . .'

'Expensive?' I suggested.

'Authentic, I was going to say.'

'Oh, thank you,' she said. 'It's not real silk, of course. A man-made material, Max, but that does not mean that you or your people are free to get it wet, or cover it in manure, dust, blood, or vomit.'

Everyone looked at me. 'Of course not,' I said.

'And a warning – the tunics are narrow so we'll give you kick pleats and the headdresses are heavy so you probably won't be able to do much running. Come back with your headdress or entangled in it, Max, but make sure you bring it back.'

'Yes, Mrs Enderby.'

We showed Treadwell the costumes completed so far. The last Big Job we'd done was Bronze Age Crete when, just for once, we women had worn the good stuff and the men wore hardly anything at all. Babylon was a little more sartorially forgiving to the allegedly stronger sex. Men's tunics were belted and with a hemline that began above the knees then slanted to mid-calf at the back. Over this, they could throw a couple of fringed shawls – one around the shoulders and the other around the waist. Low-status men wore waist strings or tiny loincloths, but none of us would be low status, for which I thanked the heavens. Markham in a Cretan woman's apron and nothing else was something I still saw in my nightmares.

As Mrs Enderby had said, women's costumes were very similar except the tunics were ankle-length. And we would all wear sandals.

'All the fabrics are elaborately decorated,' she said, pulling out a roll of fabulous cloth and unrolling it for our benefit. 'Closely woven linen and cotton, silks and so on. Gorgeous applique, embroidery, beads and so on. Favourite colours are red, blue, gold and white. Not so much of the terracota shades here. The favourite, of course, is Tyrian purple.' She looked at me. 'Do not argue with anyone wearing purple, Max.'

As if . . .

'As to how our people will look,' she continued. 'Men's hair is long and waved. Full beards and moustaches.' She frowned. 'Some of them will have to start now.'

She was right. Glass, Hyssop's youngest Half-Wit, had come to us with a massive shaving rash. Hyssop had ordered him to stop shaving but there'd been no corresponding growth. If he couldn't produce the required length and bushiness in time, we might have to glue something on. Hair was important in this era. As I pointed out to Treadwell. Certain hairstyles denoted certain professions. Get it wrong and we'd be in trouble. As I pointed out to Treadwell.

Female headdresses were intricate – obviously. I wasn't going to get away with just a linen headcloth here. My long hair would be elaborately plaited and pinned around my head, which would make it look darker and keep it under control, as well. Bed hair was probably not fashionable in Babylon.

The list of all those going was pinned on the wall – along with the usual photos and measurements.

I stared at the Security Section's photos and sighed. I had no idea how any of Hyssop's people would perform. This was never going to end well.

11

Since there were so many of us, I held the briefing in a corner of the Hall. To be fair to Treadwell, he made no attempt to impose himself, sitting quietly at the back.

People fussed around with chairs and scratchpads. As I started to lay out my files and notes I could hear Sands and Sykes settling themselves in the front row.

'Hey,' said Sands chattily. 'Did you know I work for Cunard?'

Well, even I could have told him that was a mistake.

With the air of Eowyn whipping off her helmet and declaring she was no man, Sykes moved on to the offensive. 'No, you don't.'

'No, I know I don't, but . . .'

Sykes likes to get her facts straight. 'You work for St Mary's.'

'Yes, but for the purposes of . . .'

'We all do,' she said firmly, just in case there was any doubt.

'No, when I say I work for Cunard . . .'

She put her hands on her hips. 'Which you don't . . .'

Sands appeared somewhat frayed around the edges. 'No, I know, but . . . you know what? Bloody forget it. I work for St Mary's and you're all a bunch of half-witted, humourless wazzocks with the razor-sharp intelligence of a whelk. No, not you, Mrs Midgley . . . I didn't mean . . . Bollocks.'

He shot off to placate our housekeeper.

We have a tried-and-tested briefing formula and I didn't deviate even for a second. I started by naming the teams – which took about fifteen seconds and in no way represented the hours of discussion, negotiating and shouting that it had taken to get to that point – and outlined their main areas of responsibility.

'Team One will consist of Mr Keller, Mr Glass and Mr Harper. Team Two will be Mr Clerk, Miss Prentiss, Captain Hyssop and Mr Scarfe. Team Three will consist of Mr Sands, Mr Evans and me.'

I didn't want to leave any time for argument, so moving swiftly on, I brought up large-scale maps of Babylon.

'A big city,' I said. 'Walled and gated. Ten gates – that we know of – and bisected by the Euphrates, north to south. Mr Keller's team will undertake the mapping of the town. The usual stuff – street plans, major landmarks, canals and so forth. There isn't much of Babylon left these days. Mud bricks tend to return to their original components after a while, so this should prove to be very useful.'

I turned to Hyssop. 'I'm assuming your people all have basic mapping skills.'

She looked surprised. 'Of course, but . . .'

'Good.' I moved on while she was still thinking about it. 'Mr Clerk and Miss Prentiss, Captain Hyssop and Mr Scarfe will check out the Ishtar Gate and then move on to the many temples and religious shrines with which Babylon is so well endowed. I'd like you to pay particular attention to Ishtar in her dual aspect of goddess of both fertility and war. Do not underestimate her importance – Nebuchadnezzar has built this fabulous gate in her honour. She's an important figure and will remain so until the rise of Christianity and Islam.'

They nodded, fingers flying over their scratchpads. Hyssop's people sat ominously quiet and still. People who don't take notes worry me.

I swallowed down my misgivings and pushed on. 'Mr Sands and I, accompanied by Mr Evans, will be looking at Etemenanki . . .'

'Enty . . . what?' said Keller.

'Etemenanki,' I said, the syllables rolling off my tongue but only because I'd spent all last night practising. 'Or, if you like, the Tower of Babel.'

Keller grinned at Evans. 'Rather you than me, mate.'

I continued. 'Should time permit, and after fulfilling our primary tasks, Teams Two and Three will then move on to the south-west area of the city – the poorer quarter. Miss Prentiss, I'd like you and Mr Clerk to check out the artisans' quarter, between Nabopolassar's Bridge and the Adad Gate. We suspect many of the tile works will be sited along the banks of the canal there. I'd like you to look at the method of making the blue tiles for which the city is famous.

'When we've finished at the Tower of Babel, Mr Sands and I will be looking at the commercial aspects – markets, merchants, shops and so forth – and if we have any spare time, the canal and irrigation systems and their impact on commercial life. Are there any questions?'

'Yes,' said Hyssop.

I smiled politely because I was pretty certain she meant criticism rather than questions. Still, better to get everything sorted here than stand arguing on the streets of Babylon, so I kept my face neutral and said, 'Yes?'

'I feel my team is being underused.'

'In what way?'

'Street-mapping?'

'I can assure you,' I said, 'that mapping Babylon in the time allocated will be a full-time job. If you feel it's too much, however . . .'

'I am not convinced this is the most cost-effective way to conduct this assignment. Less time on site means less cost.'

'Actually,' said Clerk, who was obviously as fed up with her as I was, 'why don't we just stay at home and open an encyclopaedia. Think how much time and money that would save.'

'Not as much as leaving our enormous Security Section at home,' were the words muttered by someone who fortunately wasn't me.

Hyssop swept on. 'As you are continually reminding me, the purpose of the Security Section is to protect historians while they carry out their missions. How can we do that if we're out surveying a city?'

'Well, firstly,' I said, 'street-mapping is a legitimate Security task. Major Guthrie mapped Troy and Mr Markham did the same for Knossos. You are following a well-trodden path. As for protecting historians, as I said, Mr Evans will accompany my team and you and Scarfe will accompany Mr Clerk's.'

She shook her head, mouth an obstinate line. 'I would prefer, in the interests of allocating resources appropriately, if Evans and Keller took charge of the street-mapping project with Glass, and Harper accompanies you, leaving Scarfe and me to accompany Prentiss and Clerk.'

167

My first instinct was to say no because that would mean there wasn't an experienced Security presence with either team, but I took a moment for second thoughts. Clerk and Prentiss knew what they were doing. They'd get on with the job no matter who accompanied them. And Hyssop, who did at least have some experience, could keep an eye on Scarfe. Sands and I could easily look after ourselves. Having Harper would make very little difference to us. Allowing Hyssop to have her way could be construed as a gesture of goodwill. I stared down at the table, thinking it through and not allowing myself to be rushed. So you could say everything that happened afterwards was my fault. I certainly blamed myself, but at that particular moment I honestly couldn't see a good reason not to go along with her scheme. They lacked experience but, to be fair, they were never going to overcome that if I had them all on street-mapping. So I looked up and made one of the worst decisions of my life.

'Yes,' I said. 'I don't see why not. Please be aware though, this will be a regimented society and there will be strict protocols. Especially in most temples and religious areas. This is not an area in which you have yet gained expertise. Please allow yourselves to be guided by Clerk and Prentiss.'

She nodded curtly and the briefing continued. But the damage was done.

I continued. 'In addition to all this, we shall be recording everything for IT to make their usual holo on our return. We shall be aiming for spectacular and colourful – which just about sums up Babylon. Have a look at this.'

I showed them a quick snippet of the holo we'd made in the Cretaceous. The bit where Sussman and I were nipping along-side and even under some pretty massive reptiles. Not many

168

people have seen an Alamosaurus from the underneath. Nor had to dodge haystack-sized lumps of Alamosaurus shit, one dollop of which could probably stun an historian for a month. Hyssop's Half-Wits were a little bit quiet afterwards. Peterson, who'd attended the briefing out of sheer nosiness, and I did not exchange glances.

I went on to talk a little about Babylonian religion and the significance of their gods in daily life. I had to do this because the importance of religion to people in ages past can come as rather a surprise in these secular times. To make things easier for everyone, I pretended I was back briefing the Time Police – all of whom have the attention span of a box of tissues – and kept it short. It was up to Hyssop to provide full details for her team and ram home some sort of understanding of what they could expect. I wasn't optimistic.

Treadwell, however, seemed happy enough with the briefing. I suspected he'd already drawn up lists of prospective customers for the holo. He did ask if there was any chance of 'bringing anything back' – like a stick of rock, I assume – and I said no, not this time; we'd stand a better chance as the city started to fail soon after Nebuchadnezzar's death in 562BC, when there would certainly be a better opportunity to do so.

He nodded, apparently satisfied.

I wasn't, but it was too late now.

Because Hyssop had been at my briefing, I felt perfectly justified in requesting to be included in hers. We gathered together in the Security Section. Cox handed me a mug of tea and I promised myself I would sit quietly and not cause any trouble.

And I did. I was as good as gold as they went through the ten thousand and forty-five ways an historian could get into trouble and what to do about it when we did. Hyssop did most of the talking. Evans and Keller said very little and the others gave the impression there wasn't anything a civilian could teach them so the civilian didn't try that hard. I'd have to rely on Evans and Keller to sort them out if we got into any difficulties.

I set the jump for the day after. We were expecting to be on site for two to three weeks, depending on how things went, and when I returned Leon would probably be back. And Matthew and Mikey and Adrian, of course. At which point Treadwell might look fondly back to the days when he only had me to deal with.

We assembled outside Number Eight. Dieter had tactfully shunted Treadwell up on to the gantry, muttering about safety lines and the need to set a good example.

Hyssop swung into immediate action, attempting to organise what she called a 'general inspection'. I suspected there was very little difference between her 'general inspection' and the normal St Mary's pre-jump check, but it was just another area she was whittling away at and I wasn't going to stand for it. I cut across her quite ruthlessly.

'Right,' I said to the Security Section. 'We've been over this, but just to reinforce: I'm leading the team in Number Eight and Mr Clerk is leading the team in Number Five. Messrs Sands, Evans, Glass and Harper are with me. Miss Prentiss, Captain Hyssop, and Messrs Scarfe and Keller are in Number Five.'

I addressed everyone, even though my words were for Hyssop and her team. 'Firstly, we check each other for jewellery, wrist-watches, anything so familiar you've forgotten you're wearing it. Then it's into the pods. Please don't forget to ensure each foot makes contact with the decontamination strip just inside the door. We'll jump and then you'll decontaminate thoroughly before we leave the pod. I believe Dr Stone has talked to you about the dangers of inadvertently bringing modern viruses with us.'

They nodded. I couldn't help noticing Harper and Glass in particular weren't half as cocky as they'd been this time yesterday.

I stepped closer. 'OK,' I said quietly. 'I'm going to say this. If anyone is having second thoughts, then say so. It's happened before and it can be dealt with and no one will ever know. Please speak up now rather than when things go tits-up at the other end.'

No one moved.

'All right then, let's go.'

We filed into our respective pods. My team settled themselves quietly. Mr Lindstrom had programmed in the coordinates – outward and return journeys – and together we checked over the console.

'Green lights across the board, Max,' he said. 'Everything topped up and working. Good luck.' The door closed behind him. Someone stirred in the sudden silence. I heard their clothing rustle.

'All right,' I said. 'Here we go. For those not brave enough to ask – closing your eyes does not help. Computer – initiate jump.'

'Jump initiated.'

And the world went white.

Babylon, 565BC. The centre of the world. Ruled over by Nebuchadnezzar II. King of Babylon. King of Sumer and Akkad. King of the Universe.

We landed about an hour before dawn and we landed gently. I'd toyed with the idea of warning our newbies to stay away from Peterson and his percussive landings but there's such a thing as overtraining. A sensitive and sensible trainer always leaves something for her trainees to discover for themselves.

While everyone else was milling around getting themselves sorted out and adjusting their shawls so the fringes hung properly, I called up the other site. Mr Clerk reported they were down and safe. I couldn't hear any sounds of arguing so presumably Hyssop wasn't trying to barge her way out of the door and take charge before they'd even switched off the engine.

We were to meet at the Ishtar Gate and spend some tourist time there, just strolling around and admiring things and getting our bearings generally before starting work properly tomorrow.

Staring at the screen now, I could see this city was far larger and denser than I had anticipated. It was heaving with activity and I couldn't wait to get out there but first things first. I had two rookies with me who thought they knew everything. This was going to be fun. Let the training commence.

'OK, everyone – Mr Glass, could you initiate decontamination, please. Yes, that control there. That's right.'

We stood still while the cold blue lamp dealt with any potential infections we might have brought with us.

'All right,' said Evans, in his role as mother hen. 'All done. Just make sure you stand on the decon strip as you exit. With both feet.'

Both Glass and Harper nodded. Neither of them had said anything yet and I guessed they were oscillating between terror, excitement and the need to be cool. I so remembered that feeling.

'At this stage,' said Evans, 'we usually ask you to check your weapons.'

They pulled out their stun guns, which were fine, and then a small blaster each, which was less fine.

Evans sighed. 'You were briefed on the importance of not killing anyone. I remember moving my lips to that effect. No unauthorised weapons.'

'Yeah,' said Harper, 'but . . .'

'But nothing,' I said. 'Please place them in the lockbox in the locker behind you. Our first line of defence is always running like hell.'

There was grumbling but they obeyed. No doubt Hyssop would be wanting a word with me later because I was damn sure Clerk would have made them do the same in his pod. I wished Markham would come back. I really missed . . . well, I was going to say his unobtrusive efficiency but I think we all know unobtrusive isn't the most frequently used word to describe him. I'd always taken Security completely for granted. They were

173

there; they did their job – I never had to worry about what was happening behind me. Now it occurred to me that I needed to worry more about what was happening behind me than in front.

Behind their backs, Evans made a reassuring face at me. At least I assumed that was what it was and he hadn't suddenly developed some major intestinal disorder, but I felt better.

We'd been on site about a quarter of an hour and there hadn't been any sort of riot or disturbance so it seemed safe to assume no one had noticed our arrival.

'If someone could get the door, please.'

Sands opened the door. I took a deep breath, 'Here we go, people,' and led them outside into the teeming streets.

So this was Babylon. Capital city of Babylonia, the most powerful kingdom in Ancient Mesopotamia – the Land Between Two Rivers. Built along both sides of the big, muddy, slow-flowing Euphrates, it was the largest city in the world, with a population of around two hundred thousand people. And it was huge. I'm still not quite sure what a hectare is but this city covered between eight hundred and nine hundred of them. That's an awful lot of hectares.

We began to orient ourselves. We were parked on the west bank of the Euphrates, just north of the main canal. The King's Gate was over to the west and Nabopolassar's Bridge to the north.

Clerk and his team were in the newer part of the city on the other side of the river, where the posh people lived. A wide canal divided that part into two main areas – religious sites on the one side and the big houses of the rich on the other. Actually, there were canals everywhere. Large ones branched off the river and smaller channels branched off of them, all the way down

174

to tiny, reed-clogged streamlets. In the desert we might be but there was no shortage of water in this city.

The canals were congested with small reed boats – kuphars, coracle-like boats made of wood and waterproof skins or leather. They came in various sizes but – and this is interesting – every single one carried at least one donkey. This was Babylonian ingenuity. Traders would row downriver to Babylon, sell their goods, and strip down and sell the wooden parts of the boat – wood has value in the desert – keeping only the leather skins and the donkey. Then they'd load the skins on to the donkey and trudge back upriver whence they came to begin the sequence all over again. Clever.

The Euphrates itself was lined with sailboats made of papyrus and wood, their square sails furled for the moment. Armies of men were unloading luxury goods of every kind – ivory, timber, gold, lapis lazuli . . . And there were warships, too, with raised platforms for the archers and, in some cases, a giant ramming device fitted at the front.

We gave our new colleagues a moment to take it all in. I knew they all had desert experience so the sudden blast of superheated air came as no shock to them. I was glad to see they had the sense to stand in the shade of the pod while they got their bearings. Because it was very, very hot. And dry. I remembered to keep my mouth closed. A hot, sluggish wind brought no relief other than to shift some of the piles of sand that had blown against every vertical surface. I imagined it was a constant battle to keep the dust and grit out of houses and temples.

I squinted in the bright sunlight. There were people everywhere. I could see men I assumed to be soldiers, with their domed helmets, either marching around in groups of six or standing idly on street corners watching the women go by. They carried tall shields and wore their swords across the front of their bodies. Quivers of arrows hung from their belts and their bows were slung over one shoulder. Their armour gleamed in the bright sunshine, and like most men here, their hair and beards were curled and oiled. Beautifully presented but competent. The shock troops of their day.

And there were plenty of women on the streets, which was encouraging. Like me they wore layers of shawls and scarves, wound around their undertunics. Not all their heads were covered, but the headdresses I could see were very intricate. My small pointed cap with the dangly bits really was extremely modest by their standards. They mixed their fabrics and they certainly mixed their colours. Most of the women on the street were gloriously dressed and with at least two or three attendants, one of whom was carefully holding a fringed canopy over her mistress. These were obviously society women. Everyone – male and female – was a riot of colour and embellishment.

Like their buildings. We were braced for the splendour of the Ishtar Gate – everyone's seen the images – but the buildings around us – private houses, shops, temples, shrines, public buildings, granaries, brothels – were also vividly painted in the favourite Babylonian blue and smothered with images of bulls, lions, flowers, palm trees and insects. With the brilliant sun bouncing off the walls around us the effect was eye-watering. I've never wanted sunglasses so badly. Anyone bringing a tray of the latest in fashionable shades would be sold out in seconds.

The men on the streets covered a much larger social span. Their costumes ranged from a tiny waist string for the very poor and slaves, to simple belted tunics with short sleeves, all the way up to fabulous concoctions of fringed shawls in rainbow colours. These were thick with embroidered thread and precious stones and swathed them from head to mid-calf. The fabrics appeared to be silks, linens and cottons – all of it feather-light.

A laden cart trundled past, kicking up the dust. The air was thick with it. Dust swirled continually, along with flies and other insects. Big, bold and persistent buggers. I noticed many people carried what looked like decorated and dyed horse's tails to whisk them away. We, alas, were whiskless, but maybe we could cobble something together tonight. And it was something to remember for the future. Hot, dry, desert town? There will be insects. Bring whisks.

The noise was everything you'd expect from two hundred thousand people and their donkeys, goats, sheep, chickens, dogs and children. Merchants and shopkeepers bellowed, each seeking to be the loudest, holding up their wares for inspection. There were children shouting behind a high wall and somewhere a baby was crying. Clucking chickens hung from a pole, their legs tied together and really not very happy about it. Wagons and handcarts rattled along, creaking under their loads.

More armed men marched past, their feet stamping in the dust and sand, with their armour glinting. Boys ran along behind them, imitating their steps. Playing at being soldiers. Adults made sure to get well out of the way, pressing back against the mud-brick houses packed so closely together. These were single-storey buildings with flat roofs and built around a court-yard. There were no windows in any of the external walls. Occasionally the outer doors had been left open, offering us brief glimpses of busy courtyard life – women crossing with pitchers and bowls, smoke rising from open fires. What looked like rugs or carpets hung from the roofs – whether they were airing in the sunshine or this was another way of decorating their houses, I couldn't tell. Or possibly they were sleeping mats. People would sleep on the roof after sundown, taking advantage of any cooling night breezes.

Yes, this was definitely Babylon. Deafening. Mind-blowing. Eye-watering. Nostril-searing. And, never forget, we were in the year 565BC and the city had been here over two thousand years already, exuding strength and prosperity. And yet, its decline was only a few years away.

Sands tapped me on the shoulder and pointed. I turned. Over everything, dominating the city, loomed the great mass of Etemenanki. The Tower of Babel. It was colossal. A huge, solid ziggurat, seven terraces high, with crenellated battlements. There were no curves. It was all angles and vertical lines and zigzags, soaring upwards to the heavens. I tilted my head back to see all the way to the top. This structure must be over three hundred feet high, and towered over everything. Nothing in the city came even close to it for size and mass.

I'd always wanted to see the Tower of Babel. Sadly, no trace of it remains in modern times, thanks to Alexander the Great. And no, he didn't raze it to the ground in a drunken orgy of destruction like Persepolis – he came across the remains of it on his travels. Rather impressed at the size of the pile of mud bricks, he issued instructions it was to be rebuilt in all its former glory. His men cleared the site, sweeping away all traces of the old tower, but that didn't matter because it was going to be rebuilt, wasn't it? And then the silly bugger died and it never was. Rebuilt, I mean. Which reminded me to put 'locate Alexander's tomb' on my bucket list for Dr Bairstow. I mean, Treadwell.

The tragedy was that in trying to rebuild, Alexander had destroyed the original building. Today there is absolutely nothing left, not even the foundations. What a bugger. Without his intervention, there was a chance part of it might actually remain today.

And it truly was a stairway to heaven – cleverly sited so that to anyone standing in front of it and looking up, all the staircases seemed to be standing one above the other. From a distance it looked like one long ladder all the way to the top. I had to struggle very hard not to hum the tune under my breath.

I couldn't wait to get to it. The tower dominated everything in the same way the pyramids dominate their own surroundings. Except the pyramids had been built for a king and this had been built for a god. A man-made mountain with a monument to the great god Marduk at the summit.

I was not so mind-blown, however, as to forget my two newbies. I watched their faces carefully. They weren't open-mouthed but it would be fair to say they were impressed by their surroundings.

'Everything is so green,' said Glass, looking around, and he was right. The broader streets were lined with avenues of palm trees, planted for dates and shade, I assumed. Ornate pots and planters were stuffed with lilies and other flowering plants I didn't recognise. Even among the poorer houses, many external stairways and flat roofs also held giant pots from which brilliantly coloured flowers cascaded down.

'The Hanging Gardens,' said Glass, suddenly.

'A good thought, but no,' I said, quite sorry to stamp on his enthusiasm. 'We discovered them at Nineveh a few years ago. Shall we go and find the others?'

The Ishtar Gate was easy to locate. We simply followed the widest street – the Processional Way – and walked north against the flood of traffic entering the city.

There were ten gates altogether in the walls of Babylon and the Ishtar Gate was the eighth. Built in 578BC by Nebuchadnezzar – as his commemorative plaque proudly proclaimed – it was the grand entrance to the city. And if that didn't knock your socks off, the southern and northern fortresses were nearby and the king's palace just over there, as well.

Before I joined St Mary's – in the days when I just wandered around from one archaeological dig to the next and European travel was a lot easier than it is today – I'd visited the replica of the Ishtar Gate in the Pergamon Museum in Berlin. I was quite keen to compare the original with my memories. I wanted to see what sort of a job the museum had made of the reconstruction.

The city walls reared above us, built of those beautiful blue glazed tiles, decorated with reliefs of dragons, lions and aurochs – don't get me started on aurochses again – representing the gods Marduk and Adad and the goddess Ishtar. The gates were opened wide, lying flat against the wall, fortunately shaded by the walls themselves, which enabled us to record them more easily because even in the shade, they dazzled the eye.

The massive gates had been constructed of cedarwood – that most rare and valuable of woods. This was Nebuchadnezzar making yet another very public declaration of his wealth and power. There really wasn't much to choose between him and Ramses II for modest understatement, was there? Although Ramses only called himself the Great. Nebuchadnezzar called himself King of the Universe. And Darius of Persia styled himself King of Kings. You have to hand it to rulers in this part of the world – they never knowingly undersold themselves.

'Look,' said Clerk in great excitement, his nose about three inches from a low relief of the god Marduk in his incarnation as a dragon. 'Look how carefully they've laid the bricks. Can you see how none of the joins run through the eyes? Every eye is complete. That is so amazing. Imagine trying to work that out without a computer.'

We pulled him away before the guards closed in.

For the first few days, everything went well and we soon dropped into our usual routines. Evans reported the survey of the city was proceeding without problems and that the new Security people were functioning. 'They're not bad lads, Max, and Glass in particular tries really hard. I'm keeping an eye on them, but everything's fine. You historians can carry on wafting pointlessly about the place like you usually do.'

We'd been quite surprised by the extent of the settlements outside the city. Not only were there whole towns out there, but each gate had at least one garrison. Evans asked permission to spend some time studying the fortifications, cleverly choosing a moment when Hyssop and I were standing together so he was able to speak to us both at the same time, blurring the lines of whom he should be requesting permission from. It dawned on me that he was managing me the same way I was trying to manage Treadwell, which was quite amusing. Hyssop and I both nodded our permission at the same time. Evans was obviously considerably more adept at conciliation than me. Perhaps I should get him to deal with Treadwell.

Clerk and Prentiss had finished with the Ishtar Gate and

were working their way around the major temples in the city – Nabu, Ishtar, Enlil, Adad – before fetching up at the big one, Esagila. Sands and I were continuing our love affair with the Tower of Babel.

Yes, everything was absolutely fine.

There had been a buzz of excitement running through the city for the last two days. We were aware something was in the offing. Additional flags and pennants had been erected and snapped over our heads in the desert breeze. Wreaths of flowers were being offered for sale everywhere. Small ones for personal use, larger ones for attaching to house doors, and spectacular, truly sumptuous arrangements for offering to the gods, I assumed. We woke up one morning and the traditional street racket was absent. The day of the festival had arrived.

We at St Mary's are no strangers to festivals. Empty bladders and full water bottles are the standing instructions. Sands and Evans knocked us up a rudimentary sunshade, knotting together three or four shawls and tying them to a couple of old wooden poles we'd found. All right – stolen. We'd put them back behind the goat shed when we'd finished with them. Evans snapped the poles in half over his knee and tied a knot in each corner of the shawls. Voilà. Sunshade for three or four people.

We now had an important choice to make. Did we stand in the dusty street with its better view or did we look for a position near the canal with its cooler breezes wafting our way? Sadly, wafting breezes tend to waft mosquitoes as well. Great clouds of them. Every morning we would leave the pod encased in a gloopy mixture of sun cream, insect repellent and our own sweat, and despite all our best efforts, the determined little buggers feasted on our flesh like tiny Nazgûl. We were all of us red and lumpy.

I remembered, some time ago, we'd had to make an emergency jump to Egypt to retrieve a weapon someone had lost there and poor old Markham had been nearly eaten alive by the local insects. He'd been in such a bad way at the end that Peterson and I had had to throw him into the Nile. For his own good, of course. I wished Markham would come back to St Mary's.

Anyway, after that small digression into the eating habits of mosquitoes, you won't be surprised to hear we chose the street.

This was not the big New Year's festival, held in March to celebrate the beginning of the agricultural year. This was something smaller and more intimate. Or as small and intimate as Babylon could get, anyway, and it certainly didn't stop the streets being lined with people who had come from all over to see the ceremony and have a bit of a knees-up and some free nosh.

Above us, the white sky was slowly turning a dirty browny-yellow again as the wind brought in even more sand from the desert.

Apart from the temples, nothing was open today. Everything had been folded up and put away. There were none of the familiar smells of street cooking. Not that we needed them. There would be sacrifices and food for all later in the day.

Groups of musicians were appearing everywhere. People danced along behind them and the streets echoed to the accompaniment of drums, cymbals, twanging harp-like instruments and horns. Those lining the streets laughed, clapped and threw flowers or small cakes. Each group was playing a different tune, of course, and it wasn't as if the music of Babylon was particularly harmonious to begin with. I suspected most of it was banging on about gods defeating their enemies and the things the king would do to subjugated peoples he considered not quite subjugated enough. The tune was probably secondary to the message.

Clouds of smoke arose from the temple courtyards, especially that of Esagila where a long line of priests were offering up sacrifices. I wondered if we looked poor enough for a nice fat haunch of goat. Don't scoff. Done properly, goat is very tasty.

The street procession was long. Spectacular, but definitely long. There were ranks of soldiers, interspersed with priests and musicians. Then more soldiers. Then more priests and musicians. Then more soldiers. This was a procession that concentrated on length rather than excitement. St Mary's had our recorders going and we grew hotter, dustier and thirstier with every minute. My ankles ached. My throat ached. My eyes ached. But finally it was over and the last soldier disappeared around the corner. Let the festivities begin.

Along with everyone else in the city, we began to make our way towards the entrance to Esagila, which had been built by the great god Marduk himself. According to legend he had fought and killed the monster Tiamat, thus bringing order to the cosmos. I had a brief vision of our own modern politicians, wearing nothing but loincloths and clutching spears, sallying forth to defeat chaos and bring order to the cosmos. Or the other way around, of course. Anyway, in celebration, they built Esagila, the Temple of Marduk, just next door to Etemenanki. This cluster of buildings was the most important temple complex in town. The axis of the world. The straight line that connected earth and heaven. So definitely a place where historians should tread lightly, then.

Behind me, Clerk and Prentiss, who understood the words *free time* about as well as any other historian, were discussing the possibility of there actually being a statue of Marduk and his wife in the inner sanctum. And if so, would they be brought out for the world to have a sight of them? It could be the most accurate representation of Marduk that we would ever see. And then the food turned up and we had other things to think about.

They'd slaughtered innumerable goats and sheep in a sacred area behind the temple, probably while everyone's attention was on the parade. Half a dozen priests, stripped to the waist and smeared with blood and worse, butchered carcasses at lightning speed. One minute the priest was dressing a whole goat carcass – the next minute he was tossing four hooves into a bucket and moving on to the next.

Plumes of smoke rose into the air, carrying the aroma of roasting meat with them. I felt my stomach rumble and I'm sure I wasn't the only one.

I don't know where the bakers' ovens were but pile after pile of flatbreads were being laid out. To be used as plates, I assumed, watching the lines of people shuffle patiently to the makeshift tables. The priests' managing-large-numbers-of-people skills were first-rate. There were no bottlenecks, no impatient people, no trouble at all. Everyone was good-humoured and enjoying their holy day.

Gorgeously dressed priests handed everyone a flatbread, more priests slapped slices of still steaming meat on top, another priest blessed both portion and recipient impartially and then we were gently eased aside by those behind us to find somewhere shady to sit. I ate with one hand, recorded with the other and was generally content with the way things were going.

Night fell eventually. I was shattered – I think we all were – but the best bit was yet to come. We watched the procession of flickering torches inch their way up the sides of Etemenanki as the priests climbed slowly to the summit. The people of Babylon stood silently, watching. We could hear the priests' solemn chanting rolling out over the city, punctuated by the occasional drum roll and clash of cymbals. It was all here. The black sky. The blaze of stars above us was mirrored by the torchlight below. My arms throbbed with trying to record it all. We had tons of material already but, as Sands said, Treadwell would reckon this was the money shot. Only when the horizon lightened in the east, and one by one the torches were being extinguished, did we pack up and make our weary way back to the pods.

The festival marked a natural halfway point in the jump and we all took a rest day afterwards. We'd been here about eleven days now and it was time to review our material and identify any gaps or areas where we felt more information was required while we were still on site and could do something about it. We had masses of raw data – figures, statistics, images, holos, notes, sketches – all safely tucked away in boxes in the pods for us to pull together on our return to make a coherent narrative of life in ancient Babylon.

Evans and his team, starting from Esagila and working out-wards, had managed to map nearly half the city, and substantial areas outside the gates as well. They uploaded daily and we sat in the evenings, watching digital Babylon unfold before our eyes. To this, we could then add specific details from various sites we'd visited. Theoretically, at the end of the assignment, we'd have most of Babylon at our fingertips. However, we still had to move to the second part of the assignment – the poorer quarter. I was particularly keen to do some work here because the flashy bits of Babylon were all very well but the less affluent areas often have a lot to offer. Sands and I were to put in some time investigating the artisans' quarters – potters, metalworkers, masons and so forth – how they lived and worked, what they ate, how they worshipped, the role of women, family groups and so on – before finally moving on to the markets and waterways.

Clerk and Prentiss wanted to spend one last day at Esagila observing the aftermath of the procession and ceremony, before moving off to investigate the giant brickmaking compounds. The final part of their assignment would be to observe the famous blue-glazed brick tiles being made.

Everything was going well. Everyone was being meticulously polite to everyone else and concentrating on the job in hand.

The newbies were performing adequately. Evans had been right about Glass. Yes, he was a little slow, but he was conscientious and gave every indication of enjoying himself, frequently staring around in an open-mouthed disbelief that was rather endearing. Even Harper wasn't doing too badly.

Scarfe, on the other hand, complained incessantly about the heat, the flies, the smells and, incredibly, boredom. Clerk reported he and Prentiss pretty much ignored him most of the time. His contributions were negligible.

Both Hyssop and I had been unable to find anything to fight over, although being quarter of a mile apart and in separate pods might have had something to do with that. There was no doubt

187

though, there wasn't the same atmosphere on this jump as I was used to. There was less joking. The two crews stayed apart and within the crews themselves, people stayed in separate groups as well. We were an assignment of two halves. Historians on one side and the new Security people on the other. Evans and Keller sat uneasily between the two.

We weren't doing badly, though. The city was robust in its behaviour, especially at night, but none of us had been involved in incidents of any kind. No one had taken a blind bit of notice of us as we pottered about, recording, documenting and working our way through our allotted tasks. None of us had gone down with anything horrible. Apart from too enthusiastically scratching our mozzie bites and making a bit of a mess of them, we were all absolutely fine. Everything was absolutely fine.

Until it wasn't and nothing was ever the same again.

It happened the very next day. Clerk and Prentiss were finally finished at Esagila. They'd covered the public areas of the temple, identified the chief priests and their functions and now just had a few loose ends to tidy up. We were all preparing for the second half of our assignment. In just over a week we'd be back at St Mary's with, I have to say, some pretty spectacular stuff. Dr Bairstow – sorry, I *was* going to say Dr Bairstow would be pleased. Treadwell, I suspected, would be mildly content and then complain about the cost. But it had been an incident-free assignment. Babylon was peaceful – probably due in no small part to the frequent patrols of well-armed soldiers on the streets.

Initially I knew nothing of it. Because that idiot Hyssop thought she could fix it herself. The first I was aware something had happened was when Hyssop herself turned up in front of me as I was packing up my gear in preparation for returning to the pod for a quick splash of cold water on my face and a drink before setting out again.

I picked up my pack and looked over her shoulder for the others, but she was alone. We'd never seen any trouble on the streets, but this was still not a wise move on her part. Why would she take such a risk?

I stared at her. She had that professionally blank expression that always means something bad either has happened or is about to happen. I felt the skin at the back of my neck tighten. Such is my lifestyle that my instincts don't usually bother getting out of bed for anything less than an apocalypse, but at this precise moment not only were they out of bed, but they were bolting down the stairs and throwing on their clothes as they went.

Trying to remain calm, I said, 'Is there a problem?'

She seemed to brace herself. 'There's been an incident.'

'Where? Why didn't you call me? What happened?'

'The Temple of Marduk.'

'Esagila.'

'Yeah.'

'What about the Temple of Marduk?'

She stared over my shoulder. For God's sake, was she standing at attention? 'We were in some sort of courtyard . . .'

'You were *inside* the temple compound?'

'Well, yes.'

'Clerk gave you permission to go inside?'

'He wasn't there. I made a decision.'

'To go inside.'

'Yes.'

'Did you remember to remove your sandals? Or wash your face and hands?'

The answer was written all over her face.

I sighed. 'Great. Did they throw you out?'

'Actually . . . there was a kind of inner room.'

It was a hundred and fifty degrees in the shade today and I went cold.

'You mean the little building at the centre of the courtyard.'

She nodded. 'It didn't look very important. It was tiny compared to the other stuff . . .'

'You're talking about the inner sanctum.'

'Scarfe had heard them – Clerk and Prentiss – talking about it and it was unguarded – no one in sight – so he thought it would be an excellent opportunity to . . .'

'Enter the inner sanctum. The place where the gods live. The holiest place in the city. And commit blasphemy.'

'Well, obviously the gods don't live there so . . .'

Shit. Shit, shit, shit.

This was exactly the sort of thing I had been afraid of. I snapped at her. 'Your opinion as to the location of the gods is irrelevant. The people here believe they do and that's what matters!'

Face tight, she nodded.

'Scarfe went inside?'

'It was easy. There wasn't even a door. Just a curtain.'

'And you let him do this?'

'He thought he could nip in and out with a recorder and no one would notice what he was doing.'

This casual assumption that people living a long time ago weren't as intelligent as modern people pisses me off no end. That the Babylonians wouldn't notice a little casual blasphemy and even if they did, they wouldn't mind. Because it was just one of their funny old gods and not important. Well, it bloody well is important. The gods of Ancient Egypt have been around a bloody sight longer than this new-fangled Christianity. And if you take a good look around contemporary time, those who lived a long time ago *were* a bloody sight more intelligent than us. By a long way.

I bit back what I'd been going to say. And I stored away the fact that a member of Security had a recorder for future thinking about.

'Well, let's take a guess, shall we – they did notice.'

Hyssop nodded. 'One minute the place was deserted and the next – priests and guards everywhere.'

I sighed. 'Well, lucky for you, Clerk and Prentiss have finished there. Tomorrow you can escort them to . . .'

Evans blasted around the corner. 'Max. A word.'

Hyssop stiffened. 'Not necessary, Evans. I'm dealing with it.'

'No, you're not. Max . . .'

'I am attempting to . . .'

'Both of you – shut up.' I turned to Evans. 'Talk to me.'

'Clerk and Prentiss have been arrested.'

It was vitally important to remain calm. I turned to Hyssop. 'And you would have told me . . . when?'

'I *was* telling you.'

'When did this happen?'

'A couple of hours ago.'

'*A couple of hours?*'

'About noon.'

'What the hell have you been doing all this time?'

'We've been looking for them.'

'Without telling me?'

'There wasn't time. Standing instructions are to search the area immediately. Which we did.'

'They wouldn't have kept them there, you clown. It's a temple. They'll have been taken away to God knows where. Have you any idea of what could be happening to them right now? Especially Prentiss.'

192

'Which bears out Commander Treadwell's theory that . . .'

'Shut up,' I said, unable to listen to her any longer.

'Yeah,' said Evans. 'I'd really shut up if I were you, Hyssop.' Which was quite a reproof from mild-mannered Evans. 'Sorry, Max. I've only just found out you hadn't been informed.'

'Watch your mouth, Evans.' Hyssop turned back to me. 'We've been looking for them,' she said defensively. 'When we couldn't locate them at the temple, I pulled Evans and his team off their mapping duties and set up a proper search grid and we've been working from street to street.'

It was only the fact that I had some really good stuff on my recorder that stopped me throwing it against the wall. Or better still, throwing her useless self against the wall. And her useless team with her.

'Have you been calling them?'

'Yes. Every thirty seconds. As is laid down in . . .'

'Mr Evans, get everyone back to Number Five. It's the closest. Everyone drops what they're doing. We'll do a head count and then attempt to ascertain from these useless fuckers exactly what happened, where and when.'

'On it,' he said and disappeared before Hyssop could stop him.

The temptation to run through the streets shouting their names is strong. To cover as much ground in as little time as possible because anything could be happening to them and all the time your brain is shouting at you to find them, find them, find them.

The *right* thing to do is to take a moment or two to stop and think. Where would they be taken? Is there a public gaol? Is

193

there more than one? Is there a public execution site? Will they be split up? What is the law? What is the punishment? Will it be the same for Prentiss as for Clerk? You have to force yourself to stop and answer these questions as best you can because lives depend upon it.

We got our maps out. Evans pulled up the uncompleted survey and he, Sands and I pored over everything, trying to identify anything that looked as if it might be a public gaol. The truth was that there were probably no holding facilities in the temple complex and the temple guards would have had them out of there at the speed of light. Something an experienced Security Section would have known. Markham would have called for assistance, stationed people appropriately and inter-cepted prisoners and guards in a quiet spot somewhere. We'd have had to run like hell afterwards, but we're used to that. In fact, if Hyssop and her people had conspired to be in the wrong place at the wrong time doing the wrong thing for the wrong reasons, they couldn't have made a better job of it.

And not a peep from either Clerk or Prentiss. No cry for help. Not even the swift tap to the ear we give when we can't talk. They were almost certainly unconscious. Or dead. I could hear Keller calling them every thirty seconds or so. On and on. Respond. Respond. Respond.

There was nothing. Not even static.

I was nearly frantic but that wouldn't help. Clerk and Prentiss were tagged – we all were – and we had tag readers, but they could be anywhere in the city and it was a big place. Worse – they might not even be in the city at all by now.

Scarfe started to say something. I don't know what it was. I only know I was furious that he should even be talking at all.

I spoke very quietly because if I didn't my rage would consume them all.

'I am certain that Captain Hyssop is punctilious in her treatment of even dickheads like you, Scarfe. I, however, am an historian and the rules don't apply to me. I couldn't give a flying duck about hurting your feelings. My first instinct is to send you back to St Mary's while you are still able to walk and to confine you to the Security Section for your own protection. However, you will be included in this search because I need the manpower. You will do exactly as you are told when you are told. You will take very good care not to irritate me in even the smallest way, otherwise I will write you off as natural wastage and leave you here for whatever remains of your sad little existence.'

'That was uncalled for,' said Hyssop, quietly.

'It was that or end his life on the spot. I'm quite happy to go with that option.'

'No, I meant he is a member of my team. If you have any complaints you should address them to . . .'

'And Clerk and Prentiss are members of mine. And they're still missing. And I have more complaints about you and your team than you can even begin to imagine. And very soon, when we've resolved this mess of your making, you and I will be discussing exactly why a member of your team took it upon himself to attempt to perform a task far beyond both his remit and his abilities and the consequences thereof.'

'Nevertheless . . .'

Something broke inside me. Weeks of pent-up tension exploded before I could do anything about it. For one dizzying moment it was as if I was crushed beneath the weight of . . . well . . . everything. I grabbed a mug and flung it at the wall.

It shattered into hundreds of satisfying little pieces. Everyone jumped.

'You still don't get it, do you? You're here to protect historians. If you're not going to do that, then there's no point in bringing you at all. In fact, we'd do better without you. Jesus Christ, Markham would *never* have allowed this to happen.'

That stung her. 'Well, he's not bloody here, is he?'

'No, but unfortunately for us, you and your people are. For God's sake, there are more fucking Security personnel than historians on this assignment and you still couldn't get it right, could you?'

Evans put a colossal paw on my arm. 'Max . . .'

'Yes, I know.' I breathed again. 'I know.'

I took a very deep breath and turned to Hyssop. 'I should have asked before – what did the tag readers say? Have you had any indication at all as to their whereabouts? In fact, that should have been the first—'

I stopped. That should have been the first thing she did. And she hadn't.

No one was looking at me.

I swallowed, and already guessing the answer, said very quietly, 'You *did* bring tag readers . . .'

Still no one was looking at me.

Oddly enough, by now I was quite calm. Probably the rational part of my brain had decided there were no words for this, so why bother.

Eventually she said, 'We didn't bring . . .'

I held up my hand because I just couldn't bear to hear her say it.

196

Sands was folding the maps. 'Max, one of us will have to go back and get them.'

Damn. We'd be down to one historian.

'I can drive a pod,' said Evans.

I blinked. 'Can you?'

'Course I can. Do you think I've been with you all these years and never picked it up? It can't be that difficult if historians can do it.'

I wasn't going to argue. And as a member of Security he'd know best what equipment to bring back. I nodded. 'All right. Harper, grab the maps. We'll get started on the search. Mr Evans, bring trackers, proximity alerts, everything you can think of. Mr Lindstrom will do the return coordinates for you so don't worry about that. Just grab whatever and whoever you can. Call me on your return. Try not to let Commander Treadwell involve himself too closely.'

Hyssop was very pale. '*I'm* in charge of the Security aspects of this mission . . .'

'Oh, really. How's that worked out for us so far?'

'We should—'

'I'm in charge here,' I said between gritted teeth. 'This is *my* assignment. Which is not something I should have to keep reminding you of. And if you'd confined yourselves to mapping the city as I requested, then we wouldn't be having this conversation. *I* wanted to ease your team in slowly. *You* were the one on an ego trip. This was your team's first assignment and they have failed. Dismally. Clerk and Prentiss are both popular and respected members of St Mary's. You and your team are neither. I'd shut up if I were you. Go, please, Mr Evans.'

He nodded. Harper grabbed the maps and we exited the pod

197

to stand around the corner. The pod blinked out of existence with no problems at all, although I don't know what I thought Evans was going to do to it.

The dust slowly settled and I surveyed my resources. Sands, Hyssop, Keller, a very silent Glass, Scarfe and Harper. And me.

'Be aware – we are now officially in harm's way. Our other pod is on the other side of the city. Too far away should we encounter any problems in this vicinity. Be aware that if anything goes wrong, your priority is to find a hiding place and when it is safe to get yourselves back to the other pod.' I looked at Hyssop. 'You know where it is?'

She nodded, tight-lipped.

'Mr Sands, you take Glass. Mr Keller will go with Harper. And Scarfe.'

Sadly, that left me with Hyssop, but this way there would be one experienced person on every team. There would be time for revenge and retribution later. Always deal with the now. With luck she'd fall into the Euphrates and a bloody hippo would eat her. And if they didn't have hippos in the Euphrates then I'd bloody well go off and find one.

I took a deep breath. 'There are too few of us for a thorough search so we'll confine ourselves to the area around the Esagila. When reinforcements arrive, at least we'll be able to say we've eliminated that part of the city. Keep your coms open at all times. Mr Keller – continue to call Clerk and Prentiss at thirty-second intervals.'

I didn't say that the chances of them calling us or even hearing us were not good. If they were in a position to communicate then they would have done so by now. I swallowed down the panic engendered by thinking about what could be happening to them right at this moment. That wouldn't help. The best thing I could do for them was not waste another second. 'Let's go.'

Sands passed me some water. 'Drink.'

We all drank. And then we set off.

We trudged the streets for two hours. It was useless. There were so many people about we couldn't see more than ten feet in front of us, let alone to the end of the street. They could have been twenty feet away and we'd miss them.

No one had heard anything on their com.

'We should shout,' said Keller, when we met on a street corner. 'They might not be able to answer their coms but they could easily be behind a wall somewhere or on a roof. Shout.'

It went against the grain to draw attention to ourselves like that, but we did. We shouted. We shouted 'St Mary's' – listened, moved on, shouted, listened, moved on. Nothing. Except a lot of very strange looks but I'd passed caring. I just wanted to find my people. I'd worked with Clerk and Prentiss for years. They'd both been at St Mary's nearly as long as I had. Clerk had often covered for me when I went on leave. I realised I was thinking about them in the past tense.

I was under no illusions. When people go missing the first few hours are the most critical and Hyssop had wasted them. She was applying military criteria to non-military circumstances. Right from the word go she'd seemed unable to get her head around the fact that we do things differently at St Mary's. We have to. And we'd been doing things this way for years because it worked. And then, in swept Wonder Woman with her *I'm young and bright and modern and I'll soon get this place working properly* attitude and everything had turned to shit.

There were minor compensations. Babylon was not a barbaric city. Contrary to the Bible – a not unbiased primary source – the Babylonians had many laws and they were strictly enforced. However – and unfortunately for Clerk and Prentiss – I was unsure what they'd be charged with – trespass at best, blasphemy at worst – the penalty for which would almost certainly be either death or enslavement.

If death, they might well be already dead. Enslavement was a different matter. We could get them back. And slavery in Babylon was not quite the same as slavery elsewhere. Many slaves were of Babylonian origin and descent. There were four types – those that were bought and sold along with the parcels of land they worked or the premises where they were employed; foreign slaves from subjugated lands; temple slaves; and private slaves who usually worked for a family and had a trade and, believe it or not, rights. A master could not maim, injure or kill a slave without just cause. If a man injured another man's slave, he had to pay compensation – not to the slave, obviously, but it was still a kind of protection. Slaves could be witnesses in court. Unlike their Roman counterparts, they weren't subject to compulsory torture to verify their evidence. And, interestingly, the law required a family to be kept together. A married slave could bring his wife and children with him. A mother could not be separated from her child. No doubt this was subject to abuse just like every other law, but it was a little bit comforting all the same. I told myself we'd find them long before it came to that.

We didn't.

Evans returned a few hours later with Sykes, Roberts and Van Owen, together with Cox, Gallacio and Lingoss.

Lingoss took me to one side.

'What?' I said.

'I have a message from Tim – sorry, Dr Peterson.'

'What is it?'

'Whatever you need – you will have. Just ask. And don't worry about what's happening at St Mary's. He's got your back. If you need him – he'll be here as soon as he can climb into a pod.'

I smiled. Things suddenly didn't seem quite so dark.

We divvied up the tag readers and all the other bits and pieces, divided ourselves into pairs, allocated areas and set off to comb the city.

I can't describe the search in any great detail because all the days merged into one another. Endless hours tramping the crowded streets, being jostled by every man and his donkey, swallowing the dust. Pausing only for a quick bite to eat and a drink and then off again. Stopping only when it was too dark to see and respectable people had locked their doors and retired for their evening meal.

Seven long, long days later we'd covered every inch and found nothing so, gate by gate, we moved outside. There were thriving communities on the other side of the walls. Towns in their own rights. Nomads, merchant trains, slave markets, herds of animals, hide tents, barracks, barns, tatty houses – we covered it all and there was no sign. No one had had even a flash on their readers. We called continually – over our coms and more shouting in the streets – but no response. When we could safely do so, we chalked 'St Mary's' on walls and gates. If they were dead then their bodies weren't in this vicinity because theoretically, we'd still be able to read their tags. Not that our tag readers were particularly reliable. I'm sure I've mentioned that before. In general, it's quicker and easier for the rescuers to shout, 'Where are you?' and the rescuees to shout, 'Over here, idiots.' But, in the end, we were forced to admit it: we couldn't find them because they weren't here.

We were running out of rations and water. We were exhausted. The mood was beyond despairing. I had to billet Hyssop and her team in a separate pod for their own safety.

Finally, I was obliged to call a halt and take us home.

14

Once back at St Mary's, I sent everyone off to Sick Bay to have their sunburn and mosquito bites treated. I decontaminated and then went straight to Treadwell, massively resenting the fact he wasn't there to meet us. Dr Bairstow would have been there on our arrival, demanding a verbal report and asking what my next plans were.

Hyssop, however, had got to him first. I hadn't hung around so she must really have motored.

Treadwell looked up as I stormed into the office. 'Dr Maxwell, this is very bad news. I take it you're here to seek permission to . . .'

I cut him short. 'I don't need your permission. It was your people who screwed this up in the first place. We're here for a few hours' rest and a good meal and then we're going straight back.' I pointed at Hyssop. 'I'll tell you now, no one will ever work with her people again – but that's your problem and I'm dumping it squarely in your lap.'

Hyssop flushed. Treadwell intervened. 'I think you forget it is I who command St Mary's.'

'I'm sure you do,' I said, 'but my priority is rescuing my

people from the situation caused by your Security Section, so I'll leave you here asserting your authority.'

'Captain Hyssop will have command of this situation.'

'Over her dead body,' I said. 'Sorry, Commander, but unless you want to treat the world to the very unedifying sight of Hyssop trying to assert her authority over a bunch of people who think she's not worth the shoes she's standing in, then I advise you to leave her and her Half-Wits behind. Perhaps, since you're so keen on women knowing their place in the world, she could do something useful in the kitchen.'

There was a rather nasty silence. I could hear my heart thumping in my head.

Treadwell came out from behind his desk. 'Three jumps, Dr Maxwell.'

I blinked. Was he saying what I thought he was saying?

'What?'

'Three jumps. Of which you have already had one.'

I took a deep breath and assembled the last rags of my temper. 'Don't be so ridiculous. You can't possibly impose a finite number of jumps on a rescue mission. No one works like that. If an airliner goes down, no one says, "You can only search until next Thursday after which we'll conveniently forget all about it and resume normal duties." They search until there's no hope of finding anyone. Dead or alive.'

'Exactly my point, Dr Maxwell. If, after three exhaustive searches, you have failed to discover any trace of the missing historians, then it makes sense to move on.'

'You mean forget my missing people, forget Hyssop's blunder in losing them and forget your blunder in giving her more responsibility than she could handle.'

'No, I mean we hold all the ceremonies appropriate and then, regretfully, resume the tasks for which we are paid.'

'And what is this supposed jump I've already had?'

'Your first search, Dr Maxwell. The one from which you have just returned. The one where you searched everywhere but were unable to find them. Face it – that was your best chance. If you failed then you're not likely to succeed in any subsequent attempts, are you?'

'Are you so blindly stupid that you think people here will just abandon their colleagues because you say so? And carry on as if nothing has happened?'

'They will if you will, Dr Maxwell. It's called leadership and it's what I expect from the Head of the History Department.'

I made very sure to speak quietly. 'Then I'm afraid you will have to brace yourself for some serious disappointment, Commander. My people are lost out there – courtesy of your people—'

'There are no your people and my people—'

'Unfortunately that is not true, because your people are a serious threat to my people and, if Hyssop has her way, very soon there won't be any of my people left. This is your fault, Treadwell, and my report will make it very clear that I hold you responsible. You insisted on deploying untrained staff. You handed Scarfe a recorder to carry out a task he was supremely unqualified to do. Your incessant urge to cut corners and change the focus of St Mary's has led Hyssop to overstep the very limited bounds of her expertise. You've taken a functioning, productive St Mary's and flung them into chaos for no better reason than to make yourself look good. Congratulations, Commander. We have *Us* and we have *Them*

205

and I am incredibly proud to belong to Team Us. In fact, let me give you some excellent advice for remedying this catastrophe of your making: fuck off. When you get there – fuck off again. And then fuck right off.'

I spun on my heel and stormed from the room. The wonderful Mrs Partridge already had the door open so nothing marred my magnificent exit.

Actually, I was so furious I could hardly see straight, but instinct must have led me to the dining room – clearly labelled Dining Room by Mrs Mack, who had been very unimpressed with the appellation 'Mess Hall'. Where I found more trouble waiting for me. In fact, we stood on the brink of a pitched battle. Possibly in a foredoomed effort at self-preservation the new Security Section – excluding Evans and his team who were conspicuously absent – had pushed the tables together to form a reserved Security Section area. And trust me, there is no quicker way to annoy Mrs Mack than to change the layout of her beloved dining room. She was there too – *sans* battle ladle but it was only a matter of time – with St Mary's lined up behind her, facing down Hyssop's people. They stood chest to chest. Food had been forgotten – an indication of the seriousness of the situation. Battle lines had been drawn and things were looking ugly.

My first thought was to back out of the door and let them get on with it, but I'd seen them, and worse, they'd seen me.

I strode forwards. 'What's happening here?'

Mrs Mack turned. 'They've moved the tables, Max. My people can't get past with their trollies and they're blocking the fire exit.'

I couldn't resist. No one could have. 'Relax,' I said. 'It's only part of Hyssop's cunning plan to kill us all off. Someone fetch our new Health and Safety officer – oh . . . wait . . .'

Hyssop's Half-Wits stood in a tight, defensive group.

'You don't want to mess with us,' said Scarfe and one or two St Mary's people laughed outright.

'Ooh,' said Sykes. 'Doesn't he look funny without his mummy.'

Scarfe raised his fist and I stepped between them.

'I'll say this only once. For your own good, go and eat somewhere else. I mean it, and if you were blessed with a leader who had any brains, she'd say the same. Obviously, she's not here – I'll leave you to draw your own conclusions about that – but I'm telling you – no, I'm ordering you – fuck off and eat somewhere else. And don't give me any crap about not taking orders from historians. Treadwell's busy selling the myth that we're all one St Mary's, in which case you *do* take orders from me. If you don't feel you're part of St Mary's – a feeling shared by everyone here – then you've no right to these facilities so just fuck off anyway.'

No one moved.

I honestly thought we were three seconds away from breaking the furniture over each other's heads but Hyssop suddenly appeared in the doorway. She looked rather pale. I wondered if she'd been blasted by Treadwell – which he certainly should have done regardless of how he felt about me. I sighed. Here was another situation for her to impose herself on.

'What's going on here?'

It was Mrs Mack who answered. 'The behaviour of your team is beyond what I can accept in this dining room. You will please remove them at once. If you phone through an order, your food will be brought down to you but until your team's attitude changes, the dining room is off limits to you all.'

Without even bothering to make sure Hyssop complied, she wheeled away, back into the kitchen.

Hyssop stared around, read the situation correctly for once and made a gesture for her team to withdraw.

Mrs Mack's team began to restore the original layout and, slowly, St Mary's returned to their tables and resumed eating.

I stood for a moment, having a bit of a think, and then caught Mr Sands' eye. And then Miss Van Owen's. Senior historians, the pair of them. They nodded and I pushed off back to my own office to try to calm down a little.

They turned up about ten minutes later with a plate of sandwiches piled two storeys high.

'You've just had lunch,' I said.

'They're for you,' said Sands, dumping the plate on my desk.

I suddenly realised I was starving.

Ham, cheese and tomato, tuna mayonnaise, beef and cold potato – I got stuck in. Van Owen made the tea. Rosie Lee was mercifully absent and I couldn't be bothered to enquire where and why.

'What's up?' said Sands. 'Apart from the obvious, I mean.'

When I could speak again, I explained about Treadwell and his brilliant new idea concerning our search and rescue procedures.

'I didn't want to say anything in front of everyone else,' I said. 'We can't have people knowing that, these days, St Mary's does leave its people behind.'

'God, no,' said Van Owen and Sands nodded.

'I've been having a bit of a think,' I said, 'and we can get round this. Picture a *relay race*.'

'Brilliant, Max,' said Sands, a phrase not uttered anything like often enough.

I nodded. 'Apparently we've had one jump – he's counting the original as our first – so according to him, we have two left. Except we don't.'

'Simple maths, Max,' said Van Owen. 'One from three equals two.'

'Yes – except – he's expecting us all to go at once. Which would constitute the second jump. I propose we tag each other. Four historians jump. After a period yet to be decided, two return and are replaced by another two. Then the other two return to be replaced by yet another two. And so on. Technically it's still the same jump. We tag each other. We could go on for months like that. There's a beginning but no end. It just rolls on and on.'

'For how long can we do that?'

'Until someone tells us to stop,' I said, which is my answer to doing anything just a teensy bit naughty. 'And the beauty of it is that even after Treadwell tumbles to it – which I expect he will sooner or later – there's still one jump remaining. And by then I'll have thought of something else.'

Van Owen grinned. 'Bloody hell, Max – genius.'

Once Bashford and Atherton were back from their own assignment at Marsden Moor, I was able to organise us into four teams.

Team One – me, Roberts and Cox in Number Eight.

Team Two – Sykes, Sands and Gallacio in Number Six.

Team One – excluding me – would return to be replaced by Team Three – Van Owen, Bashford and Evans in Number Five.

Team Two would then return to be replaced by Team Four – Atherton, Kalinda and Keller in Number Eight.

Rinse and repeat. Ad infinitum. Or until Treadwell realised what we were doing and intervened.

Hyssop and her Half-Wits were on their own in Number Seven. No one would work with them. Once we'd got this sorted, Treadwell was going to have a real problem on his hands. Once we got this sorted.

And there were plenty of other volunteers should we need any additional teams although I hoped we wouldn't. We festooned ourselves with equipment and rations and set off again.

I remained on site as the other teams came and went. We went through the city anti-clockwise this time. Each team took an area they hadn't previously covered so we could approach it with fresh eyes and the result was exactly the same. Nothing. It was a bloody nightmare. We walked every street, every alleyway. We surveyed every square and open space. We lingered outside every temple, every shop, even every palace. Roofs were pretty much private but we accessed as many of them as we could before irate house owners or their dogs chased us away.

Every night we ticked off more squares on our map. My head was full of what could be happening to Clerk and Prentiss and I'm pretty sure everyone else's was as well. We covered every inch of the city at least once – most of it twice – some of it three times or more – and there was not a flicker.

'They've been taken away, Max,' said Sands as St Mary's all gathered together one evening. I've no idea where Hyssop and her gang of useless duckwits were. The sun was setting fast and we were squatting beneath a palm tree. It wasn't safe to search at night. There was no curfew but there were a lot of other people in this city besides respectable homeowners and honest merchants. And there was no public lighting. If the homeowner didn't put a lighted torch outside his front door then the streets were frighteningly dark, and I couldn't afford to lose anyone else.

'There's no other explanation,' Sands continued. He paused. 'I think they've been sold. There are a lot of slave markets outside this city.'

I surveyed our teams. Hot, sunburned, dusty, tired. Especially tired. And tired people miss things. We'd had casualties too. Cox had been bitten by a street dog and I'd packed him straight back to St Mary's for anti-rabies treatment. A very real risk, here. Atherton had tripped over a paving slap and sprained his ankle. He spent his days in the pod coordinating the search. And Bashford had scratched his mozzie bites with rather too much enthusiasm and one of them had turned nasty. He was oozing rather more pus than I was happy with.

And then the decision was taken out of my hands. The next team brought a written command from Treadwell. He'd finally recognised my little scheme and I was commanded to call a halt and return everyone to St Mary's. The whole order was couched in terms even I couldn't wilfully misinterpret.

Sighing, we complied.

It was a good job I did go back because Leon was waiting for me. As usual, I hadn't realised how much I missed him until I saw him again. And Matthew, too. As soon as I was released from Sick Bay I walked into Leon's arms and suddenly the world didn't seem such a bad place. For a moment I allowed myself the luxury of thoughts that weren't Clerk- and Prentiss-based.

And then a big hug for Matthew, whose head, I noticed, was

now level with my chin. Not that my chin is very high off the ground but it was a reminder he was growing up.

'Off to see Auntie Lingoss,' he said, tearing himself away from his mother with no difficulty at all and shooting off.

'You look dreadful,' said Leon, St Mary's nomination for the Supportive Husband of the Year Award.

I sighed. 'One or two things have happened.'

He put his arm around me. 'I know.'

'About Dr Bairstow?'

'Yes. Commander Treadwell told me.'

'I'm sorry. I wanted to tell you myself but I've been in Babylon.'

'It's OK. We'll talk about it another time. I gather you've got a bit on at the moment.'

'Just a bit, yeah.'

We sat quietly in our room for a while, just enjoying being together, and then I asked him about Mikey and Adrian.

He rolled his eyes. 'You'd think, wouldn't you, that they couldn't get themselves into any trouble in the back end of civilisation, but you'd be completely wrong.'

I enquired what sort of trouble. 'I mean, yes, falling into rivers, getting lost, breaking an arm tumbling out of trees, that sort of thing, but as you say, you've been in the back end of civilisation. What on earth have they been up to?'

'I came across this the other day.'

He passed me a piece of paper on which were a number of incomprehensible figures, diagrams and equations.

'Oh, yes,' I said, with great concern. 'I can understand your anxiety.'

He tweaked it out of my hands and turned it the right way up.

212

'Aahhhh,' I said, equally unenlightened.

'You haven't a clue, have you?'

'Not even a little bit,' I said. 'What is it?'

'Professor Penrose thinks – and he admits it's a bit beyond him – that it's the initial theory for a portable time-travelling device.'

I frowned. 'Like a smaller pod?'

'No – like a bracelet.'

I stared at the paper. 'Oh . . . shit.'

'Exactly.'

'Leon, it was bad enough when Mikey and her brother designed a pod without any safety protocols. The last thing we need is them coming up with something like this.' I rubbed his arm. He looked as tired as I did. 'I should have asked – how's your search going?'

'I have one clear favourite and two acceptable alternatives so if you need us back here . . . We'd all be happy to pitch in.'

'Not at the moment, although I might later on. Where are you off to next?'

'I'm thinking of taking them to Skaxos for a while. Out of harm's way. By which I mean the harm they can inflict upon the universe – not the other way around.'

Skaxos is a tiny island at the eastern end of the Med. You won't find it on a map. Leon and I spend time there regularly.

'Good idea,' I said. 'They'll love it there.'

He grinned. 'As will Matthew. In fact, under the command of Professor Penrose, the three of them will probably knock up an energy-neutral hot-water system out of a rock and two twigs, install indoor plumbing, design and build an indoors to have indoor plumbing in, fall off a cliff, be snatched by aliens and

God knows what else. I'm an old man, Max. I'm not sure I can keep up. I need you there with me. And I miss you.'

I felt tears prick my eyes but only because I was exhausted and worried out of my mind. Just so everyone's clear. 'You do understand I can't leave St Mary's at the moment?'

'I do understand why you have to stay for now but try and give some thought to the future. I don't think you're going to fare well under this new regime, but I'll leave it up to you. Should I pay my respects to Treadwell before I leave?'

'What have you told him?'

'That I'm not done with my field test, that I'm still ironing out some problems and that I have to take it out again.'

'And the Archive?'

'Safe.'

I nodded. 'Don't tell me.'

'I wasn't going to. I'm sorry you haven't got to see more of Matthew. And before you ask if he still remembers you – yes, he does. It's Mum this and Mum that . . . on and on and on.'

'Really?' I said, quietly delighted.

'Yes, apparently Mum doesn't make him go to bed when he's not tired or change his socks or clean his teeth. You are a paragon of mumness.'

I smiled at him. 'Are you going now? Right at this moment?'

He smiled down at me. 'Oh, I think I've got an hour or so yet . . .'

I put my arms around him. 'I was wondering the other day – is there a square inch of our rooms where we haven't actually . . . ?'

'Don't know,' he said, grinning. 'I usually just close my eyes and pray for it all to be over soon.'

'Well, fortunately for you it usually is.'

He laughed. 'Remember, you're welcome to join us on Skaxos. In fact, I wish you would.'

'I will, but not now. Not yet.'

'Just bear in mind, Max – St Mary's isn't the centre of the universe. I know we have happy memories here, but we could easily go and make some more elsewhere. Even happier ones, perhaps. Yes, I know – not at this particular moment, but have a think about it.'

Three hours later they'd gone again and Treadwell came to see me in my office. Rosie Lee threw him one look and closed the door on her way out.

He looked down at me. 'Third and last jump, Dr Maxwell.'

I stood up. 'My people are paying the price for your people's incompetence.'

'Once again, Dr Maxwell – there are no my people and your people. We are all St Mary's.'

'Only some of us – the rest are dead or enslaved. And if, as I suspect, you intend to go ahead with your scheme to replace historians with Security personnel, you'd better get used to this. How long, do you think, before your employers query the massive number of employees you're losing? This was your people's first real jump and they made a complete dog's breakfast of it. And they're not the ones paying the price, are they?'

Treadwell ignored all that. Which is probably the best way of dealing with an enraged historian. I sighed. I seemed to be enraged all the time these days, and it was exhausting.

'You've covered the city and its surroundings, Dr Maxwell. Twice at least and there's still no sign of them anywhere.'

'We have to find Clerk and Prentiss. We never leave our people behind.'

He said nothing.

'I don't think you quite understand the conditions under which they could be suffering,' I said quietly.

Equally quietly, he said, 'Have you considered that they could be dead and you're actually putting more people at risk for no good reason at all?'

This time it was me who said nothing.

Treadwell pursued his advantage, informing me he was cutting back on the number of personnel available for the search. Apparently, other commitments and jumps were stacking up while we . . . He stopped.

I finished it for him. 'Waste our time on this?'

'Fall even further behind, I was going to say. I'm sorry, Dr Maxwell, but in situations like this, sooner or later the time comes to move on to other assignments. I understand your reluctance which is why I'm making the call on your behalf. If you like, you can tell everyone it was my decision and you resisted fiercely, but I'm sorry, the time has come to wind things down. Third and final jump. Two people only.'

'What? What can I do with two people? Are you deliberately abandoning them?'

'No, I'm perfectly happy for you and one other to continue the search as agreed, but I need to look at allocating resources elsewhere.'

'I want to continue the search.'

'We are decided then, Dr Maxwell. One final jump. You and one other. Are we agreed?'

216

I sighed. 'Agreed.'

'And then, on your return, I think you and I need to have a little talk.'

'Looking forward to it already, Commander.'

15

I considered taking Evans with me but in the end, I decided to leave him at St Mary's. He was quiet and competent and people trusted him. And I trusted him to do his best to rein in Hyssop. Without him – arguably the most important of the Security Section – there would be more Half-Wits than the original team. Yes, Evans should stay here. I mentioned this to Sands who immediately volunteered to come with me. An offer I accepted with relief and gratitude.

At least Treadwell hadn't put any sort of limits on the length of our final jump. Sands went to get the maps out – they were in a hell of a state by now – but I stopped him.

'I don't think there's any point in going over old procedures again. We've already covered every inch of this bloody city. Several times, in fact. I propose we dump it all on the god of historians. We'll just walk around. No plan – no purpose. Random wandering. Let's let chance play its part. We can't be any more unsuccessful, can we? And if we have to call a halt after this jump then at least we'll be able to say we've tried everything.'

He nodded. We had nothing else to try. By now, Clerk and Prentiss had been missing for months. The only positive was that summer had passed. And autumn, as well. We were beginning to creep into winter which made being on the streets a lot more pleasant. It was still hot, however, and would be until the rains came. They wouldn't last long but they'd be heavy. The streets would turn to mud. The Euphrates would flood, despite the massive embankments. Searching would be difficult and unpleasant so we needed to get cracking as quickly as possible.

We assembled all our gear ready for an early start the next morning, ate a miserable meal and then sat outside and watched the setting sun send long purple shadows across the city. It was all so beautiful. Stunning. Magnificent. And fabulous. There was still so much to document and record but I never wanted to see any of it again. I'd never be able to come back here without memories of Clerk and Prentiss. When I thought about how much I'd wanted to see Babylon . . .

Sands turned to me, his face grave. 'Max, I think we have to be prepared. We're not going to find them. They've been taken away somewhere out of our range and we have no idea where. Nineveh, Uruk, Assur maybe . . . It's the only explanation for us never finding a single trace of them.'

It was. Even if they were dead – if their bodies were in Babylon, then their tags should still have given us a reading.

'They might still be here,' I said, trying to hang on to hope. 'They could be right under our noses but it might just be that, after all this time, their tags are failing.'

Sands said nothing, and heavy-hearted, we turned in for an early night.

I was so tired and depressed the next morning I could barely be bothered to climb out of my sleeping module. And we hadn't even started yet. Nor likely to unless I got a move on.

'Here,' said Sands, handing me a mug of tea and taking himself off outside leaving me in peace. Obviously, Rosie Lee had him well trained.

I was only halfway down the mug when he crashed back in through the door, nearly trampling me in his excitement. 'I think I might have something.' He showed me his tag reader. I stared. Nothing.

'Dammit,' he said, giving it a good shake.

Nothing.

'Come on, you swiving useless piece of swiving shit,' he shouted, the traditional method of addressing tag readers.

Nothing. Our tag readers are shit.

I sighed. A last-moment flicker? Wishful thinking on his part, I suspected.

And then . . .

I stared in disbelief. There was a faint, a very faint spike. Then it was gone. Then a flicker. Then it was gone again.

I fell out of the sleeping module and scrambled into my shawls. Sands was waiting for me outside. 'Over there, some-where.' He gestured towards the canal. 'Close, anyway.'

I peered at the reader. 'Has it come back?'

'No – and it's only by the greatest good luck that I happened to be looking at it at the time. I suspect that was its final gasp. I think it's Clerk.'

I gabbled in my excitement. 'Oh my God. Is he all right? Has he always been here? How did we miss him? What about Prentiss?'

'I don't know is the answer to any of that. Come on. The signal was so faint I don't think he can be more than a couple of hundred yards away . . . in this direction. I think.'

He strode out – and just for Hyssop's future info, bionic foot or not I had to trot to keep up with him. We rounded a corner. We were in the north-west part of the artisans' quarter, trotting east into the rising sun, along the green banks of the wide canal separating the commercial areas. There were a lot of people on the banks already, washing, doing laundry, cutting back the reeds to make baskets. Keeping the canals clear was a continual battle. We carefully scanned every face.

There were slaves everywhere, drawing water for the three or four large brickmaking works quite close to each other. We walked past them all very slowly – the reader remained silent. And then, just as we turned to retrace our steps – a very faint bleep. We stopped dead and stared around. We were on the north bank of the canal, directly opposite the smallest brick-yard. The one on the end. There was the usual workshop – a fairly haphazard building made of odds and ends loosely tacked together, with sagging canvas awnings on poles to extend the working area. Against one wall, ten or twenty wooden crates full of bricks packed in straw stood ready to go. Wagons would turn up for them later in the day to haul them off to one of the many building sites around the city.

On the other side of the compound stood the great piles of ash, sandstone conglomerate and pebbles. The cobalt that would give the bricks their distinctive blue tiled effect was locked away and would be added at the end, painted on to the bricks which would then be fired.

Great vats of some sort of liquid stood inside more wooden frames. I had no idea at what stage of the process they were, but close by, half a dozen slaves were turning clay tiles out of the moulds and another half dozen were carrying already dried bricks across the compound and stacking them neatly.

'There – there. There's Clerk,' said Sands, careful not to point.

I stared across the canal, blinking in the low sun. 'Where?'

'There. By that pile of wooden slats.'

I would never have recognised him. Skinny. Emaciated. Filthy. Long bushy hair and beard. Burned brown by the sun. Bare feet. His sandals had either been stolen or just plain disintegrated. He was wearing a skimpy loincloth. In fact, he had more fabric twisted around his head than he had tied around his waist. I'm ashamed to say that had I encountered him in the street I would have just walked on past.

The brickyard wasn't an enclosed compound. There was nothing to stop us entering but we didn't make the mistake of galloping to the rescue. We wouldn't make a move until we were absolutely certain we could get him out successfully. We sheltered in the shadow of a nearby wood-and-reed lean-to, owner unknown, and waited for him to notice us.

After ten minutes or so he straightened up from his brick stacking, wiped the sweat from his face with the trailing edge of his headdress and accepted a waterskin from the skeleton standing next to him. Sands stepped out from under the lean-to and raised his hand to shoulder height.

At first, I thought he hadn't seen us. He stood very still for a very long time and then, abruptly, turned away, hiding his face. Sands made a slight sound.

I put my hand on his arm. 'He's OK. He just doesn't want us to see . . .' and found I couldn't go on, either.

Clerk turned back again, nodded at us, passed back the

waterskin as if nothing had happened and carried on working. There wasn't much else he could do. Two very large men did nothing very much except stand around in the shade, watching everyone else work and finger their whippy canes.

I swallowed the lump in my throat and we stood in our tiny patch of shade as the sun inched its way across the blue sky. Winter might be approaching but it was still hot. I played with my shawl, running my fingers over the design on the material, tracing the patterns. I plaited the fringes over and over until one came off in my hand. So that was me in trouble with Mrs Enderby.

The day seemed endless to me. It must have felt ten times longer for Clerk. Even in the shade the temperatures were unpleasant. I had to resist the urge to pant. What must it be like for Clerk, toiling all day and every day under that blazing sun? Insects buzzed around my head, irritating the hell out of me. There were tons of mozzies here because of all the still water around – ponds, canals, ornamental pools, the river. You could hear the frogs croaking at night and the fluttering of insect wings everywhere.

We had ample opportunity to observe the brickmaking process. The rate of work was incredible. There must be an insatiable demand for bricks. Especially good bricks as these obviously were.

I sighed and broke the silence. 'He doesn't look that good, does he?'

'No. I'm not sure he'll be able to run very far or very fast. We're going to have to plan this quite carefully.'

He was right. I suspected that initially, Clerk had been con-sidered a fairly prime specimen. Well nourished, all his teeth and so on. He'd been worked hard, begun to flag, been sold on, been worked again, deteriorated some more, been sold on again and so on. Every time he would have been worth less and less. This movement might be one of the reasons for us being unable to pick up his tag. No doubt he'd been outside the city at one of the big slave markets. By the time we got there he'd gone. Sold. He'd been out of the city when we'd been looking inside and vice versa. And all that time he'd been a slave. And where was Prentiss?

'His signal's very weak,' said Sands, consulting his reader again, 'and we're practically on top of him. The power's failing fast. I'm surprised it's lasted this long. I imagine Prentiss's packed up long ago.'

'She could still be here somewhere, as well,' I said, stubbornly, because we'd gone from no chance to every chance in just one day.

He nodded vigorously. 'You're right – she could. Listen, Max, I think our best opportunity is right here and now. Never mind going back to St Mary's for help. If they move Clerk again then we'll never find him. His tag's on its last legs. They don't seem to be heavily supervised and I suspect one of the overseers has gone off for a meal. I don't know if Clerk will be locked up at night but we can't risk it. Shall we create a St Mary's diversion?'

'Of course.'

To my non-brickmaking eyes, the compound was untidy with all sorts of materials stacked haphazardly all over the place. Which was good – lots of cover. I'd already identified a pile of mouldy-looking straw they used for packing around the tiles. And behind that, a pile of very dry-looking timber.

Promisingly inflammatory, all of it. I could saunter between the piles of tiles, pause at the straw, stare about me, toss my lighted match and stroll casually away again. I'd need to be careful. There were other people around. The remaining overseer was talking to a small tunic-clad man who appeared to be making notes on a clay tablet. Something that would normally drive me into a frenzy of excitement. But not today. Today I had other priorities.

Sands stood up slowly and stretched. I did the same and straightened my many shawls.

'All right?' he said.

'Ready when you are. I'll set the fire. You get him away. Don't wait for me. We can make our way back to the pod separately.'

'For God's sake, be careful in the brickyard, Max. I don't want to have to rescue you, too.'

I stood straight, radiating classy but strangely unaccompanied Babylonian matron, inexplicably wandering around a brickyard and what are you going to do about it, buster? 'We have to get this right. This is our one chance.'

'Understood. He knows we're here. He'll be expecting something.' He paused. 'If this goes wrong, we could all of us be working in the brickyard this time tomorrow.'

'If we're lucky.'

I crossed the rickety old bridge and began to walk slowly towards the yard. I didn't want to draw attention to myself. Within the compound, Clerk appeared able to come and go as the work demanded. He wasn't manacled or restrained in any way. And it wasn't an enclosure. There wasn't even a formal gate. The canal was one boundary, a dusty track another, the

225

next-door brickyard another, and the dilapidated old building the fourth. We should be able to do this. But if anything went wrong then the consequences – especially for Clerk – would be dire. As I'd said – we only had the one chance.

I felt for my matches. All historians carry a small stash of basic supplies. Matches, a compass, water-purification tablets . . . Box in one sweaty hand, match in the other, I set off, walking slowly along the track, because rapid movement tends to attract attention. I looked straight ahead, not catching anyone's eye, but no one shouted. No one even seemed to notice me. Past a couple of empty crates. Past the pile of old wood. I stood with my back to the straw, looking around as if lost. Most of the slaves had their backs to me. The foreman and the clerk were still engrossed in their clay tablet.

Now.

I made myself strike the match slowly and calmly. Don't stab at it. Don't snap the match. Because if that happened then I'd have to fumble for another one and believe me, I was horribly exposed at that moment. Taking a deep breath, I struck the match and waited for it to flare. Stooping a little so it wouldn't have far to fall, I dropped it on to the straw. It disappeared into the depths without so much as a flicker and believe me, that was a very nasty moment.

One endless second later – not very long but easily long enough for me to imagine every disaster under the sun – I caught a little whiff of smoke. Time to go. I strolled away, hearing the straw begin to crackle behind me. Picking up the pace, I exited the compound, hurrying along the bank and back over the canal.

I paused on the other side of the bridge, stun gun hidden in the folds of my shawl, pepper spray ready in case I was needed as back-up, but Sands was already in the compound, lurking unobtrusively behind one of the many vats of something.

Part of the brickmaking process was repeated heating and cooling and I suspected fires happened quite regularly because everyone seemed to know what to do. Three or four men seized hides hanging from a hook, apparently just for this very purpose and began to slap at the flames. Others ran for buckets and containers, including Clerk who shouted, 'I'll get water!' In English admittedly but he was gesturing at the canal and the inference was clear. Seizing a leather bucket, he ran in the direction of the canal and then veered off at the last moment, running between the workshop and the packed crates. Sands grabbed at him and began to pull him away. Somewhere a dog began to bark. I hung around long enough to make sure no one followed them. They didn't – their attention was entirely on the rapidly spreading fire and the immediate damage – and so I pressed on ahead and then looked back to see what was happening. Because that worked so well for Lot's wife, didn't it?

They weren't far behind me. Sands was holding Clerk up. His legs were all over the place – a combination of nerves, exhaustion and the weakness that frequently follows overwhelming relief. No one was behind them but an ominous pillar of smoke spiralled up into the sky. Oh God, don't say I'd burned down the fabled city of Babylon.

I ran to meet them and together we helped Clerk into the pod. I slapped the door shut on the world outside and he was safe. Whatever his life had been these past few months, that was over now. But it would take a while for that to sink in.

Clerk collapsed on to the floor and put his head in his hands, rocking to and fro. He must have dreamed of this moment for so long, used it to keep himself going during endless days of back-breaking toil. I know from experience you can keep going during the tough bits. It's the sudden relief of knowing that it's all over that knocks the legs out from underneath you.

We gave him a moment. I busied myself with the kettle to give him a little privacy and Sands helped him drink some water.

He was filthy. Smothered in dirt and dust and telltale blue splashes from the dye that would mark him out as a runaway slave. I handed him his tea.

'Don't burn your mouth.'

He sipped, closed his eyes for a moment, then sipped again. Then the rest of it disappeared faster than bathwater down a plughole.

There were so many cuts and bruises on his arms and legs which could have been occupational, but when he leaned forwards, I saw several fresh, red scars across his back. There was an awful lot of matted hair and beard, as well. He looked incredibly frail.

I was desperate to know about Prentiss, but this moment belonged to Clerk. First things first. 'Are you hungry?' I said. 'Would you like something to eat? Or more water?'

He reached out his hand to me as if he still didn't quite believe it was me. 'Max . . .'

I gripped it with both of mine. His was rough and calloused and his nails thick and broken.

'I'm sorry we took so long to get to you. How long has it been?'

'Over a year, Max.' His voice was hoarse with disuse.

I stared at Sands. Oh God. A year. A year in hell. I took in the bruises, scrapes, insect bites, the all-over damage . . .

'I'm sorry,' I said. 'I'm so sorry.'

He shook his head. 'It's me that should say sorry. I lost faith. I waited every day. Everyone who walked past – I looked up, expecting to see . . . And no one came, Max. No one.'

His voice cracked. I looked at Sands. I'd never seen him look so grim.

I passed Clerk more water. Little sips and often were the way to go.

He wiped his mouth with the back of his hand. 'Those first weeks nearly killed me. And every time I couldn't keep up and flogging didn't work, they sold me on. I don't know where I would have ended up next because you can't get much lower than the brickyards.' He grinned without amusement. 'They must have thought I was too feeble even to be a flight risk. I wasn't even worth a set of manacles. You get fed by the number of bricks you produce and I've been on less than half-rations for months. I didn't have the strength to escape – and where would I have gone anyway? – so I just got on with it. Every day.' He looked away. 'And then, after a while you just stop hoping.'

This was true. Something similar had once happened to me when I'd been marooned back in 1399. At some point, you do give up on the past – which ironically is the future. You accept your fate and just concentrate on survival. At least he'd still had that survival instinct. I wondered at what point he would have quietly given up on everything? What would have happened to him then? Sold on again? Or pushed out and left to die on the streets? Or quietly strangled, his body tossed outside the walls for the desert dogs?

Clerk went on. 'And there's none of this *let's all stick together* and *I'm Spartacus* crap. There are so many different nationalities here we could barely communicate with each other. The weakest lost their rations to the strong. I once went nearly three days without food until I stopped being Mr Nice Guy and became as ruthless and vicious as everyone else. There was one bloke – I stole his food . . . He was too weak to defend himself . . .'

Tears ran down his face.

I gripped his hands. 'It's over. It's all over. We'll find Prentiss and then we're all out of here forever.'

He shook his head. 'No.'

A terrible fear gripped me.

'She's not . . . ?' I couldn't say it.

'No, she's not dead.'

Sands looked across at me. This was an astounding piece of good fortune, but we were both thinking the same thing. We shouldn't press him too hard. Let things proceed at his pace.

'Start at the beginning,' I said. Sands found a ration tray for him and pulled the heating tab. 'Tell us what happened.'

Clerk gobbled and talked at the same time. 'Hyssop and her bloody idiots are what happened. I tell you, Max, this is the second time I've been screwed by amateurs.'

Which was true. The idiot Halcombe had done something similar and Clerk's team had borne the brunt of that as well. There had been a fish fight in Caernarvon of which we were not proud.

'What exactly happened?'

'I don't know what they did – they were behind me. We'd finished at Esagila. Prentiss and I were packing our gear and moving away. I know Hyssop was somewhere around – I'd seen her out of the corner of my eye. The temple precinct was pretty much deserted after the festival. There didn't seem to be anyone around, just a few slaves clearing away the rubbish left over from the festival. I heard that idiot – the Scottish one . . .'

'Scarfe,' I said.

'Yeah. He was behind me. I heard him say, "Back in a minute," and when I turned around, he was trotting into the courtyard. Prentiss hadn't seen any of it and was moving out. She was going one way and he was going the other. I called him back and he ignored me. I said to Hyssop to get him back and she said just a moment. He disappeared inside. Ten, twenty seconds, Max, certainly no more, and then he was back out again. There still wasn't anyone around and I was beginning to think he'd got away with it after all and suddenly – from nowhere – there were people shouting, pointing, waving their arms . . .

'It was chaos. We scattered. I don't know where Hyssop and Scarfe went. I could hear her shouting to Scarfe. I don't know what she was shouting but it certainly wasn't "Save the historians at all costs" – and then they grabbed me.

'I think they thought because Hyssop was female that it was me who had told them to violate the sanctum. That I was the one in charge. Which I should have been,' he added bitterly, shaking his head. 'I shouted to Prentiss to run. I didn't even have time to use my com. Prentiss had no idea what was happening until they grabbed her so she wouldn't have had time either. The priests started to drag us away. I thought Hyssop's clowns would intervene and it would just be a case of running like hell back to the pod but . . .' He stopped again. 'They split us up.' He swallowed. 'Prentiss was dragged away. She put up a hell of a fight. One of them punched her. She stopped screaming.'

Clerk stared blankly at the wall. 'I struggled to get an

231

arm free. To call for help. Someone hit me from behind and everything's a bit cloudy after that. At some point in the struggle I'd lost my earpiece and com. I can only assume the same happened to Paula or that she was unconscious as well. When I woke up, I was outside the city. I was there for a while. There was a compound. Full of men. I kept waiting for Hyssop. Or if not her then you. That someone would be along any moment . . . Nothing happened. No one came.' He struggled for a moment. 'And then I wondered if Prentiss might be dead and everyone thought I was as well so you weren't looking for us at all.'

He stopped again.

'We looked for you everywhere,' I said, desperate that he should know this. 'Everyone who could be spared from St Mary's was here. And a few who couldn't. Everyone pitched in. We had tag readers, proximities, the lot. We searched. We shouted. Why couldn't we find you?'

'Well, the only thing I can think is that when I came round, I was out in the desert. It was night and I was looking up at the stars. Most of my clothes had gone. I think we were at an oasis somewhere. I'm sorry I don't know for how long. Time was . . . strange. I couldn't seem to measure it.'

I nodded. One of the symptoms of concussion.

'I thought it had only been a day or so but I discovered later it wasn't. Then I was moved again. I had no idea what was going on.'

'Do you know where you were?'

'Well, I suppose you'd call them some sort of holding pens. There were a lot of people about. We were divided up into groups. I've no idea what the criteria were. I don't know how long I was out there but they fed and watered us reasonably well. Keeping us in good condition for the sale, I suppose.

'Then, after a while, I don't know how long, a load of men turned up and we were filtered back into the city again. About a hundred a day, I think. Presumably they didn't want to flood the market.

'We arrived just before dawn and I was sold before lunchtime. It's . . . a pretty humiliating experience, Max.'

I nodded.

'My first job was hauling timber. They harnessed us like horses and we pulled great loads of it through the desert. My hands bled, my shoulders bled, my sandals fell apart so my feet bled . . . after a while I couldn't work so I ended up in some sort of kitchen, I think, carrying water. That wasn't too bad but it didn't last long and then I was humping rocks for a while, until I couldn't do that any longer and then I ended up at the brickyard. I'd given up by then. I never thought anyone would find me.'

I sighed. I hadn't yet told him this was our last jump. 'Do you know where Paula is?'

'Yes, yes, I do. She's here. In the city.'

I nearly fell off my seat. 'What? She's been here all this time?'

'I don't know if she's been here the whole time – maybe something similar happened to her. Perhaps all slaves are taken outside the city. It was a big holding area and we were all men. I assume they kept the women elsewhere. Is there another tray?'

'You can have one more,' said Sands, passing him one. 'And another in a couple of hours. You can't have forgotten the drill already. Eat and drink little and often.'

Clerk nodded and pulled the heating tab.

'Prentiss,' I reminded him, gently.

'I honestly thought I was alone for the rest of my life – which wasn't going to be very long – and then . . . one day . . . I was on water detail. We have to keep the water barrels filled up. Brickmaking is like a production line and if it has to stop for any reason – such as no water – then a lot of people get very annoyed. Anyway, no one ever wants to do it. Trudging endlessly to the canal and back for water . . . it's hard work. It was my turn and the sun was sucking the energy out of me. I was filling my umpteenth pitcher and . . .' he laughed, 'I looked across to the other bank, quite casually, and there she was, filling her own pitcher. I couldn't believe it. I shouted. Typically, everyone looked at me except Paula. I shouted again. I shouted so loudly I hurt my throat. She looked up and there I was coughing like a madman. I waved but I don't think she knew who I was. She crouched there for ages, just looking at me. She didn't wave. She didn't do anything. Then she stood up. Before I could do or say anything, she picked up her pitcher and ran away. I couldn't lose her. I didn't stop to think at all. I jumped in the canal and swam across – it's not very wide at that point. People were laughing at me. I scrambled out – dripping wet – and followed on in the direction I thought she'd taken.'

He ripped the cover off his second tray and got stuck in. Chicken stew by the smell of it. Sands and I exchanged glances. A second piece of luck. Things were looking up. About bloody time.

I hardly dared ask. 'Did you find her?'

He chewed, swallowed and nodded. 'Yes. There was no way I was going to let her disappear. I caught up with her behind the back of someone's animal pen and the next thing we were

234

surrounded by a herd of idiot goats who thought we'd brought their lunch.'

Neither Sands nor I asked what passed between them. That would be private.

'Do you know where she is now?'

He nodded.

'I think so. She described the street. The shop at the end, she said. The silk merchant's. She couldn't stay. Her owner gets nervous if she's away too long. And I had to get back to the compound before they missed me . . . You don't want to be an escaped slave in this city. Or rather, you don't want to be a *recaptured* escaped slave in this city. If they caught us . . . if they chopped off our hands and feet . . . or blinded us . . . Anyway, after that I volunteered for water duty whenever I could. It's a shit job and no one else wanted it so I got down to the canal quite often, but I never saw her again. She was reasonably dressed so I suspect she's a house slave, rather than working in a brothel or worse, but I don't know.'

His voice was rising. He seemed ashamed he hadn't tried harder to escape. Looking at him now I suspected that some days, he barely had enough strength to take one step after another.

Sands put his hand on his shoulder. 'Calm down, mate. We're St Mary's. We'll get her out. This time tomorrow you'll both be back home again.'

Clerk shook his head. Hair flew everywhere. 'No, you don't understand.' He put his tray down and put the heels of his hands to his eyes. 'She was pregnant and that was months ago.'

Shit. Shit, shit, shit.

I sat back on my heels. Now we had a real problem. Not so

much if Prentiss was still pregnant. We could get her out. But if she'd had the child and it had survived, we couldn't take it out of its time. Not without bringing the Time Police down on us again. And they might – probably would – take the opportunity to reopen the Troy investigation as well, which definitely wasn't something we could afford to have happen. Especially without Dr Bairstow to keep them at bay. So, the child had to stay and if the child stayed then it was almost certain Prentiss would stay too. It couldn't be more than a few months old and needed its mum. And if she abandoned her baby and it was a female child then it might well end up exposed on one of the municipal dumps or left outside the city gates for the wild dogs to carry off. No, I couldn't see Prentiss saving herself at the expense of her child.

He finished scraping his tray. 'How long have I been gone?'

I lied. 'A couple of months.' Nor did I tell him that if we hadn't found him this time Treadwell would have written the pair of them off and they'd have been here for the rest of their lives. That wasn't something Clerk ever needed to know.

We talked for hours.

'Two options,' I said. 'We go back for reinforcements to extract Prentiss or we attempt something ourselves. Here and now.'

Sands considered. 'The downside of the first is that we lose even more time and Prentiss suffers even longer. The downside of the second is that if we fail, we alert Prentiss's owner, Clerk is recaptured, we're captured and everyone dies.'

'You go back,' said Clerk. 'You must. There can't be any argument. You have to go back.'

Sands looked at him. 'You're not saying *we*.'

He shook his head. 'I'll stay here, try and get close to Paula and tell her help is on the way.'

'We're not leaving you,' I said. 'Not again.'

'You have to, Max. I can't leave her. We've been together for years. We're partners. You wouldn't leave Peterson.' He gestured. 'Or Sands. Or any of us. I have faith you'll come back for us.'

His point was valid. We'd only have one shot at this. We had to do it properly.

'I understand,' I said, reluctantly. 'But how safe will you be? Your employers will be looking for you.'

'How long will you be gone?'

'For you, hardly any time at all. A few hours. If that.'

'In that case, I'll find a hole somewhere and go to sleep until you come back.'

He suddenly looked exhausted.

'Are you sure?' said Sands dubiously, and I shared his doubt. So much could go wrong. Suppose he was discovered in our absence. He didn't look strong enough to fight off a light breeze.

He nodded. 'If I go back, then Dr Stone will have me in Sick Bay for days. Weeks possibly. I have to be here when we get her out. She's my partner.'

'I'll stay with you,' offered Sands.

'No, I'll be fine. Just . . . please . . . don't leave us here again.'

I took his hand. 'I promise you we'll organise the rescue teams and come straight back again. I promise you we'll get Prentiss out and you'll be there to see it. I promise you we won't leave either of you here. There will be a happy ending.'

'And we'll bring you back a smart new tunic and clean you up properly,' said Sands, practically. 'We'll tidy up your hair and beard and make you look respectable. They'll be looking for a ratty runaway slave – not a minor household servant or scribe.'

I looked at Clerk. He nodded. Sands nodded.

'OK then,' I said. 'It's dark out there. Let's find you somewhere safe to sleep. We'll go back and get everything organised. We'll only be gone a couple of hours. Then we'll get Prentiss and sort out what to do next.' I looked around. 'Gentlemen, we have a plan.'

We found Clerk a safe refuge only a few yards away. Behind what looked and smelled like an old goat shed, a sagging old wall was slowly returning to the earth from which it had sprung. Between the two was a shallow depression in the ground. And it was masked by the wall. We gave him a blanket and he curled up. It was dark and unless you were right on top of him, he was invisible.

'We'll be right back,' I said, handing him a water bottle and a supply of high-energy biscuits, and, not without huge misgivings on my part, we left him there.

16

And, finally, Treadwell showed his true colours.

I fought my way out of Sick Bay and went to see him, still somewhat resentful he hadn't come to me. It's true there were few things more frightening than opening your eyes to see Dr Bairstow standing at the foot of your bed, but that's not the point, is it?

I brought Treadwell up to date and waited.

And waited. He stared at me for a long time. I could practically see the wheels turning. I stared back. What was the problem?

'You see,' he said, eventually. 'I warned you. This is a risk to which women are particularly prone. It's not their fault – they can't help it – but they're exposed to hazards that don't apply to men.'

'Prentiss won't want to leave her baby.'

'In that case she has made her choice. That's what you women want, isn't it? To make your own choices? If this is hers then I'm not going to force her to return against her will. Bring Clerk back.'

'You can't split them up.'

'I think I can.'

239

'He won't leave her.'

'He doesn't have a choice. He works for me.'

'He'll resign.'

'Then in that case I think we can assume both he and Prentiss have sundered their link with St Mary's voluntarily and we should respect their wishes. Permission refused.'

I hadn't known I'd needed permission to rescue our own people and told him so. 'Dr Bairstow . . .'

'Is dead, Dr Maxwell.'

'Nevertheless . . .'

'There is no nevertheless, Dr Maxwell. I have offered to pull Prentiss out and you say she will refuse that offer. Mr Clerk has done likewise. There is nothing more to be done. And before you exhaust us both – it is their choice.'

'We're St Mary's,' I said tightly. 'We never leave our people behind. You're ex-military – I thought you would understand that.'

'They have elected to remain.'

I struggled to put my case calmly. 'Setting Clerk and Prentiss aside for one moment – have you considered the ramifications of your decision? Do you really want this unit to know their new Director will abandon them? Especially if it becomes financially expedient to do so? Yes, we might rescue you should you find yourself in difficulties, but only if it doesn't cost too much.'

'Dr Maxwell, a considerable amount of time and resources have already been—'

I interrupted. 'Wasted?'

'*Allocated* to this operation is what I had been going to say and the end result is still unsatisfactory. I will say it again – Clerk and Prentiss are electing to remain where they are. That is their decision. And I have to say, Dr Maxwell, I am, so far, very unimpressed with the performance of your department. The Amy Robsart jump was inconclusive and I was forced to intervene to prevent you wasting more effort on something that would show no return. Now, this big Babylon jump has ended in disaster as well. I have been calculating the considerable expenses incurred so far and . . .'

'I know,' I said, with mock sympathy. 'But only two people abandoned to a life of slavery, so inside your parameters of acceptable loss, surely.'

Treadwell spoke very quietly. 'On your return to your office you will find a list of assignments I have drawn up and I would greatly appreciate you giving them your urgent attention. And your department's urgent attention as well. I have made it very clear to everyone that it is in their own interests to follow my instructions in this matter. Accept it, Dr Maxwell – it's over.'

He turned on his heel and walked away. Someone else who recognised the value of always having the last word.

I went back to my empty office, threw Treadwell's stupid list of assignments across the room, put my elbows on my desk and tried to think. It wasn't easy to begin with. My mind was filled with images of Clerk waiting, day after day, for a rescue that would never come. After I'd raised his hopes. After I'd promised him everything would be fine, and then abandoned him to live a dreadful life in that glittering city. It would have been better if I'd never found him.

After a while I got up and made myself some tea. After another while I found a piece of paper and picked up a pen. I drew a cube on the paper and carefully coloured it in. Then I

241

began to write. I drew lines to connect words. I moved them around. I fired up my data table and looked at what it told me. I took another sheet of paper and drew up the revised version. I looked at it for a long while and then, in conjunction with my data stack, made some more adjustments. I transferred those to another piece of paper. I made another mug of tea. I read through what I'd got so far. I made requisition lists. I had to make sure I missed nothing because there would be no second chance. Not for any of us.

Finally, as the sky lightened behind me, I had a list of things to do and the order in which to do them, together with another list of things to beg, borrow and steal and from whom. I knew which pod I'd be taking. I also knew I'd be going alone. Which meant I probably wouldn't be coming back. Solo missions rarely work well but there wasn't anyone else I could take. It was all very well for me to lose my job – and possibly more – but I couldn't ask anyone else to make that sacrifice. Not because they wouldn't volunteer, but because they would. The whole department would come with me if I asked, and I couldn't ask because that would give Treadwell the excuse he needed to sack us all. The end of the History Department. So it was just me. Because that's what it always boils down to in the end. You live your life and you might think you gather people around you, but at the very end, when push comes to shove, you're always on your own.

I fired off a quick message to Mr Sands, asking him to come and see me at ten this morning. Then I sat back, cold and stiff, and finished off my tea, wondering if I'd missed anything.

Around the building I could hear doors opening. Lights came on. People clattered down the stairs in search of breakfast. I bent down and started to pick up the drifts of paper around my ankles and Rosie Lee walked in. She looked at me and my mess and said, 'Bloody hell,' just as I looked at the clock then back at her and said, 'Bloody hell.'

She scowled at the piles of paper, the used mugs, the still twirling data stack. I braced myself to lie on a governmental scale.

She held out her hand. 'Pass that lot over. I'll put it all through the shredder. You make the tea. And for heaven's sake, do your hair. You look even rougher than usual and don't think Treadwell won't pick up on that.'

It is continually being borne on me that I'm not anywhere near as clever as I think I am.

I honestly couldn't think of anything to say to her so I wandered over to the kettle and made two mugs of tea while she plugged in the shredder and I decided that, actually, having a PA who knew when to shred the evidence was far more useful than having a PA who made the tea.

'David says yes, he'll see you at ten,' she said, over the noise of her infernal machine. 'Go and get your head down for a bit.'

Sometimes even I do as I'm told. I didn't sleep because if I did, I had a feeling I'd never wake up again, but I did have a shower and a bacon buttie. Not simultaneously, obviously. I climbed into a clean pair of blues and then pulled down my sports bag off the wardrobe and packed a few essentials. Change of clothes. Toiletries. Meteorite knife. Book on Agincourt. Trojan Horse. No room for my now fading red snake.

I was back in my office at five to ten and it was spotless. No piles of scrunched-up paper where I'd thrown them across the room. No dirty mugs. Just all my lists bundled up neatly

243

and placed on my desk in a file marked 'Turd Stirrer – Annual Usage'. Rosie Lee had even retrieved Treadwell's assignment list, unscrunched it and pinned it to my notice board.

David Sands was prompt, walking through the door at exactly ten o'clock.

'You wanted me, Max.'

'I do indeed. Take a seat, please.'

I looked over at Rosie Lee who'd turned her chair to face me and obviously had no intention of leaving. I strove for tact. 'I shan't need you to take any notes, thanks.'

'Good, because I wasn't going to.'

I gave up. They were an item. They lived together. He'd probably tell her everything afterwards anyway.

I took a deep breath, suddenly not sure what to say. He solved my problem for me.

'Treadwell says we can't go back, doesn't he?'

'How did you know?'

'It's all over the building. When do we start?'

'I start. You stay.'

'I don't understand.'

Now I know why Dr Bairstow always fiddled with the files on his desk. I fiddled with the files on my desk. 'David, you're not going.'

'But—'

'You're not going because I'm leaving you the most difficult part of the assignment.'

'Which is?'

'I'm leaving you the History Department. There's a very good chance I'm not coming back from this one. And even if I do survive it, then Treadwell will be a fool not to seize the

244

opportunity to sack me. Not just for disobeying instructions but for theft, improper use of St Mary's equipment, breathing, and anything else he can think of. In fact, I'll be lucky just to be sacked. I'm not involving anyone else because of that. I'm not doing you any favours. I have no doubt he'll try and impose his own Head of Department and it will be up to you to deal with that in whichever way you think best. I'm probably not the best person to offer advice. It won't be an easy time for anyone when I'm gone but I hope you understand why I have to do this.'

'I do understand,' he said, steadily. 'I just don't understand why you feel you have to do it alone. The whole History Department will come with you if you'll let them.'

'And the whole History Department will find itself out of a job on their return. If they return. This is the opening Treadwell's been waiting for and I won't hand it to him on a plate. Let him be satisfied with my head. Make him fight for everything else.'

'You'll never pull it off. Not on your own. And then there'll be three of you trapped there.'

'My mind is made up, David. All I ask is that you look after the department. They're difficult and obstinate and never act in their own best interests and you're the best person I can think of to keep them safe.'

He sighed and shook his head. 'No.'

'David – please. It has to be you. Sykes is too young. Atherton's too nice. Roberts is too volatile. Bashford is too . . . Bashford. Van Owen is my second choice if I really can't convince you but she lacks worldly guile. You don't. Anyone who can deal with Calvin Cutter can deal with Treadwell.'

He smiled a crooked smile. 'I don't really have any choice, do I?'

245

'None.'

'Any advice?'

'Don't linger here out of a sense of misplaced loyalty. The moment might come when you have to get the pods and the people out of here asap. You know what to do – you've done it before. Recognise the moment and go.'

He nodded.

'And be guided by Dr Peterson. He's pretty good at this sort of thing.'

He sighed. 'Anything else?'

'Keep them together if you can. Once they start applying for other jobs you've lost them. You'll never get them back again.'

He stared out of the window. 'Oh God, Max.'

'I'm sorry, David.'

'Answer me one question,' he said, suddenly.

'What? Now?'

'Yes. If you want me to do this, then you have to answer my question.'

Reluctantly, I said, 'OK.'

'Why did you stop me going into Rushford that day?'

Ah. *The* Question.

Some time ago I'd died at Agincourt. As you do. Especially if you're French. Or Edward, Duke of York. Anyway, obviously I hadn't been allowed to RIP for very long. I closed my eyes in 1415 and opened them in the present. In Rushford. Long story.

Anyway, in my original world, David Sands had died. In this new one he was still alive. Over the years, though, I'd noticed that things that happened there did tend to happen here, although sometimes not quite in the same way or in the same order. For instance, at Agincourt, Peterson had sustained a bad wound to his arm which left it seriously weakened, but here, in this world, he'd been injured in Rouen. Same wound. Same arm. Maybe we should just keep him out of France.

David Sands had been involved in a bad car crash that left him in a wheelchair. He'd caught a nasty infection and died in my arms. Right in the middle of one of his stupid knock-knock jokes. One of the least favourite moments of my life. Then I'd come here and he'd been whole and healthy. Until the day he decided to drive to Rushford and I stopped him and probably saved his life. Neither of us had ever mentioned it before and now he had. What could I say to him?

Very carefully, I said, 'I had a bad dream. A really bad dream. The sort you never forget. You were a trainee. You set off for Rushford and were involved in a bad car crash which put you in a wheelchair. Your health wasn't good. You got an infection. You . . . died. If you hadn't gone to Rushford that day, none of that would have happened. So when I saw you slipping out of the door, I remembered the dream and I stopped you. It was no big deal. I didn't have anything to lose,' I said, lying through my teeth because that was the sort of day it was turning into. 'So I shouted a warning and you didn't go.'

'There was a huge pile-up that day,' he said slowly. 'On the bypass.'

'In which you were not involved in any way,' I said firmly.

He looked at me a long, long while and then said simply, 'OK.' And walked out.

I tried to give Rosie Lee the day off and would you believe it – she wouldn't go. I swear I'll swing for her one day.

I became cunning and changed tactics. 'All right, if you're

going to stay – put the kettle on and make a brew, type up my final notes on Babylon and do my filing.'

I gestured at the massive pile under my desk. It's my way of avoiding Data Protection. I have this idea – rightly or wrongly – that if it never formally enters the filing system then it's not subject to the Act. And, best of all, in an emergency, I could just throw the whole lot out of the window.

She just laughed derisively.

I shook my head. 'Rosie – not today. You don't want to be caught up in this. Take yourself somewhere public and be conspicuously uninvolved.'

'No.'

'For God's sake, why not?'

'Because I'm coming with you.'

I recoiled. 'You're bloody not.'

'I bloody am.' She nodded at my requisition lists. 'You'll never get that lot into a pod by yourself.'

'You read my confidential notes?'

'Of course I did. I read all your confidential stuff.'

No wonder she never had time to make the bloody tea.

'Why?'

'It's a lot more interesting than the non-confidential stuff.'

'No,' I said patiently. 'Why do you think you're coming with me?'

'Because you don't have anyone else, Max, and I don't think you can do this alone. Plus, Treadwell might be watching the History Department like a hawk but no one ever takes any notice of admin staff. We're all invisible until something goes horribly wrong and we suddenly wake up and find ourselves in the firing line. You could argue I'm just cutting out the middleman here.'

'Rosie . . .'

'And, as you always say – someone has to bring the body back,' she said cheerfully and I groaned and laid my head on my desk.

'Seriously, Max – you can't do this alone.'

I spoke into my blotter. 'Rosie, I'm probably not going to be able to protect you.'

'Well, of course you won't. *I'll* be protecting *you*.'

I had the strangest urge to burst into tears.

I swallowed it down. She was probably right. I couldn't do this part alone. I'd accept her help on the safest part – loading the pod and so forth – and then with that safely accomplished, I'd thank her, push her out of the door and go without her. There'd be hell on when I came back, but since I probably wouldn't come back, I couldn't see this being a problem.

She and I split up. Since I was the one under observation I went after the innocuous stuff.

Taking care to look grumpy and martyred and defiant – the traditional expression of an historian who can't get her own way – I set off for Wardrobe, passing two of Hyssop's Half-Wits in the Hall – Glass and Harper. They weren't doing anything in particular, just standing around. And watching for any signs of suspicious behaviour on the part of the History Department, I suspected.

I halted. I didn't see why I shouldn't have a little fun. I called over to Sykes and Roberts.

'Guys – we've got a couple of lost Security guards here. Can someone sort them out, please? Find out where they're going and write it down for them. Use your crayons.'

I turned back. 'We really are an us-and-them outfit these days, aren't we? Fortunately, I'm on Team Us.'

'And me,' said Sykes, appearing at my elbow and grinning up at them.

'And me,' said Roberts.

There was the sound of chairs being pushed back. Glass and Harper stepped slightly apart to give themselves room.

I lowered my voice. 'I think you should go now. You're not welcome here. My department's just lost two team members thanks to you and your useless boss, and this isn't a particularly safe environment for you. Security is that way.' I pointed. 'And don't forget to hold hands – just in case you lose anyone else on the way.'

There was a long second's silence – during which the traditional tumbleweed rolled through the Hall – and then, red-faced, they left.

I picked up two sewing kits from Mrs Enderby – needles, pins, thread and so forth. I also snagged two packs of candles, a dozen boxes of matches, two packs of firelighters, some water purification tablets and some string. My story, should I be stopped, was that I was restocking the pods after Babylon. Less easy to explain were the set of knives from the kitchen – which Mrs Mack had unaccountably left out on a worktop for some reason – and a large cooking pot with a lid, into which I tipped everything. Oh – and a bucket.

Mrs Midgley stopped me in the Hall. She didn't look happy; I braced myself. 'Dr Maxwell, I had to throw away *all* the blankets from Number Eight.'

'I'm sorry,' I said guiltily. Poor old Clerk had been in a bit of a state.

250

She dropped three thick blankets into my arms, coincidentally covering the bucket and its contents 'These are the replacements. Would you take them down for me, please? I'm very short-staffed this morning.'

She winked in a manner that led me to believe she had some ghastly eye disease.

Speechless, I nodded and then ran away.

Rosie Lee was waiting for me in the paint store. At her feet was a pile of emergency rations. A month's worth. I added my stuff to the pile and I was tempted to jump there and then since we'd got away with everything so easily, but we still had clothing to acquire.

Again, we set off separately and it was just as well we did because I ran slap bang into Hyssop. Literally.

Fortunately, I was empty-handed. She had Glass and Harper with her – they must have told her what I'd said – and she'd acquired the one whose name I could never remember and Scarfe along the way. I had no idea where the others were. I hoped, for their sake, they hadn't crossed Rosie Lee's path otherwise she might, at this very moment, be concealing their lifeless bodies in the shrubbery.

The best form of defence is attack. 'Oh look,' I said, 'you've found each other. How sweet. And you didn't lose anyone along the way. Well done you.'

Hyssop flushed an angry red but I'd just seen Rosie Lee quietly nipping around the corner. By distracting them I could also get a lot off my chest – two birds with one stone.

'Is this the Security Section way of doing things from now on? Staffing our assignments with half-trained Half-Wits? Always coming back with fewer people than you set out with?'

I moved closer so only she could hear. 'I don't know who you're working for, Hyssop – it's certainly not St Mary's – but a quiet word of warning. No one here loves you. Wouldn't it be ironic if, one day, *you* were the one who doesn't come back?'

I stepped back again. 'Still – why should you worry? It's not as if it was your people sold into slavery. Have you any idea what Prentiss's life must be like at the moment? No, of course you don't. I doubt you've spared a thought for anyone but yourself since the moment you walked through the door.'

Scarfe shrugged. 'No one made her go.'

There was a moment's disbelieving silence and then a kind of blur. That's the only way I can describe it. The next moment Sands had Scarfe by the scruff of his neck and was shaking him like the rat he was.

Hyssop went to intervene and found herself sandwiched between Sykes and Van Owen.

'Go on,' said Sykes, smiling. 'I already have a reason to punch your lights out. Now all I need is an excuse.'

Hyssop froze. Sands let go of Scarfe who fell to the floor with a crash making funny wheezing noises.

Hands up all those who always knew the last thing I would ever do at St Mary's was to start a riot. However, I couldn't hang around. I turned to Hyssop.

'Treadwell won't say it but I will: you're not up to spec, Hyssop. Nor your people. You're bungling and amateurish and too arrogant to learn.'

She moved into a fighting stance. '*I'm* arrogant?'

'That's what I said. Your team's days here are numbered. No one here trusts you to have their back. Thank God we already have a proper Security Section in place. And I'll tell you this for nothing – Mr Markham would never have let people like you into the building, let alone have you on his team. I don't know why on earth you thought you'd ever be good enough for St Mary's. I'll tell you to your face, since everyone else is too polite – we're used to better.'

Behind them, Rosie Lee crossed back the way she'd come, laden with an armful of tunics, shawls and shoes. She held up two fingers. I hoped she was telling me she'd got the gear for Prentiss and Clerk as well as me – and not just instructing me to sod off. Not important – she'd got away with it. I, on the other hand, was about to be plastered across the ceiling.

It really was touch and go. Even I could see I'd pushed Hyssop too far. And in front of her own people, as well. I could only hope she was too professional to brawl in front of junior staff. An illegal jump to Babylon might be the least of my problems.

The silence through the building was absolute. I wouldn't be at all surprised if Treadwell wasn't quietly listening somewhere. I was living my last hours at St Mary's.

I risked another look around her. There was no sign of Rosie Lee anywhere. There are many alternative routes down to Hawking and if she'd any sense she'd have skirted the gallery, walked past R&D and then shot down the back stairs and out into the car park, around the building, in through the hangar – where Dieter would raise his eyebrows and look the other way – to wait in the dark paint store beyond.

On the other hand, this was Rosie Lee and it was perfectly possible she'd just stamped down the Long Corridor, alternately kicking people or turning them into stone as she went. It all depended what sort of mood she was in. And, not to underestimate my own contribution, I'd cleared her path because half of Hyssop's Hostiles were here at the moment, looking at me as if I was lunch.

A quiet voice intervened. 'Dr Maxwell, could you spare me a moment, please?'

I looked around. Peterson was standing on the half-landing. 'Of course, sir.'

I threw Hyssop a look which indicated I could tear her arms off any time I pleased but I had better things to do at the moment, and deliberately turned my back on them.

As we gained the gallery Peterson said mildly, 'I'm sure if Markham were here, he would remonstrate with you on the folly of taking on three or four adversaries without securing your exit route first. Seriously, Max.'

'Sorry,' I said. 'Won't happen again.' Which was true.

We both leaned over the banisters and watched six historians all very plainly present and very nearly correct, slowly going back to work. He looked back at me and sighed.

'It'll be fine,' I said, reassuringly.

'I'll come too.'

'No, thank you. I need you to hold the fort.'

'And suppose you don't come back? What do I do then?'

'Not my problem,' I said. 'It'll be you that has to face Leon. I'll be safely dead.'

He sighed. 'If Markham were here it would be the three of us going.'

I said bitterly, 'If Markham were here none of this would be happening.'

He sighed again. 'Just make sure you come back.'

'No problemo,' I lied.

He put his warm hand on mine. 'I've got your back here. Good luck.'

I swallowed hard. 'I've given the History Department to Mr Sands.'

He nodded. 'Understood.' He squeezed my hand. 'Max . . .'

I smiled. 'Understood.'

I left him standing there.

Rosie Lee was waiting for me in the paint store again and it was only as I closed the door that I realised just how strung up I'd been. I let my breath go in a long exhale. 'Rosie, I don't know how to thank you.'

She blinked. 'What do you mean?'

'Are you genuinely confused or has no one ever actually thanked you before?'

'I'm not the confused one here,' she scoffed. 'Bloody senior officers – I don't know how you get through the day.'

'Well, thank you, anyway. I'll take it from here.'

'No, you won't. I told you – I'm coming with you.'

'And I told you – you're bloody not.'

'I bloody am.'

'No – you're not. I won't even let my own people on this one.'

'I am *not* your people.'

Well, she got that bit right. 'I don't care. You're not coming so don't argue. For God's sake – why does no one ever do as they're told in this bloody organisation?'

She marched over to the wall and stood next to the fire alarm – the heel of her hand over the breakable plastic bit. 'I'm coming with you.'

I'd like to say my urge was to bang my head against the

wall but actually my urge was to bang *her* head against the wall. Nowhere near the fire alarm, obviously. I needed to get a move on. Treadwell wasn't stupid. By now he'd have Hyssop monitoring Hawking. And, while the entire History Department would cover for me, he was probably already demanding to know my whereabouts.

'OK,' I said. 'Help me load the pod.'

She looked around. 'What pod?'

I said, 'Door,' and a door opened in the middle of nowhere. I marched inside. I'd like to say I left her gaping but she was hard on my heels. Well, no matter. I could still push her out of the door when we'd finished loading. There wasn't anywhere for her to hide. It wasn't a big pod.

It wasn't actually my pod, either. Treadwell wouldn't find this one on the inventory. This was Leon's own pod. A single-seater with some interesting features.

We loaded it up, ramming as much as we could into the lockers and stacking the rest around the walls. Whether by chance or design, Rosie Lee ended up backed into a corner, almost completely surrounded by boxes and I remembered there was a set of kitchen knives in there somewhere within her reach. She glared defiantly at me over the bucket. Fine. I would just not let her out of the pod at the other end. She wouldn't want to stay, anyway. How often had I heard her declare we'd never get her into one of these bloody stupid things?

'I brought a set of clothes for each for us,' she said, dashing all my hopes. And not for the first time.

Quite honestly, I just didn't have the strength to argue and there was an advantage to having her along. My nose was too blunt. My hair and eyes were too light. My skin too pale. I

256

had no cheekbones to speak of. Rosie Lee, with her dark skin and hair, looked far more authentic than I did. Yes, she was completely inexperienced and I would need to keep an eye on her because otherwise that would be another one to rescue, but now I thought about it, I was glad to have her with me. To have someone who could help me pull this off. I'd have the strength of the admin department behind me. World leaders may think they're the ones who actually run things – all those shouty politicians who think they're the dog's bollocks – well, they got one part right – but it's the administrators that make it all happen. You want results? Go to the chief admin person. They've been ruling the world forever. Yes, only Rosie Lee stood in front of me, but behind her, row upon row, rank upon rank, stood the administrators of History. Back through the Victorian secretaries, Tudor clerks, medieval scribes, Roman administrators, back even to Hammurabi and his codes. All those and more stretched out behind her and I wasn't going to argue any more. Not for one minute.

'Make yourself comfy,' I said, giving in to greater forces, and she plonked herself on a handy box.

I changed back into Babylonian gear. Rosie Lee helped me with my tinkling headdress and many bracelets. I even wore my wedding ring because I had an impression to create.

After we'd done that, I helped her dress. Then I had to lay in all the coordinates which took a while. I had an anxious eye on the door the whole time. I was aiming for about three hours after we'd left Clerk. Long enough to maintain a safe interval – you can't be in the same time twice – but not long enough for him to begin to worry we were never coming back.

When I'd finished I looked around at Rosie Lee. She sat

demurely Babylonian, her hands folded, regarding me calmly. Babylon didn't know what was about to hit it.

I sighed. 'Computer, initiate jump.'

'Jump initiated.'

We landed with barely a jolt. It was definitely one of my better efforts. Rosie Lee didn't look particularly impressed. I sighed and deactivated the camouflage device. This was going to be a long day.

I made Rosie Lee wait in the pod.

'No,' I said as she opened her mouth to argue. 'I left Mr Clerk around here somewhere and I'm off to find him. I should warn you now that he doesn't look good. He's had a rough time and it's not over yet.' I pointed at the screen. 'I want you to monitor the cameras, please. You know how to operate a com and I've got my earpiece. If I miss him and he turns up here then I'll need to know.'

She nodded.

'OK,' I said. 'Coms check.'

'I can hear you,' she said.

That was because she was only two feet away from me but I wasn't going to argue with her in a confined space.

'Please do not leave the pod,' I said. 'I haven't had time to give you access and you won't be able to get back in again.'

She nodded. Admin staff are never this docile. Should I be worrying?

'I know where we left him,' I said, patting my amber necklace into place and straightening my bracelets. 'With luck, I'll be back in ten minutes or so.'

She nodded again and off I went. I closed the door behind me and looked around.

Babylon.

Again.

I remembered how excited I'd been on my first Babylon jump and now I was sick of the sight of it. I'd lost count of the number of times I'd traipsed these streets and always with the bitter taste of failure at the end of every jump.

The mud brick wall was still slowly returning to the earth from which it had been made. I called softly so as not to frighten Clerk into walloping me with a rock. There was a movement in the shadows and he emerged from behind the wall. He didn't look too bad although I suspected he hadn't slept a wink.

'I knew you'd be back,' he said, and from the way he said it I knew he'd been worried I wouldn't.

'We're over there,' I said, pointing.

I had to help him a little, realising that if he was back in the brickyard, he'd have started work by now, his body functioning on automatic. But the unexpected hope of rescue at long last, along with this complete departure from the rigid structure of his day, had taken the last of his strength. We hobbled back to the pod. Rosie had the door open, which since I hadn't shown her how to do that, gave an indication of how she'd been passing the time in my absence.

I helped Clerk inside. He caught sight of Rosie Lee and recoiled. Which, to be fair, was most people's reaction even when she *was* in her proper time and place. 'Good God.'

She glared. 'And hello to you too.'

He stared at me, probably trying to envisage the magnitude of

260

the catastrophe that had wiped out all life at St Mary's leaving only Rosie Lee available for rescue duties.

She grinned evilly and passed him some water. He reached for it greedily. He'd obviously eaten and drunk everything I'd left him.

'No,' I said. 'Just a little at a time. You know the drill.' Three sips. Wait a minute. Three more sips. And so on.

He nodded. 'Where are the other teams?'

I honestly didn't know what to say. How do you tell someone their boss hadn't authorised their rescue? That under our new regime, St Mary's did, in fact, leave their people behind.

I thought quickly. 'It was felt, given Miss Prentiss's probable position as a house slave, that an all-female team would stand a greater chance of success. Should that prove not to be the case, greater forces will be deployed. They are currently in reserve.'

Impressive – and every word of it a lie. God, I'm good.

I could see him wanting to ask why not Van Owen, or Sykes, or even Lingoss or Kalinda, but, in the face of Rosie Lee's unspoken hostility – understandably bottling out.

He turned to me. 'Is there any chance of a shower? I can't wait to get these rags off.'

'Sure,' I said. 'In you go and then I'll check over your wounds.'

'Don't drink your shower water,' said Rosie and she wasn't joking.

'We'll wait outside,' I said.

He shook his head. 'I've been paraded naked through the slave markets. I've been handled, poked, pulled about, had my teeth looked at. I've been bent over and had my anus inspected.

261

After a while, you really don't care. No offence, ladies, but I don't think either of you could top that.'

I didn't really know what to say.

'Did it pass?' said Rosie, suddenly.

He stared at her, completely bewildered. Welcome to my world, Mr Clerk. 'What?'

'Your anus? Was it acceptable?'

He grinned – a white crack in his brown face. 'As far as I know.'

'Excellent,' I said. 'And now the two of us, together with Mr Clerk and his world-class anus, can turn our attention to Miss Prentiss. Did you go back to try and identify the shop?'

I already knew the answer to that one. Of course he had. At first light, probably. His need to find her would overcome his need to remain hidden. They were on the verge of being rescued. She'd have to be warned to stay around the house and be ready for anything.

He nodded, but for the first time he couldn't meet my eye.

'What did you do?' said Rosie Lee, well versed in the ways of guilty historians.

'Well . . . I . . . um . . .' He stuck his chin in the air. 'Well, if you must know,' he said defiantly, 'I wasn't sure which building it was . . .'

'Yes . . . and . . .' demanded Rosie Lee.

'Well, I sort of . . . sang at her. From behind the wall.'

There was a bit of a pause. No one made any *Blondel* jokes.

'Well,' said Miss Lee, eventually. 'I should imagine she found that very helpful.'

I had to ask. 'What *exactly* did you sing?'

'Well, something like –' He raised a cracked voice in what he liked to think was song.

> *Don't worry, Paula.*
> *They're on their way.*
> *Just hang in there.*
> *It won't be long now.*

'Did she hear you?' demanded Rosie Lee. 'Because I'd be halfway to Nineveh if I'd heard that racket. Do *not* give up the day job.'

He said quietly, 'I don't know,' and hung his head.

I imagined him, dirty and exhausted, raising his cracked voice in song just on the off-chance that Paula Prentiss might be on the other side of the wall. Neither of them able to see or touch the other. Clerk taking comfort from imagining she was close enough to hear him and her taking comfort from knowing she wasn't alone. That help – finally – was here.

'It doesn't rhyme,' said Rosie, critically.

He refocused on her. 'Why are you even here?'

'I'm your rescuer,' she said. 'Because let's face it, if you relied on the History Department, you'd be spending the rest of your lives singing to each other over the walls. Like those people.'

He stared, mystified. 'What people?'

'When I'm calling you-ooeeoo-ooeeoo . . .'

She sang slightly less well than she PA'ed.

'That's terrible,' said Clerk. 'You can't make that sort of noise here. This is a respectable city and I've already been arrested for blasphemy once . . .'

'You say you didn't see or hear Prentiss,' I said. 'So you don't know if she's actually there.'

He lifted his head. 'I heard a baby crying.'

That was good enough for me. Babylonian law protected slave families from being split up so if the baby was there then Prentiss was there.

No one mentioned that it might be some other baby and we were on completely the wrong track. We didn't have anywhere else to look. If she wasn't there, I wouldn't have a clue what to do next. None of us would.

'Right,' I said, briskly. 'You get yourself properly showered and tidied up. Scrape off all that dirt. Scrub your fingernails. Cut your toenails. We'll comb your hair and have a go at your beard. I want you clean and respectable. There's a decent tunic for you here and some sandals. You're a trusted family servant and I want you looking the part. Ready in one hour, please, Mr Clerk.'

Rosie and I sat outside in the shade, quietly watching the morning progress. Around us, street life was getting going. Men emerged and stood in the street, scratching and yawning. Children and dogs scuttled out of doorways, either to perform household tasks, or more likely, getting out from under everyone's feet and being told to push off somewhere else. I could see wooden shutters being thrown open, and women on the roofs, shaking out sleeping mats and hanging them in the sun to air. Aromatic smoke from cooking fires wafted over the walls.

I asked her what she thought of the fabled city of Babylon.

'I've got sand in my bra.'

We sat a while longer and then she said, 'It's never good

when men spend a long time in the bathroom. Do you think he's all right in there?'

'Go and tap on the door,' I said. 'I'm his boss. It would be weird. See if he needs any help.'

She disappeared into the pod. I don't know what she said or did but it worked. Clerk emerged looking quite like his old self. Well, half his old self, anyway. He'd lost an enormous amount of body weight and he hadn't been hefty to begin with. Rosie Lee had combed and trimmed his hair and beard and made a reasonable job of it. He reeked of hair conditioner and talcum powder. His blue tunic hung off him but the quality was good. And he looked respectable. Even his feet were clean. God knows what sort of state the bathroom was in. I'd think about that later.

I asked him how his Babylonian was.

'I've got a few words. I can get us by. It's very like modern Hebrew, you know.'

We ran over the plan a few times. It wasn't much of one. We'd be winging it most of the time. The History Department motto. Eventually there was nothing left to discuss. 'Right,' I said. 'Let's go.'

It was approaching noon when we set out. Clerk walked slightly ahead in his smart new clothes, carrying the closed basket in which we would supposedly put our purchases. The trusted family retainer clearing the way and ensuring no riff-raff troubled his exquisite mistress. For anyone who isn't clear – that would be me. I wore dark blue, embroidered in gold, and had swathed myself from head to toe in fine Babylonian shawls. I was even wearing make-up, although in these temperatures, probably not for very long.

For the first time ever on an assignment, I wore jewellery.

Apart from my wedding ring it was all fake, but I glittered and tinkled impressively. Tiara, pretty amber necklace and whole armfuls and anklefuls of bracelets.

Rosie Lee walked at my shoulder, holding an embroidered parasol over my head and complaining about it every inch of the way. But the effect was perfect. I was rich. A little bit exotic – foreign and eccentric as well – but mostly rich.

We strolled through the streets, taking our time. There was plenty to look at. Most shops in this area were simple – the goods piled up on a carpet against a wall outside while the vendor sat cross-legged in the shade, swatting the flies.

The larger shops were indoor affairs. A let-down front gave a taster of the goods inside – where the better-quality goods would be away from the sun and dust and leg-cocking dogs.

We would pause occasionally outside a shop and Clerk would gently fend off the opportunity-scenting vendor. Setting the scene. Getting the message across. Not just anyone could approach his mistress.

We stationed ourselves at the corner of a short street. 'I *think* it's that one,' said Clerk, taking care not to point. 'With the blue awning. He's not a silk merchant as we would think of him – you know, upmarket shop and posh customers. This isn't a prosperous area and I think he sells anything from rough canvas to medium-priced silks. He's probably just clinging on by his fingertips and desperate to break into a better market.'

'Useful,' I said and took a moment to have a bit of a think. We were supposed to be posh. He'd probably welcome us with open arms.

Clerk nudged me. 'Max?'

'Yes, ready when you are.'

We set off, strolling slowly down the street, stopping at every shop to examine the goods offered. This time Clerk followed on behind us. I could hear him telling kids and dogs to push off.

'She won't be in the shop,' he said from behind us. He was casting nervous glances up and down the street. I didn't blame him. We weren't that far from the brickyard. I honestly didn't think we'd meet anyone likely to recognise him as their former runaway slave but he was understandably uneasy.

I noticed a public well at the end of the street. There must have been something wrong with it the day that Prentiss had gone to the canal for water. A stroke of luck. Just the one but one is usually all St Mary's needs.

'He'll have boys to assist him in the shop,' he continued. 'Female slaves – Paula – will be round the back, working in the house or the courtyard.'

Rosie Lee and I lingered at the entrance to the shop. Just far enough away to indicate we didn't expect to be served because we were just looking. I've noticed this on several assignments. I don't know if it's a cultural thing or a temporal thing but shopping habits vary considerably in different times and places.

These days, we like to walk into a shop and have a bit of a browse. We wander vaguely around until we see something we like the look of and then look round for someone to serve us. The ever-vigilant shop assistant – who probably hasn't taken her eyes off us since we strolled in – then moves forwards, all smiles and helpfulness and things move on from there.

Other cultures don't work like that. People expect to be served. From the moment they walk into the shop they expect instant service. A shop assistant will walk at their elbow at all times, showing them around, answering questions, passing them items of interest to examine and so on. At some point he'll offer refreshment and everyone will sit down. Nothing so vulgar as a transaction will occur. There will be lots of talk of the weather, the war – there's always a war – or the idiot government – there's always an idiot government – their health, their children, every subject under the sun except commerce.

Eventually, quite casually, the shopkeeper will murmur a price. There will be consternation and horror from the prospective customer. An alternative price is offered – usually about a third of the shopkeeper's recommended retail price. He will then reel back in horror, demand to know how he can be expected to remain in business in the face of such a catastrophic loss, that he has an aged mother to support and so on. He will then lower his price a fraction. The customer mentions that times are hard and the merchant around the corner is doing a BOGOF, the merchant cries that he is ruined, the customer offers fractionally more, and eventually a price is agreed. Everyone smiles at everyone else and the customer departs for the next shop to do it all over again.

We couldn't do that – no time and no money. So we stayed well back, for the time being, ostensibly looking at the merchandise on offer but actually getting the lie of the land.

'All right,' I said. 'Everyone set? In your own time, Mr Clerk.'

He nodded, looked carefully around and began to ease his way past a small group of men standing in the shade of an awning, passing the time of day. Past children playing a game with small stones and lines drawn in the dust, laughing and shouting at each other. And then he turned off the street and trotted down a space too narrow even to be dignified as an alleyway, and out of sight.

A few seconds later, a voice rose over all the street clamour. To the tune of 'Glory, Glory, Hallelujah', he sang,

> *Paula, Paula, can you hear me?*
> *We are here. Be ready.*
> *Paula, Paula, can you hear me?*
> *Get ready to go now . . .*
> *. . . Rumpty tumpty tum.*

Rosie Lee rolled her eyes. 'I cannot understand how you people get through the day.'

'I hope she heard him.'

'All of Babylon heard him. People are laughing at us.'

'Get used to it,' I said. 'Occupational hazard.'

'Not for me.'

Clerk rejoined us. 'What did you think?'

'Again – don't give up the day job,' she said.

We turned our attention to the shop. Clerk had been right. The owner wasn't a high-class silk merchant. The outside of his shop displayed rolls of canvas, linen and ordinary, day-to-day fabrics. Such good stuff as he had would be carefully displayed inside.

We paused, all ready to be tempted.

As if by magic, the vendor appeared in the doorway, sizing us up at a glance. A bit odd. Not local. Jewellery. Good materials. A woman, but accompanied, so not a street-slut. I adjusted my shawls. He bowed and then stepped back and turned slightly to one side. A polite gesture invited us to enter.

Rosie Lee gusted another sigh and in we went. The interior

269

was very dim after the brilliant sunshine outside. Rosie Lee furled my parasol.

'He's greeting you,' said Clerk quietly, as the shopkeeper launched into a torrent of words.

I didn't allow myself to be rushed, staring around the shop and very careful not to let any hint of enthusiasm show. I wanted to give the impression I'd been visiting high-class silk establishments all week and his was at the end of a very long list.

A cushion-covered divan was propped against one wall. Carpets covered the floor. Rolls of silk stood against the walls, crammed on to shelves, or swirling across a low table giving tantalising glimpses. Some were plain, some embellished. They weren't top-quality silks but he'd made every effort, placing them carefully to show each other off and tempt prospective customers. A brilliant cerise tumbled across an acid green. The favourite cobalt blue was displayed alongside an orange terracotta. They might not be high end but he'd done his best and it looked good.

I allowed myself to be seated on the divan. Rosie stood at my shoulder. Clerk moved to the back wall out of the way, unobtrusively setting down his basket. Drinks were brought by a female slave. I very carefully didn't look at her but Rosie Lee shook her head slightly. Not Prentiss.

I took a tiny sip of something fruity and set it down as if I wasn't impressed. Rosie Lee immediately waved it away.

As well as the owner, there were assistants everywhere – two outside and another inside, all male. I tried to listen over the merchant's gabble but I couldn't hear any women's voices or a crying baby anywhere.

The merchant was about my own age. Stout but not yet

270

fat, although I reckoned it wouldn't be long. His liquid brown eyes were heavily lidded and gave nothing away. He didn't look brutish. Prentiss might have been well treated although he'd obviously exercised the traditional slave owner's privilege. He'd oiled his locks and beard as all fashionable men did here and he was elaborately dressed in his own fabrics. A walking advertisement for the quality of his wares.

He and Clerk exchanged a few words and then we began. Roll after roll was pulled down off the shelves and tossed across the floor for my inspection, one on top of the other. They watched my face carefully – no language was needed. If I showed interest in something blue then other blues were unrolled and displayed. This was easier than I had thought it would be. There was no need for me to say a word. He was an expert at reading faces and body language so I made sure I remained impassive at all times.

Time wore on. I estimated we'd been here long enough. The sun was lower in the sky but we couldn't rush this. We just had to be patient. In an hour's time we could all be safely back in the pod. We'd done our best to alert Prentiss. With luck she would be ready to go at a moment's notice. What sort of state must she be in? I could not – must not – get this wrong.

I caught Clerk's eye and nodded. He slipped quietly out through the door and into the street. A comfort break was implied. Actually, he was going around to the back wall again. There was no back door. All houses were built around a central courtyard with just the one entrance which, in this case, was in full view of the shop. I hoped to God he wasn't going to start singing again.

I caught Rosie's eye. She nodded. It was time. This was it. I stood up impatiently because, obviously, nothing here was

271

good enough to interest me. Not a wise move as it turned out. As I stood up, I made a small sound and swayed. Rosie Lee swept forwards to support me. I put my hand to my forehead and said, in English, 'I think I'm going to faint.'

The merchant was in a quandary. Out on my own I might be but I'd belong to a man somewhere and no man would touch another man's woman. That was just asking for trouble. On the other hand, he wouldn't want an unconscious woman sprawled all over his special silks. And everyone knew women could have all sorts of mysterious but messy things wrong with them that decent men knew nothing about.

I let my knees sag and somehow, Rosie Lee manhandled me back on to the divan where I sprawled gracefully in a nest of medium-priced fabrics.

'Water,' said Rosie Lee, urgently. In English, obviously, but he got the message. Pulling aside a curtain concealing an archway, he shouted.

Nothing happened for a minute. Well, the merchant dithered helplessly, wringing his hands, but nothing important happened.

And then . . . She was soundless on bare feet, but it was Prentiss. She was here. We'd found her. My heart leaped. We were halfway home.

I don't know what she'd had to do to ensure she was the one who brought in the drink, but whatever it was, she'd managed it. She was closely muffled in dusty unbleached shawls with only her face showing. She carried a gilt tray with a jug and beaker. They rattled against each other. She was trembling. On the edge. I could hear her short breaths.

'Breathe,' said Rosie, ostensibly speaking to me. 'Breathe. St Mary's is here but things will probably be fine, nevertheless.'

272

Clerk slipped back in again, approached and under the guise of speaking to me, bowed and said, 'Where's the baby, Paula? Take the basket near the door. Put the baby in it. Put it back by the door.'

'No,' I said, bravely. 'I'm fine.' I tried to sit up, groaned theatrically and lay back down again. All eyes were on me, especially those of the merchant. Corpses in your shop are not good for business. People might think you keeled over because of the prices.

Prentiss left the tray beside me, eased her way through the concerned throng, picked up the basket and slipped back through the curtain.

I groaned a little more. Rosie Lee helped me sit up and sip from the beaker. I've no idea what it was but it was cold and quite nice.

From the corner of my eye I saw Prentiss slip back through the curtain and replace the basket, now with its cover fastened shut. I held my breath. If the baby made even a sound . . .

As soon as she stepped away, I stood up. Clerk tried to support me and I slapped his hand away angrily. Immediately he bowed and stepped back. The message, I hoped, was clear. No man was allowed to touch me.

We needed to be out of here fast in case the baby woke up. We'd be well and truly buggered if that happened.

I swayed again and Prentiss came forwards to take my arm. I smiled and patted her shoulder. Rosie casually picked up the basket and passed it on to Clerk who disappeared out of the door. That was the baby safely out of here. Now it was just us.

Supported on one side by Rosie Lee and Prentiss on the other, I nodded to the fibrillating merchant who just wanted me

273

out of his shop. And he seemed reasonably happy for Prentiss to assist me. We knew she was permitted to leave the house. And she'd be leaving her baby here as a deposit so of course she would return.

We dared not rush. Agonisingly slowly, we exited the merchant's shop and turned into the street. He gave us five or six paces for politeness's sake and then I heard the door close firmly behind us.

I could feel Prentiss shaking like a jelly beside me. 'You've got her?' Her fingers gripped my arm painfully. 'Tell me she's safe.'

'Clerk's got her,' I said. 'And we've got you. And in a few minutes, you'll both be safe.'

'He'll send someone after me.'

'No, he won't. Why would he? He thinks your child is still on the premises and you'll come back because of that.'

'But once he realises ... which he will ... he might already ...'

He did. Prentiss was right and I was wrong.

I could hear running footsteps behind us.

'Don't turn around,' I said. 'It might be nothing to do with us. Just keep walking.'

But it was to do with us. The merchant had sent one of his boys to escort us. Whether out of concern for me or to ensure Prentiss was safely returned to her rightful owner was unclear. What was clear was that now we had a problem. Well, of course we did.

I looked at the lad from the corner of my eye, assessing our chances of overcoming him should we have to. He wasn't a man but he wasn't a boy either. If figuring in a police report he would probably be referred to as a youth. He wasn't big – all of us combined could probably overpower him. Except he'd be yelling his head off and there were soldiers everywhere.

I sighed. And it had all been going so well. On the other hand he was paying us no attention at all, looking around him and obviously enjoying this unexpected free time.

'What now?' muttered Rosie Lee.

'Smile and keep going,' I said. 'Perhaps he's on his way somewhere else and just keeping us company.'

I don't think any of us believed that.

'We didn't do anything wrong, did we?' whispered Prentiss.

'Well, we have a stolen baby in the basket,' said Rosie Lee. 'Does that count?'

'It's *my* baby,' said Prentiss, her voice trembling.

'Not according to Babylonian law and custom,' I said. 'The two of you are a single unit but that unit belongs to the merchant back there.'

'How much further?' she said. Far from supporting me, I was holding her up.

'A couple of hundred yards,' I said. 'Nearly there.'

'We're going to have to push him into the canal,' said Rosie Lee, eyeing the youth who, in turn, was eyeing a group of young women at the well.

'That will be Plan B,' I said, firmly. 'Hang on, everyone, slow down a little.'

Rather worryingly, there was a large crowd of people ahead. We hadn't planned for this either, and the last thing we needed was our young lad alerting any of them. Mostly men, they were watching some sort of street entertainment hidden from us. Food vendors hung optimistically around the edges. I could smell hot onions on the air.

Clerk was waiting for us there. For one moment his face registered horror at our escort, who was craning his neck to see what was happening.

While he was distracted, I spoke quietly to Clerk. 'Can you and the baby lose yourselves?'

I could see he wasn't keen. He was far more vulnerable to recapture out on the streets on his own. And he didn't want to leave Paula.

'We'll create a diversion,' I said. 'Just slip quietly away. We'll meet you back at the pod.'

I tottered artistically for another few yards. Very slowly. We were almost upon the crowd which had spread all the way across the street. Anyone who wanted to get past would have to squeeze through the narrow chicane of men's backs and a largish table outside a shop selling fresh fruit and veg. And the ground here was muddy from the water a young boy was continually sprinkling over the produce to keep it fresh.

I said, 'In your own time, Mr Clerk,' and we began to ease our way through the crush.

The youth stuck close to Paula, I noticed, who in turn was sticking close to me. I gave a small cry of alarm at being in such close proximity to all these nasty rough men. Paula and Rosie Lee tightened their grips and the youth was forced to step back. Clerk and the baby just melted away.

A street vendor placed himself in front of me, grinning ingratiatingly and offering dates dipped in honey and rolled in either crushed nuts or street grit. Every fly in Mesopotamia hovered over the sweet stickiness.

Rosie Lee imperiously waved him away. He seemed reluctant to depart without a sale and in the end, it was the young lad who dismissed him curtly. I began to feel more kindly disposed towards him.

There was no sign of Clerk anywhere. 'Rosie,' I said, 'before he notices Clerk is missing – flirt with him.'

'What? Why me? You do it.'

'Don't be silly,' I said. 'I'm old enough to be his grand-mother,' and waited for them both to say no, you're not, and they didn't so I was feeling more than a little aggrieved as we plunged even deeper into the hot, smelly world of men.

'What's his name?' I muttered to Paula.

'They call him Abilsin. Son of Sin.'

'Oh, great.'

'Because he's a bit of a naughty boy.'

'Really? Don't just stand there, Rosie. Get stuck in.'

I gently let go of her arm and Paula and I began to drift to the right. Rosie craned her neck to see what was attracting everyone's attention and somehow got between the young man and us. She was smiling at him and he, poor lad, had no idea of the danger he was in. She gestured to him, giving him a sort of *what's going on here, can we get closer?* look.

He was a teenager, with an unexpectedly free afternoon and a pretty girl wanting him to show her what all the excitement was about. He didn't even hesitate.

Prentiss and I melted away behind a fat man in a too small tunic. From him we moved to another street vendor displaying some sort of pastries. I hovered artistically as if unable to make up my mind and then eased us gently around a group of boys and suddenly we were on the edge of the crowd.

We didn't look back. I walked us briskly down the street. Clerk was approaching. Minus the basket.

277

'All safe,' he said as we passed him, and I felt Prentiss sag with relief.

I patted her arm and said, 'Not far now. Mr Clerk, can you collect Rosie, please, before she injures someone.'

'On it,' he said, and disappeared into the crowd.

We were like a well-coordinated tag team. I was quietly proud.

Paula and I paused at the street corner. Within easy running distance of the pod, just in case anything should go wrong at the last moment. The wait seemed endless and by now my nerves were in shreds. We were here, alone. No back-up of any kind. If anything went wrong then all I'd done was make things considerably worse. Still we waited. No sign of Clerk and Rosie Lee. On the other hand, there was no fighting, shouting, screaming and no one had come to blows. The moments dragged by.

I turned to Paula. 'What will happen to Abilsin when he returns without you? Will he be sold on?'

'He's not a slave. He's Nabu's nephew.' I suddenly realised I'd never known the vendor's name. 'He'll probably get a clip round his ear from Nabu but not much more because Abilsin's dad is Nabu's elder brother and they're very hot about the respect due to the eldest son. And Abilsin's dad will compensate him.'

I nodded, satisfied.

More minutes dragged by and just as I was considering leaving Prentiss in the pod and going back to see what was happening, I saw Clerk and Rosie Lee emerge safely from the crowd and without young Abilsin.

Paula and I immediately set off towards the pod. So close . . .

I heard someone – Abilsin – shout.

Clerk and Rosie broke into a run. People turned and stared at them. There was another shout from the crowd.

Paula and I broke into a gallop. Bugger the heat. We flew down the street with me thanking God for kick pleats and attracting no end of amusement but not caring in the slightest. Because we were nearly there.

We kicked up little clouds of dust as we went. Rosie Lee had complained about sand in her bra but I had sand everywhere. We flew past shops, people and goats. We slowed down for the two soldiers on the street corner, obviously, sauntering past with professional nonchalance, and then picked up the pace again afterwards. All the time I was waiting for someone to come after us. Waiting for the sounds of pursuit. Waiting for the hand on my shoulder . . .

Clerk and Rosie caught us up and we all ran together. And then, finally, we rounded the last corner and there was the goat shed. And the crumbling wall. And the pod. I called for the door. One last burst . . .

Laughing – and crying a little bit from relief – we all tumbled into the pod.

18

We crashed inside, barking our shins on all the boxes and stuff stored therein.

Paula collapsed on to one of them so I couldn't help feeling it was a good job they were there. She was in tears. The unexpected rescue, the strain, the relief, the fear something would go wrong at the last moment, fear for her baby . . .

I snuck a quick look. The bits of her that were visible weren't covered in bruises. She hadn't been well fed but she'd been fed. She'd fared better than Clerk. Her voice was hoarse. She wouldn't be used to speaking. No one wants to hear what a slave has to say. She'd been here over a year, isolated by gender, status, language – the lot.

I left her to Clerk who took her in his arms. He was crying too. The pod was tiny, and crowded almost to bursting point, but we tried to give them a little privacy.

Rosie Lee squeezed into the loo – to evacuate the desert from her bra, presumably – and I fulfilled our primary function and put the kettle on.

Clerk passed the basket to Paula. She fumbled with the fastening and he had to do it for her. They opened up the basket together and stared down at the little baby. She was so small.

So tiny, but quite healthy-looking. All her limbs were straight and functioning. She had a little tuft of dark hair on top of her head. Her eyes were closed and despite our throwing her about in a basket, she was still fast asleep.

Rosie Lee emerged from the bathroom, peered over my shoulder and snorted. 'Typical historian.'

I couldn't believe it had all gone so well. I'd worried we'd have to abandon the baby and basket, or maybe float them down the canal and try to pick them up later. After all, babies were always being found floating down rivers in rush baskets in this part of the world. On the other hand, that sort of thing was frequently the precursor to exciting events and the last thing we needed was to start yet another religion.

Neither Clerk nor Paula were able to speak now, so we passed them their tea and tactfully gave them both a while to recover themselves.

Eventually, things calmed down a little.

'I have to ask,' said Clerk, moving away to give Prentiss a little space and edging himself around Rosie Lee, me, three boxes and numerous bundles – trust me, we could barely move. 'What *is* all this stuff?'

'This,' I said, 'is the beginning of your new life. We didn't just throw this assignment together. We know you can't leave your baby behind, Paula, and we know we can't take her out of this time, so we're taking you out of Babylon instead. I've been doing some research. I looked for somewhere with political and economic stability. My first choices were Carthage or Sicily but things are a bit dodgy between them at the moment. I looked at mainland Greece. I even looked at England, but there didn't seem much point because you still wouldn't be able to speak

281

the language and the climate is bloody awful. Then I started down the Ionian coast and found exactly what we needed. We're going to Patara.'

'Oh,' said Clerk, looking up. 'The Lycian League. Yes. Nice.'

'Patara?' said Rosie Lee. 'Never heard of it.'

Not many had. Founded by Patarus, a son of Apollo, and situated at the mouth of the River Xanthos in today's Turkey, Patara was a member of the Lycian League, which consisted of Xanthos, Patara, Myra, Olympos, Phaselis, Pinara and, according to who you're reading, perhaps Telmessos and Krya, as well. Patara was the administrative centre. It doesn't figure much in historical records which is usually a good sign. Hardly anything happened until 333BC when it surrendered to Alexander but that was a couple of hundred years off yet.

'A great choice, Max,' Clerk said, and I inclined my head with my usual becoming modesty.

And it was a great choice. Patara, situated on the Ionian coast, was home to the Temple and Oracle of Apollo, itself second only to the Oracle at Delphi. A thriving port and a prosperous and well-run city. In fact, the administration and government of the Lycian League was so efficient that the Founding Fathers used it as a model when setting up their own government. Wealthy and obscure, Patara was the perfect choice.

We turned our attention to Paula, now sitting quietly, clutching her sleeping baby, the tears still wet on her cheeks. Clerk hovered protectively nearby. Watching them, I rather thought the two of them might be all right. They'd been together a long time. Professionally, I mean. I had no idea what their personal relationship had been, but they were both calm, sensible people who would make this work. They were both free now but I don't think it had quite sunk in yet. An hour ago, they'd been Babylonian slaves. Now they had the chance of a new life in a new city. I felt my anger rise up at Treadwell and Hyssop again.

'There's no point in hanging around,' I said, turning to the console. 'If everyone's ready . . .'

Clerk lifted his head. 'What if someone sees us jump? There could be a bit of a commotion.'

I shrugged. Of the five of us, three were no longer historians, one of us was fast asleep, and the last one had never given a rat's arse in the first place.

'Computer, initiate jump.'

'Jump initiated.'

The world went white.

I checked the chronometer. 'It's around late afternoon. We can stay inside for as long as you like – we won't leave the pod until you're ready – but I think we should explore a little while it's still daylight. You can make some decisions about whether you're going to look for somewhere inside or outside the city walls – that sort of thing. Who's coming to look round?'

'Me,' said Clerk, standing up.

'I'll look after the baby, if you like,' said Rosie. 'You might want to go with them, Miss Prentiss. Remember, they're historians and you could find yourself living in the middle of a flood plain, or in the path of a landslide, or next to the local brothel or something.'

I think it was indicative of Paula's mindset that she didn't mention she was an historian too. She'd long since abandoned St Mary's – mentally, that is. I could sympathise. Something similar had happened to me when I was abandoned at St Mary's in

1399. There are stages. Firstly, there's denial – you rage against the fate that abandoned you there. Then there's the struggle to accept. She must have known, as soon as the baby was born, that unless she was prepared to abandon her daughter then she was never going home again. And finally, there's reluctant acceptance. *This is my life now. I have to make the most of it.*

We exited the pod and set off around the side of the hill, stumbling a little over the rough ground. I think we'd all become accustomed to the smooth streets of Babylon. The desert heat was gone. The breeze smelled of the sea. Small flowers nestled under the rocks. This was second spring. There's no autumn in this part of the world. As soon as the rains come after the scorching summer heat, everything bursts into life again. The day was warm but not scorching. And with the sea only just over there, the air was fresh and clean.

The landscape was typical Mediterranean. There were rocks. Lots of them. There were always rocks. Or building materials if you want to look on the positive side. And dotted among the pines were günlük trees. They could sling blankets up for shade during the day and sleep on them at night. When they found a suitable site they could build something more permanent. Clerk was obviously good with his hands. He even knew the secret of blue tiles – something he might be able to profit from here. Importantly, the hillside shrubs were green with new growth showing there was water present. And the city of Patara lay below us, a jumble of stone and wooden buildings following the line of the river.

The River Xanthos meandered its way from the hills over on our right down to the sea on our left. The world was perfectly silent up here and I was sure I could hear, faintly in the distance, the sound of waves crashing on the shore. The river itself was crammed, bow to stern, with shipping of all types. From big triremes, looking naked without their rows of oars, all the way down to little coracle-style boats zipping from one side of the river to the other ferrying people and goods. A constant stream of laden men carried goods on and off the ships. Once he'd regained his strength a little, Clerk should be able to find work easily. Best of all, he'd be a free man.

The banks were thick with buildings – granaries, brothels, warehouses and storage facilities. All of them built of stone, sturdy and permanent. Further up the hills from the river, the buildings became smart private homes and temples. There were plenty of people on the streets. I could see a long, paved street leading to the agora with shops on either side. An imposing amphitheatre was built into the side of a hill and only a little distance away, the bouleuterion. People bustled. There was lots going on here. Strangers came and went all the time. Clerk and Prentiss wouldn't stand out at all.

And, fed by the muddy river, the soil here was good. Cultivated patches of land were dotted both inside and outside the city. Every house had its own vines, fig trees and an olive grove. Small brushwood pens held a few goats or sheep. Away on a far hillside, I watched three or four donkeys plod a well-trodden path to disappear over the top.

'I think we'll stay outside the walls for a while,' said Clerk. 'At least until we find our way around the city. We'll find out what's where, how everything works, areas to avoid and so on and then move into the city when we're ready.'

It was a good plan. I looked around. We were standing in an east-facing hollow, concealed on three sides by a grove of pine trees. I could hear the wind whispering in their branches. It's one of the most peaceful sounds in the world. Right up there with breaking waves.

Paula nodded. 'Actually, I think here would do nicely. Within running distance of the city should we have to, but far enough away that no one will disturb us.'

Clerk smiled at her. 'Close, but not too close,' and she smiled back.

We trudged back to the pod, removed the baby from Rosie Lee's contaminating influence, laid out a blanket and piled it with all their new gear. Clerk tied the four corners together and heaved it over his shoulder. We loaded ourselves with what was left and walked with them back to the hollow. I saw Clerk stumble on the rocky ground. He and she must both be exhausted. I know I was. 'You sit down,' I said. 'We'll do all the hard work. You just tell us where you want things to go.'

We untied the blanket and laid out the contents for their inspection. I have to say, in this bright sunshine, what had seemed so much at St Mary's seemed pitifully little with which to begin a new life, but they were so delighted with everything, exclaiming with excitement as we revealed each new treasure. It brought a lump to my throat. For them, everything was special because two hours ago they'd had nothing. Things like the sewing kits would be more valuable than gold to them. And try preparing a meal without a pot to cook in. Or carrying water without a bucket. There were firelighters for when the wood was damp. Candles. String. An axe. A month's worth of rations. Blankets for cold nights. Stout shoes for winter. A change of clothes. Two cloaks. Even a small roll of muslin they could tear up for nappies. To them it was beyond price. To me it seemed woefully inadequate for their future life.

At last, it was all done. Clerk tied a length of string between two trees to hang one of the blankets over, which would give them a little shelter at night and some privacy for Paula to feed her baby, who was lying in the shade, waving her fists, kicking her legs and looking around in wonder.

I sat down beside her and asked Paula what her name was.

For the first time, she looked embarrassed.

'What?' I said. 'Is it something long and Babylonian and complicated?'

Babylonians do like to get good value out of a name. Some of them go on for half a page. Then they take a deep breath, hyphenate and carry on.

'No, quite the contrary.'

Rosie Lee got it before I did.

'Oh no. How could you? Poor little mite.'

'What?' I said, all at sea.

'They called her Max,' she said in exasperation. 'Talk about being handicapped at birth.'

Paula was scarlet. 'Do you mind?'

'No,' I said, delighted. 'Ignore Miss Lee. She has problems relating to the rest of the human race. It's a perfect name and I'm very flattered. She will grow up to be both beautiful and lucky.'

Not in the least bit like me then, but what else could I say?

And then – at last – the moment came. I don't often cry but I did then. We all did. We'd been through some stuff together and now I was leaving them here – possibly forever. And whether I would ever be able to come back was debatable. Not least because Treadwell was going to have me out of St Mary's

287

before I could even draw enough breath to argue. If I was lucky. He might well have me arrested. My future was nearly as precarious as theirs. No point in telling them that, though. They should concentrate on themselves and forget St Mary's. I'd done everything I could.

Or had I? There was no point in giving them any money, but gold has a value everywhere and anytime. I did hesitate but only for a second. I pulled off my wedding ring and handed it to Clerk. 'Here.'

He was aghast. 'Max, I can't take this.'

'You have to,' I said. 'You might need it one day. And if not, then it's a dowry for little Max.'

'But . . .'

'You can't afford to have any scruples. Either of you. This is my choice and I give you this freely. Let's hope it brings you good fortune.'

To his credit, he hesitated, but he was a practical lad. 'Thank you.'

'Right then,' I said, clearing my throat.

'Yes,' they said.

I wouldn't let them accompany us back to the pod. It wouldn't do them any good to watch the pod jump, taking us away but leaving them behind. Far better for us to leave them at the beginning of their new life in their new home. There was one last hug which we all had to cut short otherwise we'd have been snivelling again.

And so a tiny part of St Mary's was left forever on a rocky hillside in sunny Lycia. No more solid, reliable Clerk. No more cheerful, competent Prentiss. And I wasn't just losing historians – I was losing friends. Good friends. Best friends.

I turned back for the final farewell, squinting into the bright sun. There's a rigid formula for this sort of thing, which, I realised now, was designed to prevent everyone bursting into tears.

'Mr Clerk, Miss Prentiss – St Mary's thanks you for your service.'

Clerk nodded, too overcome to speak. It was Paula, shifting her tiny baby on to her other hip who held out her hand, saying, 'An honour and a privilege, Max. And thank you. We'll never forget . . .'

And that was her off, as well.

I tried to smile. 'Good luck.'

'You too, Max.'

This was a goodbye more final than I'd ever experienced before. I'd probably never know how their lives would turn out. I didn't even know if they'd survive the next twelve months.

My last view was of them standing in the dappled shade of a pine tree, surrounded by their few possessions. Paula was holding her baby and Clerk had his arm around her shoulders. They waved goodbye. I don't mind admitting – I was struggling. It went against every instinct to leave them there. I'd done what I could but it wasn't very much. And yes, I know it was their choice, but even so . . . I know what it's like to watch a pod disappear. That awful first moment when you realise you're utterly alone. That you will never go home again.

'You've done everything you could,' said Rosie Lee, disconcertingly reading my thoughts.

'I could have done so much more.'

'Not with Treadwell around,' she said. 'They will survive, Max. In fact, I think they'll prosper.'

I looked back once more. They'd already turned away. Off to make their own future.

My future, on the other hand . . .

I opened the door and we were back inside the strangely empty pod.

'Right,' I said to Rosie, 'my first priority is getting rid of you.'

'Well, there's a coincidence,' she said.

'Change back into your normal clothes. As soon as we land, nip out through Hawking. Dieter won't say anything. If anyone challenges you, you've been doing something in one of the pods.'

She stared at me. 'Like what?'

'How should I know? Why do I have to think of everything? You're quick enough with the excuses for never making the tea so I have every confidence in you to lie through your teeth. Failing everything, just turn everyone into stone like you usually do.'

She stalked off to the bathroom in huffy silence.

We landed back at St Mary's. I reactivated the camouflage device and had the screens on immediately, panning around, but the paint store was empty.

Rosie went to stand by the door, dressed in her normal clothes, all ready to leave.

I looked up from the console. 'Thank you. I couldn't have done this without you.'

'You're welcome,' she said. 'Actually, I quite enjoyed it.' She paused. 'I'll go and put the kettle on, shall I?'

'Rosie,' I said quietly, 'I won't be coming back to the office.'

I waited for the *But what about me?* It never came.

'You did a good thing, Max.'

I nodded.

'They're going to be all right,' she said.

I blinked away a tear. 'They've been dead for thousands of years, Rosie.'

She shook her head. 'You've got a crap job, Max,' and let herself out of the door.

I could only agree.

I was tempted to stay in my Babylonian gear. What would be the point of climbing back into my blues when I'd be climbing back out of them in about twenty minutes. However, let's not jump the gun. I undressed slowly, folded it all neatly because I didn't want to be accused of theft, left it on a shelf next to tins of paint marked 'Sunshine Yellow', and donned my blues for the last time.

I cracked open the door to the paint store but there was no one around. Nor in the Long Corridor, either. I began to wonder if, against all the odds, I might have got away with things after all.

Treadwell was waiting for me in the Great Hall. Of course he would be. Where he could make a public example of me in front of everyone.

He looked furious. As he had every right to be. He was a new Director, struggling to take charge of an organisation fiercely devoted to his predecessor. I'd deliberately and publicly disobeyed a direct order. I hadn't really left him any choice.

He stood in front of me and for the first time I was afraid of him. His face was tight and cold, giving nothing away as he looked down at me. The very quietness of his voice emphasised his rigid control. I wondered if he'd hit me.

I was charged, right there and then, right in front of everyone. Treadwell was making a public statement and he was using me to do it. This was the moment he finally imposed himself on St Mary's. I tried to tell myself I really didn't care, but when I looked past him, when I looked at Sands, Sykes, Mrs Enderby, all of them, I knew I really did.

I was charged with misappropriation of St Mary's property, disobeying a direct order, and finally, misconduct in a public office, which covered pretty much anything he might otherwise have missed. In other words, a dishonourable discharge. He told me I was lucky. Only my years of service were keeping me out of gaol.

'Really?' I said. 'I thought it was because you didn't want the world knowing how thoroughly you and Hyssop screwed this up.'

He looked around at the silently watching crowd of people. Everyone was there. Dieter had even brought his people up from Hawking.

He raised his voice. 'Should any of you consider following Dr Maxwell's example, I shall be happy to accept your resignations and might even manage a small termination-of-service payment as an incentive.'

'At this moment, I don't think you'll be able to dynamite anyone out of St Mary's,' said Sykes, grinning at him in a manner that made Hyssop flex her gun arm. 'I think I speak for everyone when I say we're all eager to see what Chief Farrell does when he comes back to find his wife missing.'

'Actually,' said Bashford, yanking out his scratchpad. 'If anyone fancies a small wager, I am accepting bets and giving odds on Leon of . . .'

'That's enough,' said Treadwell. 'Get her out of here.'

He wheeled away. Before he did me a serious injury, I suspected. I didn't hang around, either. I didn't want him enquiring too closely as to my mode of transport. Dieter would have no difficulty proving all the pods had been present and correct. I was hoping by the time he guessed I had my own pod it would be too late.

It was Hyssop who escorted me to my room. I was experiencing déjà vu on a massive scale. I'd done all this once before but at least this time I was prepared.

Stiffly, I climbed back out of my blues and T-shirt, folded them neatly and laid them on the bed. I dressed in jeans and a hoodie and pulled out my riding mac. My traditional getting-sacked outfit. And I made sure I moved very slowly. I made her wait for me.

I picked up my bag. If I'd thought that being packed and ready to go meant Hyssop wouldn't search my bag, I was wrong. She went through everything in it very thoroughly, but she was professional about it. She didn't throw my stuff around or break anything.

Wordlessly she produced all the paperwork. NDAs. Official Secrets Act. One month's pay. All prepared. All ready. Which was interesting. Had I been manoeuvred into this? Was this part of a carefully planned move in a whole series of carefully planned moves by Treadwell? Actually, did it matter? And did I care?

I signed everything in sight.

In silence – actually, neither of us had spoken a single word to each other – she handed me back my bag. I took it off her and walked out on to the landing. She followed me out and I very ostentatiously locked the door behind her.

'To prevent looting,' I said to her face, because what else could they do to me? Sack me twice? 'My husband will return soon and he will check our room over very carefully. If anything is missing – other than me, of course – he will come looking for you. All of you. He took down the Time Police almost single-handedly so I don't see your pathetic little bunch of incompetents causing him any problems at all.'

She led the way down the stairs.

David Sands waited for me on the half-landing. As I approached, he straightened up and offered me his arm. I clattered down the stairs to meet him.

They were all assembled in the Great Hall. Not just the History Department. Everyone. I looked for Rosie Lee and there she was, right at the back. Safe and undiscovered. She scowled at me, maintaining traditions right up until the very end.

Kalinda was leaning against the door to her office. She straightened as I walked past and inserted herself between Hyssop and me. 'You OK, kiddo?'

Treadwell stepped forwards. 'Please do not interfere, Dr Black.'

'I don't work for you, Treadwell. Although given your rate of attrition, very soon, no one will.'

'Nevertheless, you will . . .'

'Nevertheless I will be making a full report to Thirsk. I wouldn't be at all surprised if your people's dismal part in this assignment and your subsequent handling of these unfortunate events forms essential reading in all future *How Not to Manage Change* seminars.'

She turned to me. 'All right for money?'

'Yes, thank you.'

'Stay in touch.'

'I will.'

She walked off, shouldering Treadwell aside because she was tall enough to do it.

'Well,' I said to Treadwell, and was proud of my voice. 'It's only a very pale copy of the last time I was sacked but that's so typical of you, isn't it? Oh, and as I said to Hyssop: don't bother ransacking my room – our savings are hidden in the blue cushion on the sofa. Quite a large sum of money actually, for Hyssop and her team to divide between them.'

She flushed but said nothing.

Treadwell stared down at me. 'Why on earth would you keep a large sum of money in a cushion?'

'For emergencies.'

He smiled tightly. 'Doesn't this constitute an emergency?'

I'm the first to admit I'm short, but if you do it properly it's perfectly possible to arch your eyebrows and look down your nose at someone taller. 'You flatter yourself.'

His face was back to expressionless.

I rattled on regardless. 'My husband will return; I've no idea when. It's up to you, of course, but if the contents of our rooms are not in place and intact there will be a very nasty incident in which you, in your current role, will probably not survive.'

'And what role is that?'

'Scapegoat. Stooge. Fall guy. You don't know about the Time Wars. Or the Time Police. They haven't even bothered to brief you properly. I'd say your role here is not only that of scapegoat but short-lived scapegoat. Along with your people. Did they allow you to choose your own team or did they use this as an excuse to put together all the riff-raff they don't want any longer and foist them on to you?'

Great. Now I'd annoyed both him and Hyssop. There was a very good chance I wasn't going to get out of this undamaged.

Peterson saved me. As he always does. 'Max . . .'

I knew what he was going to say. I took him to one side.

'Listen, Tim, I'm gone, the Boss is gone, Markham's gone. You have to stand firm. You're all we have left.'

He leaned forwards and whispered in my ear. 'Don't forget my wedding.'

I nodded. He stepped back and cleared his throat. 'Dr Maxwell, St Mary's thanks you for your service.'

I shook his hand. 'Dr Peterson, sir – it's been an honour and a privilege.'

They applauded as I walked down the Hall. Mrs Mack and her team stood in the kitchen doorway, banging saucepans together. I waved to them. Professor Rapson had acquired some of those old-fashioned wooden football rattles and he, Lingoss and Mr Swanson were hanging over the banisters and plying them with enthusiasm. The cheering and whistling increased. Wardrobe waved strips of brightly coloured materials. None of it would do any good. Treadwell had got what he wanted. I turned for one last wave and then swung my way out of the front doors.

And that was it. I was out of St Mary's. Half my heart was breaking – the other half knew I'd done the right thing. Even now, I'd do it all over again if I had to. But I was leaving them. Leaving them to manage on their own. Thus considerably enhancing their chances of survival, said the sensible part of my brain, and I had to admit it had a point. Peterson would see them through. And Sands. They'd be all right. Or so I told myself.

It was twilight outside. And cold, because it was later than I thought.

I walked slowly down the drive, partly because I didn't want to give the impression I was running away and partly because, now that everything was over, I realised how completely knackered I was. When had I last slept? When had I last eaten?

The gates swung open as I approached and I walked through. To a new life, I told myself. Just like Clerk and Prentiss. We were all at it these days but at least I was in my own time and my own country.

I walked slowly down to the village. The street lights were coming on. No one else was about. The sky was clear and the stars were coming out. It would be chilly tonight.

I'm an ex-historian and it's always good to have a plan. I formulated as I went.

First	Blag a room at the Falconburg Arms.
Second	Something – anything – to drink.
Third	A long, hot bath.
Fourth	A good night's sleep.
Fifth	A good morning's sleep.
Sixth	The biggest breakfast in the northern hemisphere.
Seventh	Take myself off somewhere quiet and retrieve Leon's pod.
Eighth	Give said pod a thorough seeing-to before Leon saw it.
Ninth	Lunch. With dessert. Or possibly dessert then lunch.
Tenth	Off to find Leon and spend a very long time not doing anything at all. Apart from a little Leon at regular intervals.

I reviewed my proposed programme of events. Yep – all good.

Someone must have telephoned ahead. As I drew level with the Falconburg Arms, Ian Guthrie stepped out of the door, backlit by the light behind him. He'd been waiting for me. We looked at each other. I said, 'Good evening,' because Markham does like standards to be maintained.

He gestured inside. 'Come on in. We've got a room ready for you.'

'Did someone ring down?'

'No, it's been ready for you for over a week now.'

I assumed he'd known that Treadwell and I would bump heads sooner or later.

He led me into the reception area. This was the original part of the building with stone flags, a big fireplace and a small reception area. They had a new sign up on the wall.

House Rules

No singing.

No dancing.

No politicians.

No phones.

No laptops.

No wi-fi.

No TV.

No football.

No loud music.

No poncey beers.

No politicians.

Underneath, someone had scribbled, '*Sad gits only.*'

'And one just for you,' he said sternly. 'Because you're in the real world now – *no breakages.*'

I sighed and let my bag drop to the floor. Which might have been a mistake because I was never going to have the strength to bend down and pick it up.

He picked it up for me. 'Come and talk to me.'

I waved to Elspeth, serving behind the bar, and followed him into his office. 'Shouldn't you be out there in the bar?'

'No, Tuesdays are always quiet. Everyone's at home glued to *Combat Crocheting.*'

I sank into the familiar seat. He plonked a log on the fire. There was a tonic water waiting for me and I realised just how thirsty I was. I couldn't remember the last time I'd drunk anything.

He said nothing while I sipped slowly, following the same advice I'd given Clerk. When I'd finished, he refilled the glass and said, 'Sacked, eh?'

I nodded. 'Had to happen sooner or later.'

'What are your plans?'

'Hot bath.'

'No, after that.'

'Good night's sleep. And possibly a good morning's sleep as well.'

'And after that?'

'Join Leon. Am I OK to stay here tonight? I'm just too tired to do anything safely.'

'Of course.'

'I can pay for the room,' I said, just in case he thought I couldn't.

'Good, because I shall charge you for it.'

'Mate's rates,' I said.

'Depends whether you break anything.'

I smiled. I knew he wouldn't charge me for the room. Somehow, I'd have to find a way to give the money to Elspeth.

'You look really bad, Max.'

I nodded. 'I feel really bad.'

He shifted in his seat. 'I have to say, I've had this Treadwell bloke in here once or twice and he seemed quite reasonable.'

'He probably is,' I said gloomily. 'If I could work around him wanting to replace historians with a combination of drones and Security guards, and the way he costs everything down to the last penny, I'd probably quite like him.'

Ian shook his head. 'St Mary's couldn't go on as it was. Dr Bairstow shielded you all from the unpleasant realities of the world, but there have been murmurings from our overlords for quite some time now.'

I nodded. He wasn't wrong.

'It was an unfortunate beginning for everyone, Max. Dr Bairstow's unexpected death meant Treadwell didn't get the lead-in time planned. There would have been discussions as to ways to go in the future in which you would have been involved. He's a clever man – I wouldn't mind betting you'd all have come away thinking most of the new ideas originated from yourselves. Instead, everything was rushed . . . and with Markham leaving as well . . . that didn't help, either.'

'Not one little bit,' I said.

'No. Everything that could go wrong has gone wrong.'

'And now there's only Peterson left.'

'I have complete confidence in Peterson,' he said. 'Of all of you he's the one most in touch with the outside world. He'll get them through. And best of all, he'll get them through intact.'

I nodded. I had complete confidence in Major Guthrie. If he said a thing would be so then it usually was. And let's face it, without me there, locking horns with Treadwell and Hyssop every five minutes, there was every possibility things would settle down. 'The most important thing is that Clerk and Prentiss are safe.'

'Tell me what happened.'

I gave him all the details. Except about my wedding ring. I saw him cast a look at my left hand but I didn't wear the ring all the time so no clues there. I'd only worn it to Babylon to impress the silk merchant. I hoped Leon would understand.

My eyes began to close. All by themselves.

'Come on,' he said. 'Let's get you to bed.'

For some reason I thought that was hilarious. I giggled all the way upstairs.

We paused on the landing. There were three rooms available here. Two at the front overlooking the street and one at the back.

'You're at the back,' he said. 'We thought you'd appreciate the peace and quiet.'

'Very thoughtful,' I said.

He unlocked the door and threw it open.

I stepped inside. A very nice room with a pale yellow and green colour scheme that made me think of spring. The bed looked high and comfortable and there was a bathroom through the open door to my left. I could hear the bath calling out to me.

301

Ian handed me the key, wished me goodnight and left.

I closed the door and locked it, threw my bag on the bed and a voice I hadn't heard for some time said, 'Good evening.'

19

He was sitting by the empty fireplace, his chair turned slightly away from the door which was probably why I hadn't noticed him immediately. A glass of whisky stood on a small table at his elbow.

'Well,' I said, finding my voice. 'I think I should run back downstairs and ask Ian just what sort of establishment he's running here.'

He raised his glass. 'Cheers.'

I stayed still and quiet. I wasn't going to do anything until I knew exactly what was going on.

He stood up and crossed to the table under the window. 'I made you some tea.' He poured a perfect cup of tea and handed it to me and I was so gobsmacked that I took it.

He gestured to the chair. 'Do sit down.'

'Not until you tell me exactly what this is all about.'

'I shall be delighted to do so as soon as you sit down and drink your tea.'

He gestured again to the chair and I demonstrated my perpetual disinclination to do as I was told and sat on the bed. The tea was good though. I sipped and waited for him to tell me what this was all about.

He finished his whisky and set down his glass. The silence rolled on.

'Well,' I said, 'if you're not going to talk, then I'm off to have a much-needed bath.'

'Allow me to run it for you.'

'Don't you dare.'

'As you wish.'

We slumped into silence again.

I finished my tea. He took the cup from me. 'Another?'

'Not after two tonic waters, thank you.'

More silence. The only light in the room came from a shaded lamp over by the bed. I couldn't see his face very clearly. 'Why are you in my room?'

'I've come to speak to you.'

'For the purpose of?'

'For the purpose of offering you a job.'

'Me? A job?'

'I understand you are in need of employment, Dr Maxwell. Urgent need of employment.'

'And you're offering me a job?'

'I am.'

'What sort of a job?'

'Not unadjacent to my own occupation.'

'Let me get this straight, Pennyroyal. You're offering me a job as a bounty hunter?'

'Recovery agent,' he said reproachfully.

I was bewildered. 'Why?'

'I don't know why you're so surprised,' he said. 'I told you the last time we met that you would need a new job soon. I even left you my card.'

304

All perfectly true. We'd once encountered Lady Amelia Smallhope and her thug/butler Pennyroyal during an exciting visit to Scotland. They'd been pursuing a bunch of would-be assassins, we'd encountered said assassins, together with a bunch of deserting Scottish soldiers, and the whole thing had got rather out of hand. Lady Amelia looks and sounds much as you'd expect a member of the aristocracy to present themself. Pennyroyal is her butler – allegedly – and looks exactly what he is – a semi-trained thug who wrote the book on how to prepare the perfect cocktail with one hand while garrotting a troublesome guest with the other. The brutal haircut and icy eyes didn't help. His only redeeming feature was his complete devotion to Lady Amelia.

And now, here he was, in my bedroom, offering me gainful employment. At least, I assumed it would be gainful. It was always possible that after labouring for ten years my only reward would be my freedom. Or my life.

'I'm sorry,' I said. 'I should have thanked you for your kind offer. My only excuse is that I'm very tired, but I don't think I can accept.'

'Why not?'

'Well . . .'

He cocked an eyebrow.

'Well,' I said, 'for one thing, I have a family. Commitments. How long would I be contracted into this employment?'

'No contract,' he said. 'No paper trail of any kind. Payment in cash on completion of each job. Equal shares with me and Lady Amelia after expenses are deducted.' He paused. 'It's good money and you're gonna need some soon. That tutor friend of yours isn't cheap.'

305

'Stay away from Matthew,' I said. That was it. No threats. No bluster. Just a friendly warning.

'Fair enough,' he said. 'Hours are flexible – you can nip off and visit hubby any time you want. And you don't have to accept any job you don't like the look of. Board and lodgings provided. It's a good offer. What do you say?'

So help me, I was tempted. I'd been playing by the rules – mostly – and look where it had got me. Unemployed. And probably unemployable. I would be greatly surprised if Tread-well hadn't put the word out about me. Clive Ronan had once told me I danced on the edge of darkness and it wouldn't take very much for me to dance his way and his words had struck a chord at the time. Trust me, adhering to everyone else's rules is unrewarding, emotionally exhausting and not a lot of fun.

I could take a job or two, get a little cash behind me and then go back and make another life for myself somewhere. A proper family life with Leon and Matthew. With a nice indoor job where no one would try to kill me ten times a day. Something desperately dull and tedious, requiring no intelligence of any kind and very little understanding of the world around me. Local government, perhaps.

And Pennyroyal had said I wouldn't have to take any job I didn't like the look of. In a kind of twisted way, I trusted him. He'd murder me without turning a hair if it suited him but I didn't think he'd lie to me. It struck me – possibly slightly too late – that I knew some very strange people.

'How long do I have to think about it?'

'No time at all,' he said, collecting my cup and saucer and placing them tidily back on the table.

306

I gestured downstairs. 'What about Ian? What's he going to say when I'm not here tomorrow?'

He laughed. A throaty wheezy laugh to go with his throaty wheezy voice. 'Who do you think let me into your room and brought up the whisky?'

I gave in. I was tired to the bone. My thoughts, never coherent at the best of times, were beginning to disintegrate.

'OK,' I said, not having put up any sort of resistance at all. Nor asked any sensible questions. Like where this employment was. Or more importantly – *when* this employment was. Or where tomorrow would find me. 'I'll take it.'

'Good,' he said, getting up. 'I forgot to mention, you'll need your own transport. I'm assuming you've got a pod.'

I didn't look at my bag. 'I do.'

'Then let's go.'

I had to carry my own bag downstairs. It was very obvious he was Lady Amelia's butler, not mine.

We slipped down the corridor and, turning our backs on the sound of conversation from the bar, nipped out the back door that leads to the smokers' area, the garden, the car park and eventually, fields. It was quite dark by now.

'A bit too close to the buildings, I think,' I said and led him through the gate. There's a big field behind the pub where the village events happen. Peterson and Lingoss have hired a giant tent for their wedding reception here and Ian's organising the catering.

I looked around. There was no one in sight anywhere.

'Would you excuse me a minute, please,' I said.

He shrugged and wandered off to inspect the hedge.

I pulled out the Trojan Horse and stuck my thumbnail in

a place no thumbnail should ever go. The horse fell into two pieces to reveal the remote concealed inside.

Fifteen seconds later, Leon's pod stood in front of me. Still invisible, obviously.

'Ready,' I said.

He turned around, blinked and then realised. 'Camouflage device. That'll come in useful.'

'Where to?'

He passed me a piece of paper with the coordinates. You never touch someone else's pod. I don't know why but it's a rule everyone seems to adhere to. Me, St Mary's, the Time Police. And butlers, it would seem.

With a wave of his hand, he disappeared into the night. To his own pod, presumably.

It hadn't been so very long since I'd exited this pod. The smell of Babylon still hung in the air – spices, dung and hot dust. Suddenly I was back in the baking sun, the dust, the noise, the quiet desperation as we searched and searched. I pushed all that away. We'd found them in the end – try and remember *that*, Maxwell, not all the other stuff.

The pod was in a bit of a state. Leon would do his nut. There was still sand on the floor. The bathroom looked as if an ex-slave who hadn't had a shower in over a year had been in there. I sighed. I was going to have to give it a good scrub because it was my responsibility now. No more techies to run around and clear up after me. I'd have to remember to check the water and power levels regularly, as well.

I programmed in the coordinates Pennyroyal had given me and, too tired to worry about where I might end up, initiated the jump.

* * *

I had no idea where I landed. It was dark, I can tell you that. And given the smell of animals and manure, I was in the countryside somewhere. Which country and when, I had no idea. Nor did I care. My head was really beginning not to work very well.

I carefully shut everything down, which, because I was tired, took me much longer than usual, and exited the pod. Pennyroyal was waiting for me a few yards away. We were inside a large, dimly lit structure that felt and smelled like some sort of old barn. An old agricultural building anyway.

'This way, Dr Maxwell, if you please.'

'No,' I said, faint vestiges of common sense remaining. 'I can't just blindly follow you into the unknown. If I'm in the past, then I need to know. There's rather a lot of the past that already has me in it.'

'No cause for alarm. You're in your future. Not too far – just enough to avoid any inadvertent accidents. You're perfectly safe for the moment. Your temporal whereabouts are not something about which you need to be concerned.'

OK then. I followed him across a hard floor. He found his way to a doorway with a keypad. He typed in a number and pushed the door open. 'After you.'

I walked past him into a long, narrow, lighted passage that stretched in both directions.

Old house, was my first thought. To go with the old barn. There was a slight smell of damp stone. Doors on the left-hand side of the passage, windows to the right. Small windows with chintzy curtains. An odd choice for someone like Pennyroyal.

He pointed left to a door at the very end. 'Lady Amelia's private quarters. Out of bounds to everyone.' He pointed right to a corresponding door at the other end of the passage. 'My quarters. Ditto. This one . . .' he pushed open a door, 'kitchen. Lady Amelia would wish me to welcome you and say her house is your house. Please make yourself at home. Eat and drink whenever you feel like it.'

I nodded, too tired to do anything else. Quite honestly, if he'd told me the torture chamber was just next door and he'd booked me in for tomorrow at eight, I'd still have nodded, too tired to do anything else.

He looked down at me and said, 'I'll take you upstairs to your room, shall I?'

The clonky wooden staircase twisted up through the middle of the house. Shallow treads with a worn crimson carpet. Amy Robsart would almost certainly have survived falling down this one. At the top, again, the long passage stretched to left and right. Doors to one side, windows to another. My room was first left.

I opened the door to a bedroom. The curtains were snugly drawn and the golden glow from the small lamp gave everything a cosy look. There was a chimney breast with an empty fireplace. Double doors in the right-hand alcove were a wardrobe, I guessed. And a corresponding single door to the left.

'Bathroom,' he said, pushing it open. I could dimly see the usual equipment.

This was obviously someone's spare room. There were two single beds with plain white bedspreads; a bedside table with the lamp stood between them. A small table with a kettle and other necessities stood in the corner. To my right was a tall chest of drawers with a curved front which, by the smell, they'd used for storing apples once upon a time.

I was experiencing all the disorientation of an exhausted

traveller who arrives after dark and hasn't a clue what's going on. I was in another time and another place and I had no clue about either.

'I'll leave you to get settled in,' he said. 'Get up whenever you feel like it. There's nothing happening tomorrow so take your time. Sleep well, Dr Maxwell.'

It took me nearly four seconds to unpack. I stood the Trojan Horse, now with its remote control back in place, together with my other bits and pieces, on the mantelpiece in plain sight. I dumped my toiletries in the bathroom, noting the enormous number of fluffy towels provided. PJs went on the bed. I pulled open the second drawer – because the top drawer was above my eyeline – and laid underwear on the left-hand side, a spare pair of jeans in the middle and two T-shirts and a sweatshirt on the right. Job done. My shoes went under the bed and my riding mac behind the door. That was it. I'd moved in. I undressed, left my clothes on the chair, used the bathroom and crawled into bed. A small part of my mind was telling me I really should carry out some sort of recce; anything could happen while I slept. But sometimes you just don't care.

The bed was cool and comfortable. I pulled the covers around me and closed my eyes. It had been quite a busy day.

20

I woke slowly, wondering where the hell I was. I didn't recognise the room. All the furniture was strange and in the wrong place. I could smell apples. What the hell was going on?

I'm never brilliant first thing in the morning – although I rather suspected this was slightly past first thing in the morning. At St Mary's – where I obviously wasn't – no one would ever come near me until I'd had my second cup of tea. I could see a kettle from where I was. And a bowl of tea bags. And a matching sugar bowl. There was even a plate of lemon slices. Tea seemed the obvious way to go.

I made myself a mug, wandered over to the window and pulled back the curtains. I don't know what I was expecting but what I got was a country landscape. A long lawn stretched in front of me, down to a line of willow trees fringing the banks of a stream. An old, battered table with four chairs sat on the grass under the trees.

I opened the window and leaned out. I was in a very long, low, red brick building. An old farmhouse, I guessed. I counted eight windows on the ground floor and, I think, eleven along the first floor. It was difficult to be sure without actually falling out of the window.

The building was very old. Looking at the style of the windows, either late 1600s or early 1700s. If it had ever been modernised it had been very well done.

I looked left and right. Part of the building was covered in a creeper similar to the one at St Mary's. The one that turns red in autumn. This one was green so it was still summer here.

A long hoggin drive led up past the lawn and disappeared under an archway in the building.

I stood sipping my tea, and as I looked, one of those quad-bike things that farmers race around on shot out of the arch and headed down the drive. Apart from the crunch of tyres on the hoggin, this one was completely silent. Electric, obviously. Two sheepdogs raced alongside, their tongues lolling.

OK, I was in the country somewhere. Northern Europe. Possibly England. Probably England. Possibly. Somewhere rural. A working farm judging by the smell.

I sat on the low windowsill and sipped my tea. It was all very peaceful here. Other than the bloke on his quad-bike thingy, there wasn't another soul in sight. A couple of crows called from a group of trees to my right and behind them rose a series of low hills, patchworked with fields. A few cows grazed. So peaceful . . .

I finished my tea, ignored the temptation to climb back into bed and have another half hour or so and wandered off to have last night's bath. I washed my hair – there was even a hairdryer provided – and dressed in yesterday's clothes because there wasn't a lot of choice. That done, I went downstairs.

Pennyroyal was in the kitchen, sitting at the table doing some paperwork. He actually had a small pair of spectacles on the

313

end of his nose. Now he looked like an *intelligent* psychopath.

'Good morning, Dr Maxwell. Did you sleep well?'

'Very well, thank you.'

'Help yourself to anything you want for breakfast.'

The message was clear – he cooked for Lady Amelia and no one else.

I couldn't be bothered to do anything for myself so I made a couple of slices of toast and poured some orange juice. The day looked lovely and I felt the need for some solitude while I thought things through, so I took it all outside to the little table under the willows. Everything was very still. I could hear the stream burbling over its stony bed and then a voice behind me said, 'What ho, Max.'

I dropped my toast on the grass in shock.

'Oh my God. Markham? Is that you?'

'The one and only,' he said. 'Whatever you do, don't turn round.'

'Why not? Are you here in secret?'

'No,' he said nonchalantly. 'You just look better from the back.'

I leaped to my feet, toppling my chair and crushing my toast, and gave him a massive hug. With Markham here the world was suddenly a very different place.

He gave me a massive hug back. We stood for a long time and then he said, 'Good to see you again, Max. Did you miss me?'

I stepped back to look him up and down. 'I'm sorry – have you been away?'

'Not so's you'd notice, obviously.'

'You look well.'

314

He grinned his usual sunny grin. 'Yeah, not too bad.'

I looked around. 'Hunter's not here, then?'

'Why do you say that?'

'You're wearing odd socks.'

'Oh.' He looked down, helplessly.

In some exasperation, I said, 'Don't you have another pair?'

'Well, yeah, but they're exactly the same.'

We grinned at each other.

'How's Flora?'

'Beautiful. Well. Growing. She can hold up her head now.'

'Not something you've ever managed to do.' I looked around. 'Where are they?'

He shook his head. 'Not here.'

'Why not?'

'They're somewhere safe. I see them regularly.' He changed the subject. 'I gather you've been sacked. Again.'

I sighed. 'It's all gone to shit. I'm sorry, but I have some bad news for you. Dr Bairstow . . . has died.'

'Yeah, I know. Pennyroyal told me. I didn't believe him to begin with.'

'I didn't believe Treadwell, either. It just doesn't seem possible, does it?'

He shook his head. 'No. I thought he'd go on forever. He couldn't, of course, but even so . . . It's a bit of a bugger, Max.'

'I know.' I started on my depressing catalogue again. 'You're gone, I'm gone, the Boss is gone. Clerk and Prentiss . . . I have to stop doing this.'

'What?'

'Listing all the people who aren't with us any longer.'

'Peterson's still there.'

'Yes, true. But God knows what's going to become of St Mary's.'

He straightened my chair and we sat down. 'Well, you could say it's not our problem, Max. We're not part of St Mary's any longer and we have ourselves to worry about now.'

I nodded, picking pieces of grass off my toast.

I expected I'd have to talk about Hyssop and her gang of clowns and what had happened to Clerk and Prentiss but Markham was as up to date as I was. A line of communication clearly ran from Ian Guthrie, through Pennyroyal, directly to Markham. There wasn't anything I could tell him he didn't already know.

I gestured around. 'How long have you been here?'

'Oh, a while,' he said vaguely and I remembered there's no getting any information out of Markham if he doesn't want you to. 'It's not bad here and the pay's good.'

'You've been working for them?'

'I've done a couple of jobs, yeah.'

'What sort of jobs?'

'Picking up people, mostly. Pennyroyal tracks them down, I lure them into a dark place, incapacitate them by whatever means seem best at the time, cuff and stuff, then Pennyroyal takes them back to TPHQ and returns with a wad of money, some of which he gives to me.'

'You're working alone?'

'Only at the moment. Lady Amelia's off somewhere, doing something to someone, so I've had Pennyroyal teaching me the ropes – which I will now pass on to you. Apparently, you and I are the B Team.'

I sat back. So – now I was a bounty hunter. Sorry – recovery agent.

I finished my breakfast and Markham showed me around. There was a whole farmyard behind the arch. A proper old-fashioned farmyard with ancient but still working brick buildings built around a square. The long farmhouse formed one side. On the left was a large barn in which nestled their pod – or possibly one of their pods – and now my pod as well – and a couple of smaller barns with normal, more agricultural contents. A row of four stables stood on the south side, unoccupied for the moment. Four pigpens – again unoccupied because their owners were vacationing in the field behind the pens. On the right-hand side there were sheds storing colourful but complicated pieces of farming machinery and a Dutch barn full of hay at one end and straw at the other.

'It's a working farm,' said Markham. 'Owned by Lady A, I assume, but worked by the Faraday family, who hang out in a bungalow about half a mile away. They go home every night.'

'What on earth made Lady Amelia want to live here?'

'It's a good choice. Easily defended. Long low building. Accessed only through the archway which is gated and locked at night. Poor access from the rear because of all the buildings. To say nothing of three or four dogs running around so don't venture out there at night unless you want to be a canine midnight snack. Plus, we're miles from anywhere, there's only one road in and out . . .'

'All-terrain attack vehicles?' I said.

'Really boggy ground. Streams come off the hills every-where.' He gestured. 'Really, without installing minefields and gun turrets and deploying a battalion, they couldn't be much more secure. And, of course, they can easily get to their pod without leaving the building.'

I nodded. Not a bad set-up.

'There's a job coming up,' he said, moving to stand behind me as a chicken approached too closely. Markham and the animal world are frequently at odds and he always comes off worse. Even Angus bullies him and she's a sweetie. 'I expect Pennyroyal'll give you a couple of days to recover – got to say, Max, you're looking rough, even for you – and then we'll get stuck in.'

He was right – I had three days off to get some strength back and then there was a job waiting for us. We gathered around the heart of the house – the kitchen table.

'Josiah Winterman and Jack Feeney,' said Pennyroyal, laying two images on the table in front of us. Markham had explained they did very little electronically. Should anyone unfortunate appear through the door it would be a simple matter to pick up the files and dump them all in the kitchen range. Electronics leave a trail. Apparently, you had to know this sort of thing when you were on the wrong side of the legal establishment. If apprehended by the forces of law and order, the correct procedure is to demand a lawyer and then utter, 'No comment,' over and over again until they either go mad and release you or go mad and shoot you. 'Can go either way,' he said, serenely.

I expressed some doubt.

'Oh, come on, Max,' he said, grinning. 'Admit it – you've been training for this your entire life.'

'I do sometimes wonder whether Pennyroyal and Lady

Amelia have ever been tempted to the dark side. Do you think they sit planning bank heists during the long winter nights?'

'Nah,' said Pennyroyal when I mentioned this. 'We're on to a good thing here. Those bastards in the Time Police tolerate us as long as we do a good job and I will say this – the buggers pay well. We'd be idiots to jeopardise that.'

Back to the files on Winterman and Feeney. Not their real names, apparently. Pennyroyal wouldn't tell us those in case we inadvertently let them slip. Which showed he'd judged his audience correctly. These were the names they were currently using in the 19th century and these were the only names we needed to know.

Winterman was – had been – some kind of gang boss. His image showed a benign-looking silver-haired gentleman with a prominent nose. I thought he looked rather like a 19th-century clergyman. What that said about either him or 19th-century clergymen I don't know. He'd caused endless trouble and misery for countless numbers of people. He had started small and traditional – selling drugs across county lines.

Feeney was his enforcer. A younger man with curly hair and a cheeky grin. Not what I'd been expecting at all and certainly not the traditional muscle-bound goon, so his methods of ensuring unquestioning compliance with his boss's instructions must have been both imaginative and effective.

From these humble beginnings they'd moved into prostitution and trafficking – so far so yawn-making – but from there they'd somehow acquired a toehold in the construction industry and things really began to look up. For them, that is. The term 'compulsory purchase' took on a whole new meaning. People had stood in their way, of course – although only very briefly – because now rumour had it they stood – or more probably lay – in the car park of the award-winning motorway services station just outside Gloucester.

At this point this precious pair had made the evolutionary leap to respectability. Far from consorting with drug dealers, pimps, arsonists and murderers, they'd graduated downwards towards politics – 'Makes you wonder if they noticed any difference,' said Markham – and moved into the promising areas of blackmail, bribery, cronyism and so on. And since they had in no way relinquished their old skills – drugs, women, protection rackets and such – the two businesses merged seamlessly.

They overreached themselves, of course. They pushed someone too far and a cabinet minister hanged himself, but not before leaving several damning recordings all over the internet. The police closed in on Messrs Winterman and Feeney, who immediately buggered off to live in 1893. We were to fetch them back to face the wrath of the Time Police. I asked why the Time Police didn't do this sort of thing themselves. There were enough of them and it wasn't as if they were short a pod or two.

'They do,' said Pennyroyal. 'But they're busy, same as everyone else. Obviously, they don't want people knowing they're swamped. Lady Amelia spotted a niche in the market and we made them a gift of one or two people they'd been wanting a word with for quite some time, and now we're their go-to guys for when things get hectic. Or sometimes for those cases that require a more . . . informal approach.'

'Do they know about me and Markham?' I asked.

He shifted in his seat. 'We tend to keep things on a need-to-know basis. Shouldn't be a problem.' He frowned at us. 'As long as you're discreet.'

I beamed at him and Markham assured him discretion was our middle name.

'I'll leave these two buggers to you, then,' Pennyroyal said, getting up. He pushed over the files. 'There's the London address, together with the best layout of the house I could get.'

'Habits? Routines?' said Markham, rummaging through the papers.

Pennyroyal had kept the bad news until last.

'They rarely leave their house,' he said, kicking into touch my favourite approach, which is always to nobble people in a back alley and drag them into the pod before they know what is going on. 'I suspect they're paranoid about being found by the Time Police. You'll have to get inside somehow, overcome them and then get them both outside. I'll wait round the corner with a closed carriage. You whistle when you need me. We'll bundle them inside. Back to my pod. Job done and go.'

He disappeared to his room. Well, suite of rooms. I'd counted the windows and he had three rooms, including the armoury, at one end of the house – and Lady Amelia had four at the other end. Markham and I had a room each in the middle. No man's land.

We laid everything out and read it all. When we'd finished, we read it all again. Interestingly, there was no mention of the mechanism that had removed them from their own time to relocate them in another. I made a mental note to think about this later. Pennyroyal had provided writing pads so I wrote. Peterson and I used to do this all the time. On the occasions where we had to interact directly with contemporaries, we would devise scenarios to account for our presence in an unfamiliar environment. After about half an hour Markham and I exchanged pads.

'No,' I said. His idea was that I'd infiltrate the house as a maid of some kind – according to the notes they found it difficult to keep staff and I could guess why – and, once in, I was to drug them. Or something. He was a bit hazy on the detail.

My much better idea was that I gain access to the house somehow – charity donation, new neighbour, twisted ankle, whatever – and having lulled them, *then* incapacitate them – drug them, stun them, liaise with Markham, who would be effecting a more informal approach at the rear – i.e. breaking and entering – call up Pennyroyal, and then bundle them into the carriage, etc., etc.

'I'm female,' I said. 'There aren't many women in the Time Police. I'm obviously not young and fit – in fact, I'm so outside the accepted parameters of Time Police personnel that they won't suspect anything at all.'

Markham pulled a face but agreed. We made a colossal plate of sandwiches and a giant pot of tea, and got stuck in.

I have to say, it's brilliant being on the wrong-ish side of the law. Comfortable accommodation, good food – I should have done this years ago. Lady Amelia and her thug were professional to their fingertips. The facilities here were magnificent. There was everything we could possibly need. A whole room was set aside for costumes and equipment. Lady Amelia was a little taller than me but our colouring was similar and I had no hesitation picking out a rather smart outfit in a kind of teal blue. Striking and unusual and definitely not the sort of thing a discreet undercover agent would wear, as I informed Markham, who had selected a quiet cut-away coat with matching black trousers and a conservative bowler.

I scoffed and held up my costume. 'Are you sure you don't

want this one? It's ages since you've worn a skirt. I don't mind if you want to be the girl this time.'

He informed me I was the noisy distraction and he was the dark and deadly professional and could I stop calling him Oddjob.

I had to shorten the skirt – which caused me some problems until Markham threaded the needle for me. It took me the best part of an evening to tack it up. And I reinforced it with sticky tape at strategic points. As I said to Markham, it was only for a couple of hours.

I also acquired a small, old-fashioned clothbound notebook, and with a copy of Debrett's propped up in front of me, I spent a fun morning making imaginative entries. One or two in ink, the rest in pencil. In beautifully flowing copperplate, obviously, because as a child I'd had a girls' school inflicted on me and had therefore received an education based on social conditions in the 1850s.

Lady Hounslow	*£0 10s 0d*
Mrs Heppleby-White	*£0 12s 6d*

That would be Mrs Heppleby-White not wanting to be seen as less generous than her ladyship.

The Hon Mr M.H. Phrynne	*£1 1s 0d*

A whole guinea! I decided the Honourable Mr Phrynne must have won at his club last night and be in a good mood this morning.

323

Mr Wm. Allison	*£0 5s 0d*

William had lost his shirt to Phrynne and couldn't afford a larger sum.

Lady Ryde	*£0 10s 0d*
The Misses Cowley	*£1 1s 0d*

Only a guinea between the three Misses Cowley, I decided, because their father's recent death had revealed he'd gambled away half the family fortune and they were now living in newly straightened circumstances.

And so on and so on. About six pages of entries altogether. Then I tossed the little book about a bit, cracked the spine and dog-eared a couple of pages. I have to say, I did rather a good job there. It really looked as if it had been dragged in and out of someone's muff ten times a day.

On the morning in question I dressed carefully in my rather attractive outfit. White blouse, high at the neck, tight-fitting jacket, practical, ankle-length skirt and a jaunty little hat with a feather that curved over my right eye and which, I was pretty sure, would drive me insane before the day was out. If I lived that long.

I spent some time loading my muff. Notebook. Pencil. Two pencils, in fact, in case something happened to Pencil One. Pepper spray. Stun gun. Handkerchief. Spectacles in case there was an emergency and I had to read something. Unfortunately, they were too modern to be worn normally as part of my outfit. If I was going to do this full-time, I would have to acquire something less contemporary. Perhaps I could peer haughtily at the world through a lorgnette. I made a note to mention it to Markham on our return.

I knew there was a considerable armoury locked away in Pennyroyal's quarters. I, alas, was not allowed access. Not that I wanted to go in there – for all I knew he lived in some sort of cave littered with the bones of his victims . . . but I couldn't help feeling that a nice little lady's pistol . . . but sadly, no. Apparently, the Time Police deduct for damage to the merchandise. Given they're famous for shooting anyone who looks at them wrong – what a bunch of bloody hypocrites. However – no guns.

We took all the info with us although we'd have to leave it in the pod. Pennyroyal had the coordinates ready – I laid them in – and away we went. Markham and Maxwell – bounty hunters.

Sorry – recovery agents.

21

London 1893. Victoria was still on the throne and with a few years left to go yet. Industry and commerce reigned supreme. Black chimneys reared skywards belching their smoke into the already dirty air. A glittering aristocracy at one end of society – extreme poverty at the other. The British Empire spread across the globe. Hunger at home. Exactly the sort of place where our two fugitives could exercise their natural talents. God knows the sort of damage they could do here. There was very little legislation to protect women, children and the poor. I remembered the state of Matthew when Leon eventually rescued him from being a climbing boy. I couldn't remember anything from school about the Factory Acts. In fact, I was pretty sure I'd been asleep. Typically, my school had veered away from interesting History – pharaohs, curses, murders, regicide, bloodshed, violence and plague – and dragged me, fighting and kicking every inch of the way, into 18th- and 19th-century social History. I left them to get on with it and immersed myself in the probably less worthy but far more interesting Ancient History. It seemed a safe bet, that our two targets not only knew less than me but cared less than me as well. If such a thing were possible. However, from their point of view, the nineteenth century was a wonderful place to bring several dozen big bags of gold and make a fresh start. Within a very short space of time they'd have even more bags of gold, courtesy of their own particular brand of bribery, corruption and terror. And no real police force to worry about. I wouldn't be surprised if half the industrialists of this age were from the future.

Anyway, we were only interested in two of them. Josiah Winterman, who'd made his fortune in various unspeakable ways, and Jack Feeney, Winterman's enforcer who was probably even more unpleasant than his boss. Two evil men who'd made their own time too hot to hold them and thought they'd nip back to the 19th century to avail themselves of the many opportunities to do it all over again but better this time.

Or so they thought. Because now they had Markham and Maxwell on the job. It should have been Maxwell and Markham but we'd been unable to agree and apparently, rock beats scissors. I'd gone along with it because Markham's other big idea had been that I go as a prostitute – for no better reason, as far as I could see, than we could then call ourselves *Pros and Cons*. He'd been very keen on the idea. I wondered why I'd ever missed him.

We'd both rather liked the idea of *Slippery When Wet* as a team name but Pennyroyal put his foot down over that one. There'd also been a bit of a confrontation over Markham's call sign. *Combat Wombat* had been his preferred designation. Pennyroyal's silence was eloquent.

'Could be worse,' I said. 'It used to be *Horse's Arse*.'

His look gave us to understand that fifty per cent of that call sign had been correct.

*   *   *

327

We landed in a kind of ill-defined no man's land between two rows of modest dwellings. They weren't quite back-to-back hovels but they weren't much further up the social scale. And the site was a little more public than I was happy with.

Peering at the screen I could see the ground was rough and muddy with deep ruts where laden wagons had passed, presumably on their way to the smoke-belching edifice I could see in the distance. It had been raining so these ruts were now filled with oily water. A few wooden shacks crouched nearby but there were no fires – no signs of life. No dogs barked. No men shouted. We waited a few moments, just in case, but no one appeared. Not even a small crowd of curious boys and their dogs. Everyone was obviously out earning a dishonest crust.

Cautiously, we opened the door and got our bearings.

The day was cold and windy. Very windy. I had to hang on to my hat and the wind whipped up my skirts in a way I was pretty sure would get me arrested for reckless ankle-revealing if I wasn't careful. At least it wasn't raining, which was a good thing because even the most dedicated fundraiser wouldn't be out in that sort of weather. I skewered my hat more firmly to my head and hoped for the best.

Markham had put himself firmly in charge of navigation. His map, as far as I could see, consisted of a sheet of paper with a few streets and squares drawn on it in pencil. He was certainly embracing low tech.

'This way,' he said confidently. 'We pick up this street here, turn left at the end into Stratford Street there, and Swan Court should be on our left. About a mile.'

London was filthy. There was very little difference between the rough ground where we'd landed and the streets leading off it. The mud and shit were so deep in places that if you wanted to cross the road and couldn't find a small boy with a broom to sweep you a path then you stood very little chance of reaching the other side unburdened by waste product. Both animal and human.

I'd been to Victorian London before when Kal and I had set off to find Jack the Ripper and he'd found us instead. Something about which I still have the occasional nightmare. And I'd come back again to sort out old Ma Scrope. I had forgotten the dirt, the grime, the way you could actually taste the soot at the back of your throat; the way everything felt gritty to the touch; the rich, ripe smell of horse dung – nearly knee-height in some places; the noise of metal-rimmed wheels clattering over cobbled streets and the incessant clip-clop of hooves over the same cobbled streets.

There were chimneys everywhere – on houses and factories – all of them belching out dirty yellow smoke that seemed to climb about twenty feet into the air and then just hang like a sinister cloud over the city.

Looking in through the windows as we went, many houses had already lit their gas lamps. In one house, a middle-aged man and woman sat either side of a cheerful fire, each holding a glass of something. Sherry, probably. They were talking together and just for a moment I felt a slight pang for the sort of domestic peace I probably wouldn't enjoy very much. Or so I told myself.

A young paperboy, muffler under his chin and his hands black with newsprint, stood on the corner, piles of newspapers around his ankles, shouting something incomprehensible. Occasionally, a man would toss him a coin and take a paper. It's funny how some old customs linger. Leon always prefers to get his news from a newspaper. I, on the other hand, always feel that nothing interesting has happened since 1485.

The streets were a living tangle of horses, carriages, carts, dogs and pedestrians. Driving on the left had been mandatory since 1835, although actually, in this country we'd driven and walked on the left since the Romans had decided on our behalf. Apparently, it was to keep your sword arm free. Incidentally, it's not true that Napoleon forced Europeans to drive on the right. They were all on the wrong side of the road long before he turned up. Anyway, looking at the street in front of me, I don't think anyone had any idea of the correct side. Coachmen yelled at draymen who shouted at wagoners, and jarveys roared at everyone.

Pedestrians were moderately better behaved. Most women were accompanied, their male escorts walking on the outside – theoretically to protect them from oncoming traffic. All the men tipped their hats when stopping to speak to someone. Their formal manners shone like jewels among these dark satanic mills, although given the moral standards of the day, they then probably went home, knocked their wife senseless and rogered the parlour maid over her unconscious body.

I mentioned this to Markham who rolled his eyes.

'It's only just around the corner,' he said, attempting to distract me, I suspected. He consulted his map. 'On the left. Swan Court.'

'Nice name.'

A nice name for a nice court. A small open square was set back from the busy road, with three large terraced houses down each side and two detached houses facing us. Eight altogether. In place of the garden normally found in the centre of a square, railings enclosed the biggest London plane tree I'd ever seen and very little else.

'Fun Fact,' said Markham and I groaned because I thought I'd got away with it this time but there's never any escape. Not unlike Leon's approach to sex, all you can do is close your eyes and pray for it to be over with as soon as possible.

'The oldest London plane was planted on land belonging to the then Archbishop of Canterbury – although he probably didn't do the actual digging himself – back in 1685 and is still living today. The tree – not the archbishop.'

He gazed fondly at the magnificent specimen. 'They don't plant them like this any more. Modern planes are smaller and less long-lived. Most of the originals succumbed to plane tree wilt in the 20th century but there are a few still left.' He sighed. 'I wonder if this one will make it.'

'Number Six is on the right,' I said quietly and he nodded, still staring at the tree, presumably willing it to survive the centuries.

Right from the moment we exited the pod we'd agreed to assume there would be eyes everywhere. I wouldn't have been surprised to discover Winterman and Feeney had a network of young boys watching the surrounding streets, all ready to sound the alarm should anyone suspicious come into view, which was why we'd parked so far away. There wasn't a soul in sight on this windy afternoon but I was sure they'd be there somewhere, and who knew what eyes lurked behind those gleaming windows?

We moved smoothly into character, supposedly pausing to confer over who would take left and who would take right side of the square but we'd already agreed right would be me.

Possibly over-optimistically, we'd decided a woman would be less likely to arouse suspicion. Markham conceded that might actually be true right up until the moment they met the woman in question.

Our cover was that we were collecting for charity. I would go in openly through the front door. Markham was to nip round the back and enter by whatever orifice he could find that would accommodate him. There had been vigorous discussion on which charity we would be representing and we'd finally gone with Seamen's Missions which seemed to be a fairly popular and non-controversial fundraising initiative. My choice of Women's Suffrage was deemed to be too inflammatory.

'Another Fun Fact,' said Markham, labouring under the mis-apprehension that I cared. 'The first collection tin appeared in the temple of Jerusalem and religions have been separating the faithful from their dosh ever since.'

'Shut up,' I said, without any hope that he actually would.

'Samuel Pepys mentioned collection tins in his diary. They were collecting to rebuild London after the Great Fire. He banged on about what a nuisance they were.'

'Well, there's a coincidence.'

'The RNLI started their street collections in 1891 and—'

Sometimes you just have to be brutal. 'Will you shut up about collecting tins. We don't have any so it's irrelevant. We're collecting subscriptions.'

'I thought you'd be interested,' he said, hurt.

'Straighten your cravat. You look like a street urchin.'

He wrenched at the offending article of clothing, making things slightly worse, but at least it stemmed the flow of Fun Facts. 'How's that?'

'Perfect. Are you ready?'

We wished each other luck and split up. He moved left to knock at the first house.

The first door on my right, Number Eight, was opened by a portly butler. I summoned all the confidence engendered by my smart outfit and subscription book, greeted him brightly and asked for the mistress of the house. Obviously wise to the ways of me and my kind, he bade me wait in the hall, relieved me of my subscription book and disappeared through a door to my right.

I had been offered a seat but I was too keyed up so I wandered around, admiring the paintings on the wall. Not that there was much to admire – there was the usual depressing stuff – Caledonian landscapes where the most prominent feature was mud, and still lifes (lives?) of bowls of fruit and dead pheasants tossed carelessly across highly polished tables. The Victorians had some very strange habits. Overheated brains, I suspected, caused by wearing all those too-tight clothes and staring at dismal landscapes.

Before I had time to develop any of my own strange habits, the butler returned with my subscription book on a tray, open at the appropriate page. It would appear that Mrs Tregaskes, obviously unwilling to be outdone by Lady Ryde, would contribute one guinea.

I retrieved my book, asked the butler to convey my thanks to his mistress and allowed myself to be ushered back down the steps to the pavement.

On the other side, Markham was just mounting the steps to Number Two. He was slightly ahead of me. I reminded myself this was not a race.

I plied the knocker on Number Seven. A very smart maid answered. The mistress wasn't in, she said, tossing the ribbons on her lacy mob cap, but the master was available. Telling myself this would be good practice, I stepped over the threshold and was shown into some kind of parlour.

Ten minutes later I was no longer surprised the mistress was out. If she had any sense, she was halfway to a colony by now. I personally would have worked my passage. Good God, Horace Leyton, as he introduced himself, could bore for England. I listened politely and attentively to various anecdotes he mistakenly thought demonstrated his intelligence and business acumen. In my new role as someone labouring for the good of mankind, I forbore to enlighten him, but don't think it wasn't a struggle. He moved smoothly into relating the ultimate fate of some fellow who'd tried to cheat him over a horse and I whiled away the time staring at the portrait of a very pretty dark-haired woman over the mantel. The wisely absent Mrs Leyton, I assumed.

He went on and on. By now I was panicking that Markham would get to the back of Number Six before I got to the front, so, in desperation, I thrust my subscription book under his nose and smiled winningly.

He scribbled in my book, inviting me to come and look over his shoulder as he did so. I declined that particular treat because the brandy fumes would probably have knocked me over, rang the bell myself to summon the maid, whipped my book out of his hands as soon as she entered and whisked myself out of the door so rapidly that I practically trod on her heels in my efforts to get away.

Seemingly unsurprised at my determination to leave as

quickly as possible, she opened the front door, wished me a very good afternoon and I was out into the much-needed fresh air.

Good grief – so far, I'd visited two houses. In one I'd been left in the hall like an old umbrella and in the second I'd had some ghastly overweight drone with halitosis boring me to death. And the next house held a couple of murderers, drug dealers, traffickers and arsonists so the day wasn't going to get any better. I'd envisaged spending the afternoon being given tea by little old ladies in fingerless mittens while fat cats purred in front of the fire and that hadn't happened at all. I wondered how Markham was faring. With his luck he'd be up to his withers in little old ladies and was, at this very moment, scarfing down fairy cakes as fast as he could go.

The wind still blew. Straightening my hat with its irritating feather, I squared my shoulders and approached the House of Doom. The very epitome of a middle-class Victorian matron with a social conscience and a lot of time on her hands.

From the outside there was nothing to distinguish it from its neighbours. The steps were neatly swept, the windows clean, and the brass door handle and knocker gleamed. A fine example of Victorian respectability. I had no doubt the occupants would appear to be – on the surface at least – pillars of the community. The house would be impeccably furnished, and presided over by a traditional butler and any number of starched housemaids.

I don't know anyone who gets things as wrong as me. The door was opened by Jack Feeney himself which surprised me so much I was temporarily speechless. I knew it was him imme-diately. Pennyroyal's staff work was impeccable. I'd had a full description and images of both our targets. Feeney – late forties. Dark, curly hair and brown eyes. Around five foot ten. Slim build. Winterman much older. In his sixties. Grey-haired. A little stooped. The tips of two fingers were missing – an old gangland punishment, apparently. Winterman had been the leader but looking now at the man standing before me, I wouldn't mind betting Feeney was the more dangerous of the two. He'd been the enforcer, with everything that entailed. I looked at the person regarding me with polite enquiry, while my hindbrain shouted to turn around and walk away because we could always come at this from another direction.

I smiled brightly. 'Good afternoon. I wonder if I might speak with the lady of the house.'

His eyes twinkled. 'Alas, madam, it is of continuing regret to me that there is no lady of the house.'

I wasn't quite sure what to do next. He wasn't dressed as a servant so I couldn't ask to see his master and I wasn't supposed to know their names.

'Oh,' I said, crestfallen. 'My name is Mrs Farrell and I am collecting subscriptions on behalf of the Seamen's Mission in Rotherhithe. They do such good work there. I have been collecting in your square and everyone has been very generous. I wondered . . .'

I let my voice tail away and looked at him.

He looked me up and down in a way that Mrs Farrell didn't much care for but for which Dr Maxwell would give him a good kicking at the first opportunity.

And then I got the cheeky grin. The one I suspected had been the last thing ever seen by anyone who crossed him. He held the door open wider.

'Won't you come in, madam. Mr W is always busy at this time of day but perhaps I can be of assistance.'

I allowed myself to hesitate. 'Well, if there is no mistress on the premises, perhaps I should return with my companion . . .'

As I spoke, a nearby church clock struck four. 'Ah,' he said cheerfully. 'Surely you can put aside your scruples for a few minutes, Mrs Farrell. I know how you ladies like your tea. Don't make me drink mine alone.'

'Well,' I said. 'I must admit . . . I do enjoy a cup of tea around about now.'

'As do we all, madam. As do we all.'

'Well,' I said again, and with the air of one crossing a social Rubicon, stepped over the threshold. The door closed behind me.

The hall was very cold and very dark. Small, intricately patterned black and white tiles on the floor added to the gloom and induced a slight sense of vertigo.

'This way, Mrs Farrell,' he said, gesturing me towards a closed door on the left. 'There's a nice fire in the parlour.'

I stood my ground. I was Mrs Farrell, do-gooder and independent woman, solid middle class and respectable, with all the social invincibility that entailed. 'I regret, sir, you have the advantage of me.'

'Ah, yes, of course. Jack Feeney at your service, madam.'

I said haughtily, 'Delighted to meet you, Mr Feeney,' and preceded him into a large room overlooking the street. A small fire burned in the grate but it wasn't much warmer here than in the hall.

'Do sit down, Mrs Farrell.'

'That's very kind of you but I mustn't linger. Will Mr . . .' My lips formed around the first syllable of Winterman when I suddenly realised I wasn't supposed to know his name. I was going to have to keep my wits about me and be a lot more careful. 'Will Mr W be joining us?'

He crossed to the fireplace and rang the bell, saying cheerfully, 'I shouldn't think so, madam. He's always occupied during the afternoons. Now – do draw closer to the fire. It's a trifle nippy this afternoon.'

I have to say, he had the mannerisms off pat. A Victorian gentleman with a roguish smile and a very faint brogue. So faint that you had to listen hard for it, but the tantalising trace was there. I wondered if he'd had lessons on how to behave in this century. It seemed likely. Victorian society was mannered and very rigid. Feeney and Winterman might not care about that but unless they wanted to stand out like tits on a bull – which they obviously didn't – full integration would be important. And they couldn't pick it up as they went along. They'd have to arrive fully briefed. Was there actually an organisation dedicated to helping criminals conceal themselves in time? That might be a thought to take back to Pennyroyal. A useful avenue of enquiry for the future. Or, knowing him, another lucrative area for him and Lady Amelia to move into.

I didn't want to sit down so I drew closer to the fire and held out my hands. As I did so, the door opened and two maids entered. I stiffened. I'm not wise in the ways of housemaids – you want Markham for that. Trust me, housemaids love him – but I'm pretty sure they don't usually travel in a pack. Two stood in the doorway with an older woman – the cook, perhaps – at their shoulders. There was something in the way they waited . . .

None of them spoke. Their eyes flickered around the room. No one looked directly at Feeney. They stood just inside the

338

room, waiting with their hands behind their backs, eyes on the carpet.

Mr Feeney greeted them jovially and demanded tea – quick as they could, please.

Silently they bobbed curtseys and backed from the room. But not before I had noticed a fading bruise on the taller one's cheek. And the other one appeared to have some sort of bandage on her wrist. I could just see it peeping from under her cuff. I began to have an inkling of what sort of house this was.

Feeney was smiling at me from the other side of the fireplace. A sensible woman would march from the room, let herself out of the house, meet her colleague on the pavement outside, go down the pub and rethink the whole situation.

I smiled back, sat down, settled my muff on my lap, pulled off my gloves and looked around the room. Just a silly woman so armoured in her own complacency she couldn't see what was under her nose. Sometimes I can do that without even trying.

The house was utterly silent. Whatever Mr W was up to upstairs, he was doing it very quietly. That was a thought – how likely was it that the doors had been soundproofed?

I decided to take control. Pulling out my little book, I said brightly, 'Well, Mr Feeney. How much can I put you down for?'

He rubbed his chin thoughtfully. 'I'm not sure what would be appropriate for such a fine lady as yourself,' and I don't think he was talking about the subscription.

I passed over my book. 'Perhaps it would be helpful to see what I've raised so far.'

He took the book and pretended to flip through the pages.

'Ah, yes. I see you squeezed something from that windbag Leyton next door.'

'He was very generous.'

'And the lady of the house?'

'Sadly, his wife was not at home. I shall return another time, perhaps.'

He gave a crack of laughter. 'I can save you the trip, my dear. She's upstairs at this very moment. Having tea with Mr W.'

It took a moment for his words to register and then my stomach turned over. There could be no good reason for Mrs Leyton to be upstairs. What was going on here? I remembered Horace Leyton, who, despite his drunken bragging, was, I suspected, a complete idiot. Had he done something to place himself in the power of these two? Debt? Was he gay? Something unforgiveable by the standards of the day, anyway. Was the contemptible worm using his wife to keep his neighbours quiet? I swallowed hard.

And what should I do? To linger would surely arouse his suspicions. But I couldn't leave.

I fell back on social protocol. I pretended I was royalty. They never hear impertinence and neither should I. I smiled a bright, impervious smile and waited.

In films and fiction, the heroine – who is always madly attractive but doesn't know it because, presumably, she doesn't know how to use a mirror properly – is, sooner or later, placed in a position where she has to make herself attractive and . . . flirt. The victim is always completely fooled by this, makes his move and the rescue team leap in and rescue her before her virgo is no longer intacta. I could see all sorts of problems with this scenario. However . . .

I stuffed my hands in my muff, took a firm hold on my pepper spray, looked him straight in the eye and said, 'As I look forward to tea with you, Mr Feeney.'

Well – that gave him something to think about. I'd almost put him off-balance. He looked at me speculatively and I could feel my heartbeat begin to pick up. God knows how that moment would have ended but then, thank God, the tea arrived.

I've never been so pleased to see a teapot in all my life because this man was not only more intelligent than either Markham or I had given him credit for, but he was considerably creepier as well.

I needed to keep him occupied while Markham broke in and found his way upstairs to deal with Mr W, and a teapot would be perfect. With the added bonus of being a useful weapon, should it come to that. I could either bludgeon or scald him. Or both. Having rendered him *hors de combat* I could then zap the bugger senseless, signal through the window and assist Pennyroyal in getting him into the carriage. Markham would have located Mr W – whose attention, if Feeney was to be believed, would be elsewhere, which could prove useful – and dealt with him. And possibly Mrs Leyton from next door as well – if she really was here and Feeney hadn't just said it to see how I would react. I wouldn't put it past him. He struck me as the sort of person who plays with his victims first. Like a pitiless cat.

We would also have to avoid the ten billion servants with which Victorian households were packed; although, given what I'd seen so far, I wouldn't mind betting Feeney's staff would hold the doors open for us. There had been fear – real fear – in their eyes. This man smiled and smiled but inside he was black and stinking to his core.

341

He was regarding me now. 'Mrs Farrell?'

'I'm so sorry – I was thinking of something else. A bad habit of mine. Did you speak?'

'I wondered if you would like to pour.'

'Of course.'

We'd discussed drugging our targets and reluctantly decided against it. We'd expected to find them together and response times sometimes vary wildly between individuals. Unless they both passed out at the same moment which was most unlikely, it could be too risky. I never thought I'd say this but the Time Police way – zapping and zipping – is usually the best approach.

I was regretting our decision now, however. It would have been so easy to lift the lid, stir the pot, drop in a little something that would almost certainly make my afternoon proceed more smoothly, and watch him fall face down into the fireplace.

'Have you lived here long?' I enquired, pouring myself a cup. First out of the pot. The only one worth having. I am aware many people prefer their tea to be the colour of an American president on the campaign trail, but not for me. Occasionally, my duties at St Mary's sent me to Thirsk in Yorkshire, where I always worried the inhabitants would stone me. And then reward themselves with a beverage the consistency and colour of tar. With milk. Because tar cordial isn't evil enough on its own – you have to add the Juice of the Devil to make it completely undrinkable.

I became aware my mind was wandering again. It does that. Especially in a crisis. Sadly, it never takes me with it.

He was smiling at me and I didn't care much for the glint

in his eye. Still, I was holding his attention, which was my intention at the moment.

'Not long,' he said, evasively. 'You like your tea very pale, Mrs Farrell?'

'I do,' I said defensively, because there are a lot of people in the world who have trouble with that. 'And you, Mr Feeney?'

'Me? I prefer mine black. Black as the devil's heart.'

I passed over a cup of tar.

'Tell me, Mrs Farrell, how long have you been collecting for this worthy cause?'

'Two or three years now.'

'Rotherhithe? Is that not a little too far east for a lady such as yourself?'

I wondered whether he actually suspected I wasn't who I said I was or whether he automatically suspected everyone who came to the house. I rather thought the latter. I can't think of anyone who looks less like a Time Police officer than me. To mutual relief, I suspect.

'Well, it's mainly my husband's concern. He's an explorer and one of his men mentioned the good work they do there.'

'And what sort of good work would that be, Mrs Farrell?'

'I am involved mainly with supporting the widows and orphans,' I said firmly, having no knowledge of seamen in any way. Other than the fact that they were men who went to sea, of course. 'We educate the boys wherever possible and find respectable places for the girls.'

'Very commendable,' he said, sitting back and stirring his tea. 'And quite a coincidence. Mr W and I are always willing to give a decent girl a good start in life. We've had several come through here.'

343

Yes – that I could imagine.

I sipped my tea and said brightly, 'Then perhaps I could add you to our list of prospective employers?'

'You might,' he said thoughtfully. 'Would this be instead of the subscription?'

'Oh no,' I said, holding his eye. 'Having come so far, I could not possibly leave without a subscription.'

He smiled over his cup. 'Well, aren't you the little tease.'

I fumbled my cup and saucer back on to the table and while I was busy doing that he got unhurriedly to his feet, strolled across the room and locked the door.

OK – not sure that was supposed to happen.

22

I've been in situations similar to this before, but usually with
the full might of St Mary's behind me. Although sometimes
having St Mary's with you is helpful and sometimes . . . less so.
Today, I was on my own. Yes, Markham was around somewhere,
breaking and entering with a bit of luck, but not here and not
just at this moment. At this moment it was just me. Mrs Farrell
and her trusty pepper spray. Indefatigably labouring for the
good of others and occasionally tossing out the sort of remark
that could easily be misinterpreted. Keeping him just slightly
off-balance until I could see my way clear.

I allowed myself to look alarmed. Not actually that difficult.
'What are you doing?'

'Oh, come along, Mrs Farrell. You've wrapped it up in a
cloak of fine words and good intentions, but here you are, like
every other woman in the world, wanting money. The only
question for us now to resolve is – what will you do for it?'

'I think you mistake my purpose here, sir.'

'Oh, I think not.'

He began to walk towards me.

My mouth went dry. I don't know why I'd likened him to a

cat. He was a snake. A king cobra, staring into my eyes, freezing me in my chair, unable to escape. Unable even to move . . .

He lifted off my hat, set it on the table and gently ran his finger down the back of my neck, finding nerves and sensitive areas I didn't know I had there.

I drew a sharp breath.

He smiled some more. 'Well now, Mrs Farrell, that's a lovely outfit you're wearing today but why don't you take off your coat. Relax a little with me in front of the fire. It's a filthy day out there.'

I swallowed and quavered, 'I think not, sir.'

He wandered over to the desk. I was surprised – and slightly offended – that he'd given up so easily. Rummaging in his pocket he pulled out a small key and unlocked a drawer. Smiling broadly, he pulled out a roll of banknotes.

Even though I knew it was locked, I ran for the door and artistically tugged at the handle while he was over the other side of the room.

'Locked,' he said, laconically, undoing the roll. 'Here you are, Mrs Farrell. Cash in hand. I've never yet come across any woman who didn't like cash in her hand and I don't suppose you so-called ladies are any different. Take off your jacket now.'

I wheeled away from the door and allowed myself to cry a little. Would it be wrong to say a little bit of me was quite enjoying this?

He was all concern. 'Now Mrs Farrell, don't you upset yourself. It'll soon be over. Just think of the benefits. Take off your jacket and show me the pretty blouse underneath.'

I lifted my chin. Every inch the plucky little woman standing firm. 'I shall do no such thing.'

346

'You'd rather I did it for you?'

'I shall scream for help.'

He shrugged. 'Be my guest. No one hears the girls and believe me, in this house, they scream quite often. No one ever hears, Mrs Farrell. No one ever comes to help.'

'But . . . Mr W,' I said.

'Oh, believe me, Mr W is, at this very moment, causing someone else to scream. Don't worry, you won't hear anything. He's at the top of the house. It's his way of passing the long, boring afternoons. Now, time's passing, Mrs Farrell, so let's get down to it. You take off your jacket or I'll do it for you. That earns you . . .' He held up a large white banknote. 'Five pounds. Not bad for less than thirty seconds' work. Removing your blouse will earn you another five.'

He placed the second note alongside the first.

'And then,' he said, 'you'll lift your skirt and events will proceed very profitably. For us both.'

He placed the whole roll of banknotes on the desk.

'And then afterwards, Mrs Farrell, you and I will talk a little about these respectable girls of yours and the opportunities Mr W and I might be able to offer them. For a suitable remuneration, of course. You will find neither of us ungenerous.'

I drew myself up to my full unimpressive height. 'You are speaking of prostitution.'

'I am.' He smiled. 'Theirs . . . and yours.'

'Are you out of your mind? My husband . . .'

'Oh, you're going to tell him, are you? Well, that's entirely up to you, Mrs Farrell, but what exactly will you say? You called, uninvited. I asked you in out of the wind. We had tea. I was about to make a very generous donation to the Seamen's

Mission when you had some sort of woman's moment. I tried to call one of the maids but your behaviour, Mrs Farrell, was . . . well, I don't like to say such things about a lady. But I don't think you'll mention any of this to your husband, will you? I like to touch – that's all, Mrs Farrell. It's really very lucky for you that you didn't get my boss. He likes all sorts of things your little middle-class mind couldn't even begin to comprehend. Whereas me – I just like to touch.'

He showed his teeth suddenly. '*And bite.*'

I slapped on the door panels. 'Help. Help me.'

He laughed, seized my skirt and dragged me back across the room. To the fireplace. And my muff. 'You're still wearing your jacket, Mrs Farrell.' Suddenly his voice was different. 'I shan't tell you again.'

This was going well. Target A acquired and happily occupied. The exact location of Target B unknown but Markham would be all over that. And if he wasn't breaking in somewhere downstairs at this very moment, then he and I would be having words later on. And best of all, I could reach my muff. Time to turn the tables.

I thought of the two maids I'd seen. Bruised and terrified. I thought about what might be going on at the top of the house at this very moment. I thought of these two men who'd contaminated their own time to such an extent they'd had to flee to another. And the opportunities in this century were so much greater. These men were monsters. I began to regret Pennyroyal's firm instructions about not damaging the targets. However . . .

Markham spoke in my ear. 'There's an unexpected third party up here, Max, but I'm on it. Can you have your man ready in five minutes? No more.'

I yanked my skirt free of Feeney, seated myself at the tea table again, picked up my cup and smiled at Feeney. I too could enjoy myself.

I nodded in the direction of the money. 'How much is there?'

'A goodly sum.'

I sipped my tea. 'I could match it without blinking.'

He laughed. 'You think you can buy your way out of this room?'

'I don't have to. You'll open the door and let me out of your own free will.'

'And why would I do that?'

I smiled. 'Because I say you will.'

'A challenge? By God, Mrs Farrell . . . I'm going to enjoy you.'

'No, you won't, I'm afraid, but that's your problem. Now – open the door, please.'

He sat down and folded his arms. 'Make me.'

'After my tea. Would you like some more?'

He smiled, mocking. Completely in control of the situation. 'Thank you.'

I turned the teapot so the handle was facing my way. Five minutes, Markham had said. No problemo.

I swirled the dregs of my tea three times in the traditional mystic manner and upended the cup over my saucer. Righting it, I took the saucer away and peered into the cup, twisting it this way and that, remembering the portrait over the mantel next door.

'I see a small dark woman.'

He scoffed.

'Very young. Very frightened.' I looked over at him. 'Quite alone.'

349

He smirked.

'But not as alone as she thinks.'

He sat up but I swept on.

'A romantic stranger has entered her life. He has travelled far. Across remote continents, vast mountain ranges . . .' I paused. 'The Oceans of Time itself.'

Now I had his full attention. I could see him struggling to place me. Was I some do-gooder from this time who just happened to have made a lucky guess? But that comment about time? Was I Time Police? Surely not. Too old, for one thing. Was I someone hired by the desperate and despicable next-door neighbour to extricate himself – and his wife, if it was convenient and didn't cost too much – from the situation in which his folly had placed him?

'Tall, dark and handsome, I suppose.'

'I'd like to be able to say yes, but actually, short, fair and disreputable.'

He sneered. 'Her prince has come.'

'How strange that you should say that.'

He narrowed his eyes. 'Who are you?'

'Oh, let's not talk about me. Let's continue to speak of Mrs Leyton whose life is about to take a very unexpected turn.'

I swirled my tea leaves again. Mr Feeney owned a very efficient tea strainer and there were actually only about three tea leaves in the bottom of my cup, but trust me – from three tea leaves it is perfectly possible to extrapolate an entire plantation.

'Oh, look.'

It was instinctive but Feeney managed to stop himself leaning forwards. He smiled. 'Mrs Leyton's affairs have taken an unexpected turn for the worse, I think you'll find, Mrs Farrell.'

I frowned. 'No . . . no . . . that's not what it says here. I see Mrs Leyton leaving her husband – no great loss there, I think we can both agree. I see her leaving London. I see a pretty house. By the sea. And a little garden.'

I squinted into the cup. 'In fact, I see a long and happy life for Mrs Leyton. Who'd have thought?'

He'd recovered himself. I'd hardly jolted him at all. 'Alas, madam, I fear your talents with the teacups are very imperfect. Mrs Leyton is unlikely to be leaving this house at all in the near future. Not without physical assistance, anyway.'

This was it. This was my moment.

Very softly, I said, 'Which she is, at this very minute, receiving.'

He couldn't help himself. Just for one moment, one very brief moment, his eyes flickered up to the ceiling. But one brief moment was all I needed.

I ripped the lid off the teapot with my left hand, surged to my feet and in the same movement, hurled the contents straight into his face with my right. He screamed but not anything like loudly enough so I threw the teapot at him as well. It was a classically shaped, beautiful blue and cream china affair, with a perfect dribble-free spout, and it deserved a better fate than bouncing off Jack Feeney's forehead and into his lap.

Hats were being worn on top of the head this year and so my hair was bundled in a big knot at the back of my neck. I pulled out something shiny and sharp. Sadly, he was fully clothed, Victorian style, and I doubted I'd get penetration – so that was both of us disappointed this afternoon – so I slashed at his face. From the corner of his eye to the corner of his mouth. I have to say there was rather more blood than I was prepared for.

He screamed. He actually screamed. What a baby. And it wasn't as if I'd actually stabbed him – which had been my first impulse.

There was certainly more blood than he was prepared for. He staggered backwards, yanked a cloth off a small table and held it to his face. His language was worse than mine. What sort of words were those to use to a lady?

I pulled out the pepper spray. There was no real need but I'm a nasty person and I saw no reason at all why he shouldn't suffer a little, so I aimed for the open gash and pulled the trigger.

He reeled again, colliding with yet another knick-knack-laden table, which this time toppled over with a very satisfactory crash. And I was perfectly safe from interruption – the door was locked, although I was certain the maids would be under very strict instructions not to intervene no matter what they heard happening in this room. They probably thought it was me doing all this girlie screaming and falling over.

He had his hands to his face. Bad mistake. In this situation you should always keep your hands away from your eyes. They only make things worse.

No – actually I'd got it wrong. He wasn't as helpless as I had thought. Far from rubbing his eyes, he reached around to the back of his neck, pulled out a knife and slashed blindly. A nasty low slice that should have disembowelled me. He was badly scalded, cut, peppered and bleeding but it was so fast and unexpected he nearly got me. I jumped backwards and my skirts saved me from injury. The knife caught in the material. He jerked blindly and I lost my balance, fell, and, because he hadn't let go of the knife, I dragged him down with me.

Shit. This wasn't good. I really should have zapped him

first. Not gloating is always the way to go. The gloater gloats over his fallen victim – the gloatee. The gloatee pulls himself together, launches a desperate attack, frees himself, overcomes the gloater and hey presto. Victory snatched from the jaws of defeat. Although not for the gloater, obviously. Clive Ronan never gloated. He just pulled the trigger and strolled away. He's not exactly a role model for me but in the area of non-gloating – very sound. I really should have followed his example and just zapped this bugger as soon as I entered the room. Something to remember for the future.

I rolled away from him as quickly as I could. He grabbed blindly for my skirt again. I kicked out and my foot caught something. The tea table. The whole lot went over with a crash. He yelled again. Typical. Obviously one of these people who can dish it out but is less enthusiastic about it being dished back again.

Unfortunately, he still had hold of my skirt and was using it to pull me closer to him. My muff was only a fingertip away. If I could get to it. I kicked and kicked but he gritted his teeth and hung on. I couldn't shift him and in a second or so he'd be close enough to do me some real damage.

'I'm done up here,' said Markham chattily in my ear. 'Everything all right with you?'

I grunted, 'Absolutely fine,' and stopped kicking because I could see my pepper spray. I stretched for it, felt something tear – not me, I hoped – grabbed it, sat up from the waist – which wasn't something I'd done in years but trust me, you can do it when you have to – and gave him another quick squirt.

Feeney was roaring and flailing with his fists. One hit me on the top of my left shoulder and my whole arm went numb.

I had to get out of range. If he hit me and I went down, I'd never get up again.

'You sure?' enquired Markham. 'There's an awful lot of noise at your end.'

'Absolutely certain,' I said, grittily.

'Well, OK then. I've got mine, by the way. He's in a heap on the floor having the shit kicked out of him by a young lady who had the sense to keep her boots on. How's yours?'

'Scalded, kicked and sprayed. Still won't go down.'

'Do you need rescuing?'

'No.'

'You sure? I'm not doing anything at the moment.'

I instructed him to go forth and multiply.

Feeney was proving more difficult to shift than the failed leader of a political party. I needed to use my brains. I said urgently, 'Mr Feeney. You need to keep very still. You're practically in the fire. You'll burn your legs.' And he was so surprised that for a second, he did just that.

I kicked viciously because there's no point doing it any other way, rolled away, grabbed my muff, found my stun gun and gave him the good zapping he deserved. Probably more and for longer than I should but ... well ... what the hell.

Panting, I scrambled to my feet. My hair was coming down. My skirt was torn. I was covered in tea and tea leaves and my hands were stinging so I guessed I'd got pepper on them.

There is a use for milk after all. Who'd have thought? I carefully washed my hands in the remaining contents of the milk jug – I'm really not fit for polite society – and dried them on the tray cloth.

The room was a bit of a shambles. Overturned tables, smashed china, and tea soaking into the rather nice carpet. The teapot had survived but both cups were history, together with most of the contents of the little knick-knack table.

I could hear Markham at the door but first things first. I pulled Mr Feeney's hands behind his back and zipped him firmly. And his ankles, too. And then just for good measure I yanked off a cushion cover and pulled it over his head. Then I really couldn't think of anything else to do to him, so I kicked a helpless man a couple of times because that really does make you feel better.

The door key lay on his desk, alongside the money. I let Markham in. As usual, he was surrounded by housemaids. It's his USP.

'Good God,' he said, surveying the devastated room. 'What on earth happened here?'

I shrugged. 'He tried to put milk in my tea.'

'What a bastard.'

'Where's yours?'

'In the hall.'

'Conscious?'

'He was, but I left him in the care of some of his staff so probably not any longer.'

I lowered my voice. 'What about his . . . guest?'

'She's still upstairs.'

A housemaid was already slipping away. 'We know what to do, madam. Leave her with us.'

Again, I spared a second to wonder what the young woman from next door had done to merit the attentions of Mr W. I couldn't believe that any action of hers could possibly have placed her in the power of these men. Her husband, however, the worthless Horace – yes, I could easily believe that something he'd done had landed him in big trouble, been found out by these two charming specimens, and he had used his wife to buy his way out of it. Well, that was all over now.

I wondered what she would do. Divorce was possible in this day and age and if Leyton had any sense, he'd keep his mouth shut and sign everything put in front of him. The Married Women's Property Act would allow her full control of her own property. Perhaps my little fantasy of a cottage by the sea was not so unrealistic after all.

I gestured to the crowd of servants in the doorway. 'So much for quick and quiet.'

'Yeah, sorry, Max, but when I saw what Winterman was doing . . .'

'Yeah,' I said in my turn and we both surveyed the slowly-returning-to-this-world Jack Feeney, while I got my hair back together again.

He groaned and then cursed, his words muffled by the cushion cover. Then he shouted for Maggie. Then for Kathleen.

Two maids pushed past me in a rustle of starched aprons. Maggie and Kathleen, I supposed. One reached for the poker but I shook my head and handed her the shovel instead. She bobbed a curtsey and thanked me politely.

I am continually being told that violence is never the solution to any problem, so I stepped back and considered the issue carefully, finally coming to the conclusion that that was a load of complete codswallop and that, in this instance, violence and retribution were actually doing these young girls a very great deal of good. There's nothing like suddenly realising you're not as much under someone else's control as you thought. That in the end, ill treatment gets its just deserts, and it's extremely satisfying to be the one doling out those just deserts.

I dusted myself down, straightened my clothing and followed Markham out into the hall.

Pennyroyal had been waiting further along the square. Markham stuck his head out of the front door and gave him the signal. A closed cab, pulled by a single horse, drew up at the foot of the steps.

'You two get them out,' I said to him. 'I have something to do here.' I turned to the maids. 'Who's in charge?'

The cook elbowed her way through. 'Mrs Proudie, madam. Cook.' She gestured at the young maids, not one of whom looked over twenty-one. 'I look after them. As best I can.'

'Come with me.'

I went back into the sitting room. Her eyes widened as she took in the full extent of the mess.

I grinned. 'He takes some fighting off, doesn't he?'

She nodded, grimly. 'He does, madam. I think that's the bit he likes best.'

'Not any longer,' I said, crossed to the desk and pulled out a drawer. In addition to another roll of banknotes, there were several soft bags that clinked when I placed them on the desk.

'Were you all paid last quarter day?'

She shook her head. 'Nor the quarter before that.'

I sighed. What a life. Servants were almost completely at the mercy of their masters. Especially female servants. The lack of a male butler or footmen was clearly deliberate policy by Feeney and Winterman. We had here five or six young girls – orphans, I was prepared to bet – with no relatives to speak up for them, or even come looking for them should things get out of hand – which I was prepared to bet they did occasionally. Always hanging over their heads would be the threat of dismissal with no references. Fatal for any chance of future employment. Or worse, several small ornaments would be discovered to be missing, and the police called. It would be the master's word against theirs and theirs counted for nothing. Yes, the doors were locked and they were probably physically unable to leave, but they were trapped more completely than that. No pay – nowhere to run to – and then, when they were too badly damaged to be of any further entertainment, they'd be kicked out into the street to fend for themselves. Or die somewhere. Anywhere as long as it wasn't here. If they healed, they'd be on the streets trying to earn a living, and dreadful things happened to unprotected girls earning a living on the streets. And things weren't any better if you did have a pimp. What a choice. Perhaps, since abuse seemed inevitable, they preferred to have the dreadful things happen to them here, where at least there was food and a roof over their heads. Perhaps they saw it as the lesser of two evils and these two bastards had traded on that. I hoped Markham and Pennyroyal would manage to drop them down their own steps a couple of times.

One bag contained a quantity of sovereigns.

'How many are there of you?'

'Five altogether, ma'am. Although Sarah ain't been able to work for a while.'

I pulled out ten sovereigns and handed them to her. 'Two for each of you.'

The other bag was loose change – half-sovereigns, crowns,

half-crowns, shillings, sixpences, and so on. Probably about fifty pounds' worth. I handed it to her. 'Divide all that among you. Don't touch the banknotes. Your masters are being taken away. You will never see them again. They will never come back here. But, sooner or later, enquiries will be made. Tidy up this room and carry on as normal. You know nothing. You'll all be questioned and they'll look for signs of pilfering, so leave the rest of this money exactly where it is. Take nothing. Say nothing. Any of you. Do you understand why that is so important, Mrs Proudie?'

She nodded. Her bright currant-like eyes were shrewd. She was middle-aged and experienced. I was satisfied she'd look after them.

'There's enough there for you all to start again somewhere. When the moment is right.'

'We're from the agency, ma'am. Mrs White's. She sends a lot of girls here.'

Ah – that explained why he'd been so excited over the 'respectable girls' from the mission. Another source of income and entertainment.

'Well, don't go back there, whatever you do,' I said. 'Register with a reputable agency but don't be in a hurry. You have enough to keep you going for a while. And don't let them spend it all at once. It's possible the police will watch you for a while. Make the girls understand why they have to be so careful.'

She frowned. 'Believe me, ma'am, these girls know how to be careful.'

'Will you be able to keep an eye on them?'

'I can, ma'am. We'll do as you say. Carry on normal like, answer any questions, leave the valuables alone. Rest assured, ma'am, these girls will take care. They won't want nothing like this ever happening to them again.'

I nodded. 'I must go.'

She passed me my hat and muff. I could hear Markham calling for me in the hall. The coach had stopped at the foot of the steps – Pennyroyal really couldn't have got any closer – but someone might have seen something. We shouldn't hang around.

'Good luck, Mrs Proudie. And look after each other.'

'We will, ma'am. And thank you.'

I nodded.

Markham was waiting in the hall. 'He says he'll meet us back at base. Are you ready?'

I settled my hat as best I could, checked I had everything I'd brought with me, shook out my skirt to hide the worst of the tear and pushed my arm through his. 'Ready when you are.'

Mrs Proudie herself saw us out, curtseying politely as we passed through the front door. Pennyroyal's coach was just disappearing around the corner. Typical Pennyroyal, he must have pulled straight out because we could hear the shouting, barking, neighing and screaming of dislocated traffic all the way from here.

'Well,' said Markham, as we made our dignified way down the steps. 'I thought that went rather well. I could get used to this.'

I nodded. Reprehensively, I'd rather enjoyed putting the boot into our Mr Feeney. So, I'm a bad person – live with it. And the constant worry about upsetting History, or inadvertently changing something, or setting off something apocalyptic – there was none of that in this line of business. You just went in, did whatever was needed to get the job done, and got out as soon as possible. Oh, dear God – I was turning into the Time Police.

There was no tedious aftermath to cope with, either. No reports to write, no time in Sick Bay – just decontaminate and go. Markham and I both had a giant slug of something that could loosely be construed as extremely beneficial, and decided, medically speaking, that that would do.

Pennyroyal had disappeared off to Time Police HQ with the prisoners. Markham and I tidied our own pod, set everything to charge, went back indoors and poured ourselves another congratulatory shot of medicine. And then another one, because why not?

'Here's to *Pros and Cons*,' said Markham, and I was feeling so mellow I let it go. He scrambled some eggs while I did the toast – which both of us mistakenly thought would be the easier task. It was as we were sitting around the table, congratulating ourselves on a job well done, that he said suddenly, 'Are you going to Peterson's wedding?'

'Well, I don't see why I shouldn't,' I said. '*I'm* not wanted by the law.'

'Well, technically, neither am I. I just pushed off before the law decided I was. Wanted, I mean.'

I waited.

'I was supposed to be his best man,' he said gloomily, riskily holding the ketchup bottle over his head to see why nothing was coming out. 'That won't happen now. God knows what sort of a mess he'll make of things without me there to keep an eye on him.'

A large red blob slid reluctantly from the bottle and splatted unpleasantly on to his eggs.

'You could still go,' I said with alcohol-induced bravado. 'In fact, we both could. It should be easy enough. They're getting married at the village church, not the chapel at St Mary's, because apparently it's not big enough for all their friends and family.'

We took a moment to contemplate people less fortunate than ourselves. Those burdened with innumerable friends and family.

'We could still go.'

'Yes,' he said with enthusiasm. 'Lightly disguised, of course.'

I admit I was slightly uneasy at his use of the phrase 'lightly disguised', but on the other hand, if the authorities really were looking for him . . . I'd heard nothing official but if Markham had taken the precaution of removing himself and his family from public view, then I was prepared to trust his judgement. Suppose they guessed Markham would be unable to stay away? That here would be a good place to snatch him? Quick and quiet.

And I certainly didn't want Treadwell taking the opportunity to have another go at me. Weddings are stressful enough without one guest making her getaway by having to club another with a headstone.

Markham nodded again. 'St Mary's will think we're friends and/or family, and friends and/or family will think we're St Mary's. Yeah. That could work.'

I sat back, alarmed. 'I'm not going with you if you're going to wear a dress.'

'Actually, I was thinking of a false beard.'

'What?'

'No one will expect to see me in a false beard, will they?'

'I hate to break it to you, but I doubt anyone will be surprised. I don't think you'll be able to move for people saying, "Have you seen Markham and his ridiculous false beard?"'

He sighed. 'A false moustache?'

'Dear God, no. Sunglasses. That's it.'

'What's it?'

'Your disguise. You can wear one open-bracket figure one close-bracket pair of sunglasses.'

He considered this. 'OK – sunglasses are cool. I am, after all, the epitome of cool.' He struck an attitude. 'Markham – king of cool.'

I began to regret saying no to the dress.

He grinned. 'While Pennyroyal's away the mice will play . . .'

It was easy. I knew the exact time, date and location. Which was a lot more than I usually had for a lot of our assignments. We ransacked the costume room again. Pennyroyal had not been best pleased with the condition of my Victorian clothes – ripped, soaked and covered in tea leaves is not, apparently, the correct state in which to return things – and I was worried he might have locked the room in his absence, but I was worrying for nothing. He hadn't.

'We'll be back before he is,' said Markham, rifling through the suits. 'He'll never know anything about it.'

Personally, I doubted this, but what the hell. Rules were for people on the right side of the law. As Markham said, we were badass fugitives, living wild, walking the mean streets and not to be trifled with and what did I think of this pink tie?

It was a summer wedding so he chose a quiet grey suit. I had rather more to disguise – hair, build and so forth – so I chose a jumpsuit in a dramatic black and gold pattern, because people would see the pattern and not me, together with a wide-brimmed hat to hide my hair and shade my face, and a pair of giant sunglasses. Or possibly a giant pair of sunglasses. I never know which way round it is and I really should find out one day. I went for ballet flats too, in case I needed to make a run for it. Although, as I pointed out, yet again, I wasn't the one wanted by the law and Markham pointed out, yet again, that it was only a matter of time.

I have to say – if you smother me from head to ankle in a jumpsuit, cover my hair and plonk a pair of sunglasses on my nose, there's not a lot left to recognise. Just the tip of my nose and a bit of chin.

Markham looked unusually clean – I told him no one would know him – and he'd slicked his hair back with product which made him look much older. I wondered again – how old was he?

We surveyed each other, side by side in the mirror. I suddenly couldn't think of anything to say. Peterson was getting married.

'It'll be fine,' said Markham. 'And if not – well, how many people can say they've had St Mary's Security Section, the police, the military, members of British Intelligence and probably a couple of black helicopters at their wedding?'

I nodded. 'Peterson should be grateful to us. It would probably have been quite dull otherwise.'

'Exactly. Shall we go?'

*   *   *

I put us down in the woods opposite the church. Coincidentally, not that far from the place where I'd been abandoned around six hundred and fifty years ago. I shook my head. Sometimes I felt as if my past was overwhelming me which, let's face it, was perfectly possible because I had a hell of a lot of past to be overwhelmed by.

We exited the pod carefully and looked around. The world was green and full of birdsong. Shafts of sunlight slanted through the trees. We made our way cautiously along the path, emerging almost opposite the church.

The church gate was open and wedding guests were already arriving in small groups. I didn't know most of them. I drew Markham back under the trees. We'd talked about this and we had a plan. We'd wait for the ceremony to begin and then creep in and sit at the very back. We'd be able to watch what was going on but unless anyone actually turned around – and why would they because they should be looking at the bride and groom? – we'd be lost in the dim shadows in a dark corner. And then, just before the ceremony finished, we'd nip outside, through the gate and back to the pod. No one would ever know we'd been there.

Well, that was the plan anyway.

It began well. We stood under the trees, watching people arrive, passing the time by criticising their outfits and agreeing we looked the dog's bollocks and everyone else didn't. Most of the St Mary's men had run true to form and wore their formal uniforms. The women, however, had made an effort. Mrs Shaw, Peterson's PA, looked very smart. As did Mrs Enderby and Mrs Mack. Sykes wore a pretty summer dress in yellow that contrasted nicely with her dark hair. Bashford walked on one side of her, Roberts on the other. Occasionally, they glared at each other over her head. Sykes walked imperturbably onwards, a small smile on her face.

Van Owen wore a striking fuchsia dress with a white jacket over. She and Polly Perkins had their heads together. Mrs Partridge wowed in a plain, cream silk dress with a black hat and gloves. As far as I could see, everyone was there. I could even see Treadwell in his usual pin-striped suit but rocking a white carnation. I'd like to say he looked ridiculous but actually he looked quite distinguished. On the other hand, he was surrounded by people from St Mary's so there wasn't a great deal of sophisticated competition.

Hyssop wasn't there. None of her people were. I wondered if they were actually still at St Mary's, told myself it wasn't anything to do with me any longer, and tried to concentrate on those entering the church.

I was amazed at how normal Lingoss's parents looked. Neither of them had Lingoss hair. In fact, he hardly had any hair at all and hers was a rigid, iron-grey bob. They looked quite normal. Kindly, even.

'They are, Max,' Lingoss had once said to me. 'I don't want anyone getting the idea I was abused or anything. I mean, yes, they didn't notice me much but when they did, they were great. And now I'm at St Mary's.'

I knew what she meant. Eccentric, argumentative, noisy, St Mary's was a typical family and she'd found us. Does everyone find their family sooner or later?

With Markham gone, Peterson had selected David Sands to be his best man. I could see Peterson was nervous from the moment the two of them got out of the car. They stood just outside the gate, checking each other over. Force of habit. Rings, tattoos, wristwatches and so forth. I saw Sands pat his pocket – reassuring them both about the wedding rings, I suppose, although sensible Sands was a good choice for best man. I could see Markham judging him on style and presentation.

They talked quietly. The sun shone, a pleasant breeze blew, the churchyard was tidy and no sheep were eating the dead. For a St Mary's gig, it couldn't have gone any better.

Eventually, Sands looked at his watch, said something to Peterson, and they walked slowly up the path. As they passed through the door, Peterson looked back over his shoulder. For a moment, I thought he looked directly at the place where we were standing. He couldn't possibly have seen us – we were in deep shade and he in bright sunlight – but I stepped back anyway. And then they were both inside.

Silence fell. We were just waiting for the bride now.

'All right?' said Markham, although I don't know why he would ask.

'Absolutely fine,' I said.

I had no idea who the bridesmaids were. Two tiny little tots with wreaths of flowers in their hair. I couldn't help thinking it was all a bit conventional for Lingoss.

And then we heard the clip-clop of an approaching horse. Markham craned his neck.

'I'd have thought arriving by horse and carriage was a bit traditional for Lingoss,' I said.

Markham nodded. 'I was rather hoping for a steam-powered tripod from *The War of the Worlds*.'

We underestimated her. I've seen brides arrive in horse-drawn vehicles. The beautifully decorated horse trots smartly

368

to the gate and pauses, posing and posturing while the bride carefully alights.

We didn't get any of that. For a start, Lingoss was driving, while Professor Rapson sat beside her, clutching his hat and the bridal bouquet. It was hard to tell who was about to be married. Mr Strong, magnificently accoutred in red and black, clung on at the rear.

They arrived at a fast canter with Lingoss leaning forwards, urging the horse on. I suspected both she and Turk were channelling Ben Hur. Turk's gigantic hooves struck sparks from the tarmac. Lingoss's veil streamed dramatically behind her. Both of them were obviously enjoying themselves immensely.

'She terrifies the wits out of me,' muttered Markham.

The bridal conveyance screeched to a halt outside the church gate. Turk too was bedecked with summer flowers. And wearing his traditional thunderous expression, of course. Lingoss began to manoeuvre her dress in order to climb down and Turk passed the time by trying to eat the bridesmaids' wreaths. Or possibly the bridesmaids themselves. It was hard to tell at this distance.

On the other hand, he looked magnificent. Our bony, flower-bedecked brown horse gleamed in the summer sunshine. Red ribbons decked his mane. Another was tied around his tail – less for decoration and more to advise the unwary he was a kicker. And don't make the mistake of thinking you're safe if you just stay back out of range – he was perfectly capable of farting an adult to death from twenty feet away.

Mr Strong, in his smart black and red uniform and with the traditional bowler, spoke sharply to him and he desisted with the bridesmaids. Although I didn't give much for their chances later on when he was really hungry.

For those who want to know – Lingoss wore white. But, of course, this was Lingoss, so she also sported frothy black underskirts. The whole effect was of shifting, swirling greys. And she carried a bunch of blood-red roses because you just can't keep a good girl down. Today's hair was jet black, tipped with crimson, and her veil was secured by a wreath of the same colour roses. She looked like a cross between Snow White and the wicked stepmother – who's always been a favourite character of mine. Snow White was such a wuss. All that housework. Looking after seven men. *And* she sang while she was doing it. That girl was not bright.

Professor Rapson climbed down after her. He was, nominally, giving her away. Lingoss straightened his tie, checked he was all zipped up and pointed him in the direction of the church. He set off, remembered his responsibilities and came back for her. I saw one of the ushers dart back inside the church and the organ music changed to the traditional opening chords of 'Here Comes the Bride'.

'That's disappointing,' whispered Markham. 'I bet Evans a fiver it would be *Phantom of the Opera* or something from Rammstein.'

Miss Lingoss and the professor, followed by the so far uneaten bridesmaids, disappeared into the church.

'Ready?' said Markham. Suddenly reluctant, I stood still. Come on, Maxwell.

'If you'd rather go down the pub,' said Markham, 'that can be arranged.'

I shook my head. How stupid to come so far and not actually go in. Move yourself, Maxwell. Just a few steps. Why was I so reluctant?

The last notes of the organ died away. If I was going, then now would be a good time. Beside me, Markham said nothing. I tried to take a deep breath, to be calm, to remember how to walk . . .

'I think he'd like you to be there,' said Markham softly, and he was right. Tim had always been there for me. The least I could do was be there for him. So I was. But don't think it wasn't a struggle.

We slipped in the back just as the Rev Kev was welcoming everyone. The church was packed – there was no way we'd have got all these people in the chapel at St Mary's. I mean – no way *they'd* have got all these people in.

It was cool and dim inside, even though the sun was streaming through the stained-glass windows, setting the floor and pillars on fire. Blood-red roses drooped at the end of every row of pews, all setting off Lingoss's white dress. You had to hand it to her – she really knew how to knock your socks off with colour.

We sat close to the door in the shadow of a fat pillar and watched the ceremony. I tensed when we got to the bit about just cause and impediment – I think everyone else did as well – but no just cause or impediment materialised and with barely a break, we carried on.

Lingoss made her vows quietly but firmly. Peterson, with his deeper voice, was less clear. I saw them exchange rings. She reached up and wiped something off his cheek and at that point I had to put my sunglasses back on. Markham nudged me and just before the service came to an end we tiptoed back out into the sunshine and heat.

By rights, we should have returned to the pod and jumped away. We'd pushed our luck just by coming here today.

371

'Lovely day,' said Markham.

'Nice to see everyone.'

'Even if they don't know they're seeing us,' said Markham.

'Their loss,' I said, and we went off to hide behind the little shed where the sad pieces of broken angels and gardening tools were kept.

The little churchyard was silent in the sunshine. I could hear bees buzzing. And then all of a sudden, the organ crashed a triumphant fanfare. Echoes of Mendelssohn bounced off the tombstones as the organist really put her back into it, and here they came.

They paused for a moment in the doorway and then Peterson almost ceremonially escorted her up the doorstep and out into the bright sunshine. Into their new lives together.

They couldn't see us – I doubt whether they saw anyone but each other – but I drew back further into the shadow. Without looking, Markham took my hand. Just for a moment. And then the guests came pouring out of the church.

There was the usual milling around. St Mary's was present so the milling was even more chaotic and noisy than usual but everyone looked so happy. There was a great deal of laughing and hugging. Peterson stood quietly, having his hand shaken by everyone present. Even Treadwell, I noticed.

Snatches of conversation drifted towards us in our hiding place. Professor Rapson was fretting over whether he'd left something on the boil. Polly Perkins and Van Owen were discussing a cottage somewhere in the village. Bashford was worrying whether Angus had yet noticed his absence. Apparently, he'd been all set to bring her. They'd been practising with him leading her on a red ribbon but Mrs Lingoss had allergies and even Bashford had conceded it would be unkind to exclude the mother of the bride on her daughter's special day.

Sykes was telling a joke. Buttonholing Atherton, she said, 'Hey, Atherton. Here's a good one for you. I work for Cunard.'

He laughed. 'You certainly do. That's hilarious. Good one, Sykes.'

Sands looked around. 'What?'

'It's a joke,' explained Atherton, while Sykes stood quietly, perfecting her 'butter wouldn't melt in my mouth' expression.

'I know it's a joke,' said Sands, between gritted teeth. 'I've heard it before.'

'Good one, isn't it?'

'No.'

'Perhaps you didn't get it. Let me explain. When Sykes says she works for Cunard . . .'

Believe it or not, it was Bashford who intervened and led Sands away.

Then there were the photos and holos to be taken. Combinations of bride, groom, parents, friends, the uneaten bridesmaids and so on, culminating in the big group photo. The one with everyone in it. The photographer began to shunt people around, making sure everyone would be visible in the shot.

I looked at Markham. Markham looked at me. Sometimes you don't need words.

I pulled off my hat and fluffed up my hair. My sunglasses went into Markham's pocket, along with his own. We walked quietly around the shed and joined the wedding group from behind. Markham slipped along the back row to stand at the other end. I found myself standing behind Treadwell.

We were all instructed to smile, so I did. A big, bright smile for Peterson on his wedding day. I knew Markham would do the same.

'One more,' called the photographer. 'Look at me, please. Smile, everyone . . .'

I smiled again and held up two fingers behind Treadwell's head. Something flashed somewhere. I wondered what Peterson's reaction would be when the images came back. When he realised we'd both been at his wedding after all.

Markham appeared behind me because now it really was time to go. As far as I could see, no one was paying us any attention at all, but we'd both learned not to push our luck. As the group began to break up and move towards the gate, we strolled slowly around the side of the church and stood in the shade behind a convenient buttress.

People were laughing and shouting. Markham nudged me. 'Uh-oh.' Rather ominously, Professor Rapson and Dr Dowson were disappearing behind a cluster of tombstones. 'Is that what I think it is?'

It was indeed. With a sinking heart I recognised the professor's late and very unlamented rapid chicken-firing gun. I had nightmarish visions of some pretty perturbed people panicking as portions of putrid poultry plummeted precipitately. These were nice people. Nice, normal people. This was supposed to be Lingoss's wedding day. What was he thinking?

I think I must have been acting on automatic pilot because I made some sort of strangled *What the hell do we do now?* noise and Markham patted me reassuringly. 'It's not your problem any longer, Max.'

Oh – no, it wasn't, was it? I tried to relax and waited to see what would happen next.

There was a series of small pops – I remembered the word 'rapid' figured first in the professor's description of his equipment – and a huge shower of brilliant red fountained heavenwards. Oh God – had they somehow disembowelled a cow? Or even an elephant?

No – it was rather beautiful. Vast quantities of red rose petals fell softly through the air, coating everyone's heads and shoulders. People gasped and applauded. The tiny bridesmaids ran hither and thither with cupped hands, trying to catch them as they fell. There was a small round of applause. It was a lovely finish to the ceremony. Well done, professor. I should have had some faith. He was very fond of Lingoss and she of him. He wouldn't have done anything to spoil her day.

And Peterson's day, of course. I watched him, still shaking hands and smiling. I saw him thank the Rev Kev, who himself was wreathed in smiles. Everyone was having a great time. Everyone was happy for them. Peterson had finally done it. He'd finally married Lingoss. The movement of the crowd brought them back together again and, just for a moment, they were the only two people there. He kissed the palm of her hand and folded it over. To keep the kiss safe. She smiled up at him and he touched her face and I had to look away because this was a private moment and belonged to them alone.

I became aware Markham was watching me. 'What?'

'Nothing. We should leave, Max.'

I nodded. We should. I swallowed it all down and flashed him a bright smile. 'Ready when you are.'

He said softly, 'Max.'

'Oh, look. Here's Turk back again. Doesn't he look smart?'

There was a short pause and then he said, quite normally,

'Yes. Can't believe he hasn't eaten anyone. All those hats . . . all that exposed flesh. He's obviously on his best behaviour.'

'As are we all,' I said, gaily.

Mr Strong pulled up outside the gate. Turk's nose was dusty so I guessed Mr Strong had kept him occupied with a nosebag. The happy couple climbed aboard. There was more laughing and cheering and clapping. It had been a beautiful wedding. Perfect in every way. The weather, the setting, everything . . . And then they were gone, trotting down the road to the Falconburg Arms and the reception.

I watched them go. In my head I could already hear the chink of glasses for the toasts, hear Sands making the perfect speech – God knows what Markham would have said – and then the music would start up. The happy couple would step out on to the dance floor and Peterson would immediately have started moving in mysterious ways because he truly can't dance.

St Mary's, never slow when food was involved, followed hard on their heels and the more normal guests followed after them, laughing and calling to each other as they made their way down the hill. Within minutes, they were all gone. Silence returned. Crimson rose petals swirled slowly in the breeze, fluttering among the gravestones. A pollen-covered bee buzzed past. Just a sunny afternoon in an empty churchyard.

We went home.

24

That night I couldn't sleep. I tossed and turned, my covers tangled themselves around my legs, my thoughts became unbearable, and in the end, I got up and went downstairs.

At some point Pennyroyal had returned and despite the late hour, was sitting in his shirtsleeves at the kitchen table, reading his newspaper and drinking a glass of whisky.

'Come in,' he said, as I stopped in the doorway. 'Can't sleep?'

I shook my head.

'Why not?'

I sat opposite him and shook my head again. My thoughts were not for sharing.

'Must be a reason,' he said, turning a page.

Perhaps there's something about sitting with a psychopathic butler in a dark kitchen in the middle of the night that encourages people to unburden their soul. Of secrets being safely told. He'd asked a question – I'd answer it and if he didn't like the answer then that was his problem.

'I have no job and no home. I haven't seen Leon for months. My son has probably forgotten me. I have no idea how my life is going to pan out and my best friend got married today.'

He folded his newspaper and laid it down.

'Well, you do have a job – and a good one – here, for as long as you and her ladyship want. Your husband's not stupid. He can find you through Guthrie. Your son's reached the age where he wants to stretch his wings a little. There might be more important things in his life at the moment but if you've done your job right, you'll always be his mother. But none of that is what's really bothering you, is it?'

Not looking at him, I shook my head.

'It wouldn't have worked, you know,' he said, getting up.

'Markham said that once.'

'Not as green as he's cabbage-looking, that one.'

'No,' I said.

He began to rummage in a cupboard, pulling out two or three dusty bottles. Taking down a glass he began to slosh in vast amounts of liquid, apparently at random.

'I'll tell you what would happen,' he said. 'Let's suppose you and your best friend do get together. You sneak around behind everyone's backs, lie to everyone whose good opinion you value and do the deed. The pair of you are so riddled with guilt that everyone guesses what's going on. Your husband finds out. Only you know what that will do to him, but you will lose him. Then you'll lose your best friend – because the two of you won't even be able to look at each other. You'll have lost the respect of everyone who knows you, including your other best friend upstairs at the moment, who relies on you more than you know. You'll have devastated your kid's life and soured every memory your friends at St Mary's have of you. Has to be one hell of a shag to risk all that, don't you think?'

There was no sympathy. No understanding. Just a blunt,

378

brutal, bleak and, I suspected, very accurate foretelling of my future. Of the destruction I could cause. Of the damage I could do. Of the lives I could ruin.

'And it's all down to you,' Pennyroyal said, stirring the contents of the glass. 'If you lift your finger, he'll come running. You know he will. So unless you're prepared to weather the storm – best you don't lift that finger, eh? Drink this.'

My hand wasn't quite steady. I sniffed. It smelled liquoricey. 'What is it?'

'A closely guarded secret.'

I sipped.

'Straight down.'

I tilted the glass. Whatever it was, it tasted thick, dark and not unpleasant.

'Thank you,' I said, wondering what I was thanking him for.

He took the glass off me. 'Back to bed now or you'll be passed out on the floor in thirty seconds.'

'Strong stuff,' I said, getting up.

'Yeah. One measure's usually enough. I gave you three. Let's hope you wake up in the morning, eh?'

'I'll make every effort,' I said. 'If only to save you the embarrassment of explaining to Lady Amelia that you've inadvertently poisoned twenty-five per cent of the team.'

He raised an eyebrow and I thought, for a very swift moment, there might have been a gleam of amusement. 'You'll do,' he said. 'Off you go, now, because I'm not carrying you.'

I did wake the next morning. Pennyroyal greeted me and Markham as if he had no idea we'd sloped off to a wedding and he and I had never had a midnight chat. The three of us went out and sat under the willows with a pitcher of fruit juice. Markham and I wore our best angelic expressions that wouldn't have fooled Dr Bairstow for an instant and I suspect not Pennyroyal either.

He handed us both a piece of paper with a list of disbursements down one side and a credit on the other. The difference between the two had been divided into four equal portions. Even divided into quarters, this was still a considerable sum of money. There were rather more noughts than I was accustomed to seeing in my monthly pay cheque. Wow. Take it from me, the wrong side of the law is a lot more profitable than the right side of the law. Considerably less effort and considerably more money. I was impressed.

'These sums will be paid to you,' he announced. It would probably have been polite to thank him, but just for a moment, Markham and I were bereft of speech. And that doesn't happen often.

I asked him if he'd mentioned our names as he'd handed over our prisoners to the Time Police. He shrugged. 'It never came up.'

Which suited both of us.

We were just beginning to think about lunch when a tiny car raced up the drive, engine roaring, gravel flying and seriously terrifying a couple of blameless fat pigeons who had nothing more on their minds than their own lunch.

'Ah,' said Pennyroyal, presumably in case we hadn't noticed. 'Lady Amelia has returned.'

Rising, he followed the little car under the arch.

I looked at Markham. 'What do we do? Go and greet our host politely or give them a moment to discuss whatever it is bounty hunters talk about when they've been apart for a couple of weeks?'

'I think we should give them a few moments, don't you? If they want us, they know where we are.'

So we sat tight and after a few minutes, Lady Amelia Small-hope appeared through the arch and strode vigorously across the grass.

'Hello there. Welcome. I hope Pennyroyal has made you comfortable. We rather thought we owed you a spot of hospitality after your invite last Christmas. Everything all right, I hope. Pennyroyal's bringing margaritas. I know it's barely lunchtime but I left London before dawn so as far as I'm concerned it's more than cocktail hour. Although if you plan things right it's always cocktail hour somewhere. And here he comes.'

And indeed, Pennyroyal, now wearing his formal jacket, was treading across the grass towards us, bearing a well-laden tray.

'Cheers,' she said, seizing the frosted glass tenderly placed in front of her. 'Bottoms up. Or up your bottoms, as dear Papa always said.'

I sipped appreciatively. Margaritas at barely noon was a habit I could really get used to.

Silence fell. Pennyroyal sat down but didn't drink. There was an air of waiting for something.

'Well,' she said, and suddenly her voice had a crisper, more business-like note. 'Now that we're all together . . .'

I put down my glass. Something was going on here.

She looked at Pennyroyal. 'What do they know?'

He shook his head. 'As far as I know, nothing, my lady. I haven't said a word. As per your instructions.'

'Good man. Stick another in there, will you.' She pushed her glass across the table.

'Well then, I suppose it falls to me to break the news.' She looked at us. 'It took a while but I was finally able to locate Mrs Brown.'

'Is she still alive?' I asked, suddenly hopeful. 'The last I heard she wasn't expected to survive.'

She fixed me with a glare. 'There's nothing wrong with her at all. Well, she's under house arrest, of course, and I had to go over the roof.' She looked over at Pennyroyal. 'Could have done with you that night, Pennyroyal. A chimney is no substitute for a good butler.'

'As I believe I pointed out when we discussed the arrangements, my lady.'

'You did indeed, Pennyroyal. Apologies. I shall certainly listen to you next time.'

I exchanged glances with Markham. He shrugged slightly. I was glad I wasn't the only one without a clue what was going on.

'However,' she said. 'Not the most important news du jour.'

Markham put down his barely touched drink. 'Which is?'

She turned to us. 'Mr Markham, Dr Maxwell, I bring good news. Dr Bairstow is not dead.'

My first thought – and I'll admit the margarita wasn't helping – was that he had somehow risen from the grave. As I'd always suspected he would do one day. Fortunately, before I could make an arse of myself, more conventional second thoughts shouldered that piece of nonsense aside.

Markham repeated, very carefully, 'Dr Bairstow is not dead?'

'Even better,' she said cheerfully. 'Not even injured.'

I had a sudden flash of enlightenment. 'There never was a car crash, was there?'

'Not even a little one. They drove out of St Mary's gates and were detained shortly afterwards. They didn't even get to Rushford.'

'Where?' demanded Markham. 'Where are they?'

'They've been split up. Mrs Brown, as a fairly high-profile member of society, is now under house arrest in London. Dr Bairstow is in a secure establishment which is, I believe, not unknown to *you*, Dr Maxwell.'

I stared. I didn't know any secure establishments. I probably should do. There are those who say I should be in one – which is rather unkind, don't you think? I think my mind was running along the lines of Broadmoor, or Wormwood Scrubs or that big new place just outside Redditch where they put the real dregs of humanity, and then common sense kicked in. They'd want somewhere quiet and discreet for Dr Bairstow. They wouldn't want him mixing with hordes of unstable troublemakers – as if he didn't do that on a daily basis at St Mary's – they'd want him somewhere out of the way. Somewhere no one knew anything about. Not officially, anyway. And then I had it.

'The Red House.'

She beamed. 'Well done.' I felt as if I'd scored the winning goal with the clock ticking down the last seconds. Presumably this was how her ancestors encouraged the peasants to hurl themselves at the slings and arrows of outrageous fortune while they themselves remained quietly on their horse out of harm's way at the back.

I, on the other hand, was not beaming at all.

The Red House is a very discreet, very upmarket medical

facility to where the great and good can be shunted off after their latest headline-grabbing exploits while their defence lawyers get their act together. Red House clients are mainly politicians although they do have important and relevant people there sometimes. They had once lowered their standards sufficiently to offer me and Leon the use of their facilities. It hadn't gone well. Which, when you think I was only there for about two hours, said a lot for both it and me. My brief stay there is also the reason Leon's car doesn't start well on cold, damp days, but we don't talk about that. Well, I don't and Leon also says nothing at all but in a completely different way.

The less well-known aspect of the Red House is that they also offer secure accommodation to people whom the government want out of the public eye. For the public good, of course.

The person in charge – and I'm back to the Red House now – Alexander Knox, had died shortly after I met him. Although executed would be a more accurate description. I saw again that cold tundra. The sprinkling of snow on the iron-hard ground. Heard the moaning wind. Saw the blood on the snow.

When I resurfaced, Markham was asking how long Dr Bairstow had been there.

'Longer than a month,' she said, gesturing for another refill. 'As far as I can ascertain, he was never taken more than a few miles from St Mary's.'

'How do you know all this?'

'We were hired to find out,' she said shortly.

'By whom?' I asked, without any hope she would tell me. Clients were confidential. Apart from the Time Police, of course. As Pennyroyal said, we'd always know when we were working for those buggers because of the number of noughts on the bill and I'd had no problem with any of that. 'Someone hired you to find them when they disappeared?'

'Someone hired us to find them *before* they disappeared,' she said. 'Sorry – confusing sentence. To clarify – we were hired before the event in question could occur.'

'By someone who knew it was going to happen?'

'By someone who suspected Dr Bairstow and Mrs Brown would be removed from circulation at some point.'

'Why?' I asked.

'Why would they be removed or why were we hired?'

'Both.'

'Didn't ask,' she said crisply. 'You do know people just employ us, don't you? No reasons given, usually. They say, "Ho there, good people. Take this money and do such and such," and we take the money and do such and such. The whole transaction is usually over in the very short amount of time it takes us to perform the task, grab the money and run.'

Actually, I didn't believe this. I was pretty sure they didn't take just any job. And if they didn't want to do the job then there wouldn't be enough money in all the world to change their minds. And if you were foolish enough to persist, then there was every possibility you'd wake one night to find Pennyroyal grinning down at you.

I tried to establish a few facts. 'Dr Bairstow is definitely still alive?'

'Yes. Well, as of a few days ago, certainly, and I've no reason to believe that's changed.'

'And he's being held at the Red House?'

'He is. Hit me again, Pennyroyal. I'm gagging. That last one

385

had less impact than flinging a chipolata into an aircraft hangar. Thirsty business, this driving.'

'Well,' said Markham catching my eye, 'I wonder if it would be possible for Dr Maxwell and I to request a week's leave. Things are quiet at the moment. I don't believe we have much on. This would, I think, be a good time to . . .'

'Au contraire,' boomed Lady Amelia, startling the crows in the trees. They rose, flapping and cawing into the sky. 'We have a very great deal on at the moment. Before you begin to pout, however, I do believe our interests are about to coincide – very profitably, I think – and we need to get busy. Lunch first and then a staff meeting at . . . say . . . two. Don't be late.'

Seizing her glass, she strode off across the grass. Pennyroyal followed on behind. And he took the pitcher with him.

I looked at Markham. 'We're going to rescue Dr Bairstow, aren't we? All four of us, I mean.'

'Oh, I think so, otherwise why would they tell us where he is?'

'Did someone pay them to locate Dr Bairstow and Mrs Brown?'

'Well, obviously, or they wouldn't have done it otherwise.'

'Before the supposed accident?'

'So it would seem.'

'Who?'

'God knows. I'm still struggling to get my head round the fact he's not dead. Or Mrs Brown.'

'And who's funding all this?'

He frowned. 'All this?'

'Well, yes. Who arranged for them to employ us? Suddenly you and I are out of St Mary's and equally suddenly, two bounty hunters who always work alone offer us gainful employment. Exactly the right people for the job are all assembled together in one place and raring to go. For more than adequate remuneration, of course. So who's providing the adequate remuneration?'

He shrugged. 'If we work through it logically, we should start with Mrs Brown herself. She will have powerful friends both in a personal and private capacity.'

'Including a daughter in the Time Police,' I said. 'Mrs Brown is probably the best-connected person on the planet. It could be her.'

'Well, since you've brought them up – how about the Time Police themselves?'

I shook my head. 'I don't think so. I can't see the Time Police paying good money to save Dr Bairstow and St Mary's, can you? Why would they do that? Anyhow, the way Treadwell is going there won't be any St Mary's in six months' time. Their wildest dreams will come true and they won't have to lift a finger.'

Markham played with his glass on the table. 'All right. How about someone in the government? Someone who wants St Mary's to survive. For some reason that escapes us for the moment.'

I looked at him. 'It's not you, is it?'

Markham is not who you think he is.

He shook his head and lifted his glass. 'No. It's not me.'

'Only your accent's disappeared again.'

He smiled but shook his head. 'No, it's not me.' The accent was back.

'Major Guthrie said you were a Geordie in the army.'

'Why aye, man.'

'We are going to get him out, aren't we?'

'Your mind jumps about like a frog on a hotplate, but yes. We'll get him out. And Mrs Brown too, because I suspect her welfare will be the first thing he asks about and if we can't come up with an acceptable answer, we'll be subject to the Bairstow Stare.'

'God forbid,' I said.

'Indeed,' he said.

'I can't believe he's alive,' I said, my mind still on the implications. What this would mean for St Mary's. 'So what's next? We get him out and then . . . ?' I stopped because, well, what then?

Markham grinned. 'As the saying goes, "With Dr Bairstow, anything is possible."'

I frowned. 'Shouldn't that be God?'

'What?'

'That saying – I'm sure it should be God.'

'Sorry. With Dr Bairstow, God is possible.'

We downed the remainder of our drinks and went in to lunch.

Which was unexpectedly grand. Pennyroyal's famous slow roast pork with rosemary and apple. He'd obviously known Lady Amelia was on her way home even if we hadn't. I told Pennyroyal it was lucky Treadwell had accustomed me to this new mushroom environment.

He raised his eyebrows.

'You know,' I said. 'Kept in the dark and fed on shit.' And then realised, too late, he might take that as an adverse comment on his cooking.

No business was discussed during lunch. Pennyroyal and

Lady Amelia spoke of mutual friends, Lady Amelia's visit to the Royal Ballet, shopping, the traffic, the weather and other trivia. Markham and I ate and listened.

Outside, the sky had darkened and rain began to fall.

'We'll have our meeting in here, I think,' announced Lady Amelia. 'It's warm and the cocktail shaker is close by.'

'Right,' she said, after we'd cleared away the lunch things. 'Despite its posh appearance and high-class patients, the Red House is no different than any other secure establishment. Authorisation paperwork is required to transfer any prisoner to another location. All documents and movement orders originate from the Home Office, along with details of transportation and approved escort. Everything must be checked and cleared well in advance. We can't just breeze in and expect them to hand him over.'

'And from where do we obtain this paperwork?' said Markham. The accent had disappeared again.

'Well, obviously the first stage is to submit a request to move the prisoner and the second is to obtain official permission to do so.' She rummaged in a briefcase and plonked a large white foolscap envelope on the table. 'Everything we need.'

'Wow,' I said. 'You actually managed to get all that forged at such short notice?'

'Of course not,' she said. 'A really good forgery actually takes considerably longer to manufacture than simply obtaining the real thing. And is much more expensive. No, these documents are genuine. These will pass the strictest scrutiny because they are the real deal.' She regarded the envelope fondly. 'They are the dog's bollocks of genuine documents.'

I looked at the envelope but left them where they were. Even genuine documents lose their credibility if covered in greasy fingerprints.

Markham continued. 'Will we need to produce details of the prisoner's ultimate destination?'

'No. Once you have signed for the prisoner then the original establishment relinquishes all responsibility. With an official prisoner it is sometimes in everyone's best interests that the final destination remains unknown.'

'Are you able to talk us through it? What can we expect?'

She took a healthy swig of her post-lunch margarita.

'I think our plans must, of necessity, be very loose. None of us has the faintest idea how things will go down, so specific instructions are just a waste of time, don't you think?'

The words 'wing it' were not spoken but made their presence felt nevertheless.

Her plan had two parts. Lady Amelia and Pennyroyal would handle the London end and Mrs Brown. They had the entrée, they knew the lie of the land, they fitted in; common sense dictated they handle that part of the mission. Which left me and Markham to deal with Dr Bairstow.

'At least he isn't in a secure military prison,' said Lady Amelia. 'The Red House, although not without its own security, is a considerably easier proposition than, say, the Tower of London.'

I did not look at Markham.

'You and Markham would be members of the armed forces,' she continued, prompting a battle between the two of us over who would be the ranking officer.

'Well, me, obviously,' said Markham, 'given that *I* was actually in the army. I look the part. Let's face it – you're just a hot mess.'

'You could have stopped after hot.'

'No, I couldn't.'

'It should be me,' I said. 'In these days of positive gender . . .'

'Don't give me that cr—'

I played my winning card. 'And if it all goes horribly wrong, then I'll distract them and buy you the time to get Dr Bairstow safely away. Which you're much more likely to achieve than me. That's more important than who has the higher rank.'

He scowled. 'Well, all right then, but don't think I'm happy about it.'

We spread a clean cloth carefully over the table and familiarised ourselves with the paperwork.

'This is top-quality stuff,' said Markham, admiringly, feeling the paper between finger and thumb because, according to him, forgery is easy – it's getting the correct paper on which to forge your forgery that's the difficult part. 'This feels just like the real thing.'

'That's because it is the real thing,' said Pennyroyal from the other end of the kitchen. 'As we told you. Kindly keep it out of the apple sauce.'

We read it all through very carefully.

There were copies of the request to move the prisoner, the movement order itself to transport the prisoner Bairstow from the Red House to 'an alternative destination', together with our personal authority to do so, our IDs, vehicle details and registration number. Everything was signed, stamped, and, as Lady Amelia informed us, in perfect order.

'Because we have already submitted our paperwork and obtained the relevant permits, they should have the prisoner ready and waiting for you. Once you have proved your identity, there will be a simple handover and you can be on your way. You could be in and out in twenty minutes.'

'And if something goes wrong?'

'Well, if they don't like the look of you then you'll be arrested as soon as you come through the front door. Or if your documents don't pass muster. Or if you say or do something to arouse their suspicions. In any or all of those cases they'll arrest you. Or just shoot you on the spot,' she said jovially. 'However, please remember your paperwork is genuine. You will be presenting genuine documents signed by a genuine member of the government – Dr Bairstow's friend Mr Black. Who has rather stuck his neck out on this one, don't you think? But going back to your question – it's only the two of you who won't be. Genuine, I mean.'

'Will they question us?'

'Before they shoot you?'

'No – on our arrival. Before they hand over the prisoner.'

'Probably. You'll need a brief backstory. Any questions you can't answer, simply invoke the Official Secrets Act, clam up and say nothing. My advice is to keep the talking to a minimum and don't allow yourself to be drawn into conversation with anyone. Get in – take delivery of the prisoner – and get straight back out again.'

I asked if there would be any other on-site checks. 'I remember from my previous visit there's a checkpoint in the drive. And on the front desk, too.'

'You won't be going in the front door. There's a discreet door around the back, which is where the more sensitive patients are taken in and out. You'll have to show your ID as you come in through the gates but remember they'll be expecting you. That's the whole point of submitting all the paperwork in advance. Theoretically, any problems should have been ironed out long before you turn up.'

'And if there *are* any problems?'

'Mr Black, as the official signatory, will handle any difficulties that might arise. Your job is at the unskilled end of the spectrum.'

'Nothing new there, then.'

'Getting yourself into the Red House shouldn't present any problems. I do advise spending some time on your exit strategy – just on the off-chance things don't run quite as smoothly as we would like.'

'And while we're at the Red House, you'll be getting Mrs Brown out?'

'Yes, we'll be in London where, I suspect, we will be more at home than you.'

In other words, they got the civilised end of the assignment while we were responsible for the less subtle part.

'Markham and Maxwell,' I said gloomily. 'The blunt instruments of bounty hunters.'

'Recovery agents,' said Lady Amelia gently.

Lady Amelia had acquired the appropriate military police outfits. We didn't ask how. Markham said they looked amazingly
genuine and I couldn't help wondering if she'd just marched
into a barracks somewhere and stolen a couple of uniforms. Not
as unlikely as it sounds. Can I just say again how much easier
life is when you don't play by other people's rules?

We unpacked them carefully and I kept the plastic bag away
from Markham because according to the warning label, it wasn't
a toy.

'Redcaps,' said Markham, feelingly. Obviously this was not
his first encounter with the military police.

'Problem?' I said, wondering if he was still on someone's
wanted list from his army days.

'They're a bunch of evil, Satan-worshipping, psychotic bastards in uniform so no, not really.'

I tried on my peaked cap. The red clashed horribly with my
hair. 'Not known for their nurturing qualities, then? They don't
ask you how you're feeling today?'

'Only after they've belted you with their batons half a dozen
times. Sometimes then they ask you how you're feeling.'

I spent the afternoon having my uniform tailored to fit. By Pennyroyal. I don't know why I was astonished.

'An inch off the cuffs and another inch off the hem,' he said. 'Nothing fancy.' And he was right. Trust me, military uniforms aren't fitted half as stylishly or flatteringly as films and TV would have us believe. And then I wore it for a couple of days so it looked as if we belonged together. Markham did the same. He was a sergeant and I was a major.

'You're too old to be a captain,' said Pennyroyal, apparently under the impression he was complimenting me. 'They'd wonder why you never achieved your majority. You're just the right age for a major. And he . . .' he nodded at Markham, 'is your experienced and trustworthy SNCO.'

'Make sure you appreciate him,' said Markham, still admiring himself in the mirror. I made a note not to tell him he looked like a stunted robin. 'Sergeant, eh? Must remember to tell Major Guthrie when I see him next.'

'If you ever see him again,' I said, still not convinced this operation wasn't all going to end in tears. This wasn't an historian entangling herself in History with a knowledge, however vague, of who everyone was, what their motives were and how everything was going to turn out. This was all contemporary stuff and I hadn't got a clue how it would go down. Badly, probably. Unexpectedly, certainly.

The plan was simple. Pennyroyal would drop us off in his pod. We would collect the perfectly legitimate hired car, attach the military number plates and drive to the Red House.

Once there, we would wave our papers to gain access – I was able to brief Markham on security measures as they had been a few years ago, during my extremely fleeting visit. I didn't tell Smallhope and Pennyroyal how that had ended. Markham knew, but said nothing, contenting himself with making little swimming gestures to remind me of the unhappy combination of me, the lake and Leon's car.

We'd take the back entrance, flourish our immaculate paperwork, pick up our prisoner and drive away. What could possibly go wrong?

'Have you any thoughts how you'll play things?' said Lady Amelia, striding into the room as we were packing everything away. 'What's your backstory?'

'I shall be the professional woman,' I said. 'Brusque, polite but slightly impatient, and continually on the watch for gender discrimination. That always makes people nervous.'

'I shan't say anything at all,' said Markham. 'I shall finger my weapon and look for an excuse to shoot someone.'

'Does Dr Bairstow know about this?' I said. 'Will he be expecting us?'

She hesitated. 'I think assuming he doesn't know about any of this will be your wisest course of action. You'll need to sign for him,' she continued. 'From that moment onwards, the prisoner will be your responsibility.'

'Won't they query such a small escort?' I said.

'I'm five foot six,' said the escort indignantly.

'I mean – there's only one of you.'

'You only ever need one of me,' Markham said smugly.

'I'm sure you'll think of something to tell them,' said Lady Amelia. 'Once you've signed for Dr Bairstow do not hang around.'

'Will he be restrained in any way?'

'I don't know but take handcuffs or zips just in case. Be

prepared to have to return their own restraints before you leave. You know how cheap government establishments can be.'

We nodded. We knew.

We practised. We had a slight idea of the layout and what would be where. We chalked outlines out in the yard, shunting nosey chickens out of the way. Markham tried holding a chicken's beak to the line because he said it hypnotises them, only it didn't and he was badly pecked by an indignant Scots Dumpy. And then its friend turned up and had a go at him, too.

My job was to secure the handover. Markham's would be to protect me, the prisoner, and secure our exit. If we got into any difficulties then I would create a distraction and drop off Markham's radar of responsibility. His priority would be to get Dr Bairstow out safely. If he had to leave me behind then so be it.

He said he'd come back for me, I told him he'd better not. 'If you've got Dr Bairstow then get out of there as quickly as you can. I won't come to any harm in just the few hours it will take for them to think about what to do with me. If they shoot me then I'm already in a medical facility. Do not jeopardise everything by coming back for me.'

Markham nodded because I was talking sense. As he said – who'd have thought?

We went through it over and over again. What to do if I stood there. Or over there. Or if they tried to split us up for some reason. We needed to be aware of each other's position at all times so we choreographed it – like a dance. The most important thing, said Markham, was to look as if we'd done this hundreds of times before and were completely accustomed to working with each other. Which was nearly true.

We practised with him standing on my right, my left, behind me, in front of me, over in the corner, standing on the ceiling. We practised for three guards accompanying Dr Bairstow. Then for five. Then for a whole gang of them.

We talked about the Red House staff we were likely to encounter and how to address them. The security staff were all on eighteen-month postings and it seemed most unlikely anyone there would recognise me from my previous visit.

We talked about whether they would bring him to us – the most likely scenario, Markham and Pennyroyal thought – or whether they would take us to him. In which case, if anything went wrong then we were a long way from the door.

'Straight out of the window,' was Markham's advice. There were only two storeys in that part of the facility so if we landed on grass, we'd probably be fine. Should I have to jump into the car park I was instructed not to land on my head. If we were in the basement and something went horribly wrong, I was to treat it as a fire and make my way calmly to the nearest exit. And to be sure I had noted said exits on the way in.

We looked at images of the exterior of the building – the car park, the gardens, likely cover, blind spots, areas where we'd be completely exposed, other areas where we could expect some cover.

'I'll pull up outside the door,' I said. 'The sign says no parking, but I don't think I'll be the sort of person who would take any notice of that sort of thing.'

'You've never been the sort of person who takes any notice of anything,' said Markham. 'It's only because you can't actually park a car that you don't hold the world record for parking tickets.'

There was another brisk discussion, the end result being that to allay any fears, he, Markham, would be doing the driving. It had been unanimous. No discussion. I'd had to agree.

In another part of the house Lady Amelia and Pennyroyal were going through exactly the same preparations for rescuing Mrs Brown. Both operations had to take place simultaneously so there would be no chance for anyone to warn anyone else, should everything go tits up.

It was Pennyroyal who finally called a halt, saying there was such a thing as overpreparation. It was all very well to try to anticipate every contingency, but in his opinion, something always happened completely out of the blue and all the preparation in the world couldn't cover everything. Improvisation was often the only way to go.

We spent the night before having a quiet dinner. I'd noticed the two of them never socialised in the local area if they could help it. If they wanted a night out, they went to London. The nearest village was about four miles away and as far as the world knew, only the Faradays lived and farmed here, and the Faradays themselves were very handsomely paid to maintain that myth. I wondered if the local people were even aware of Smallhope and Pennyroyal's existence.

Anyway, we dined at home. Beef and chianti lasagne followed by orange sorbet. Pennyroyal served wine but none of us had more than one glass.

I had an early night, leaving the three of them sitting around the table. I'd deliberately kept myself concentrating solely on the operation and its mechanics. At no point had I allowed myself to think of Dr Bairstow. Of the possibility of getting him back and what that would mean. I couldn't afford that luxury. Get through this. Get him back. And then think about it.

I stood in my room, looked at my major's uniform hanging in the wardrobe, the red cap on the shelf and my shiny shoes neatly lined up on the rack. I opened my briefcase, checked over the documents one last time, tried not to think about where I could be this time tomorrow, had a long, slow bath, picked up a book, read three paragraphs and fell fast asleep.

26

Pennyroyal dropped us off in his pod. The hired car with its fake military plates was exactly where it should be. The journey was a bit of a blur for me. I sat in the back of the car and ran through everything. Moment by moment. Action by action. What to do if this happened. What to do if that happened. What to do if everything went pear-shaped and we had to run for it.

Markham drove quietly and well within the speed limits, mirror, signalling and manoeuvring as carefully as if he was taking his driving test. Fields and signposts zipped past.

We drove for about an hour and a half, avoiding motorways and big towns. The car was quite comfortable and showed no signs of the digestive troubles that so often afflicted Bashford's Chariot of (sometimes literally) Fire.

I sat in the back because, as I told Markham, I was the officer, my briefcase on the seat beside me. Neither of us said very much. I was concentrating on not panicking.

As we drew closer, I began to recognise familiar landmarks. Pubs, mostly, because St Mary's was only about twelve miles away in that direction. Markham slowed as the lanes narrowed. The Red House was out in the middle of nowhere, as befitted its need for discretion and privacy, because no one is ever reassured by discovering half the government is in desperate need of psychiatric assistance and the other half is already getting it.

We were in late summer and the farmers hadn't yet trimmed the hedges. The occasional branch whipped at the windows. The grass verges were overgrown and thick with unseen hazards. I knew from experience that a combination of concealed objects in grass verges and a determined driver could do a great deal of damage to an unsuspecting car.

'Nearly there,' said Markham, and I turned my thoughts from the past to the now.

He slowed. I smoothed my hair, settled my hat on my head and squared my shoulders. He indicated left, easing the car through the gates.

The security check was just inside the main gate. A guard stepped out and waved us to a halt. One walked around the car, checking the registration plate against his list.

Markham opened his window to show the second guard his ID. I simply held mine to the closed window because I was a major and making things easy for people wasn't part of my remit.

There were no problems. We were on the list. And for the right reasons, just for once. Everything checked out. We were instructed to take the left-hand fork, up went the barrier and we were waved through.

Markham thanked them politely, and we crawled up the drive.

'Nice grounds,' he said, and they were. With immaculate lawns and well-planted borders, even at the dusty end of summer, everything still looked colourful and fresh.

'That's the Annexe over there,' I said, pointing to a separate building. 'That's where the arts and crafts centre, gym, swimming pool and so on are. Something tells me Dr Bairstow will not have been availing himself of those facilities.'

'We go this way,' said Markham, turning left off the well-kept drive and on to a slightly rutty lane. Towards the non-public area. We twisted around trees and shrubberies, eventually arriving at the back of the building. As expected, there was the small car park and our destination – a door marked *Authorised Personnel Only*. Markham very carefully turned the car around so it was pointing in the right direction should we need to get away quickly. I sat in the back, ostensibly arranging my paperwork while he checked out the CCTV cameras.

'OK,' he said. 'Let's say you need to get away in a hurry and I'm not with you, the keys are in the ignition. The car's in neutral. All the doors are unlocked. Put Dr Bairstow into the back. Throw him in if he won't cooperate. Get into the driver's seat and drive away. Don't wait for me. Don't look back. You know where to go. You know what to do when you get there. Everything's all set up and waiting. I'll join you if I can but wait only for as long as is safe. Then go without me.'

I nodded. 'And the same applies to you, too.'

'All set?'

'Yes.'

He jumped out and held the door open for me. I could get used to this.

I stepped out and looked around. The door was off to my right. Our car was parked in the space nearest to it. Pointing outwards and all ready to go. I checked the car park exit. There was no chain nor any apparent means of barring the exit. No bollards. No sleeping policemen. Three more cars occupied spaces at the other end. Staff probably, given the location. And the age of the cars. Security isn't a terribly well-paid occupation. Markham can drone on about it for hours.

There was no one in sight.

Markham looked at his watch. 'We're exactly on time. Hope it's all going well in London. Ready?'

He walked ahead of me and rapped sharply on the door. A disembodied voice instructed us to step back and look up at the camera. We did so, holding up our IDs at the same time and trying to look as if we did this sort of thing several times a week.

The door clicked open.

'After you, ma'am,' said Markham, ushering me in.

I found myself in a small anteroom, about twenty feet square, with one corner converted into the traditional glass-fronted cubicle, occupied by a uniformed security guard. He looked up as we entered.

I left Markham to deal with him while I took a look around. Excluding the one we'd come in by, there were three doors in this room – one in each wall. The one to the left was actually encased by the glass-and-wood cubicle and led, I suspected, to the guards' lockers and restrooms. The one to my right would lead to a room with an outside window, so I guessed that might well be the superintendent's office. The door ahead of us probably led into the facility proper. The keypad alongside bore out this theory. And no handle. In fact, none of the doors had an external handle. No access from this side. So, at least three rooms led into this one but there was just the one exit. The one behind us and only the security guard could buzz us in and out.

It made sense. This was a holding area. In or out, all traffic must come through here.

A table stood against the right-hand wall with a quantity of incredibly ancient magazines spread thereon. Seriously, a social historian would have had an orgasm over this collection. A few bleak wooden chairs were pushed against the wall nearby. Something told me the public never saw this part of one of the most expensive medical facilities in the country.

I could smell that institution smell – disinfectant, floor polish and people. All the surfaces were washable. Everything was old and scruffy, but spotlessly clean.

The uniformed man behind the glass held out his hand. 'Your identifications, please.'

We handed them over.

He scanned them and then handed them back again. 'If you could sign the book, please. And enter the car registration, here. Thank you.'

He passed a plastic tray through the hole in the glass. 'If you could deposit your weapons, please. Thank you.'

We'd expected this. Silently we made them safe, showed them to him for verification and dropped them into the tray, which was then placed in a pigeon hole. One of many behind the desk. All the others were empty. It looked as though we were the morning's only guests. Markham never took his eyes off his gun, giving an excellent impersonation of an unhappy SNCO parted from his weapon.

The guard spoke into his intercom. 'Major Bradley is here, sir.' He turned back to us. 'The superintendent will be with you in a moment, ma'am.'

I nodded and turned away to examine the ancient magazines.

As far as I know, the *BBC Knowledge* magazine ceased publication some considerable time ago. I was itching to turn the pages but first things first.

I knew that contrary to its own publicity material and because of the mysterious disappearance of its former director – an event with which I was not unconnected – there were now two superintendents here at the Red House. James Washburn, in charge of the medical side, and Martin Gaunt – security. The public face and the private. Our appointment was with Martin Gaunt.

Time ticked on and still no sign of the security superintendent. We had an appointment. He knew we were coming. Was he genuinely busy or was he, as I was beginning to suspect, exercising his control by making us wait?

I knew the worst thing I could do was to show signs of impatience, but things were happening in London. Pennyroyal and Smallhope would already be in place. It was vital the two operations occurred simultaneously. We didn't want anyone phoning here to warn them.

I stared at the table. What if this was a game of nerves? What if he was quite happy to make us wait all day?

I said, 'Sergeant, what's the time?'

'Ten past one, ma'am.'

Damn. I turned to the guard in the cubicle. 'I'm on a schedule today and can't wait any longer. Please could you inform Mr Gaunt that I'm sorry he was unable to have the prisoner ready for us. I'll report this failure back to London and they'll make arrangements for another day. Although they won't be happy.'

My suspicion we were being watched was confirmed. It

couldn't have been a coincidence. At that very moment the right-hand door opened, the security superintendent entered, and my heart sank.

We didn't have much info on Martin Gaunt. He'd served in the police, rather than the military. He was in his mid-sixties and I suppose, subconsciously, I'd imagined someone just putting in the final few years before collecting his government pension and retiring to grow marrows. Or a fussy little man being a big fish in a small pool at everyone else's expense.

Wrong again.

I think everyone's initial impressions must have been un-favourable. I saw a very tall man – well over six feet – whose domed, shaven head made him look even taller. God knows what he saw when he looked at me but he certainly wasn't impressed.

Gaunt wore an impeccably tailored black suit that shouted, 'I'm too good for this place.' All his visible skin was a deep shiny pink as if he scrubbed himself down three times a day. With hedgehog skins. With his slightly underhung jaw, he looked like a shiny pink shark.

The worst part, though, was his eyes. He wore those tiny round spectacles that reflected the overhead lights and made them difficult to read. And then he stepped out of the glare and I wasn't any better off because they were so dark, I couldn't tell where pupil ended and iris began. They were just black pools. The whites of his eyes were disconcertingly white. Seriously bright white. As if he'd scrubbed those as well.

He had authoritarian written all over him. Relationships, family life, sex, outside interests – I suspected everything had been subjugated in his quest for complete and absolute control over everyone and everything around him. I'd finally come across someone who made Treadwell look appealing. If St Mary's had got Gaunt instead, there would have been deaths.

The slightly good news was that he had a folder under his arm, containing, if we were very lucky, his version of our transfer documents.

He checked our IDs again, taking his time over it. The naughty part of me itched to ask for his, but before I could get us all into trouble, he said abruptly, 'Papers?'

The courteous approach would have been to introduce himself, ask after the journey, enquire re current bladder status and invite us into his office to review our documents.

We obviously didn't rate any of that.

I wasn't going to hand them to him. I walked to the table, opened my briefcase, swept the magazines aside and laid out my papers, one after the other.

He was going to play games with us. I was certain his next move would be to shoulder me aside and manspread over as much space as he could manage while ostentatiously examining our immaculate documents. I'd end up crushed against the wall.

I stepped back, ignored him completely and went to stand by Markham, who was waiting, wooden-faced, by the exit. There was no handle on his door either, but there was an emergency door-release mechanism on the left. Fire regulations, I guessed.

The remark about the tight schedule had been a mistake. Gaunt took his revenge by making us wait. Relishing his moment, he picked up each sheet of paper and meticulously read every single line. Every now and then, just to demonstrate his superiority over lesser mortals, he would refer back to something on a previous page.

I stood quite still but I could hear telephones ringing inside the cubicle. I told myself to relax. This was a busy place. Not everything was about us. But it was nerve-wracking, nevertheless. I had to work at standing still and keeping my face calm. Especially when the telephone in his own office began to ring. It rang on and on. I didn't dare look at Markham.

Fortunately, Gaunt was more concerned with playing with us. Whoever had called would have to wait for Gaunt to finish here. Because he was an important man and everyone should always be very aware of that.

I don't know if the phone diverted elsewhere or whether the caller just gave up in the end but eventually it stopped. The silence was even worse.

It was eighteen minutes past one by the time he'd gone over everything at least once. According to our schedule, we should have our prisoner by now and be heading towards the door. A faint frown puckered Gaunt's shiny pink forehead. I suspected it was because he'd found nothing to pick at.

I took a brief moment to wonder how prisoners fared under his regime. I didn't imagine for one moment he actually physically tortured anyone, but here he had complete control over people whose poor life choices had left them with no power at all. No rights. No civil liberties. I wondered how much autonomy he had. And how had he fared against Dr Bairstow? And, more worryingly, how had Dr Bairstow fared against him? That his people feared him was very apparent. The guard behind the glass sat at attention, not making a move. Not a sound.

And neither did we. Until Markham yawned ostentatiously, breaking the tension.

Eventually, Gaunt gathered up our papers in one contemptuous handful and thrust them back at me. 'Everything appears to be in order.'

I put them back down on the table and began to arrange them neatly. Now he could wait for me.

'Why now?' he said, suddenly.

I kept my attention on the papers. I'd presented them to him in perfect order. Simple courtesy required him to return the compliment. 'Why now what?'

'Why today? Friday is the usual transfer day.'

We'd left the *Reason for Transfer* box empty. It wasn't mandatory.

I said brusquely, 'I'm in a hurry.'

He folded his arms. The message was clear. No one was going anywhere until he'd squeezed every last little bit of pettiness from the situation.

I thought I'd have a bit of fun. Well, why not.

I glanced at Markham, then at the guard behind the glass – who probably couldn't hear a thing anyway and was probably too scared of Gaunt to try – and took a step away to the centre of the room, quite curious to see whether Gaunt would follow me. Move from his turf into mine. Oh, the games people play.

He did. Without looking at him directly, I said very quietly, 'Someone screwed up.'

It was exactly the right thing to say. A rigid disciplinarian himself, other people's mistakes would always be another reinforcement of his own superiority.

Matching my tone, he said, 'Who? London?'

'Treadwell. Treadwell screwed up.'

'I've never met the man,' he said. 'What did he do?'

I suspected that should he ever meet Treadwell, this would be something to hold over him. This was how he operated.

I compressed my lips and then said tightly, 'He let Maxwell go.'

He blinked. Good. He wasn't in the loop. That would rankle. 'Who's he?'

'The one person who knows almost as much about St Mary's as Bairstow.' I let anger bleed into my voice. 'Maxwell is – was – Head of the History Department and has walked out of St Mary's and vanished off the face of the earth.'

'Someone's got him?'

'No one knows. Thanks to Treadwell, Maxwell's in the wind and anything could happen. There are heads rolling in all directions over this. Word has gone out. No more Mr Nice Guy as far as Bairstow's concerned. We transfer him to London and he tells us everything he knows, like it or not, and if it kills him . . . well.' I looked Gaunt in the eye. 'I can't afford to waste any time.'

'In that case, why didn't you bring a helicopter?'

Because Markham, while quite happy to TWOC pretty well everything that wasn't nailed down, had drawn the line at helicopters. Besides, we didn't need a chopper.

'Standing by,' I said.

Gaunt nodded, opened his folder and produced his own paperwork. 'Sign here.'

'When I've seen the prisoner,' I said, leaving my briefcase on the table as I'd been instructed by Markham.

'There shouldn't be any trouble,' he'd said, 'but keep your hands free at all times. Just in case.'

411

Gaunt nodded to the guard in the cubicle. The door ahead of me buzzed. A metallic voice announced, 'Door opening. Door opening.'

A uniformed security guard came first. Unarmed – or apparently so. He paused, looked around and caught Gaunt's eye. Apparently satisfied I didn't represent a massive security threat – ha, little did he know – he nodded over his shoulder and they brought in Dr Bairstow.

Another guard escorted him – or supported him would be a better description. My heart sank. For the first time I realised he was elderly. He looked bedraggled; his little bit of hair had grown and fell lankly over his face. He shuffled like an old man. He was wearing grey sweats – normally he would have gone to the stake rather than publicly appear in such garments – and just generally looked seedy and frail. He and his escort waited silently in the doorway.

Dr Bairstow's glance passed over me. Completely uninterested. I wondered if perhaps he was drugged, which might be a problem if we had to make a run for it.

I made a show of looking critically at the prisoner and then said to Gaunt, 'Can he manage for himself?'

'Oh yes. He's uncooperative but no trouble physically. You should be able to get him in and out of a car without difficulty. Do you have far to go?'

I smiled politely and ignored the question. Need-to-know.

I was actually very pleased. Everything was going exactly as Smallhope and Pennyroyal had said it would. We'd walked through the procedures so many times I felt quite familiar with everything going on around me.

412

'If your people could bring him through, please, Mr Gaunt, my sergeant will take it from here.' Assuming Gaunt's consent, I continued, 'Sergeant . . .'

Markham crossed to the cubicle and held out his hand. 'My gun, please.'

The clerk reached for the tray and set it down on the counter. Markham took his gun.

Gaunt held out his own paperwork again. All I had to do was sign . . .

Dr Bairstow shuffled towards me. I was pleased to see no one hustled him. He looked so ill. I hoped he could walk as far as the car.

Markham had his weapon. Mine was still in the tray. Dr Bairstow was shuffling across the room. Gaunt was standing by the table. The two guards stood by the inner door, watching closely. Everyone was exactly where they should be.

Gaunt laid a double sheet of paper on the table. I leaned over it, read it carefully because this could still go wrong and signed A. B. Bradley (Maj) with a flourish.

We were going to get away with this. This was going to work.

Gaunt picked up the paperwork, tore off one sheet and handed it to me.

'The prisoner is now officially yours, Major Bradley. You have responsibility.'

'Thank you, Superintendent Gaunt.'

Behind us, the red light over the internal door began to flash again. The same metallic voice intoned, 'Door opening.'

Gaunt looked over his shoulder and back to me again. 'Goodbye, Major.'

'Goodbye, superintendent, and thank you. After you, Sergeant.' I reached out to pick up my briefcase.

The clerk behind the desk pressed the control and opened the outer door for us. I could see the car park. I could see our car. I could see sunshine and trees. Markham took Dr Bairstow's arm in a firm grip. 'Now then, sir, this way, please.'

Dr Bairstow began to shuffle through the outer door.

And then a voice shouted, 'Stop that woman.'

Bollocks.

Markham didn't hesitate. Actually, neither did Dr Bairstow. Cunning old bugger, I suspected he'd been waiting for just this moment. In fact, I wouldn't mind betting his first words would be, 'What took you so long, Dr Maxwell?' He was transformed. Gone was the frail old man barely aware of his surroundings. He might not have his stick but it was very apparent he was perfectly capable of getting out of here by himself.

He moved at some speed through the door.

'Black car,' shouted Markham after him. 'Get in the back.' He himself stood blocking the doorway, gun raised. Gaunt, over by the far door, was shouting instructions at the clerk behind the glass, who frantically stabbed at the door controls, but there must have been some sort of safety device that prevented this heavy metal door slamming shut if a person was in the way.

My gun was still in the tray and I was too far away to get at it, so I spun around to deal with this unknown threat behind me.

I don't swear anything like as often as I used to – despite being a mother – but I swore now.

Fuck. Fuck, fuck, fuckity-fuck.

Standing just inside the door, staring at me with hatred in their eyes, were Halcombe and Sullivan and, as if that wasn't bad enough, pushing past them to see what was going on, Captain Hyssop.

Again – fuck.

My first thought was – what the bloody hell are they doing here?

My second thought was not to be so silly. Where else would they be? The Red House was a select medical establishment where the government stashes those whose personal problems are becoming an embarrassment to the nation. That weird cabinet minister was here for a while – you know the one I mean – and tellingly, six months later, they hosted her husband as well, so God knows what was going on there. Discreet and effective – but not cheap – the nation's leaders could be nudged back on to the straight and narrow before anyone became aware their behaviour had been any more bizarre than usual.

And the Red House wasn't that far from St Mary's – where else would they send a couple of inconvenient nutters? It really should have occurred to me, although, and I think everyone will agree, I've had a lot on recently.

It had all gone so well. They hadn't been expecting trouble. Why would they? Our paperwork had passed the closest of inspections. We'd passed muster, we'd taken legal possession of the prisoner, one more minute and we'd have been driving out of the car park. And now – this.

Well, at least my role was clear. We'd talked about this. I knew exactly what to do. I shouted, 'Go.'

His gun raised, Markham backed out through the door. With the obstruction removed, the door swung shut and locked. I heard the clunk. I was trapped on the wrong side.

Well, there went my escape route but at least Markham and Dr Bairstow had made it out. My job now was to hold the door. Alarms pealed everywhere. Lights flashed. Throughout the building I could faintly hear the crashing doors of lockdown. Security teams would already have been deployed. If Markham lingered for even one moment . . . if he waited for me . . .

We'd discussed our exit strategy. What to do if things went wrong. According to Markham, the trick of successful escaping is to do the unexpected. Not for him the expected escape route down the drive taken by the law-abiding. He'd be smashing his way through the gardens, the car digging great ruts in those perfect lawns, flattening rose bushes and shattering garden ornaments. And he wouldn't have to go far. There was a small grove of trees about four hundred yards away, just inside the perimeter fence, and behind that grove a secluded spot where a small pod could be concealed until required as a getaway vehicle. Obviously, we hadn't been able to arrive in the pod because it was important to appear in a conventional vehicle. We couldn't just appear from nowhere and expect them to hand over Dr Bairstow. That would never have worked.

Had things gone according to plan we'd have driven through the gates, turned right, gone a couple of hundred yards down the lane, turned right into the fields and accessed the pod from there. We'd have had to leave the car there. Pennyroyal – or whoever's identity he had borrowed – would lose his deposit if it was discovered before we could retrieve it, but recovery of Dr Bairstow was the priority. And I still had my part to play in that. I should get on with it.

Once in a bad dream – a very bad dream – I guarded another door so someone dear to me could get away. Every second had counted. Every second.

Now I stood against the door to the Red House. I honestly don't know what I thought I could do but whatever it was, it wouldn't have to be for very long. Just long enough for Markham and Dr Bairstow to find the grove and call up the pod.

On the other hand, this was Halcombe and Sullivan in front of me and both of them were very familiar with the existence of small hut-like structures with unusual properties.

'Get her out of the way,' roared Halcombe. 'After them. They'll get away.'

Well, that was a big mistake. I could have told him there was no way Gaunt would appreciate anyone attempting to trespass on his turf.

In a perfect world they would have argued among themselves, giving Markham the time to get clear and I wouldn't have to do anything. Sadly – and I don't know if anyone's noticed this – we live in a very imperfect world.

Things continued to happen at a rapid rate.

Sullivan, coming alive at the thought of action – or, more likely, coming alive at the thought of revenge – grabbed me. Too late, I remembered how strong he was.

I was hoping very much that Gaunt wouldn't let them shoot me but on the other hand I'd just made a bit of a fool of him and he wouldn't be feeling that friendly. He might well decide to let them have ten minutes' fun with me.

Fun, however, was not what Sullivan had in mind.

I was forced down on to my knees by a man who never cared how much he hurt people. I heard the crack as they hit the hard floor and for one moment I wondered if they were broken. Seizing both my arms, he dragged them back and up. Long past the point of pain. Great pain. The position forced my head and shoulders forwards. All I could see was the floor.

I heard a door opening somewhere. Gaunt shouted, 'Red alert! Immediate lockdown. Alert the main gate. One intruder. One inmate. Shoot on sight. Search the premises and grounds and if that dozy wazzock Washburn starts whining about his precious patients then shoot him too. Just find them.'

The door closed, cutting off his voice as he passed through. All his attention was on retrieving his prisoner. The one he'd been tricked into parting with. He would be on fire to rectify his mistake. Although it wouldn't be *his* mistake. This would be someone else's cock-up. At the moment he had no interest in me, which was a shame because from my point of view I reckoned I'd have been better off with him. With all his many faults, he was at least mostly sane, whereas I had grave doubts about Sullivan and Halcombe. And Hyssop, in whose charge they apparently were, was just a complete waste of a pair of shoes.

Sullivan forced my arms even higher. The pain was excruciating. Overwhelming. I couldn't think of anything else. No coherent thoughts. No clever plans. No witty remarks. Just horrible, brutal pain. Agony rippled up and down my arms, through my shoulders, into my neck and even around my ribcage.

This was a form of *strappado*. A torture very popular with the Catholic Church during the Spanish Inquisition, which tells you how effective it must be. And efficient. You didn't catch the

419

church wasting long hours in the torture pit. An hour of this was enough to kill you. Even just a few minutes of it could lead to long-term nerve and tendon damage. Girolamo Savonarola – our old friend from the Bonfire of the Vanities – was tortured by this very method and it was allegedly used at the Salem Witch Trials as well. Because it works. If done properly – if the victim is hung from a rope with their arms tied behind them and taking the full weight of their body – then they die.

I could believe it. The bastard put his knee on my back for leverage and hauled again. All I could do to try to ease the pain was lean forwards some more. My forehead touched the icy floor. The only thing saving me was that most of my weight was being taken by my knees. My shoulders were being wrenched from their sockets. I clenched my teeth but there was no holding it back. And why would I even try? A scream burst out of my mouth. And again. I was in agony. He was dislocating my shoulders a fraction of an inch at a time. Arms aren't supposed to do this. Shoulders aren't supposed to take this strain. Imagine pulling a chicken wing apart. Remember that gruesome little popping sound? That was going to be me any second now.

And then, just when I was convinced I was going to pass out from the pain, gasping for breath, screaming and dribbling, the agony seemed to ease a fraction.

My relief was short-lived. Something cold and hard bored into the top of my head. Shit – he must have grabbed my gun from the plastic tray. Halcombe yelled, 'This time. This time, you bitch! This time you're going to die.'

I actually didn't care. I was enveloped in a ball of flaming pain. I tried to fall sideways but Sullivan had me in a firm grasp. He shoved his knee between my shoulder blades and pushed again, his arms pulling mine backwards. Every part of me was screaming in red-hot pain. Physically, I think this was the worst thing that had ever happened to me.

I couldn't tell what Halcombe was yelling. He had to yell because I was making a hell of a racket. I couldn't hear anything over the throbbing inside my own head. I think I might have shouted, 'Just do it, for God's sake,' but I don't know. I could feel dribble running from the corner of my mouth. My throat was raw. My screams were no longer screams, just hoarse, long, drawn-out wails of suffering.

Halcombe himself was still shrieking. His loss of control was frightening. Words spewed everywhere, a torrent of abuse spilling from his lips. 'You took my life, you . . . Do you know the things I've had to do just to stay alive? Never mind what I did for food. Well, I've done it. All of it. And worse. And the one thing that kept me going was the knowledge that one day – one day, Maxwell, you fucking b—' There was a long string of vile words. The gun jabbed again. 'I knew one day I'd have you and now I have. And then I'm going after your kid. Trust me – life as a climbing boy will be a picnic compared with what I'm going to do to him. And every single second I'll make sure he knows it's all your fault.' He was crying – nearly hysterical – completely out of control. 'That you're the reason! All the pain and humiliations – the vile, unspeakable things done to me – I'll do them to him. And then I'll sell him on. For others to do even worse. He'll learn to hate you as I do. But first, I'm going to blow your fucking brains up that fucking wall.'

The gun jabbed again. I knew this time I really was going to die. Gaunt had pissed off – he had other priorities. I spared a thought for Markham. Had he and Dr Bairstow got away? I

421

don't know what the guard in the cubicle was doing. Pulled out by Gaunt, I suspected, who wouldn't want any of his people involved in this. If I died, then Hyssop would carry the can. Gaunt would make sure of that.

The pressure on my arms eased again. I stopped screaming. In the silence I could hear my own panting. And the snick of the safety catch coming off. All this had taken only seconds. Far, far less time than it takes to describe.

'The last thing you hear,' Halcombe said quietly, 'will be the shot that kills you.'

I wondered if I would. How quickly would it happen? Would I actually hear the shot that killed me?

Yes. Yes, I did. There was an enormous explosion at one and the same time both inside and outside my head. The echoes resounded around my skull, ringing from one side to the other. Back and forth. Back and forth. The world went black. There was nothing. There was nowhere. There was no one. Everything stopped.

Death – the all-encompassing darkness we drag behind us from the moment of our birth . . . the one from which there is no escape . . . the one that inevitably overwhelms us when our time is done . . . here was mine. My time had finally come. For years, I'd always been one hop, skip or jump ahead of it, laughing as I got away every time but now, now I'd finally stumbled. My death pounced, smothering me in its dark embrace. This truly was the end.

I . . . died.

28

The world was a negative. All black and white. And very cold.

I looked down. I was standing up to my ankles in snow. The ground was white. The trees were skeletons against the black sky. The lake, off to my right, was black, deep and motionless. There were no stars in the sky and no light reflected in the lake.

A ghostly wind whispered among the ghostly trees but nothing moved.

I was back at St Mary's, standing in our tiny graveyard. Was this my funeral? Had I been buried already? Was that it? And now I was doomed to stand here for all eternity, cold and alone?

St Mary's itself had disappeared. The whole universe had shrunk down to just this tiny spot surrounded on all sides by the whispering darkness of death. Who knew what waited for me in there? Lisa Dottle, broken and betrayed and blaming me? Or Isabella Barclay, her gaze fixed on me as her lifeblood soaked silently into the dirt, her hatred of me the last thing to die. Or Clive Ronan, with his broken spine and ruined face, the black hole of his mouth cursing me with words I didn't want to hear.

They'd walked behind me while I was alive. They'd waited patiently for the inevitable and now, finally, here I was. Guest of honour in my own private hell as the souls of those whose death I'd caused feasted on mine.

The silence was vast and everlasting. And had always been so. Time stood still here. This was not part of the world I had known.

I looked around. Neat rows of headstones were laid out in front of me. The names were obscured by snow but that didn't matter because I knew them all. Every last one of them.

The black and white silence stretched on and on and on.

There's a story somewhere. Every year a bird flies around the world and comes to a mountain. He strikes a rock with his beak and flies away again. And the next year and the next and so on. Until the rock is worn away. Then he moves on to another rock and then another and then another until finally, the whole mountain is worn away to nothing. And even though it has taken the little bird hundreds of thousands of millions of years – all those years are only the first second of the first minute of eternity.

The cold was striking up through my feet. And my heart. Someone stood behind me. I dared not move. I couldn't move. I was paralysed with fear. My head spun. The world began to skid away from me. I was lost. They'd come for me. This was my end. It was as if I'd always known I would end this way.

A voice said, 'Max.'

I opened my eyes.

I was in Sick Bay. Light streamed through the window. Dazzling, eye-watering sunshine. A dark figure sat on the window seat, silhouetted against the brilliant light.

There was a sigh of exasperation. 'I can't find my bloody lighter.'

I swallowed. My voice wouldn't work. I swallowed again and croaked, 'Peterson has it.'

'Ah.'

I heard a match strike and then I could smell cigarette smoke, see it even, floating across the room, hazy blue in the sunlight.

'You shouldn't be here, you know,' she said, puffing her smoke out of the window. 'That's so bloody typical of you, isn't it? What's the phrase – wrong time, wrong place? Bloody historians.' The figure was already fading. As insubstantial as the fast-disappearing smoke.

'Wait,' I said urgently.

'You need to sort yourself out. And quickly.'

I said stupidly, 'I can't. I'm dead.'

'No, you're not.'

I could still hear echoes of the shot that had killed me. 'Yes, I am.'

'For God's sake – who's the bloody doctor here?'

'But . . .' I looked around. 'Where am I?'

'The most dangerous place in the world.'

That figured.

'You're inside your own head, Maxwell. WAKE UP.'

Well, that was nasty. I did as I was told and opened my eyes. I was in a small hospital room. On my right was a window. Just an ordinary window with the sash pulled up to let in the summer sunshine and with an ordinary sill. No window seat.

The room was bare of everything except a bed and a small locker next to it, a plain blue plastic chair and a waste bin.

The smell was familiar. Shit – I was still at the Red House, which meant I was probably still under Gaunt's jurisdiction. This should be fun.

The throbbing pain in my shoulders and arms didn't seem to have lessened even the tiniest fraction. I squinted down. I was wearing a cotton hospital gown and covered with a light blue blanket. My army uniform had been tossed over a chair on the other side of the room with my shoes tucked neatly underneath.

I'd like to say I ignored the pain and tried to sit up. That's what heroines do. They're always ignoring the pain. Daft bats. Sadly, it's not that easy. I rolled on to my side and discovered my right hand was handcuffed to the bedrail. I don't know why they'd bothered. I could barely move as it was.

And that was the least of my problems because Treadwell was standing in the doorway. He'd obviously arrived from St Mary's. I wondered how much time had passed. And what of Markham and Dr Bairstow?

He walked forwards to stand at the foot of the bed. 'Well, Dr Maxwell?'

I swear, if he said, 'Here's another fine mess you've got yourself into,' I would not be responsible for my actions.

I found my voice. 'You lied to me,' I said. 'Dr Bairstow and Mrs Brown are alive. I don't know what's going . . .'

'Oh, for heaven's sake,' he said impatiently. 'Haven't you worked it out yet?'

Since I hadn't worked out anything yet – let's face it, until not long ago I'd been unconscious and exploring the unpleasant bilges of my psyche – I said nothing, but kept my end up by looking as if of course I knew everything but there were just one or two teeny-tiny points that still required elucidation.

426

Treadwell sighed. 'I know what you are thinking but I am not the person you should fear.'

'Who then?'

He sighed. 'Edward Bairstow is . . . a friend of mine.'

Well, that stopped me in my tracks. Not the statement itself but the fact that Dr Bairstow had friends. And this friend in particular.

A penny began to drop. 'He set all this up,' I said.

'We did, yes.'

'We?'

'Commander Hay, Bairstow, Mrs Brown and I put all this together. We thought we'd give the box a good shake and see what fell out.'

'Why?' I jiggled my handcuffs. I don't know why I did that. They weren't just going to unlock themselves, were they?

I said again, 'Why?' And then I had it. 'You wanted to see what the idiot Halcombe would do.'

He nodded.

'And where he went. And who he met.'

'That's right – and there he was, all set to be released back into the wild – all ready to lead us to the answers – and who should walk through the Red House door?' He sighed. 'You possess a gift, don't you, Dr Maxwell? A strange and wonderful gift.'

I said flatly, 'I thought I was dead. If I listen, I can still hear the shot.' I wondered if I'd hear it for the rest of my life.

'I know,' he said gently. 'I'm sorry about that.'

Well, that took the wind out of my sails.

Annoyingly, he was answering all my questions. I was determined to find something to be grumpy about, however, so I said,

427

'So . . . did he miss? Halcombe, I mean. I know he's an idiot but even so . . . it was point-blank range.'

'It wasn't he who fired the shot,' he said.

'Who, then?'

'Hyssop.'

'Hyssop shot me?'

'No one shot you,' he said impatiently. 'Can we move on?'

'But there was a gunshot. I heard it. I don't think I'll ever stop hearing it.'

'Hyssop shot Halcombe. She was only a few feet from you which must be why you confused who had shot whom. She saved you.'

I refused to be grateful. 'What was she even doing here?'

'Supervising the removal of Halcombe and Sullivan to a halfway house from which they could eventually be released and, with luck, lead us in some very interesting directions.'

'So she's nothing to do with Gaunt?'

'No.'

'And, presumably, not part of your plans for Halcombe.'

'No. She was here solely in her function as Head of Security at St Mary's.'

'Why would she save me?'

'Well, as to that, she seemed to feel she owed you.'

'Why?'

'You must ask her that.'

'But I've been unconscious,' I said, determined to make my point. 'Because I was shot.'

'You've been unconscious,' he said, 'because you fainted.'

'I bloody didn't.'

'Sorry. I should have said you succumbed to the cumulative

428

effects of shock, pain, stress and pants-wetting terror. On my recommendation, they've kept you under for an hour or so while the lovely Mr Gaunt concentrates on damage limitation here. I hesitate to say there's nothing actually wrong with you when there is obviously a very great deal wrong with you, so let's just say you are unharmed.'

'Not dead.'

He sighed. 'No. Captain Hyssop moved swiftly and competently to deal with the situation, relieving Halcombe of your gun and shooting him before he could do any harm.'

'Is he dead?'

'No.'

'She didn't by any chance shoot Sullivan as well, did she?'

'No. He was persuaded to let you go.'

I sighed in a dissatisfied manner.

'If I could just remind you of my original plan, Dr Maxwell – having no history with either Halcombe or Sullivan, I could legitimately let them go. With Dr Bairstow safely "dead", and a new order established at St Mary's, we were working on the assumption that they would feel safe enough to resume at least some of their former dealings and we could monitor their movements. A plan which now is on hold until Sullivan's leg heals because a certain someone walked through a door she had no business walking through. If anyone should be expressing dissatisfaction, it should be me.'

Time to move on. 'Where is Dr Bairstow now?'

'Well, thanks to you, no one knows at the moment, do they?'

'So you're still in charge of St Mary's?'

He sighed. 'Define *in charge*. Bairstow said he'd warned me, but he really didn't tell me the half of it.'

'I'm not going to apologise,' I said defiantly.

'No one ever expected you to.'

'Prentiss,' I said angrily. 'And Clerk. Did Hyssop's team deliberately . . . ?'

'No, no. Not at all. It was just something that could have happened to anyone at any time. Just a normal, everyday mishap. That it took so long to rescue them is regrettable. Believe me, you didn't say anything to Hyssop she didn't say to herself.'

'She's useless,' I said bitterly, quite overlooking the fact she'd saved my life. 'In fact, at one point they were so rubbish I was convinced she and her Half-Wits were Time Police.'

'*They're* not, no.'

This was one of those moments when the Universe stops in its tracks and waits for me to catch up.

'Alas, Dr Maxwell, I fear you must brace yourself.'

No. No, no, no, no, no, no, no, no.

I fell back on my pillows. Pain raced through my shoulders. 'Oh, shit.'

He was genuinely amused. 'Oh, shit indeed.'

'You're Time Police.'

'Yes, I am.'

Well, bloody bollocking hell.

I couldn't speak. I was see-sawing between anger at being duped and mortification at being duped so easily. All that crap he'd fed me about not knowing who the Time Police were. I suddenly remembered I hadn't had to explain to him about the weird and wonderful Time Police sentencing policy. He hadn't queried why Halcombe and Sullivan had only been away a year but aged thirty. He must have been laughing his socks off at me. And I'd explained Bluebell Time in words of one

430

syllable to a member of the organisation who identified and defined it. And all that guff he'd given me about wanting to bring stuff back. I realised, with some indignation, that he'd been winding me up. All this time he'd been enjoying some sort of joke at my expense. And I'd fallen for it. Bastard Time Police.

'Problem?' he said, obviously relishing the moment.

'I wish I hadn't been so restrained when commenting on Time Police policy and performance, but not really. Although I must ask – why?'

'We have concerns about St Mary's. Oh, not St Mary's itself, but it has occurred to both Commander Hay and Dr Bairstow that should Temporal Tourism ever become legal, there's an organisation here already set up. Pods, equipment, premises, personnel – all there for the taking.'

'We've fought people off before now,' I said, feeling I should keep up the St Mary's end. 'Including the Time Police, I believe.'

'One of our off-days,' he said seriously. 'Trust me, if I'd been in charge of the Time Police then that would never have happened.'

'Clerk and Prentiss,' I said angrily, zigzagging from complaint to complaint. 'You would have just left them in Babylon. Just to give yourself some credibility.'

'No,' he said calmly. 'I know St Mary's regularly clambers on its high horse, intoning, "We never leave our people behind," but you're not the only ones. I had a team of Hunters on stand-by, all set to get them out if anything had prevented you, although I was pretty certain you'd be off there as soon as I particularly forbade you to do so.'

'You knew I had my own pod?'

431

'I was banking on it. And for your peace of mind, teams have visited Clerk and Prentiss regularly, taking supplies and medicine and little luxuries. They lived long lives and were prosperous. A great deal more so than had they remained at St Mary's, probably. Their children thrived. As did their grandchildren. They enjoyed a gracious old age. They died peacefully within a few months of each other and, in line with St Mary's tradition, I've had their names inscribed on the Boards of Honour. Which reminds me . . . they asked me to return this to you with their love and gratitude.'

He held out my wedding ring.

I went to take it and realised I was still handcuffed. Frustrated, I yanked on the handcuffs again because I never learn and that set my shoulders and arms off all over again.

Treadwell sighed. 'I want to make it absolutely clear, Dr Maxwell, that my next action does not, in any way, constitute a binding arrangement on my part.'

'Same here,' I said.

He slipped the ring on to my finger.

I hadn't finished. 'And Matthew – the one person who might have recognised you?'

'Safely out of harm's way. Well, when I say out of harm's way, I don't know what he and those other two tearaways are up to at the moment, but I'm sure Chief Farrell will be more than equal to the challenge.'

He tilted his head. I could hear Gaunt's voice in the distance, giving someone hell.

He moved closer to the bed. 'I know in situations like this it's traditional to shake hands and say I wish I'd been able to know you better, but the very tiny glimpses I've had of you make

432

me more than ever inclined to exterminate you with extreme prejudice. And now I must go.'

'What?'

'I was brought here to make a formal identification, Dr Maxwell. Having done so I see no reason to linger.'

I couldn't believe it. 'You're leaving me here? Oh, yes – that's what you do, isn't it?'

'I am leaving you in the wind. An impediment to friend and foe alike.'

'What?'

'You make things happen, Dr Maxwell. I am simply leaving you to fulfil your full potential.'

Gaunt's voice drew closer.

I became cunning. 'Wouldn't you prefer to have me inside the boat pissing out rather than the other way around?'

'I'd rather not have you at all, Dr Maxwell. Floating face down with no boat in sight would be my first choice, but I work with what I can get.'

Gaunt was almost upon us. I threw a panicked look at the door.

He was still amused. 'You went to so much trouble to get here it seems churlish not to let you benefit from an extended appreciation of the facilities.'

'Bastard.'

Gaunt swept into the room, followed by a uniformed nurse with rather nice ash-blond hair and bearing a jug of water on a tray. I suddenly realised how thirsty I was. Although he might be about to waterboard me, of course. I looked at his posh suit. No – he wouldn't want water all over that.

He approached the bed but looked at Treadwell. 'Well, Commander?'

Treadwell nodded and said, 'I can formally identify this person as Dr Maxwell, dishonourably discharged from the St Mary's Institute of Historical Research for misconduct in a public office. Well done, Mr Gaunt – you may have let the big one slip through your fingers – only temporarily, I'm sure – but this is a very acceptable alternative. And by the way, Dr Maxwell . . .'

I turned my head from Gaunt to Treadwell and he slapped me. Quite hard. Although he did have the decency to pull it at the last moment, his open hand made a very satisfactory sound. From where Gaunt was standing it must have looked very convincing.

I fell back with a cry and then struggled to prop myself on my elbow again, glaring at him.

Treadwell straightened his cuffs. 'Feel free to carry on where I've left off, superintendent,' and strode from the room. I felt like shouting after him that you can take this undercover business too far, you know.

The nurse was hovering in the doorway, looking from me to Gaunt and back again. Presumably the medical staff belonged to the medical superintendent. That dozy wazzock Washburn, if I remembered correctly.

Gaunt regarded me impassively. There are times when being handcuffed to a bed is fun and there are times when it isn't. I knew which this was going to be.

He beckoned the nurse forwards. The water wasn't the only thing on the tray. He picked up a rather large pair of scissors.

I struggled to lean away from him. Which turned out to be a complete waste of time.

When I'd set out this morning, I'd subdued my hair with a ponytail and then I'd plaited it tightly because it makes

434

shoving it and keeping it in a bun much easier. At some point my bun had come unravelled and now I had just the plaited ponytail.

But not for long.

Before I knew what was happening, Gaunt leaned over me, grabbed it and began to hack away. I could hear the blades scrunching through my hair. Small pieces of hair fell around me. I tried to struggle and twist but between him, the pain and the handcuffs I wasn't going anywhere.

It sounds such a tiny thing. It was only hair. It would grow again. But it wasn't just a tiny thing. For as long as I could remember, my hair had been part of my identity – not just as an historian but as part of me, Maxwell. To be wrestled with and cursed, yes, but part of me nevertheless. To have someone lay hands on me like this and just hack it off . . .

It took him only a few seconds and then it was gone. Gaunt stepped back from the bed, scissors in one hand, long plait in the other, and then he turned and just dropped it into the bin. There was a slight metallic sound as it hit the bottom. I stared down at it, coiled and completely separate from me. I wouldn't be gluing that back on.

'There are standards to which all prisoners must conform,' he said. 'That was one of them. There will be others.'

And on that splendid last word, he strode from the room, brushing past the nurse who only just got out of the way in time.

I pulled uselessly at the handcuffs, starting up all the little rivers of pain again.

The nurse stood in the doorway, watching him go, and then came further into the room with the tray.

'How are you feeling?'

'Absolutely fine as long as I don't laugh.'

'That's sex with me out, then.'

I sighed. My day was not getting any better. 'What are you doing here?'

'I'm here to rescue you. You pulled me out on Crete. I'm returning the favour.'

'I'm not some useless princess, you know,' I said with dignity. 'I can rescue myself.'

'No, you can't. You'd have got impatient and attempted something stupid and – hey – get it? Impatient? But you're actually a patient. So not impatient.'

Oh, dear God. Someone who made David Sands look good.

'Come on,' he said, pushing a wheelchair into the room. 'I've got everything all lined up and waiting for you. All we have to do is go.'

I cut straight to the heart of the matter. 'Why are you dressed as a woman?'

'I'm not dressed as a woman. I'm dressed as a nurse. Not the same thing at all.'

'Can I be there when you tell Hunter that?'

He twitched the blanket back.

'You're handcuffed to the bloody bed.' He looked around. 'Leon's not here, is he?'

'Shut up.'

He was lining up the wheelchair. 'So how exactly were you going to rescue yourself?'

'You can dislocate your thumb and . . .'

'No, you can't.'

'Yes, you can. I've seen it in movies.'

436

'God save me from amateurs. Well, I'll nip off and have my tea while you try to dislocate your own thumb and release yourself from a set of military-grade handcuffs, shall I?'

'Like to see you do better.'

'Well, I can, but there's a temporary setback because all your hair seems to have fallen off.' He began to rummage in the bin. 'But where there's hair there's . . . one of these.' He waved a hair clip.

I scoffed. 'That's an even bigger myth than the dislocated thumb thing.'

'Want to bet? Watch and learn, historian.'

He opened up the hairgrip, removed the plastic bobble off the end, inserted the clip into the keyhole and bent it back. Removing it, he did the same again but in the opposite direction this time.

He held it up and surveyed the angle critically. 'Yep, that looks good,' and inserted it into the lock. There was a click and the whole cuff-thing fell away. Four seconds. Possibly five.

Well, bloody bollocking hell.

At this point the Legal Department would like me to make it very clear that this is a very wrong thing to do. Especially if the use of handcuffs had been authorised by the police or military authorities in the lawful execution of their duties and that the publishers, printers and all allied trades in no way condone the improper use of hair accessories. By anyone other than Markham, of course.

Another nurse appeared in the doorway. A proper one this time, wearing proper scrubs and not some random nursing uniform gleaned from God knows where and a really rather good ash-blond wig. Holding a tray of something, she was halfway across the room before she saw Markham, her cheery greeting dying on her lips as she tried to work out what he was.

He moved faster than I would have thought possible. In less than a second, he had his arm around her and was ushering her into the bathroom. 'Now then,' he said soothingly, 'we don't want to make a big fuss and upset the patient, do we? And most of all we don't want to upset that bastard Gaunt, so you just come with me.'

Pausing only to scoop up my stockings from where they were lying across the chair with the rest of my clothes, he swept her into the bathroom. Five seconds later he shot back in again and ripped my pillows from underneath me. I fell back with a thump which did my shoulders no good at all.

'What are you doing with my pillows?'

I think I thought he was going to smother her and she hadn't done us any harm at all.

'Just making her comfortable.'

'Where is she?'

'In the bath, nicely tied up. Pillows for her head and a couple of blankets to keep her warm. It's not her fault she walked in at the wrong moment.'

He shot off into the bathroom. I could hear him talking reassuringly.

Reappearing again, he began to strip the bed around me. Sheets, blanket, the lot. I found myself lying on a bare mattress.

'Are you insane?'

'If anyone comes in, they'll think you've been legitimately transferred and the bed is stripped in readiness for the next patient. Believe me, nothing is more suspicious than an empty bed, but a stripped bed tells a completely different story. Clever, eh?'

I stared up at him from my bed of pain. 'Promise me – just promise me – you will never rescue me again as long as you live.'

He disappeared back into the bathroom to cosset his nurse.

I swung my legs out of bed and, handcuff dangling, began to hobble to the wheelchair. Which was when, despite the burning pain in my shoulders and arms, it became apparent I'd had some pretty hefty painkillers. One leg went east and the other declared it had been a long day and refused to work at all.

'Whoa,' said Markham, grabbing me before I crashed to the floor. He stuck his head out of the door and withdrew it almost immediately. 'Bugger.'

I would have panicked but my world had gone pink. 'What?'

'Gaunt's coming back.'

'Ha,' I said, losing all control of my outlying regions. 'Leave him to me.'

'No, I don't think so. This way. Time for Plan B.'

'Wow – that was Plan A? What's Plan B?'

'I told you when we were prepping. Window.'

'What?'

'Don't scream now.'

And then the bugger threw me out of the window.

29

Believe it or not, I was fairly relaxed about this. Half of me was in a kind of pink painkiller haze and the other half was convinced Pennyroyal was around somewhere and would catch me.

Well, that didn't happen.

Fortunately, I landed on a nice piece of well-kept lawn although I had a nasty suspicion I'd have gone out of the window anyway, even if it had been the car park. Or a bed of spikes. Or a snake pit. Being rescued by the Security Section is not always a blessing although they get quite upset if you mention this.

Barely had I even begun to cope with that happening than most of Markham landed on top of me.

'Bloody hell, Markham.'

'No, no,' he said bravely, straightening his wig. 'I'm fine.'

'What happened to *do no harm*?'

'Doesn't apply to nurses.'

'I'm pretty sure it does.'

He rolled off me and sat up. I stayed where I was. What with the horror of his dress rucked up around his waist and displaying incorrectly worn tights, my fiery arms, wonky legs and crushed lungs, I wouldn't be making any substantial contributions to our getaway any time soon.

'I didn't need rescuing,' I said into the grass.

'Really? You were just going to take up your bed and walk, were you?' he said, disentangling himself. 'The one you were handcuffed to?'

'I told you,' I said as he hauled me to what were passing themselves off as my feet. 'Thumb. Dislocate. Escape.' My knees gave way.

He heaved me over his shoulder. 'Bloody hell, Max. Less chocolate. More exercise.'

Muscle weighs more than fat – which has been my lifelong excuse – and finally my moment of justification had come. I made my case as he staggered across the grass and I flattered myself I was both articulate and persuasive which, considering I was upside-down and with my arse in full view, was impressive.

'Where are you parked?' I said, displaying a polite interest in his plans for the afternoon.

'By that green tree.'

I tried to squint around him. My face was dangerously near his backside – although not as close as his was to mine – so I was willing to look anywhere else. 'They're all green, you pillock. Your ignorance of the plant world is as great as your ignorance of the animal world.'

'Look, much more criticism from you and I'm buggering off down the pub and leaving you to make your own way back to the pod.'

'Bet I still get there before you.'

'I could hear the pair of you a hundred yards away,' said Pennyroyal, appearing in the pod doorway.

441

I was dumped unceremoniously on to the floor.

'Why aren't *you* dressed as a nurse?' I said to Pennyroyal's feet.

'For so many good reasons.'

Markham got the door closed. 'Can we go, please. I've only had her for ten minutes and that's eleven and a half minutes too long.'

The world might have gone all the colours of the rainbow but believe me I was far too gone to care.

The pain in my arms and shoulders woke me up. I shifted my position slightly to try to ease things a little and managed to pry one eye open. And then the other.

'What took you so long, Dr Maxwell?'

Dr Bairstow was sitting in a chair by the window, hands crossed on his stick – not his usual stick, I noticed, with true historian talent for focusing on the trivial.

I looked around. I was back at the farmhouse. It was night-time. The little bedside lamp threw out a gentle light. I could smell apples again. Everywhere was very quiet. It was just me and Dr Bairstow.

He stood up. 'I have been instructed to give you these in a glass of water.'

He ripped open a foil strip and dropped two tablets into a glass where they fizzed and frothed.

'Painkillers. Can you lift your head?'

I could.

'Please drink it all.'

I did.

'Would you like a cup of tea?'

442

I would.

He clicked the kettle on and busied himself. I lay back and looked up at the ceiling while I tried to piece together the events of the last twenty-four hours.

He pulled two pillows off the spare bed and propped them behind me so I could sit up a little. And the handcuffs had disappeared which was good news. I'm not sure what was in that foil packet but I was beginning to feel much better and who needs to be able to see the corners of their bedroom anyway. Take it from me – corners are overrated.

He put a mug on the bedside table beside me.

'Only half a mug,' he said, demonstrating his usual faith in me. 'In case you spill it.'

'Will I get the other half for good behaviour?'

He smiled and went to sit back in his chair. I carefully held the mug in both hands and closed my eyes and sipped. It was good tea. I'd have happily stayed like that forever but, as usual, curiosity got the better of me.

'So,' I said, trying not to wince as I twisted to set down the mug. 'Not dead.'

'Rumours of my death have been greatly exaggerated,' he said.

I nodded. 'That Gaunt's a bit of a bastard, isn't he?'

'An unpleasant personality type,' he said.

'He cut off my hair,' I said, personal grievances rising to the fore.

'Ah – I did wonder. I was reluctant to comment in case this was the latest style and you had, in fact, paid quite a lot of money to achieve that . . . unusual . . . effect.'

'Mrs Brown?'

443

'Asleep at the moment, but very well.'

'Can I have the other half?'

He poured out the rest.

'What now?' I asked. 'Back to St Mary's? Or are we all criminals now?'

'I think I can safely leave St Mary's in the very capable hands of John Treadwell. For the time being, anyway.'

'You organised *all* this, didn't you?'

'Yes, in conjunction with Mrs Brown and Mr Black but not, sadly, with Mr Gaunt, which might have been an error. Together with Commander Hay and a few others from Thirsk, we put together a plan to be implemented should events take a sudden turn for the worst. The main thrust of which was to scatter various elements of St Mary's, thus ensuring, should anything happen to me, there would always be others to carry on.'

'Leon,' I said.

'And the Meiklejohns and Matthew – all safely stowed away.'

'Markham?'

'Here, with the very excellent Lady Amelia. As intended.'

I sat back. 'They're working for you, aren't they? Smallhope and Pennyroyal, I mean.' I sighed. 'Everyone works for you.'

'Well, not quite,' he said modestly, 'but for the purposes of this conversation, yes.'

Well – devious old bugger. Hang on a minute . . .

'You couldn't know I'd be sacked,' I said.

He raised an eyebrow. 'I think use of the word "inevitable" might be quite appropriate here.'

'Are you saying that Treadwell deliberately wound me up? What about Clerk and Prentiss? Were they a price worth paying?'

'No. That was completely unexpected. I understand the

commander has instituted a programme of monthly visits and medical checks. As much as could be done – he did.'

Well, that was true, but it didn't make me feel any better.

'And bloody Hyssop?'

'That was regrettable. I think, without blowing my own trumpet, that had I remained in place a little longer, I would have been able to smooth the path of your working relationship somewhat. It was unfortunate for Hyssop that she became linked with Treadwell and my reported demise.'

'So,' I said, trying to sum up. 'St Mary's is safe. Ish. The Archive, Leon, Matthew and the others are safe. Mrs Brown is safe. Markham's safe. You're safe.'

'Yes,' he said, interrupting my catalogue of safeness. 'Everyone's safe. Even you.'

'I'm a wanted criminal,' I said.

'Well, I think that's an issue that can be discussed when we can see a little more clearly, I think.'

'All this? All this is exactly what you had planned?'

'That is correct.'

'So what now?'

'That is to be discussed when everyone is feeling a little better.'

'But why? Why this . . . ?' I nearly said 'over-elaborate charade' but I was in enough pain without asking for more. 'Why is all this happening? All these wheels within wheels. Moving people around like chess pieces. What's going on?'

He tweaked the curtain and looked outside. Still dark. He let the curtain fall back.

'Well, we're not sure why and we're certainly not sure how, but to use one of your sayings – something's gone horribly

445

wrong somewhere. I am not alone in thinking this. Commander Hay is in complete agreement with me. Somehow, somewhere, something has happened. Or not happened. Something is accelerating events – bringing them forward and setting them on a whole new path.'

He sighed and sat back down, his face full of shadows. 'I'm sorry to say this, Max, but we think – in fact, we are convinced – that we are in the opening stages of the Time Wars.'

THE END

ACKNOWLEDGEMENTS

2020 has been designated as the Year of Patara. It really is the most amazing place and should we ever be released from captivity, I do urge anyone who can to visit both the magnificent ancient site and the fabulous beach half a mile away.

Thanks to Phil Dawson for his advice on what's involved in moving a prisoner from A to B. His opinion of the military police is entirely his own and I suspect not completely unbiased.

Thanks as always to my prosecco-knitting agent, Hazel.

And to my excellent editor, Frankie, and all the staff at Headline who work so hard on my behalf.

Thanks to Nicola Reynolds who came up with the name R2-Tea2 for Markham's assistant. Of whom I feel reasonably sure we haven't heard the last.

I usually go on to express my apologies and thanks to all the people who had to put up with me while I was writing this book but a lot of it was written during lockdown, which, while brilliant for my productivity, didn't do either my sanity or my waistline much good at all. The highlight of my week was thumping my saucepan for the NHS. Yay, NHS!

ACKNOWLEDGMENTS

Have you met the Time Police?

A long time ago in the future, the secret of time travel became known to all and the world nearly ended. And so an all-powerful, international organisation was formed to keep the timeline straight. At all costs.

Enter Jane, Luke and Matthew. The worst recruits in Time Police history. Their adventures kick off in . . .

And they're back for round three in . . .

SAVING TIME

October 2021. Available to order now.

**Discover Jodi Taylor's gripping
supernatural thrillers**

There are some things in this world that only Elizabeth Cage
can see. Important things. Dangerous things.

But what is a curse to Elizabeth is a gift to others – a very
valuable gift they want to control.

And they'll stop at nothing to do so . . .

WHITE DARK
SILENCE LIGHT

And the series continues with . . .

LONG
SHADOWS

August 2021. Available to order now.

To discover more about

JODI TAYLOR

visit

www.joditaylor.online

You can also find her on

Facebook
www.facebook.com/JodiTaylorBooks

Twitter
@joditaylorbooks

Instagram
@joditaylorbooks